THE
SERPENT'S
HEIR

THE SERPENT'S HEIR

THE HATCHLING IS ALREADY AMONG US

VLAD V. IMAKAEV

The Serpent's Heir
Vlad V. Imakaev

CONTENTS

There was a man in the land of Uz whose name was Job, and that man was blameless and upright, one who feared God and turned away from evil. There were born to him seven sons and three daughters. And when the days of the feast had run their course, Job would send and consecrate them, and he would rise early in the morning and offer burnt offerings according to the number of them all.

Now, there was a day when the sons of God came to present themselves before the LORD, and Satan also came among them. The LORD SAID TO SATAN, "FROM WHERE HAVE YOU COME?"

SATAN ANSWERED THE LORD AND SAID, "FROM GOING TO AND FRO ON THE EARTH, AND FROM WALKING UP AND DOWN ON IT."

AND THE LORD SAID TO SATAN, "HAVE YOU CONSIDERED MY SERVANT JOB, THAT THERE IS NONE LIKE HIM ON THE EARTH, A BLAMELESS AND UPRIGHT MAN, WHO FEARS GOD AND TURNS AWAY FROM EVIL?"

THEN SATAN ANSWERED THE LORD AND SAID, "DOES JOB FEAR GOD FOR NO REASON? HAVE YOU NOT PUT A HEDGE AROUND HIM AND HIS HOUSE AND ALL THAT HE HAS ON EVERY SIDE? YOU HAVE BLESSED THE WORK OF HIS HANDS, AND HIS POSSESSIONS HAVE INCREASED IN THE LAND. BUT STRETCH OUT YOUR HAND AND TOUCH ALL THAT HE HAS, AND HE WILL CURSE YOU TO YOUR FACE."

And the LORD said to Satan, "Behold, all that he has is in your hand. Only against him do not stretch out your hand." So Satan went out from the presence of the LORD.

The oxen were plowing and the donkeys feeding beside them, and the Sabeans fell upon them and took them and struck down the servants.

The fire of God fell from heaven and burned up the sheep and the servants and consumed them.

The Chaldeans formed three groups and made a raid on the camels, took them, and struck down the servants with the edge of the sword.

His sons and daughters were eating and drinking wine in their oldest brother's house, and behold, a great wind came across the wilderness and struck the four corners of the house, and it fell upon the young people, and they were dead.

Then Job arose and tore his robe and shaved his head and fell on the ground and worshiped. And he said, "Naked I came from my mother's womb, and naked shall I return. The LORD GAVE, AND THE LORD HAS TAKEN AWAY; BLESSED BE THE NAME OF THE LORD." In all this, Job did not sin or charge God with wrong.

And the LORD said to Satan, "Have you considered my servant Job, that there is none like him on the earth, a blameless and upright man, who fears God and turns away from evil? He still holds fast to his integrity, although you incited me against him to destroy him without reason."

Then Satan answered the LORD AND SAID, "SKIN FOR SKIN! ALL THAT A MAN HAS, HE WILL GIVE FOR HIS LIFE. BUT STRETCH OUT YOUR HAND AND TOUCH HIS BONE AND HIS FLESH, AND HE WILL CURSE YOU TO YOUR FACE."

AND THE LORD SAID TO SATAN, "BEHOLD, HE IS IN YOUR HAND; ONLY SPARE HIS LIFE."

So Satan went out from the presence of the LORD and struck Job with loathsome sores from the sole of his foot to the crown of his head...

Book of Job

PROLOGUE

How do you really know if someone's crying is genuine? Different tears have different meanings, and you should not always trust them. They say that there will be no tears in Heaven, none at all. Here on Earth, however, everyone has cried at least once in his life. Some cry for a specific reason, and others simply from an inability to control their overloaded emotions. But it is an even greater challenge to understand those who do not cry at all.

Today, even the sky found itself unable to hold back its tears.

Summer had ended three days ago, and it seemed as though it would never again return to the Patterson family. Over the night, a cold winter wind had brought heavy dark clouds from the ocean, and now they bore down impulsively onto the trees, making them cry and creak as well. The wind sang his dark eternal song, playing the power lines like the strings of a violin, all the while whispering something into Lisa's ear since she alone had agreed to listen to him. She let him stroke her hair and caress her skin because her husband's touch stung everything inside each time he tried to comfort her.

No, it was not his fault, but she could not even look at him. He had aged so much over the last three days: his hair had gone half silver, his skin was pale and lifeless, and his eyes, once a vibrant blue, took on a sickly appearance void of all color. They looked as if someone had spilled bleach on them, leaving two eerie black holes on a chemical-gray canvas. How could she speak to him? Would she ever be able to speak at all?

Could he forgive her? Ever? No, it was too painful to think about it, and better that she let the wind embrace her shoulders and whisper to her. At least his words did not remind her of her loss.

With a blank stare, she greeted everyone who approached. She looked at each of them but could not recognize a single person, and she definitely was not listening as they offered their condolences. Those who knew her found the absent and emotionless look on her face disturbing and almost oppressively so. The cold, bronze statue of Holy Mary standing in a niche slightly behind boasted more life than Lisa. She was as good as dead, all life having drained away from her together with her tears over the last few nights. Unfortunately, she could still breathe, while her daughter could not. There were no more feelings and no more tears, only a great emptiness that spoke to her through the wind.

Everything proceeded in such an unrealistic manner: the memorial service, family and friends in mourning, her little Vicki's body in the cavernous coffin. She did not hear a word of the pastor's eulogy while she stared at the toys and Vicki's favorite stuffed animals positioned among dripping candles and flowers. A smiling portrait of her baby stood to one side, with a black ribbon wrapped around the bottom right corner.

Maybe it was all a bad dream? All she wanted to do was to wake up from this nightmare. If only she could go back to the beginning of the week, she would get up, run to the second floor, and find her daughter asleep in her princess-themed bed. She would kneel next to her and lay her head on Vicki's tiny chest and listen to the beating of her small, strong heart…If only she could…She would stay there forever.

A few of the assembled mourners helped Lisa outside, but others were still coming forward and offering platitudes. Many wept. People spoke in hushed tones about what had happened. Lisa's nightmare just would not end.

"The poor girl, she was such an angel. I still can't believe it happened in our neighborhood," whispered one woman to her companion, wiping another tear with a completely wet tissue.

"It's so painful just to look at them."

The ladies stepped aside and drew closer to Vicki's portrait. She had just turned six years old, and with deep blue eyes and a head of golden curls, she indeed looked angelic.

"Everything happened in front of Lisa...I saw it, too." The woman closed her eyes and shook her head, trying to fight away the bad memories and floating images that would haunt her until the end of her days. "And Brad...He loved her so much. He got home just before the ambulance arrived. I get goosebumps thinking about how he yelled. Part of him died right there. He called out her name, tried to wake her up. He didn't even notice the blood all over his face and clothes."

"Look at Lisa. My God! She's like a mummy. No tears, no words. Is she even breathing? I'm worried that she's losing her mind."

"I know...I know." The other woman covered her face and started to sob.

"Did they find the fool who did it?"

"There was no need. He was so scared right from the beginning, and later, he came to the sheriff on his own and turned himself in. It's the ex-husband of that blonde who lives in the corner house next to Caroline, you know, the one who drives the Jeep with the open roof?"

"You don't say! And where were his eyes? How could you not see the kid on the sidewalk?"

"I don't know. He'd had a big fight with his ex—you could hear them streets away. He just popped like the cork out of a bottle, slammed the door, jumped into his car, and hit the gas. After that, it all happened so quickly..."

Her lips started to tremble.

"Lisa was outside with Vicki, waiting for Brad to come home from work. She was watering the plants and just turned away for a moment when Vicki's ball went into the road." Almost choking on the last words, the woman took a deep breath...but could not hold back anymore.

The neighbor hugged her friend and allowed her own tears to stream down freely.

The wind pushed about with renewed strength, and the rain became an annoying, repetitive drizzle. Nobody hurried to leave. Those who had already spoken to the heartbroken parents broke into small groups, trying to decide who would go on to the cemetery and who would go straight to the Pattersons' house to set up food for the wake. Some collected money. Of course there was no amount that could help them fill the abysmal loss, but at least it would ease the burden of paying for funeral expenses.

Only one person slipped back into the sanctuary where the memorial service had just ended. He walked slowly through the rows of empty chairs and stopped right beside the lonely coffin. The men from the funeral home were busy loading flowers, portraits, and toys into the hearse, and they still needed to procure enough folding chairs and umbrellas to go along in a separate truck. But their presence did not matter—he would have just enough time, twenty or thirty seconds...He did not need any more than that.

Cautiously and silently, he lifted the coffin lid and looked upon the porcelain face of the lifeless girl. He gently stroked her golden hair, touched her forehead lightly, and moved his fingers along the stone-cold cheeks as though admiring a statue. He remembered how when she smiled, those same cheeks boasted such cute dimples. Now they were gone. He beheld the straight, white, polished mask that remained of the angel; it was nothing more.

"You should smile more often, Vicki," he whispered, taking her cold hand. "Wake up! You went to sleep too early..."

Everything outside had calmed down to an uneasy silence, the likes of which you sense only before a giant of a storm hits. The crowd could even hear the traffic from the highway on the other side of town. There was no longer any wind or rain, and the sound of chirping birds and whispering of mourners was muted by the deafening silence.

Lisa felt as though Death itself walked around her. Maybe it had come to take her along with her daughter. What a sweet relief that would be! She closed her eyes and faded into the depths of her mind...Something inside the funeral home fell to the ground with a crash, and an otherworldly scream ripped through the silence.

One of the funeral ushers ran outside from a side door, looking like he was trying to escape a fire. He saw none of the people in his way of escape and only pushed people aside and knocked over the portrait. Dashing straight to his car, he fumbled with the keys, started the vehicle, and immediately sped away from the parking lot. Everyone looked around, perplexed. Some were frightened, and others were curious as to what was going on. An unseen presence drew their attention toward the side door from which the man had just run. Nothing. Only the same heavy and unbearable silence emanated from within.

Rapidly, as though escaping from captivity, a wall of rain hit the street. Streams of water flowed down like waterfalls onto the helpless yellow leaves strewn about the sidewalks.

Lisa started to shake like one suddenly taken with fever. Through the corner of her eye, she perceived someone descending the dark steps of the sanctuary toward the hall. With small, timid steps, the figure drew near the open door.

Thunder rolled over the sky, gripping the gut of each person present. They felt as if their intestines tangled and fought like snakes dueling to the death. The sky seemed to fall apart as a crack ruptured through the heavy clouds, releasing a bright ray of sunlight that filled the bell tower, the side entrance, and the little girl who stood in it. Her golden hair radiated in the surrounding light, briefly blinding the crowd. Death had fled in terror, and life seemed to pour out through the doorway, penetrating everyone present.

"Mommy?" called Vicki, peering meekly toward her parents. Lisa, who moments earlier could not find it within her to cry, dropped to her knees and wept hysterically.

Squalling and bawling filled the air. Chaos bred from panic and fear enslaved the witnesses. Some turned and ran, some screamed, frozen in place, and a few simply passed out onto the dampened ground.

CHAPTER 1

I t was raining for the second day in a row. If it continued this way, then really soon, US 61, the highway coming from Louisiana to Minnesota, would join with the river and forever disappear from the maps. The GPS Navigator was having a hard time, and the recalculating sign appeared more often than the map of Lake City itself. Who knows, maybe such a small town had been flushed out with the flood and was currently drifting down the Mississippi River. Last week, Lake City was just a tourist resort of around five thousand people, and today, it is one of the hottest subjects on the Internet. Someone had published a video on YouTube from one of their funeral houses, and in hours, it had almost a million views.

The road made a sharp turn, and a car driving along it almost flew off the cliff side.

Maya Polanski, one of the lead editors of the *Chicago Voice*, began hissing the most colorful curses toward her absent chief. Actually, over the past six hours of driving, she remembered all the spoken and unspoken curses and metaphorical epithets that she would love to use in writing his obituary.

It was already dark enough because of the rain and the heavy storm clouds, but after six, when night started pushing on, the driving became nearly impossible. To make her life more miserable, the fuel meter started blinking at her with its annoying orange eye. Really soon, the light would become steady, and from that point, she would have gas for another ten to fifteen miles.

What to do after that? Call for emergency road service? Ha! That would be funny since she had lost coverage right after Winona. So, she supposed that if something did not show up soon, she would need to sleep in the car that night because there was no way she would walk anywhere in rain like that. Who knows, maybe another car would notice her (but to be honest, she had not seen any cars in more than thirty minutes).

On top of everything, the only working radio channel was more and more overcome by white noise, with only rare bursts of distant voices and barely recognizable tunes. It seemed that one of the local stations was trying to tell Maya something that she already knew. Dangerous driving conditions on the highway, forecasts of rain for the whole evening, and unusually cold weather for September. After another burst of mumbling, the music faded into a static scratching sound, and the display went blank.

"Perfect! Science freaking fiction!" Maya concentrated all her frustration into one finger and started hitting random buttons on the panel, trying to readjust or switch to another channel.

Static. White noise. Static. More static. More noise! Why had she not thought to take along a couple of CDs from home? As if anyone these days listens to a CD in the car—who needed that when you had wireless coverage and a whole music library one click away? But not here.

"Piece of crap!" She picked up the book that was lying on the seat next to her and began smashing the innocent control panel as if it would solve all of her problems. The noise stopped. The display blinked a couple of times and then went absolutely dark.

With a furious roar, she threw the book behind her. It hit the back seat and fell to the floor, opening to a page with a bookmark in a chapter on "How to tell your family about your cancer diagnosis."

The wipers worked at full speed, scraping from the windshield enormous amounts of water with each move. The rain had stopped falling in drops and turned the air into a wall of water. The headlights could barely break through that wall, and it made driving near impossible.

A little ding grabbed Maya's attention, and it was a good sign. After many miles of driving in the middle of nowhere, her phone finally established a connection to the nearest cell tower. She tried to reach her phone from her purse, but in her way was everything from an extra set of keys and makeup items to a wallet and numberless bottles of pills. She glanced down for just a moment when, out of nowhere, a loud honking accompanied by huge blinding headlights rattled the silence. Returning both hands to the wheel, she swerved to the side, almost slipping from the highway. Maya had not noticed that she had driven into the middle of the road, where a fully loaded truck almost ran her over. No harm done, but he kept honking for another five seconds until the rain muted the sound.

"I love you too, moron!"

From her purse came another ding, but she decided not to bother anymore. That would be the great irony if, after finally accepting her sickness and the beginning of her upcoming chemotherapy, she should die in a car accident in the middle of…

"And where am I?" Like it had understood what Maya was asking, the GPS popped up with another "recalculating new route" sign. "Whatever! Oh, I swear, Bill Sawyer! I swear I'm gonna kill you!"

In the pitch-black surroundings, a distant light finally blinked. On reflex, Maya looked at the GPS but did not see anything new. The light grew steady, and it seemed that something glowed around it as well. Maybe it was not a city, but any type of civilization was better than nothing at all at this point. Trying to slow down, she noticed an old sun-bleached sign with a gas pump pointing toward a washed-out exit. If she had not been paying attention, she might easily have missed the road leading from the highway.

Carefully looking to both sides, she followed the exit. It was not clear who was responsible for building and leveling that "piece of art," but it was not practical, especially for the Audi she drove. Trying to avoid bumps and water-filled potholes, she managed to make it all the way to a small group of buildings.

There were a couple barns and a half-empty garage with old and unused tractors that probably had not worked in years. An empty church building without a door stood nearby with a huge hole in the roof from where God's rain literally flooded the sanctuary. Five or six abandoned houses, covered with graphite and dark marks left from what resembled petard explosions, looked small and lost. It seemed that no more than twenty years ago, there was a productive working farm here, but something had gone wrong, and now it looked like a cemetery. A huge pile of old metal parts next to the only living building, which itself was covered with rust and depression completed the picture like a cross carelessly stuck in a grave.

One house still looked functional, and from the top of its roof shone the same light that had captured Maya's attention. The windows were clean, and the curtains behind them looked friendly and carefully adjusted. A blue light glowing from within might have belonged to a TV or a computer screen.

It was not easy to scare Maya, and while some might pass by those ruins in hope of finding a less frightening gas station, she decided that it would work just fine, even if zombies were running the place. Next to an old-looking gas pump was a huge board where prices per gallon had been written in chalk, but of course, the rain had washed away the numbers a long time ago. She did not care about the price either at that point.

"Full tank, a full tank! My kingdom for a full tank!" She lightly pressed the horn. The melodic "beep" echoed through the church, garage, and empty buildings. It also seemed to catch the attention of whoever was living in the home. The curtains parted, but it was too dark to see who was there looking through at her.

Whoever it was, the person did not rush to help her. She blinked with her high beams, hoping the owner would take this as a sign of friendship and not annoyance or impatience. To be honest, she was more annoyed than friendly, but with God as her witness, she could act kind and lovable, even if she totally hated and despised everyone in sight. Some might call it hypocrisy, but she would say it was a necessary talent in the world of journalism.

A light came on behind the main door, and a lamp hanging outside lit up—a welcoming sight in the darkness. She waited for a couple of minutes in the hope that someone would come out, but it seemed that the clerk did not want to get soaked for a mere twenty bucks. Maya did not want to leave her car either. Maybe her Audi was no tank, and the glass was not bulletproof, but still, she felt safer inside, especially in weather like that.

"Fine, you win..." She pulled her raincoat from the backseat, then opened the glove compartment and pulled out a small gun. After double-checking that it was loaded, she slipped it into her purse and took out a pill from one of the bottles.

As soon as she opened the door, rain and wind invaded the Audi, wetting Maya's face, wheel, and purse. It was refreshing and challenging at the same time. Without hesitation, she walked away from the car and, trying not to sink into a huge puddle, ran toward the house.

An old man cracked open the door just slightly as soon as she came close enough for conversation. He didn't look like a maniac, at least not from first sight. He was in his late sixties, dressed in a simple gray T-shirt and a pair of jeans whose knees were pointed and white with age. On his head, he sported an old cap with a faded logo for some cheap casino, but to his credit, despite his clothing, he was clean-shaven. He was a man of the old school, perhaps a veteran? Maya knew that every person was a castle with many gates and locks, and all she needed was to find the right key to begin a conversation. She took a deep breath and put on her best smile...

"How can I help you?" The man was faster than she was, and by the tone of his voice, he was not happy.

"Good evening. Sorry for bothering you." She smiled, knowing that her voice of caramel and butter worked perfectly on almost every man. "I would like a full tank of gas and a map. My GPS betrayed me."

As if chewing something, the old man moved his lips from side to side, carefully staring at Maya, trying to decide whether he should let her in.

"I hope I am not too much trouble?"

"No...Not at all!"

Bingo! With a man like this, you must play weak. They want to be heroes, and they will never admit that you've bothered them beyond what they can handle. The door was wide open now. Maya, like a cat, slipped inside with one step, trying not to leave muddy marks on the floor, though water dripped from her coat all over.

The house was divided into two parts. On the left side was a long hallway leading to what Maya assumed was the owner's living area. She guessed that he lived alone because there was only one old leather chair in front of the malfunctioning TV. To the right was a small shop with a counter, a couple vending machines, a stand with postcards and other souvenirs, and two big thermoses for coffee.

"Go on in there. I'll bring you some paper towels." The old man flipped another switch, and the lights came on in the shop.

Maya smiled gratefully and even nodded, showing her best behavior. She noticed a rifle in his other hand, but it did not look like he planned to kill her now. If she lived alone in God-knows-where, she would also greet everyone who pulled up with a gun in her hand. Her own was still concealed in her purse, and she kept one finger on the trigger the whole while. Maya walked into the shop area, and for some reason, she felt safe and finally calmed a bit, as if the biggest of her troubles was now behind her.

Everything would get better now, she thought. Though she was never really superstitious, Maya always trusted her gut, and in her line of work, that was important. And right now, her gut was telling her that all was well. Maybe, though, it was just the painkiller she had taken before entering that was dulling her judgment. She let go of the trigger and began looking at a shelf of old, sun-bleached postcards. Maybe she would buy one and send it to Bill?

Speaking of Bill, Maya reached again into her purse and dug around for her smartphone. No reception.

"Sorry, there's no coverage," said the man, having returned, as he promised, with a new roll of paper towels in his hands.

"Do you have a payphone?" she asked, pulling off a good amount of the roll and wiping it over her wet face and medium-length dark red hair.

"Nope. But I can let you use mine if you tell me what brought you to our area." He picked up his glasses and turned on the register. Maya had not seen such an old-fashioned machine for a long time, and she had the feeling that by some evil cosmic sense of humor, she had fallen through time and would now be stuck here rusting and collecting dust together with the old vending machines and unwanted postcards.

"My damn job." Maya smirked and kept walking around and looking at the other items for sale. Surprised, she noticed two copies of today's *Chicago Voice* on a newspaper stand.

"Job, you say? A cruddy job, if you ask me. You're not a local, right?" The man readjusted his glasses and looked more carefully at Maya. "Or from the area?"

"Oh, no! This is my first time here, and hopefully not my last!" This time, she smiled with just a hint of flirtation, even though she knew for sure that no matter what price she was offered in the future, she would never come back.

"Your face…You look so familiar somehow," explained the curious owner, struggling to make the registrar start working. It took a couple good hits on its side before the cursed thing started up and made some sounds. "Are you sure you've never stopped here before?"

"I'm sure I would remember." Maya smirked.

"So, you asked for a map? I just have those for ten bucks," and he placed one in front of her.

"Not a big deal. Can you show me where we are?"

"Sure…Sure…I still think I know you. How much gas do you need? Full tank?"

"Depends on how far it is to Lake City."

"An hour, no more. But with weather like this, I wouldn't rush."

"Twenty dollars then."

The man gave her a haughty look and then nodded toward a sign on the counter reading "self-service." Maya sighed deeply, trying not to lose her smile. The rain outside seemed to pick up its speed and started hitting the window with renewed force.

"I can give you an umbrella," offered the shop owner, with a slight mocking tone in his voice.

Maya looked over at the corner where a basket of old, dusty umbrellas sat. They were covered with cobwebs and something that resembled mold.

Now, her smile looked more like a grin, but she had no other choice. Carefully, she picked through them until she found the least dirty, checked whether it opened all right, and with her sweetest voice, she thanked the owner.

As soon as she stepped outside, the wind almost ripped the umbrella from her hands, but she was not about to give up without a battle. Moving quickly, she maneuvered over puddles back to her car, opened the gas cap, connected the nozzle, and signaled to the owner, who was looking at her through the window.

It was the first time, to her memory, that it took nearly five minutes just to pump five gallons of gas. At one point, she thought of hiding in the car until it was finished but then saw no point as she was already as wet as if she had come straight from the shower. She fought the temptation to just throw away the umbrella and leave without paying simply to get back at the owner for the self-service, but unfortunately, she still needed a map, so she was destined to go back inside.

"I hope you accept credit cards. I just discovered that I don't have much cash on me." The water was dripping from her all over the floor, and not trying to be polite anymore, she tossed the umbrella back into the dusty corner.

"I hope so, too." The old man took out a portable card slider, pressed a couple of buttons, and from somewhere behind the counter, Maya heard the noise of a dial-up modem.

"Can I use your phone now?"

"As soon as the transaction goes through," he said, looking at her like she was a small child asking the stupidest of questions. But after a minute, he smiled and placed an opened *Chicago Voice* on the counter. "By the way, I finally know where I recognize you from."

Maya's photo took up an eighth of the page and had been printed with every Saturday edition for the last two years since she had become the local star of the *Chicago Voice*. She started out working for the *Voice*, second only to the *New York Times*, as a clerk in the marketing division.

Later, they let her process and rearrange public announcements, and after a year, she was one of the obituary writers for nearly two years. It was not the most positive sort of work, but some people's relatives were ready to pay big money for a beautifully written hundred-word write-up. Sometimes, it was love for the departed, and sometimes it was guilt that motivated those requests.

Of course, while someone walks among us, we are too busy to say how much we appreciate him, but after he has died, we feel the need to print our sentiments in over a hundred thousand copies. This was in addition to the flowers, memorial cards, and unnecessarily expensive coffins. Such a pricy box for a piece of meat. But even though Maya could write some beautiful parting words, she did not believe in all these ceremonial procedures. That is why, when she found out about the cancer, she made clear notes in her will instructing that she be cremated or donated as a cadaver for medical research.

It seemed like a rotten deal to die in the middle of one's thirties, but what could she do? No, no, she would fight and take all of the available treatments, but she would not be afraid of death itself. She valued life, and as much as she despised death, she was not afraid of it. Her attitude was in stark contrast to that of some of her friends. This is why she had not yet told anyone about the growing mass on her neck. She could not tolerate all the sad eyes and words of comfort. Sometimes, just for a laugh, she would write an obituary for her friends on their birthday. The more superstitious of them did not appreciate her dark humor, but she always thought that you have to laugh at death while you still can.

Popularity had come to her two years ago after a tragic accident. On a rainy day just like this one, a Boeing A320 crashed just ten miles away from the airport. Of 150 passengers, only eighteen survived. Maya was returning from a conference when the plane, failing to maintain balance, crashed into a cornfield. Like a good journalist, she always carried her camera with her, but when she heard voices screaming from the broken tail of the plane, she dropped the camera and rushed inside to help.

A week later, the eighteen survivors agreed to give an exclusive interview just for Maya Polanski. The *Chicago Voice* sold a record number of copies for that specific issue, reprinting it three times. And that was how Maya won her Pulitzer Prize and two pages in every Saturday's edition where she could write about anything she wanted or publish articles of new, promising authors.

"It's funny how anyone can recognize me from that photo. I hate my hair in it!" Her smile came back.

To be honest, she loved that photo; she had chosen it over a hundred others. Stanley, her photographer and good friend, said that it was the last time he would ever take pictures of her. Well, she did have high standards, which were not easy to meet, and that is probably why she was still unmarried. She loved the attention, though, and the celebrity treatment she often received just for a silly double-page article in a newspaper.

"Oh, it's finally working. Give me your card, please."

Maya gave him a credit card with the *Chicago Voice* logo on it and stepped closer to the window. With cruel irony, the rain finally stopped; if she had known, she would have waited a while longer rather than getting soaked. Actually, she would rather have waited at home. On rainy days, she preferred to sit on her couch wrapped in a long, plaid throw next to the floor-to-ceiling window in her apartment. She imagined herself there, on the twentieth floor, looking out over gloomy Chicago while listening to vinyl records and the purring of her cat.

"So what happened in our area that's brought Maya Polanski herself?" The shop owner's voice totally changed after the transaction went through. He even put a map into a little bag for souvenirs, along with a receipt.

"I wish I knew for sure!" Maya playfully moved her finger over the top of a dusty coffee thermos, leaving a visible line.

"Sorry, I don't have visitors very often, but if you want, I can brew some fresh coffee. Or tea?"

"No, no worries, I need to go anyway. Seems the rain has finally stopped, so I guess I should use the opportunity while I can. Oh, I'm going to need to find a place for the night."

"Right. I can tell this pause isn't going to last long. When it starts raining around here, it rains for weeks. But I still think you should dry out a little and have a hot drink. You said you needed the phone; here, make your call. Just push nine first. I'll go make some coffee and look for an address. I have a friend in Lake City who works in one of the motels. I'll call her after you've finished, and she'll prepare you a room."

"Wow, aren't you a handy gentlemen! Why did they stop making men like you?" That was her first honest smile since she had been there, and the old owner smiled back.

"I'll go so I won't bother you. If you need to, you can use my chair," he said, rolling the squeaky thing toward her before leaving the shop.

Maya felt like a conqueror who not only had won the throne in a castle but who had tamed the king as well.

Carefully and with slight disgust, she pressed the sticky buttons on the phone, dialing the *Chicago Voice*. As soon as the machine started playing the recorded greeting, she punched in Bill's extension number. Normally, he stayed in his office until late.

"Mr. Sawyer's office."

"Hi, Alison, it's Maya."

"Oh, Miss Polanski, how's the trip?" Bill's secretary seemed happy to hear her voice.

"It's a total disaster. I'll tell you everything on Monday. Can I speak to Bill?"

"Sorry, he left a couple hours ago. I thought you knew about his dinner with the mayor."

"Damn it! I totally forgot! That's why he's not answering his cell."

"He left me the number in case you called asking for him. Do you want me to bridge you?" Alison was the most clever and resourceful secretary that Maya knew. On more than one occasion, she had thought about stealing her from her ungrateful chief editor.

"Yes, dear, please! I would LOVE to talk to this bastard."

"One moment!" Alison started to giggle and put Maya on hold while trying to connect with her boss.

Maya calmed herself, repeating in her head everything she wanted to say to Bill. He hated her yelling, so if she wanted to tell him exactly what she thought about him, she would need to keep her voice calm, or otherwise, he would just hang up on her. She appreciated that he expected her call and left a number where she could reach him. It would be interesting to know whether he had left it in case of an emergency or simply to find out about her research as soon as possible. Did he really believe the story about this resurrected girl was more than a scam? Normally, they never printed anything scandalous or sensational like that. They wrote about corruption, robberies, murders, city events, dirty politics, international relations, or anything that generated public interest, like stories on a rare animal or cute puppies who swam across the Chicago River. But what they did not print were stories about aliens, magic, curses, and mysterious resurrections. That was the kind of nonsense for the *Chicago Twilight*.

The hold music changed into the sounds of a party, and a strong masculine voice overshot the din.

"Hey, girl! So, what's up?"

"What's up? Well, not my self-esteem, apparently. I can't believe I let myself agree to this. Bill, I feel like I'm in the belly button of the United States—dirty, smelly, full of lint and rotting food crumbs."

"Did I ever say how much I love your poetic language?"

"I hope you're enjoying the party."

"It is nice. The mayor is a man of great taste. You should see the ice sculptures. Oh, and I asked them to put aside a bottle of your favorite champagne. We'll open it when you get back...I miss you already!"

Normally, Maya never mixed her personal life with work, but what she had with Bill was hard to call a personal life—they just slept together from time to time. Yes, they had great sex, but nothing more. It was physical satisfaction without all the romantic stuff. They were both so busy with work and careers, so they simply did not have time for dating or looking for the perfect match.

"I want to go home. Seriously, Bill, this is a terrible place. Even my GPS doesn't know where I am. The weather is a total nightmare."

"I'm sorry...So what about the girl?"

"Are you kidding? I'm still on my way, and who knows if I'll get there alive?

"Well, luckily for you, people come back from the dead there!"

"I will hang up! I am tired, wet and hungry. All I want is to find a hotel with a nice warm bed."

"Will you think about me?" It seemed like Bill had had a bit too much champagne.

"Yes, especially if there are bed bugs!"

"Hey, I offered for you to fly to Twin Cities and rent a car there. No, you decided to drive all the way from Chicago."

"You know that I hate rental cars. They smell like mothballs and tobacco, exactly like my nana."

Bill broke into laughter.

"Well, Maya, if someone else publishes an interview with the Pattersons, instead of going on your European vacation, you'll be writing criminal chronicles…Every day!"

Of course he was joking, and Maya knew it. She was too popular to move back to routine work. But she really needed the vacation time next month. She was not going to Europe, though. She would start chemotherapy and would write her articles from her apartment in Florida all the way until her surgery in December. People said her doctor was the god of oncology and that he performed real miracles. If she had any chance, it was only with him.

"Bill, I feel like I'm wasting my time."

"Don't say that. You know that I have a sixth sense with stuff like this. The man who ran over the girl was in jail, and now he's free again. The parents didn't even press charges. There is medical proof that the girl was dead. Eleven broken bones…Maya, they did an autopsy! You know what that means? So if this girl is not a zombie, then she's a symbol of faith— they're even sending an expert from the Vatican."

"I don't know…"

"But I do! We need this. This story might be your next Pulitzer, and it could bring back our sales. The parents avoid everyone, but if someone can find a way, it's you!" Bill knew how to manipulate her. Maya knew what he was doing, and she hated herself for letting him get into her head, but she could not say no to that. "And if you get this, I'll pay for your tickets to Europe. First class."

"I make enough to buy my own tickets."

"Then what do you want? Anything you ask—it's yours!"

"Ha, you said it!" She laughed evilly, knowing that she would find the best and most inconvenient way for him to compensate her for her struggles.

"I am serious, so start thinking, but I need to go. Call me as soon as you find something."

"Fine, fine. Say hi to the mayor and Mr. Cloudy."

"I will. Drive safe."

"Don't forget my bottle!" Bill did not seem to catch her last line and, on the other side, sounded the long tone of a disconnected call. "Jerk!"

Into the room walked the shop owner with a clean coffee pot full of dark magic. The old man had removed his cap and was even wearing a nicer shirt now. Maybe she had applied too much flirtation to her voice… She decided it was probably better to leave before he offered her his heart, but the smell of coffee was so good. Maya chose to stay for a cup or two, and maybe the old man would know something more that she could use. But afterward, she would jump back into her Audi and would proceed to do what she did best—searching out the truth.

"Oh, Billy, I hope it's worth it," she whispered and picked out the biggest of the plastic cups set out for coffee.

CHAPTER 2

The alarm clock broke the silence. Maya hated that device with every fiber of her soul.

In recent years, she had worked only when she wanted to work or when she felt the inspiration, rather, and it was only around inspiration that she built the rest of her life. She could sit up until two or three o'clock in the morning writing an article and then easily could sleep until noon without any hesitation or guilt. She did not always have to make an appearance at the office and usually only did so in those cases where she wanted to show off her new outfit or when something went wrong and she had to pour out her anger on the subordinates in the department.

But this time, she needed to get up early. Really early—at ungodly 6:00 AM, in fact. And without the alarm, she would not have woken up. Yesterday's traveling had drained her emotionally and physically. Lately, she had been tiring fairly easily, and Maya was not sure whether she should blame the cancer or the variety of pills that she took on a daily basis.

The motel, recommended by her new friend, was not as bad as she had imagined. It had nice Southern-style decor, quiet surroundings, and, most importantly, it was clean, dry, and supplied fresh-smelling bed linens. They had given her a nice room with a view of the lake and a large TV with a shiny, clean remote control. This was nothing new, actually. When business owners found out who she was, they tried their best to impress her because Maya often would recommend the places where she had eaten or stayed. Of course, this motel was not remotely as grand as the Plaza where she normally stayed, but they tried really hard, even sending fresh flowers and a bottle of cider to her room.

But for all their trying, Maya fell asleep right there in her clothes as soon as she lay down and turned on the TV. It was later, around three, having woken from the pain, that she took her medication, turned off the lights, set the alarm, and crawled into bed.

She would have loved to sleep more, but knowing that as soon as she met the Pattersons, she would be free to go home gave her motivation and even an energy kick. Maya took a long, hot shower, playing through her mind different scenarios and approaches to how she would pin down the camera-shy family for an interview. She was debating between an attack accusing the parents of pulling off some sort of scam so that they would agree to clear their names or trying to offer them peace, saying that if they gave an interview to a big newspaper, the rest would leave them alone. Personally, she preferred plan A, but she promised Bill that she would do her best, even if that meant plan B.

She always traveled with three or four sets of clothes for different situations, so the light brown pantsuit would be perfect for this particular case. She needed to look professional and well-to-do but not too snobbish or intimidating. She applied a reasonable amount of makeup, ate the breakfast that had been delivered to her door (this was her first motel with room delivery—a miracle indeed), and by eight, was ready to go on the hunt.

Thank the saints, the rain had finally stopped, but the sky was still gloomy and dark. She was not even sure whether the sun had risen, and if so, from which side? The clouds were so low that Maya started to feel a little claustrophobic. If they came any lower, it seemed that the invisible pillars holding the heavens up would break apart, leaving the sky to collapse onto the heads of unsuspecting humanity.

At least the GPS was working fine today, and the home of the resurrected girl would not be so hard to find. Most of Maya's time was spent in either Chicago or Miami and even when she had business trips, they were usually to other megalopoli where life never ended. That is why Lake City seemed to her like a town under some sort of sleeping spell. There were almost no cars in the streets, not many people about, and no typical city noises. The random citizens who did show up along her way looked almost identical, with no personality or identity. Boring! A town like this was probably best for meeting your death. You could escape from everyone and become one of the many faceless shadows, waiting for the cancer to eat you up. Maybe that is what she should do. If the chemo and surgery failed, she would sell her home in Florida and move here.

"Oh, stop it!" How in the world had she become so passive? She decided to blame it on the gloomy surroundings. "Suck it up, Maya!"

The subdivision where the Pattersons lived was another cookie-cutter reality typical of small cities. More empty streets and sleepy houses. From one of the windows, someone looked out at her and then hid back behind the blinds. She had seen cities like that in videos about nuclear tests— those towns that the government would build in a remote corner of the Nevada Desert to find out just what kind of damage their bombs were capable of unleashing. If she had had a button that would blow this town to kingdom come, she would have pressed it without any hesitation.

Unless…

Finally, something impressed her and made her shark-like instincts wake up. Next to the Pattersons' home were parked about thirty cars, most of which were covered with the logos of different TV channels and newspaper firms.

"Shoot! Bill's going to kill me!"

Who knows how long they had been "fishing" there? Maya looked around, searching for any familiar faces. No, it seemed that only the most unwanted and least ambitious people were here. So many were young journalists with tired eyes and messy hair. They might have been sleeping in their cars. Well, they were at the beginning of their career, so she could understand their desperation. What she could not understand was what the hell she was doing there.

With the press right outside their house, the Pattersons would sit inside like an oyster in its shell—tight and quiet. That was good and bad news at the same time. The good news was that no one would have gotten anything yet. Otherwise, the cars would already be on the way back, hurrying to tell the world elements of the sensation. So what could she do that had not already been tried by the others? She decided to wait for an opportunity to present itself.

Maya lowered the back of her seat, made herself comfortable, and prepared her photo camera, making sure it had enough battery and that the memory card was properly formatted. Then she took her book and, keeping an eye on the house, began reading.

"Cancer: The Battle Inside" was written by Maya's psychologist. She herself had gone through that hell six years ago and came out victorious, and that is why Maya chose precisely her. She needed someone who would understand her, who she would trust without having to fear exposure.

At the same time, not everything in the book resonated with Maya. The author suggested that you share the journey with your friends and family, enlisting them to help fight the battle with you. Oh, no! Maya left her parents' house as soon as she had finished high school, and for them, she was an example of stability and a source of pride. She could not let them pity her. She could not see Bill worrying about her; the thought of him being gentle and supportive nauseated her a bit. She definitely would not tell her subordinates! All those puppy eyes and the endless "How are you feeling today?" would make her want to murder someone. No, they need to see the she-wolf in her, the one who fights to the end to subdue her prey.

What really made her mad was that she had never smoked for fear of lung cancer, she always ate organic food to avoid stomach cancer, and she never used a tanning bed because she thought it was the best way to get skin cancer. And after everything, she ended up with a spinal tumor near her neck. It was not aggressive, and on most days, she did not even remember it was there. But it was slowly draining her energy, growing like an unwanted baby, an invader. It demanded no sacrifices, at least not yet, but she needed to eliminate it before it turned into a puppet master, pulling Maya's strings however he liked or cutting them all at any moment.

As soon as the garage door slowly started upward, everything around came to life. People with cameras and microphones started running from their cars. Photographers rushed ahead, trying to stake out the best spot. She stepped outside as well but did not even try to push through the craziness. Dozens of voices turned the sleepy morning into a croaking bazaar of vultures.

"Mr. Patterson, is it true that you're not going to press charges against…"

"Where is Vicki right now? How does she feel?"

"Is she eating? Does she speak to you?"

"Mr. Patterson, is it true that the coroner is your school friend?"

"Has a Vatican representative contacted you yet?"

"Do you think it's a miracle or a medical mistake?"

Brad Patterson finally turned to look and charged the paparazzi. Before he was able to say anything, flashes from different cameras started to blind him. There were more questions, more noises. They pushed closer, almost to his face…

"BACK OFF!" he yelled. "Leave us alone, please! We're glad that our daughter…"

"Are you sure it is your daughter?"

"Did she tell you what she saw during her time of death? Was she in hell or Heaven?"

Brad pushed away the camera of the photographer who had the nerve to ask the last question, and Maya thought that with his other hand, he would sock him in the mouth…No. At the last moment, he regained control of himself and stepped back.

"Get off of my property, or I'll call the cops. I'll go get my rifle!"

How interesting…Maya was intrigued now. Either this man was a great actor and played his part really well, building up interest and tension, or he really did not like all of the publicity. But if Maya accepted the latter, then she would have to believe the girl had been resurrected for real. Otherwise, what was the point of making such a show of the funeral and then hiding from everyone? Maybe money? Maybe they did not want to share their story with everyone but with some specific source who would be willing to pay an exclusive amount for an exclusive interview. She guessed that she should call Bill and ask how much he was willing to pay for this story.

"You have no right to hide this from the public!"

"Do you know what or who helped your daughter?"

"How is the mental health of your wife? Are you not afraid to leave her alone at home with your daughter?"

Brad jumped into his car and pulled back from the garage straight into the mass of journalists. They darted around but would not give up on their questions. They tried filming and taking pictures of him all the way into the street until he closed the garage door with his remote and hit the accelerator. Several cars followed straight after him, picking up their respective journalists on the way. Only four other cars remained in the subdivision with the hope that maybe Vicki or Lisa would look through one of the heavily covered windows.

Maya, though, was looking into a different window. According to a copy of the police report that Bill managed to get her, somewhere living here was supposed to be an eye-witness of everything that had happened, and if Maya played her cards right, she might get more information from that one woman than all of those idiots who were trying to chase Brad Patterson.

She waited until the rest of the journalists returned to their cars, but only after they saw her leave would they go. Trying not to draw too much attention to herself, Maya made a loop around a few blocks and circled back, parking right next to the house opposite the Pattersons'. Seeing that she had driven off, the others figured there was no reason to stay. The scene was hers for the taking.

Psychology is a big part of journalism, and Maya's skills were flawless. All she needed was an opportunity to start a conversation, and if she could get that chance, then more than likely, she could get anything she needed. Some said that she used hypnosis. In college, they called her "Queen Cobra" because her voice and stare made so many dumb "bunnies" do or tell anything she asked.

Acting casually, she approached the door. She could hear that someone inside was already waiting for her. Maya adjusted her jacket and fixed her hair, tossing it back confidently. Yes, she knew that whoever was inside was watching her, but she took her time all the same. After stretching her shoulders to relieve the soreness, she removed the voice recorder from her purse. Excitement behind the door came to a boiling point. As soon as Maya pressed the button, the door immediately opened.

"Yes, yes?!" A lady in her late fifties with a fluffy cat in her hands tried to show so much surprise that it came off ridiculously cheesy.

"Good morning, I'm Maya Polanski, *Chicago Voice…*"

"Oh, dear, of course I know who you are! Come in, come in! Make yourself at home!" The lady grabbed Maya's hand and almost dragged her in, locking the door right behind her. "I'm Josie. Josie Crogan, at your service. I can't believe it, Maya Polanski at my house!"

Josie acted slightly crazy but was nothing dangerous. Maya met fans really often, and most of them were stay-at-home mothers or women like this who spent the biggest part of their day watching the shopping channel, working in gardens, and petting cats. This was her target audience for the romance novels she wrote using a pseudonym. Under that name, she had written some erotic stories for popular magazines, and her Florida home was attached to that name. In the beginning, it was just a game, a double life. Now she started to think that maybe she would not die and that only Maya Polanski, the journalist from Chicago, would get eaten by cancer, but Lala Flint, the author of bestsellers from Miami, would keep on surprising the world with new stories and novels.

"Do you want tea or coffee?"

"I've already had coffee today, so a cup of tea would be great."

"Oh gosh, I have great tea! Straight from India. You will love it! You'll love it so much that I wouldn't be surprised to read about it in the next *Voice*!" Josie started to giggle, embarrassed like she had told the stupidest of jokes, but Maya understood that this was the price she had to pay if she wanted to get information.

"You know me too well, Josie. You know how much I love to write about my adventures. And your town is a real digging site for treasures!"

"Believe me, it is! Oh, I can tell you everything you want to know! Come! Come on into the kitchen!"

While Josie was twittering on about her love for Maya's writing, which Saturday issue was her favorite, and how she read every article at least three times, Maya was looking around for clues. Well, there was no need to be a detective to figure out that Josie was a spinster. She had no pictures of kids or any man, no toys or extra shoes, and everything was bright and shiny, like after a visit from Mr. Clean. And he must be the only male who would visit her since not a single normal man could survive in a house like this. No, this was not even a home. It was the set for a soap opera, where everything was too pink, too sweet, and too fluffy. And Josie looked like an elderly Barbie in her unfulfilled dream house, but instead of Ken, there were cats—at least five that Maya could count.

"Please, dear, sit! You must try my pumpkin pie. I got the recipe from my grandmother."

"You're too kind. I'm so lucky to meet you."

"Oh, yes, you are!" and Josie carefully but purposefully tapped Maya's hand.

Maya hated being touched, especially by lunatics like this one, but she kept smiling.

"So what are you writing about?"

There was no need to postpone anything. Josie was ready to tell everything she knew and maybe even more. Maya placed her voice recorder on the table, asking if it would be okay if she recorded their interview. Josie had nothing against it, and more than that, she fixed her hair and straightened her necklace as if the voice recorder could care how she looked.

"So, I'd like to ask you what you know about the accident at the Pattersons' house."

For the next ten minutes, Maya simply zoned out, making serious faces, nodding, pretending to take notes, and checking the recorder. She had only a couple sips of tea and found that it was bad, but not compared to the absolutely disgusting pie. Josie chirped on about everything, starting with her decision to move to Lake City and about the day when the Pattersons moved into the house across the street. She talked about Brad and how he had been working at the visitor center. She talked about Lisa, how great she was, how beautiful her wedding dress was, and how cute she looked during the pregnancy. There were stories about Vicki and how her parents would take her out in a stroller made to look like a little royal carriage.

Another five minutes passed, and Josie was telling about the bad feeling she had that tragic day and how important it was to listen to her inner voice. She even related to Maya a couple examples of when her "feelings" had saved her life. And just because of those feelings, she had been next to the window that day expecting something to happen. She told Maya about the new blonde neighbor and how she often fought with her husband, blaming that on magnetic storms.

After a small lecture about bad ecology and explosions on the sun, she moved on to the accident. If Maya had been in charge of the Oscars, she would definitely give one to Josie. Maybe even two, for both leading and supporting actress—anything to stop this terrible performance. But when Josie started to imitate Brad's bitter cry of anguish, Maya decided to give her one more for best actor as well. Oh, how Josie cried, how she cried!

Maya felt obligated to shed a couple tears as well, even though all the theatrics were starting to play on her nerves.

Only after she had taken a moment in respectful silence, and her tears had finally dried…and she loudly blew her nose…and took a long chain of sips from her teacup, was Josie ready to tell about what happened during the funeral.

Maya tried not to interrupt. Yesterday, she was certain that all this resurrection nonsense was just a con to bring about attention and popularity, but today…Normally, people who were looking for publicity did not run away from cameras. Today, little Vicki should have been in the studios of every single talk show and invited to the White House and the biggest churches in the country. But no, all that everyone kept showing was a blurry video recorded on a cell phone. Rain, a crazy man running from the building, and a beam of light toward the door where the resurrected girl appeared. It was not much, but people watched again and again, debating whether it was possible or if the girl just decided to "wake up" or if someone had helped her.

"Well, Josie, it's indeed a really interesting story."

"You want to say my interview will be on your page?" Josie blushed, and her eyes started to sparkle.

"More likely—yes." Maya smiled back. She knew, probably, that this was the only story that she would be able to bring back to Bill. "I am sure my chief will love this cover."

"Oh heavens, my friends will die of envy! We're all huge fans of yours. HUGE! You should come see—we even keep a book in the library made from Saturday pages. You can't leave town until you see it!"

"That's flattering." For some reason, the name Misery King popped into Maya's head, and she started looking toward the door. She turned off her recorder and put it back into her purse. "Unfortunately, though, you won't become too popular."

"I'm sorry?"

"Well, you see, stories like yours are going to be in almost every single paper. Did you see how many reporters were outside?"

'But I wasn't talking to anyone else. Deep inside, I knew you'd show up!"

"Yeah…But you weren't the only one who was there during the memorial service. And I'm sure my colleagues will have found someone who could tell me exactly what you've told me."

"There were a lot of people, it's true. Almost our whole church was there."

"What is the name of the church, by the way? And how many members are there?"

"Love of Christ. Around a hundred."

"You see? Almost a hundred other lovers could offer something like you have, and even if I try really hard, your story is going to be just one of many…Unless…you tell me the truth. Then every other paper would fight over the right to reprint your testimony."

"What kind of truth?" Josie looked confused.

"Oh, come on, you really thought the girl was dead? You seem like a well-educated, intelligent woman; don't tell me that you really bought their performance."

"What do you mean by performance? I saw everything with my own eyes!" Josie jumped up from her chair so fast that her cats, startled, ran out of the room.

"I'm sorry if I offended you. I didn't mean to at all. But don't you think that maybe someone just wanted you to see exactly what they wanted to show?"

"My pastor thinks it was the hand of God! And I am not going to question how He does His work!"

Maya tried so hard not to roll her eyes.

"I totally understand! I'm a faithful Catholic, and so I'm really careful not to judge others or question the ways of our Lord. I do want to believe you and make others believe, too. The world needs to believe that miracles are back, that God is still alive, and that the miracles the Apostles did can be done today as well!" Maya could not believe what she had just said, but that is what you need to do. If you want to gain a lunatic's trust, you have to act like one of them. "But don't you wonder if someone might be trying to make things look like a miracle to steal glory from our Lord? What if we tell everyone that it was a divine act, and then later, they find out that it was all a hoax? What then?"

"I don't think so…" said Josie, trying to defend her position, but Maya could see the change in her eyes.

Oh, that was too easy.

"So, let's try to think back again. Maybe…maybe there was something suspicious. Anything that would make you question it? We know that really soon, a Vatican expert will be here, but let's try to beat him and get to the facts first. If there are no gaps, and it is all real, that's great! But if not, we're going to need to understand how they staged all of it."

"Very well." Josie sat back at the table and took a deep breath. Her face changed. It became cold and distant. Gently, she adjusted her teacup and spoon. "Look, Miss Polanski…I am sure if you dig deep into this story, you will definitely find something to support your theory. But I saw with my own eyes how the Jeep hit Vicki. I heard it! I wish I could erase it from my memory, but I can't!

"Look at Brad. Look at his gray hair. I wish you could see Lisa a week ago and now. She's not the same person anymore. Her face had gotten ten or twenty years older. Death and great pain changed them forever. You can't fake that. We're not in a Hollywood movie, Miss Polanski. I saw Vicki dead. I saw her in her coffin. Not a single kid could lay that still for that long.

"You know…you can write whatever you want, and I can't stop you, but one thing I want you to know is that starting today, I will never buy a Saturday issue of *Chicago Voice* again! And now you'll need to excuse me. I have plenty of things to do around the house. So if you're finished with your tea, get the hell out!"

CHAPTER 3

"No, you heard me correctly. I'm leaving!" Maya was picking up her things in the motel room.

"I can't believe you didn't find anything!"

Her phone, the speaker on, lay on the nightstand next to a half-packed bag.

"Bill, I promised to come and check it out. I came, and I checked! Tomorrow morning, I'm leaving."

"Listen, maybe you need to offer them money."

"You know what? *You* come here and try to give them your money." Maya stopped with a hair drier in her hand and pointed it toward the phone as if Bill could see her. "You think I was born yesterday? Bill, they are crazy! They don't need fame or money! This whole town is nuts! I talked with two neighbors, with the security guy from Brad's work, with the pastor of their church, and some people in a local coffee shop. They're all brainwashed!"

"If they're not telling the truth, then maybe…"

"Don't! Do not even go there! A little bit more, and I'll start believing it myself, and if that happens, I'd rather stay here and not spread this mental illness onto others."

"You're so skeptical…And I can't understand how you, of all people, can give up that easily!"

"That easily?! Are you freaking kidding me? Well, you have plenty of interns. Send them up here. They'd love to sleep on the rug under the Pattersons' door for you, just for a chance to take a picture through the window, unless Brad shoots them. I have a feeling that really soon, we'll need to resurrect a couple dozen annoying journalists. But me...I am done. With the first rays of the sun, I am out of here. Actually, I'm not sure they even have a sun here!"

Bill was disappointed. He was not saying anything, but from the sound of his heavy breathing, she knew he was quite angry.

"Seriously, Billy...It's not worth it. Believe me, it was a bad idea in the first place. They're liars. I'm not sure how many people are involved in this fairy tale, but they all cover up for each other." This last bit, she said with a softer tone, not like his subordinate, but like the one who fell asleep on his shoulder those nights when she felt too tired to drive home.

But Bill's reaction was shocking, almost as if someone else had replaced him on the phone. His voice became cold and distant. His phrases were sharp, and their hits destructive like the swings of an ax.

"You knew from the beginning? Bull shit! Yes, once you were good, maybe one of the best, but now you're just a lazy, spoiled, disrespectful brat. You act like a diva, ignoring your responsibilities! Did you even bother to ask about other miracles?

Maya kept silent, partly because she had not expected such an attack.

"I didn't send you there because I don't have anyone else to do it. It wasn't a punishment for you. It was a reward. For the last three years, a lot of weird things have been going on in Lake City. The whole of their society is covering it up. Tell me, did you speak with any journalists there? How many locals did you interview? And not just for a checkmark, but to really talk to them and get some answers?

"What am I supposed to ask? 'Have you seen any flying saucers lately? Any little gray men renting a boat for fishing?'"

"Stop it! I'm not in the mood!" He was almost yelling at this point, and it made Maya's stomach turn into a stone. A wave of cold heat started bubbling up from the deep vaults of her anger. "We are not looking for a UFO!"

"Then what?!" she yelled back. "How do you imagine I can do something if I have no idea what's going on?"

"I can't tell you. You need to find out everything on your own!"

"Are you kidding again? What, are we in middle school, and you've decided to create a scavenger hunt for me?"

"Anything I would say could change the course of events!"

"Do you even hear yourself, Bill? What a pile of..."

"Maya, listen! And listen really carefully!" Suddenly, he lowered his voice, almost like he had decided to whisper something into her ear. Maya picked up the phone, switching off the speaker. "I know it sounds insane. I know you have questions, but believe me, if I tell you more, you might lose your job, and I might lose something way more valuable."

"Are you threatening me?"

"Maya, you don't listen..."

"Oh, I do, and I've heard enough. And you know what? I'm done! You want to fire me? Fine! You really think I won't just find a new job? Ha!"

"Maya, slow down..." A slight tone of fear penetrated Bill's voice.

"No, Bill, you were totally clear! You'll fire me if I don't keep playing the idiot over here."

"Maya, there are really powerful people who need you to do the..."

"People. Your mother? Or your dad, who left you as chair of *Chicago Voice*? You know that the *New York Times* called me almost a year ago asking me to work for them?"

"They might kill me for telling you..."

"Kill you for the resurrected girl story? Are you serious? You're so pathetic! Take some paranoia meds, okay?"

"Maya! MAYA! Ask people about the Water Walker!" shouted Bill, his voice cracking like he had just said something really stupid and wanted to take it back.

"I'm leaving in the morning. I'll stop by the office in the evening to pick up my stuff, so I would appreciate it if you wouldn't make a scene there."

"No, please. I'm sorry...Please, Maya. Please just let me..."

Maya hung up on him, partly from anger and partly from confusion. If she kept listening, he might have started crying right then and there. Bill?! Crying?! Nonsense!

Well, this was all for the best. Maybe now she could better concentrate on her health. A vacation would be too complicated to manage, but now that she was unemployed, there was no need to stress over deadlines and come up with fake pictures from Europe. She had enough money in her savings account to survive this disaster, but only if she was destined to survive.

The phone started ringing again. It was Bill.

"Nope, I've heard enough."

She rejected the call and turned off the phone completely. Luckily for her, she had not told him the name of the motel where she was staying, so there was hope for a good and peaceful night's sleep.

*

It was almost four when Maya gave up trying to fall asleep. A couple of times, she almost did, but as soon as she started dreaming, something would kick her back to reality. Medicine helped kill the pain and calm her down a little after the fight with Bill, but it did not remove the terrible feeling that scratched her soul inside out. Now, like after a heavy hangover, a headache and nausea made her get up and run to the bathroom.

She threw up her late dinner, and for the moment, she felt better. That was the first time since the diagnosis. Maybe it was just stress, or perhaps the steak had not been cooked well enough, making her sick. She got up, washed her face, and looked at herself in the mirror.

"What should we do now?"

Her reflection looked back at her with emotionless silence.

Maya replayed the dialogue with Bill in her head a hundred times and looked at her phone. She was sure that as soon as she powered it on, there would be a dozen text messages and a full voicemail box, but she was not ready to read them or listen to his voice right now.

If she survived her valley of deathly shadows, should she really move to New York or just work as a romance writer and sell her flat in Chicago? She loved to travel, but starting from scratch with a different news firm... Well, time would show, but for now, she needed to hit the road. If she started feeling tired, she would just take a nap in nearby towns along the way.

She threw the rest of her things into a bag and left the room, closing the door with great satisfaction as though she had overcome a major milestone in her life.

Luckily, there was still a light on at the front desk, so she would be able to check out without having to do so over the phone. She prepared her key and the newspaper's credit card and went straight to the desk.

A teenage girl, who slightly resembled the owner of the motel, was sitting on a couch in the lobby wrapped in a blanket and watching some scary movie on her old laptop. The quality was terrible, either from using the wrong codec or because it was a pirated version of the film. The story looked familiar, but Maya could not recall the title. In the nineties, when she was in college, films like this were on belt production, and nearly every week, something bloody involving naïve college students would come out on the market. Maya's roommate had worked part-time at a video store, and every day, she would bring back something new to watch.

"Good morning. I'd like to check out." Maya tried not to scare the girl, but it seemed she was not the type to be easily scared.

"Leaving?" The girl paused her movie and got up from her couch, walking toward the computer. "What room?"

"Twelve." Maya placed the key and card on the counter. Apparently, not everyone recognized her face, which she found a little bit offensive.

The girl picked up the key, pressed a couple of buttons on the keyboard, and an old dot matrix printer started spitting out papers. Maya did not know there was still a company that could produce ink for these ancient machines. Who would keep junk like this when, for fifty bucks, you could buy a newer and faster device?

"It might take a while. We have some coffee and freshly baked cookies if you want."

"Why not?" Maya did start to feel a little hungry. Maybe her stomach had decided to work again, so she picked up a Styrofoam cup and filled it with hot coffee. She covered it with a lid because she would rather drink it on her way, and then she picked out a couple cookies.

"You paid for three nights. Do you want money back on your card?"

"No need. Keep it as a tip." Maya smiled. "It's my company card, they wouldn't mind."

The girl did not respond, taking the gesture for granted. Or perhaps people always left her hundred-dollar tips. Whatever. All Maya wanted to do was leave. She took the papers and signed where the girl had left marks.

"I wonder how many more will leave today." The teenager smirked while returning the card to Maya.

"Excuse me?"

"More journalists. You're not the first one who's going home tonight."

Maya was not surprised. The town was small; it was obvious that everyone here knew everything going on.

"I guess someone was smarter than I if they left earlier."

"It was a stupid idea from the beginning." The girl finally looked at Maya, and something scary was in her stare. Her eyes were those of an old woman who had lived a long life and who had grown tired on the last stretch. That sort do not expect anything new, and they give up trying. All they want is rest.

Maya had heard so many stories about family businesses and people who get trapped in them for their whole lives. Minneapolis was not that far from here, and all she needed was to say "no" to her parents and go to college to live her own life. No...Maya had a different mentality toward home. Most of her high school classmates still lived in Alaska, working in small shops, on fishing boats, or building civilization through the miles of forest and mountains. Her own four brothers still lived in the same town as her parents. But Maya herself limited her involvement with family, even on holidays when she would just send gift cards and make Skype calls.

"Why is that idea stupid?"

"Because no one wants to deal with 'Love of Christ.' They're all weird and paranoid."

No, Maya, no! Home! She must go home. But she could not resist.

"Seems like you don't really like them?"

"Why should I like them?" The girl picked up her blanket and moved back to the couch. "They're not a real church, just possessed fanatics! Everyone from the pastor to the ushers."

"You know them well?"

"I wish I didn't. My parents took me there all the time. Sunday school and other things. You know what I'm saying?"

"So why'd you stop going there?"

"I had my reasons," and with these words, she looked again at Maya, but this time, it was a little wolf looking at her, not an old lady. "And they'll pay for it!"

"Want to talk about it?"

"Why do you care? The story's too ugly for your Saturday column. Better go home before it starts raining again."

The girl picked up her laptop and pressed play again. Maya felt confused, put the card and receipt into her purse, and rolled her case toward the exit. She was angry but not able to overcome the boiling question inside her when she stopped next to the door and asked.

"Is the Water Walker related to the church?"

"Hell, yes. Otherwise, why would they be so uptight about it?"

"And you know who it is?"

The disgruntled youth looked at Maya again, and now it was the face of an ex-member of 'Love of Christ' there. She might hate them for some reason, but she was not willing to give up their secrets to an outsider.

"Look, Miss *Chicago Voice*, you'd be better off going to Scotland to try to get a picture of Nessie or to Idaho to interview some yeti. You'd have better luck with that than here."

*

Maya was speeding along in her car, cursing everyone and everything.

Maybe it would have been smarter to wait until dawn, but she could not wait any longer. She needed to leave this place as fast as possible. She passed the whole town in less than two minutes and jumped onto the highway, ignoring the stop sign on the corner. How stupid she felt for even agreeing to this adventure! How stupid to let Bill fool her! And how stupid ever to doubt that it was a con!

In six or seven hours, she would be back in Chicago unless the rain caught up with her on the road. Even now, because of the fog coming from the lake, the road was slippery and wet, but that was not going to slow her down.

Out! Faster and farther!

She pushed the accelerator even harder, and the speedometer slowly climbed toward the mark of 80 MPH. Please, as if some cop was actually going to patrol this area at this ungodly hour.

What a great feeling it was to blame yourself and swear at others while speeding on an empty highway! 90 MPH!

Changes! She needed more changes! Maybe she would cut her hair and color it deep black like crow feathers. A leather jacket and a bike? She always wanted to have a motorcycle, and she even had a license. Or maybe she would go to Europe, for real, for the whole two weeks until they started the treatment.

100 MPH.

Her left hand was on the wheel, her right hand held the cup of coffee. It tasted old and probably had been requested by someone who had left before Maya unless they were required to keep hot coffee out the whole night long.

Reporters. Cigarettes and coffee. A terrible sleep schedule. Long hours of putting together the articles from bits and crumbs of information. Being someone's slave. No, this would all be in the past. She should open her own newspaper. She would be a chief editor who would decide what to print and what to…

Her headlights cut a huge silhouette from the fog.

Completely on reflex, her feet slammed the brakes. Letting the coffee cup go, she clenched both hands on the wheel. The hot liquid went all over her lap, but she did not care about that right now. The car was moving toward a giant creature. Maya pulled the wheel to the right.

An adult elk, a rare sight in that area, expected Maya no more than she expected him. The Audi started spinning on the wet road.

HIT!

The airbags shot into Maya's face, but she still heard the bellowing elk and the crash of the windshield. Ignoring the impact, the car kept moving. Maya pulled the hand break, and as soon as she did, the world stopped spinning horizontally and began rotating vertically. Very soon, even that stopped having any meaning, and she was caught in the middle of a centrifuge. The sound of crashing metal and heavy "booms" echoed each time the car hit the road, creating an alternative reality around her where time slowed to eternity and memories flashed through her mind at the same time.

Another hit! But this one was different because afterward, she sensed that she was falling. After a long silence, there was a deafening splash!

Panic hit her stronger than the airbags, collapsing the air around to a claustrophobic minimum. She felt the cold water grab her ankles and start creeping toward her knees. She had flown off the road and was now in the lake!

There was no time for hesitation or weakness. The water poured inside too fast, and if she did not act immediately, then very soon she would be drowning.

Maya pushed aside the airbags and looked out a window. The water level was almost up to the top, but she could just see the shore. The car could not have flown out that far unless she had fallen from a bridge, but there was none in sight. At most, there were no more than forty feet to the shore, and she could easily reach it as long as she got out of the car first. Maya tried the door, but it was locked, and more than likely, the electronics had given up. She tried the door on the passenger side— same story. She could not even roll down the windows or the moon roof. Luckily for her, the windshield was already cracked, so all she needed was to push through without cutting herself to death.

Maya took off her shoes and jacket, as less wet clothing would make it easier to swim. She picked up her purse and put it over her head and one shoulder. For a moment, she considered turning on the phone and calling 911, but she might drown before help was to get there. Concentrating all of her strength and anger into her feet, she pushed on the windshield, but it only made the water flow in faster. She was fighting the opposing pressure of the lake.

"Damn it!"

She pushed again. The windshield started to crack even more, letting water in from another two spots. Maya leaned back and, this time, pushed with both of her feet with all the strength she could muster. Victory! The way was open, even though the car quickly filled up. Pushing herself off from the seat, she managed her way outside and to the surface, watching as her favorite car disappeared in bubbles and dark water. Cold needles start to poke her whole body.

"HELP!" she yelled as loudly as she could, but her voice seemed to vanish together with the car.

Condensed fog turned everything around into a limitless plane of water without anything to orient her. Maya could catch no glimpse of the shore, and she looked to the sky, hoping that the stars would tell her where to swim. The deep, empty space of the universe as it appeared right now was even scarier than the cold abyss that tried to swallow her. She felt so small and empty, like a little dot placed on a line divided into eternities.

"He-e-e-e-elp!" She tried again, but cold water pushed on her chest, suppressing her voice.

Her slacks weighed down with water, started pulling at her, but at least her legs were not freezing like her hands.

"He-e-e-e-e..." She accidentally swallowed some of the water and began to choke from the disgusting taste of mud and slime.

"Somebody help!"

Only resounding emptiness came to give her a last kiss and a solemn farewell.

"Ple-e-e-e-ase! Help!"

She did not know which direction to swim. Fog—the deep, white, omnipresent god of the lake—was covering her with his attention.

A sharp pain struck her leg, stiffening the muscles. Maya began hitting her leg, but the cramp was spreading all the way to her feet. With one fast movement, she pulled off one of her earrings and poked her leg with the sharp end as hard as she could. It helped, and the cramp left her alone with the feeling of a great bruise. She knew that with water as cold as this, her whole body would soon be fighting cramps. She needed to swim, no matter what direction. It was better than not moving at all.

She had never wanted to live like she did in that moment. Swim!

Overcoming herself and the cold water, she started to swim toward the rising moon. Why? Simply because if she were to die, then at least she could enjoy the view. Each movement was painful and cost her more energy. She felt like she was trying to fight against invisible razors that cut her to the bones.

Light!

"He-e…e-e-e…elp…" She pushed the words out, but her voice left her completely, and she could hardly hear her own wheezing.

Swim! She must keep swimming. Stay on top!

Her clothes got heavier like they had put down anchors and roots, trying to pull her under the water. No! She must keep fighting. Help is there. They just need to see her.

Pain struck her hand, and Maya screamed, but no sound came from her open mouth. She lost control and momentarily sank under the water, swallowing the lake and its darkness. Maya made attempts to push herself up, but the darkness told her not to worry. It was okay. She tried. She really did. She was just unlucky.

Maya agreed with the darkness. It was too much pain to deal with now.

The cold water did not hurt her anymore, and it even felt calming and loving, like the first warm hug from one's mother. Maybe things were better like this, instead of leaving the world bald, poisoned by chemicals, and under the wrath of a scalpel in three months. Death could be merciful and dignified. She just needed to take another deep breath of darkness. If she let the lake fill her lungs, it would become a part of her, and everything would go away.

Deep-deep darkness. She was sinking deeper and deeper. How long would she keep sinking? Maybe the darkness had no end. She did not deserve Heaven, but would her hell be an eternity of sinking into this cold abyss?

Before her last thoughts and desires disappeared forever, Maya felt someone grab her wrist and pull her back to the moonlight.

CHAPTER 4

She was alive!

With pain in her chest, a swollen eyelid, and the taste of slime on her lips, Maya woke up feeling every bruise and every scratch on her body. The sunlight coming through the window stung her eyes, and she squinted in pain. This could not be Heaven because there is no pain in God's Kingdom. But it could not be Hell because there would not be so much light! It was still life, though Maya was afraid to believe it.

She felt sickeningly disappointed, and the realization caused her more nausea than the aftertaste of lake water in her throat. Why disappointment? She was alive, so she should be happy. But Maya was angry that as soon as she had agreed to die and finally had made peace with the cold darkness, someone had the nerve to bring her back. Or perhaps she was disappointed with herself for having given up too easily. Help had been there, and she only needed to fight a little longer.

Someone saw her and came to the rescue. The light she saw on the shore was real. But who was it?

Maya's eyes finally adjusted to the light, and she was able to look around, trying to understand where she was. The room looked remarkably clean, with abundant sunlight and fresh air, but it was not a hospital. It seems that her savior had decided to bring her to his place, so they must have been confident that she would be all right without any medical attention. Or maybe Lake City did not even have a hospital.

Maya checked her bruises, some of which were huge. Nothing appeared to be broken, and there was no evidence of bleeding. Pajamas?! Someone had changed her clothes. They undressed her? Completely? Well, it was the right move since she had been in nearly freezing water. Whoever they were, they had placed her in a clean bed with two warm blankets on top of her. Of course they needed to take away her wet clothes; in the hospital, they always do. To be honest, she was more ashamed than angry.

Maya tried to sit up.

The room was large and bright, with light curtains decorated with butterflies. Next to the bed, she saw a desk with a pile of textbooks, and across the room was a bunk bed with carefully made bed sheets and funny-colored pillows.

Next to the half-opened door was an open futon with a couple of pillows and a blanket. It seemed that someone had slept there to keep an eye on her. The walls were covered with large posters of different actors, a sweet-faced Canadian singer, and some popular British boy band. Outside the open window, dozens of roses peered inside, filling the air with a pink aroma. Above the desk, she soon noticed a few photo frames decorated with glitter and girly stickers. Kids—so many kids were in those photos! All of them looked so happy, and most of them closely resembled each other.

"Good morning!" said someone with a voice like a little golden bell.

Maya turned and saw a girl of roughly five years standing in the door frame and wearing an adult-sized T-shirt for pajamas. The shirt nearly reached her feet, which were sporting long socks of different colors. The girl looked at Maya with such concern and concentration, almost looking through her, trying to decide whether she was friend or foe. Only kids and deer stare that way, and it made Maya smile. She raised a hand and waived to the little one.

"Hi, cutie!" Maya's voice, nothing like a bell, sounded like an old trombone after having yelled so desperately for help. A sting in her throat indicated that she had caught a cold, which was not surprising, considering her icy swim the night before. "Do you live here?"

The girl hugged the door frame, hesitating, thought about stepping inside, and just nodded in response.

"Is this your room? It's really pretty."

"I sleep over there, on top." The girl finally smiled and pointed toward the bunk bed. "And Masha sleeps on bottom."

She spoke with a slight Russian accent, which was cute and original.

"And who sleeps here?" Maya asked, pointing down to the bed she occupied.

"Tanya. But she slept today here on futon…Did you really drown in lake?"

Maya smiled. Well, if she had really drowned, she would be dead and unable to speak. She guessed that English was not the child's first language. But what a sweet kid! She was still skittish around her, as if Maya were some kind of zombie who had died in the lake and now was invading their house.

"Are you home alone?"

The girl shook her head "no."

"Mama, me, and Venya, we are the smallest; the rest at school."

"And Dad? Is he at work?"

"We don't have a dad, just Mama…"

Maya looked at the child, who was absolutely at peace mentioning the absence of her father, and she felt a bit ashamed now for having asked. But if there was no father, then who saved her? Would a mother of so many children risk her life jumping into a lake to save an unknown person? Or had she been rescued by someone else who then left her at the house of a lady with a kind heart? Either way, she felt grateful. Kindness toward strangers is a rare treasure these days.

"Do you know who brought me here?"

"Misha…but others call him Michael. He said he saw how your car falled into the lake from a boat ramp."

From a boat ramp? Well, that explained why she was so far from shore.

"Michael—is he your brother?"

The girl nodded.

"But he's at school now."

"I guess I'm really lucky that your brother was around."

"He is always praying there. He almost never sleeps, so he go on lake all the time." The shy child smiled again, and her cheeks turned a little red. Maya could tell that she was really proud of her brother but too shy to brag about him.

"Алиса!" a voice came from somewhere in the house. "Найди Веню, и идите завтракать!"

"Мамочка, тут тетя уже проснулась."

Maya was from a family of Polish emigrants, so another Slavic language was somewhat familiar to her but not completely. She figured out that the mother had called the kids to eat, and the little one, whose name was Alisa, had informed her mother that Maya was already awake. After a second, a woman appeared in the doorway behind her daughter.

"Oh, poor thing, how are you? Is Alisa waked you up?" The mother of many was near Maya's age, maybe a little bit older. She had a heavy Russian accent but such a friendly face and such a kind smile that Maya could forgive her broken English. Something about this woman resonated with Maya. She had the strange feeling that though she was meeting her for the first time, she had known her forever. Neither too tall nor too small, with a little bit of healthy weight, the woman had long hair made into a perfect bun, no makeup, and beautiful features. Wearing a house robe with an apron and a kitchen towel over one shoulder, she reminded Maya of her own mother. This kind of woman does not live in the big city, especially the kind that are that young and natural. She was not just an exemplary housewife. She was the ideal female stereotype in Slavic culture from the last century.

"No-no-no, don't worry! I woke up on my own." Maya tried to get up from bed. "Sorry for my intrusion. I'll go…"

"Don't tell nonsense!" The woman spoke with a tone of playful scolding as if Maya was one of her children. "Rest, take your time. There is no need to hurry. Let me feed small ones, and I will make something for us. What you like: coffee, tea, milk?"

"I feel so awkward. You've done so much already. I don't know how I can ever repay you and your son for what you've done."

"Repay? What are you talking about? We are humans; we are supposed to help each other!"

Maya smiled sadly; this naïve truth had been disproven in practice so many times in her life. People do not help each other unless they see some gain in it.

"Thank you again. Well, if you insist. I would love to have some breakfast, but I am done staying in bed. I'm not that kind of person."

"Very well. Алиска, принеси из прихожей тапочки для мисс Полянски."

The girl left the room and came back with slippers for Maya. The mother seemed to know who she was. So was all the hospitality just because of her popularity? Here we go. It seems that Maya had just found the reason behind all the kindness.

"So, it looks like you know my name already. Can I ask what yours is?"

"I am Valya, but for you, it might be better call me Valentina."

"No, Valya is fine. My parents are Polish, and we had many Slavic friends in Alaska, so I got used to names like that. You can call me Maya, but I'm not sure if there is a longer version of that name."

Valentina smiled, nodding with understanding.

"Nice to meet you, Maya. Well, we will wait on you at kitchen. Shower is over there, and your clothes in dryer right now. Should be done in no time."

The dryer?! Maya did not say anything, but her silk shirt that she had brought in France could not be machine washed, and it definitely should stay away from any dryer. And her pantsuit would have shrunk by at least one size. But Maya said "thank you" and did not even express a single note of disappointment. She was lucky to be alive and would have been willing to go home in her pajamas.

"By the way, what time is it?"

"Almost ten. I did called sheriff, and told him that you stay at our home. They trying to get your car out of water, but he recommend you not keep your hopes up."

"Crap..." said Maya, immediately closing her mouth and looking apologetically at Alisa, who started to giggle. Valentina gave a slight look of disapproval.

"I hope you have insurance."

"I do, and I'm sure they'll be thrilled to hear what's happened."

*

It was quite a cozy kitchen, though at least half of the space was taken up by a long table with twelve chairs. All the walls were covered with funny paintings made by children of different ages and featured different styles and themes. On the fridge door, there was no empty space, and it boasted not only hand-drawn pictures but a number of happy family photos as well. Looking around, one would notice a juice maker, two microwaves, a stove with six burners, a big oven, a small working TV, a dishwasher, a separate freezer, and a gigantic teapot. All of these items had their own special place.

Maya walked around, taking it all in while Valentina set the table. Everything smelled so fresh and clean. The windows were spotless, and the Lake City sun, finally making an appearance, shone through them without any impediments. The tablecloth was glaringly white, which seemed a miracle in a house with so many kids. Maya touched the tulle curtains at the sides of each window, and it brought back fond memories from her childhood.

She felt suddenly nostalgic. Her family had left their home, just a couple miles away from Warsaw, when Maya was the same age as Alisa, but to this day, she remembered their room arrangements and the old garden behind the house. Maybe now that she was free from work, she would visit her parents before her treatment began and tell them what was going on. Maybe her mom would decide to move in with her down in Florida to help her out. Maya felt a needle prick her chest and then both eyes. Before she knew it, her eyelashes were wet with tears. Control yourself, Maya!

"Come, sit! Everything is ready!"

Indeed, it was everything. Maya felt a little bit ashamed for all the trouble she had brought on this family, and now Valentina had set up a whole feast fit for a party. But no, there were just the four of them— Maya, Valentina, Alisa, and the three-year-old boy, Benjamin. Maya would be lying if she said she did not enjoy the meal. Oh, how she did! She loved everything! The omelet had chicken and tomatoes. There was toast with sour cream and herbs, fried sausages, pancakes with honey, and strawberry jam. A glass jar of compote with a mix of apricot and plum sat temptingly nearby. She finished things off with a large slice of apple pie and a cup of the best herbal tea in the world.

When Maya had completed her feasting, she was afraid to breathe lest her pantsuit, now a size smaller, should just rip apart.

"Valya, that was delicious! You should open your own restaurant. I would come here all the way from Chicago just for breakfast!"

Valentina laughed, and Maya noticed the same red color on her cheeks that Alisa had, even though they did not look alike. Not at all! And what was more was that Benjamin looked like neither his mother nor sister.

"Thank you, but Maya, what you talking about? I barely have time cook for my kids. But not going to lie, I love to cook, and I love to have people over."

"By the way, how many kids do you have?"

"Eight!" answered Valya proudly, and she took one of the photos from the fridge.

"Wow. My mom had five of us, not counting my dad, and she barely was able to handle anything. But you?! It's cleaner than a museum here."

"Probably your mother was working."

"No, she couldn't handle the English language, so Dad was the only one who worked...I mean, officially. Mom, me and my brothers would do some little things, like if the neighbors needed help, but that was nothing. I think Mom never got over the culture shock, and sometimes I suspect she's still mad at my dad for leaving Poland." Maya was so full, but her hand still moved after another piece of pie, and Valentina refilled both of their cups with tea.

"My kids help me a lot, and I am not working, so we think it better keep house clean every day, to not make huge mess to clean over the weekends."

"Does their father have a good job?"

"The Lord is their Father." Valya smiled, and Maya stopped chewing, trying to understand if her new friend was serious or joking. Another Virgin Mary, but with eight kids? That was more than impressive...It was probably time to leave. "The kids...I am not their biological mother."

Now Maya's jaw dropped. She looked at the picture again, and everything came together. None of the children looked alike. They were all adopted.

"Their parents left them, and least what I could do for them was try to become their mother. So I am their mom, and Lord is their dad."

"You are my hero. I'm serious! Believe me, I am the most spoiled person in the world, and I would never be able to do anything remotely as sacrificial as you have. I mean, I live alone with a cat who has probably already peed on all my clothes for leaving him, and he even sometimes gets annoying by invading my personal space. But kids! Eight! You know what? I need to write a story about you!"

At first, Maya thought all the hospitality was to bribe her for a story, but now, she wanted to write one on her own. The only problem was that since she had quit the *Chicago Voice*.

"No-no!" protested Valya, and for a moment, Maya thought she seemed scared by the offer. "I am doing this not for nice words."

"But someone might end up feeling sympathetic and decide to help. I'm sure you wouldn't mind some financial help. The government can't cover all of your expenses."

"Please, no need to write about it. We have enough for the food and bills, and also I have a garden, ten chickens, and last year the mayor bought a cow for us. Also, our church helping us a lot with clothes and groceries."

Maya was about to ask what the name of the church was when her attention shifted to the picture on the TV.

"I'm sorry. Can you make that a bit louder?"

"Sure!" Valya picked up the remote and turned up the volume.

On the screen was the building of the *Chicago Voice*.

"...Currently, the official police version is that it was a suicide. The office of Mr. Sawyer was locked from inside, and no one had been seen going in or leaving over the course of the night. No security cameras were found in the office of the chief editor."

Maya felt the Earth spinning under her feet. It could not be true. Was this somebody's evil idea of a joke? Bill's picture flashed again on the screen. It was the same photo they used in the paper whenever Bill would write something himself.

"…Was it really suicide? Employees of *Chicago Voice* are insisting upon further investigation. A day earlier, Bill Sawyer had been one of the speakers during the mayor's birthday celebration and had mentioned the plans and goals of the firm for the next five years. It seems unlikely that he would kill himself without a significant reason…"

"Maya, are you okay?" Valentina was afraid to move, looking at the white face of her guest.

"I don't know." She quietly pushed the words out, feeling hysteria coming over her as she listened to the report describe how great a person he WAS, how many friends he HAD, and how much he would be missed. Today's *Voice* had been canceled, and instead, they would be releasing a special issue dedicated to Bill's life.

"…Police are trying to contact a Miss Maya Polanski…" On the screen appeared a picture of Maya, the same photo from her Saturday column. "…According to the phone log, lead editor Miss Polanski was the last person who spoke to the chief editor."

"My purse? Do I have my purse…?" Maya, staring blindly at the TV, no longer saw or heard anything they were saying.

"It is here. I took everything out so it would dry." Valya pointed to a table on the porch where all the items from Maya's purse were carefully arranged in old newspapers.

Not feeling her legs, Maya was barely able to stand, and she walked outside to pick up the phone. She did not have much hope for the survivability of that model. Sure enough, the phone did not respond to any combination of buttons she pressed, but she had expected as much. Maya ripped off the back panel of the thousand-dollar device, threw away the wet battery, and carefully removed the SIM card. All she needed was a store where she could buy any cheap replacement, as all of her contacts and the address book were stored on the card anyway, and her photos and documents were kept in the "Cloud." The voice recorder was water and dust-proof, so it woke up as soon as she touched it.

Her wallet was dry on the outside, but the inside was a total mess. Thankful that she did not often use cash, she removed only her credit cards and put them into one of the pockets in her pants. Wiping mud from her license, she pocketed it as well.

Her purse was still wet and exuded a strange smell, one that did not evoke the best memories. She decided, rather, to buy a new one, and this once-glorious Prada item could make a nice toy for Alisa. Maya picked up the two bottles of medication, the rest of which had probably gotten lost in the accident, her key chain, and an unopened pack of gum. The rest she dumped into a trash can next to the table.

"Valya, where can I rent a car?"

"We don't have anything fancy, I know that for sure, maybe some small rentals. But we can go ask 'Jimmy on Wheels,' he has car shop on Main Street. Or take my old Mazda. It has couple hundred thousand mileage, but it is still running."

"Oh no, I'm not going to take your car. You've already done so much for me. And I was thinking more of something I could use to speed along the highway to Chicago."

"Are you sure you will be okay to drive?"

Valentina had a point. The adrenaline boiled her blood with such intensity that she felt as though her head would explode at any moment.

"I hate busses, but do you have any here?"

"Yeah, every hour until midnight, we have some to Buffalo City and Minneapolis."

"Can I call for a taxi?"

Valentina looked at her as if she had just spoken silly nonsense, the way some might look at an overly excited child.

"Maya, what you talking about? Let me change Benjamin, and I will take you to bus station. Oh…Sheriff wanted to see you about your car. We can stop by unless you don't want to deal with it right now."

"No-no, I'd rather talk to him now. I'm sure he's already reported to Chicago that I'm here, and he might have some answers for me."

"Well, give me five minutes. I saw your phone is dead. If you need to call, Alisa will give you mine."

"Thank you, Valya. What would I do without you?"

Valya smiled and waved her away.

"Алиса, приниси тете Майе телефон." On that command, the girl jumped down from her chair, running away, and in a moment, she returned with a simple cell phone in her small hands.

There were no passwords or tricky unlock patterns, and even the screen was a simple monochrome.

"Thank you so much!"

"No worry, I will be back. Алиса, пошли!" Valentina picked up her son from the highchair, and they left Maya alone in the kitchen.

Maya knew that the police were looking for her, and if the sheriff had not been here yet, that meant they really believed it was suicide. But Maya remembered the last words Bill said to her before she hung up on him. "They might kill me just for telling you…"

What was that supposed to mean? For telling her what? She was so mad at him at that moment that she was not closely paying attention. They were arguing about a stupid article. Why would someone kill Bill because he had told her to stay there?

She needed to call the office and clarify what exactly had happened. All the numbers were on the SIM card, but she did remember the general line and five or six extensions for the people who could actually help her.

Unfortunately, the line was busy, which was not really surprising. Perhaps *Chicago Voice* had turned off the phones since normally they were the ones who made the news, not the ones who became the news. She tried a couple of times to call the marketing division, still remembering her old number from the time she worked there, but had no luck with it either. Of course, people would love to have a spot in the newspaper whose chief editor had been on every screen in Chicago.

Bill…

She really needed to buy a new phone and get to her voicemail, more specifically to the messages he had left. The thought gave her an idea, one that was intensely painful but necessary for her peace of mind. Not understanding how, her fingers punched in his cell number, one of the few she remembered, and she began listening to the long beeping tones on the other end.

One. Why was she doing this? It would not bring him back.

Two. She just wanted to hear his voice, his stupid voice machine recording, the one she hated so much when he would not pick up his phone.

A third beep. Almost there. She prayed stupidly, hopefully, to unknown gods, asking for this small favor to make it all a huge misunderstanding. To make him alive.

Four. Yes—yes, he must be there. He could not be dead. It was just a bad joke, and he would pick up…

"Hello?" asked someone on the other side, and Maya almost dropped the phone.

"Hello, who is this?" Maya looked at the screen for a second, thinking maybe she had dialed the wrong number.

"This is Detective Ramirez. Who am I speaking to?"

Emptiness.

Everything became endless, like someone had taken and stretched the universe around her. She talked to the detective, barely understanding anything he asked her. She told him where she was and promised to show up at the precinct as soon as she returned. He most likely understood that Maya was in shock, and there was no reasonable need to keep her on the phone, so he let her go.

But Maya continued to sit quietly, looking into the emptiness around her.

Bill was really gone.

She was always good at memorizing speeches or interviews, and she could easily find the required piece or sound bite on her voice recorder in no time. But now, trying to reconstruct her dialog with Bill, she drew a blank.

"Miss Maya, Mom asking if you want some pie with you to go?"

"Tell Mom I said 'thank you,' but I will eat something on the road. I wouldn't want it to go bad on the bus."

"Too bad you can't stay a little longer. Michael was waited for you so long."

"He waited for me to wake up?" corrected Maya. It seemed that the second language was confusing Alisa. "I also really want to meet him."

"He talked about you so much!"

Maya smiled and gently petted Alisa's hair.

"You know what, as soon as I am done with my stuff at home, I will be back."

STOP! What was she talking about?! She wanted to get away from this place and try to erase every memory of the town from her mind. But her car was still on the bottom of the lake with a couple bags and her laptop. Of course the computer would have been destroyed, but she still might try to recover the hard drive.

No-no-no, she could not look for excuses to come back! Yet she wanted to return with bags full of food, new clothes, and different gifts for the kids and Valya. As soon as she figured out what had happened to Bill, she would drive back to Lake City, even if it was only to say thank you, in person, to her savior.

"Promise?"

"Yes! I promise. And tell your brother to get ready for an interview. I'm going to make him a national hero!"

"Hero?!" Valentina appeared in the doorway with Benjamin, now dressed and squirming in her hands, and she looked more frightened than happy.

"Of course, what else would you call a boy who jumped into cold water to save a stranger? Most people would call it crazy! In conditions like those, very few could swim well enough or far enough to come to the rescue."

"Michael don't know how to swim..." Alisa laughed, but her mother gave her a stern look, which made the girl cover her mouth with both hands.

Valentina looked even more scared and confused. Perhaps she had seen something else in the news that caused her to build this sudden wall between the two of them.

"Okay, we better keep going if we don't want to miss the bus!"

If Maya recalled correctly, there was a bus leaving every hour, but she decided not to argue. She just smiled and followed along.

Something had happened, but what it was, she did not yet know. Yet.

CHAPTER 5

She returned to her apartment long after midnight.

A sleepy cat walked out from Maya's bedroom, regally and acting as though he had not been sleeping on the pile of clean laundry. He gave her a lazy "meow," rubbed against her leg once, and, thinking the greeting more than enough, shuffled into the kitchen to his food dish.

Home. It was a two-bedroom flat with no doors and stylish partitions instead of walls. Normally, she loved the design as it gave her more space to think and walk, and the wall-to-ceiling windows gave her the feeling that Chicago's downtown was part of her territory. But now she felt small and alone and wished that she had blinds at least.

Maya looked through a pile of new mail on her coffee table and touched one of the plants, knowing the soil would be wet. She would have to buy something as a "thank you" gift for the lady who lived next door. And who says it was dangerous to leave a key with your neighbors? It was really practical! Maya did not travel much lately, but when she did, it was a relief to know that someone kept an eye on her flat. Otherwise, who knows what the cat would do to her plants and books? They say that cats are a reflection of the owner's soul. If that was true, then he was the male version of herself during her period. Once, he slashed her pink Italian pantsuit just because she had not left the window to the balcony open for him. To be honest, she hated pink anyway.

Maya took off the sneakers she had bought at a small marketplace in Lake City, followed by the pair of jeans and a gray hooded sweatshirt from the same shop. After Valentina had left her at the bus station, she bought a double ticket to Minneapolis to make the traveling experience less painful. For that reason, she had changed into more comfortable clothes. The meeting with the sheriff was fast and easy. He brought her the papers to sign for the insurance company about her car.

According to him, they were able to pull the car out of the lake, and it would be taken to the junkyard parking lot for the next couple of weeks without charge. That should give her some time to figure out what to do with it. He let her know that the Chicago office had already contacted him with a request to make sure that Maya got on the bus, which he thought was a bit ridiculous. He recommended that Maya check in with the detectives as soon as she got home; it seemed that they were anxious to close the case.

Under other circumstances, she would perhaps have used the opportunity to ask about the Pattersons, the Water Walker, and other strange happenings in the area, but she decided to save her energy for the long day ahead.

On the bus, something strange had happened to her. One of the passengers riding a couple seats back looked so familiar to Maya, but she could not remember where she had seen him before. Her journalist memory had years of experience memorizing faces and names, but in this case, she could not even outline a simple setting where she may have met him. During one of the stops, she said "hi" to him, but he just nodded in response and turned back to the window, listening to music from his phone. Well, everyone makes a mistake now and then.

After five hours on the bus, Maya faced another challenge. There were no business class tickets to Chicago, so she flew next to a crying baby and his mother, who kept pushing her large breast to his small face. Maya was not sure if something like that would make her stop crying or if it would scare her to death or traumatize her till the end of her life. There were brief moments when the baby would stop for a couple of minutes, but only to catch his breath and start again with renewed strength. During the landing, he burped up a white fountain of breast milk, which covered the mother's face with an even layer like a sour cream mask. Maya barely kept herself from doing similarly. The smell of vomit was haunting her even now.

After landing at O'Hare, she took a taxi and went to the precinct where she had spent the last three hours. Bill had been a close friend of the mayor, and so everyone was trying their best to find out what really had happened. With Maya, they were polite and patient—after all, they probably knew about their untitled relationship. She left the police department near eleven, but six blocks away from her apartment complex, the cab got a flat tire, so the rest of the way, she walked alone. Maya was not afraid, and, given her mood, it would be the potential attacker who ought to be afraid.

It turned out that nothing happened, and now she was finally home. She took off her remaining clothes, donned a bathrobe, and went into the kitchen to pour herself a glass of wine. She stopped pouring halfway but then continued to fill the glass nearly to the top, remembering that her pills, which interacted with alcohol, were somewhere at the bottom of the lake. Slowly sipping from the tall glass, she went to the bathroom and began filling the vintage tub with hot water. After adding a double portion of bubble gel, she watched momentarily how the white foam rose up along with the steam. What could be more calming than lying in a hot bath, having a glass of cold wine, and listening to the bubbles popping and the foam settling?

Slowly easing herself into the water, she drew a deep breath as the heat caressed her skin. Peace…

Not for long! Her home phone started ringing with an annoying persistence.

"Oh, for the love of God!"

Perhaps it was the vengeance of the phone gods for her not having checked her voicemail. She had noticed the blinking light next to the flashing number "42," but who in their right mind would listen to forty-two voice messages? Unless one of them was from Bill.

Maya looked at the clock. Almost 1:00 AM. None of her friends or family would call her this late, even after hearing the news. The closest people in her life knew that in those stormy moments, Maya needed to be left alone. She had never been good with sharing feelings; people generally annoyed her, and sympathy just irritated her even further. It was more than likely one of her colleagues trying to build a story and wanting to get a couple words from her. Or maybe another groupie had written a brilliant article that Maya had to publish in the next *Voice*. No! Everyone could go to hell as far as she cared. It was her time to relax and recharge, and she definitely deserved it.

The ringtone finally stopped, and the voicemail started with its greeting message.

"Hi, this is Maya Polanski. I can't answer your call, but if you leave a message, and if it's good enough for me to call you back, I'll do so when I get a chance. Ciao."

Right now, nothing could raise her interest more than a glass of wine and a bubble bath.

"Miss Polanski, forgive me for calling you this late..."

No-no-no...She did not care.

Taking a deep breath, she slid down under the water, and peaceful silence gave her a long kiss. It was so good to be in control. Who would have guessed that just yesterday, she was similarly in the embrace of the lake? Peace and sanctuary. The whole world became distant and meaningless, and the echoing drops of water from the tap synchronized with her own heartbeat.

She needed a breath of air. It would be ridiculous to drown in her own bath after having survived the ordeal in the lake.

"I know you're home. We really need to meet!" the voice of an unknown man with a Russian accent continued dictating the message. "Please, pick up the phone. I have information about Mr. Sawyer...It wasn't suicide, and I have proof."

For a few seconds, she did not move, trying to understand if she had heard correctly. The police showed her reports from the expert on ballistics, and it was a suicide. The trajectory and position of the gun, along with signs of gunpowder on Bill's hand, all pointed toward the simple conclusion. He had used the gun in his desk, and Maya knew it. The fingerprints were from the left hand, and Bill was left-handed. There were no other prints, just his…

"Miss Polanski, please, I think I've been followed. My life depends on you."

Even in the hot bath, she felt cold goosebumps on her skin. Bill's voice came from deep inside of her, repeating, "I know it sounds insane. I know you have questions, but believe me. If I tell you more, you might lose your job, and I might lose something way more valuable…They might kill me for telling you…"

Maya jumped out of the bath, grabbed the towel, and, leaving wet footprints all over, ran to the kitchen where her phone was. She nearly slipped on the parquet, but keeping her balance, she stretched out over the counter and picked up the phone.

"Hello?! Are you still there?"

"Thank God…Yes! Yes, I am here! Thank you for answering."

"You didn't leave me a choice. So you know who shot Bill?"

"This is complicated. He did shoot himself, but it wasn't suicide."

"Hold on!" Maya took a deep breath before continuing. "Someone made him bite the gun?"

"I have proof!"

"Okay. Have you shown it to the police yet?"

"No, Miss Polanski, I can't! The police can't know about it!"

"And why is that?"

"You need to see the video. I'll give it to you, and you can decide later what to do with it."

"O-o-o-o-okay…" Maya did not like the idea, but she had already witnessed so many conspiracies in her life. In one of the big cases she had worked on last year, she exposed a whopping lie about the previous mayor. Thanks to his advisor, Mr. Cloudy, she was able to write an explosive article after which the mayor was impeached, and more than twenty political figures and police captains were replaced. This was partly how she became a close friend of the new mayor, who, from the whole office, decided to keep only Cloudy as his advisor. Sometimes, you cannot trust the police. Maybe this was payback to Maya and Bill for destroying the old regime. Vengeance of an ex-mayor?

"When can I get the video?"

"In ten minutes at the ABOB near your apartment."

"Ten minutes? Do you know where I live?"

"Fine, fifteen. And it's cold, so you'd better dry your hair. And no police or I'll just walk away."

The short tone signal hummed.

Maya froze with the phone in her hands. Then, slowly turning, she wrapped the towel more tightly around her, half expecting the mysterious caller to be right behind her.

No, she was alone. Special tinting on the windows would have prevented anyone outside from seeing her, but how did he know about her wet hair? And he wanted her to know that he knew about it. Was it a threat? Maybe he was setting up a trap? Then why would he be willing to reveal himself? No, something else was going on. It was probably a warning so that she could understand that he would know whether she decided to call the cops. But she could do that from the closet or the hallway outside, and then how would he see?

No, she would try to do this without the police, especially since he wanted to meet her inside a restaurant and not in a dark alley. Maya knew she did not need to be scared. She needed to be confident again, and it was time to turn the table and take charge!

She removed her towel, not caring who could see her, and freely, proudly, like a lioness after the hunt, wandered over to the walk-in closet. Was he watching? Fine. She had nothing to be ashamed of, and after all, confusion was one of her greatest weapons.

*

"ABOB" was one of those places that Maya would visit only if she had come home way too late, the fridge was way too empty, and she was way too hungry. Having one of those 24/7 places across from her building was not a necessity but a nice addition to city life. Thanks to happy hour, after midnight, there were always a lot of people, so it was the logical choice for a meeting if you were afraid of being killed. The great amount of light inside and in the parking lot gave the place a feeling of safety.

All over this part of Chicago were tech support buildings and companies with a variety of call centers, and that made the restaurant a popular dining choice for geeks and nerds. They all looked the same as Maya, with their messy hair, pale skin, red eyes, and ridiculous T-shirts with badges displaying their pictures and names. They seemed almost proud of working in software design and making computer games.

Maya took a seat at an empty booth near the kitchen and ordered a cup of tea and the "famous" pancakes with strawberry jam. She was not sure if her mystery man from the phone was already there, and no one seemed to make eye contact, so she sat back in her booth and sighed deeply. Out of habit, she closed her eyes and started to massage her neck, realizing for the first time that there was no pain or heaviness in her spine. She had been too busy today to notice. Maybe her cancer had decided to give her a day off? Well, first thing tomorrow morning, she would visit the pharmacy and restock her medication before it got worse again.

"Thank you…"

Maya opened her eyes and found him standing there in front of her. He was around thirty, with a gray face and an equally gray T-shirt, small glasses, and huge red eyes. His longish hair was stuck behind his small, pointy ears, and his trembling lips looked dry and sore.

"For what?"

"For not calling anyone." Her mystery friend sat cautiously across from Maya and placed a small laptop in front of him.

"Are we waiting on someone else?" Maya hated when people looked around more than they looked at her, especially when they planned to have a conversation.

"I hope not." He tried to smile, but it looked pitiful and unnatural.

"Oh, I need to say 'thank you' to you too."

"For what?" he repeated with almost the same intonation as Maya.

"For watching me bathe and not placing it on the web."

The man turned red like the bottle of ketchup on the table.

"Let me know where you were watching from so I can wave to you next time or at least sit in a more flattering position."

"I'm sorry..."

"Don't bother!" She was angry and pondered smashing him over the head with his own laptop.

"No, really, I am sorry. But I only hacked your webcam to know when you were home."

Maya looked at him again and had the crazy feeling that she knew this guy as well, but the one she remembered was more clean-cut and less shaky.

"Have we met before?"

"Yes...I was in your office last week. I'm Vlad. Vlad Kalinovsky from SafeGate."

Maya tried to remember, but nothing came to her mind. Even the name of the company sounded suspiciously new. But last week, they had been so busy with deadlines that she could barely remember her own name.

"*Chicago Voice* hired us to update your firewall; I was connecting your server to our system."

"That's right! Thanks to you, we almost failed with last week's issue."

"No! It was an attack on your office, and we helped to recover everything!" For the first time, he looked alive, and it seemed that Maya had accidentally offended his sense of professionalism, a grievous sin against the geek code.

Up to the table strutted a server with Maya's tea and a huge plate of hot pancakes. Her tray also held a dish with a few different packs of jam—as she seemingly forgot which flavor Maya had ordered—and a bottle of maple syrup. The waitress asked Vlad if he wanted anything, but he shook his head so fast that one might think she had offered him something naughty and indecent. The server stepped back, gave both him and Maya a curious look with one overly-plucked eyebrow arched high, and then left.

"So, Vlad…" Maya cut a big piece of pancake with her fork and dipped it into the jam. "Now, can you tell me why in the world I'm eating pancakes at two in the morning instead of being warm and cozy in bed?"

Vlad looked around and leaned toward her.

"Miss Polanski…"

"Screw the formality! You saw me naked already, so call me Maya. Oh, please. Stop blushing like a sorority girl at her first party. Show me the video. Isn't that what you have on your laptop?"

"Yes. It is." Vlad opened the laptop, looked around, and entered a long and complicated password.

"Marasmus Simplisium!" sighed Maya, imagining what kind of nerdy password he might have. She rolled her eyes and cut another piece of pancake.

"You see, we always check each other's work. You guys had a big attack, and we were updating not only your firewall but the video monitoring system as well. My coworker wrote the script, and I remotely tried to hack it."

"So…?" Maya had stopped caring, actually, and decided that after she finished her late meal, she would pay and go home because it seemed that she was talking to a crazy person.

"I got it. I got through and was able to hack into the security cameras."

"Nice try! Bill didn't have a camera in his office."

"Really? Then how do I know what you did on his desk three days ago around eleven PM?"

Maya stopped chewing.

"I'm sorry…I shouldn't have. We had just broken through, and we didn't mean to see anything. We thought no one would be there that late…"

"We? Who else saw that?"

"My coworker—Mike, you met him too…I understand that you're upset. You can write a letter of complaint, but it's not relevant right now."

"Keep going!" Maya pushed aside her plate, having just lost her appetite.

"So, Mike fixed the bug, but I had already left a backup door."

"I'm not going to ask why, or one of us will go home and sleep while the other takes a ride to the city morgue in a body bag…with this plate in his head!"

"I'm…"

"You're sorry, I get it!"

Vlad looked around again before continuing nervously.

"So I attached a small script that would let me know if something was happening in Mr. Sawyer's office. And yesterday, when I got a notification, I thought…and I decided to record…but for private viewing."

"I feel way better, thank you! How sad! My dreams of being a porn star just got crushed! Okay, show me what you got."

"No! First, you need to promise me that you will not reveal my name!"

"My sweet boy, I'm a journalist. I can promise anything, or I can just use force if you don't stop toying with me."

"I know you keep your word. Some people might not like you, but everyone respects and trusts you. I wouldn't harm you, and I'm sure the people who did that to Mr. Sawyer would be afraid to do anything to you. But me, I am no one. Just an immigrant whose green card expires next month."

"Oh, so you want me to help you stay here?"

"No! Just promise me you won't tell anyone my name, especially the police. Because they were the ones who deleted the security footage from your servers!"

"What you talking about?"

"The people who made Mr. Sawyer shoot himself must be really powerful if the police clean up after them. So just make this video public, talk about it, and then they won't be able to do anything." Vlad removed a small flash drive from his pocket.

"Okay, I can say that someone dropped it on my doorstep or in my mailbox. That happens all the time."

"Thank you again."

Vlad plugged the drive into the USB port, clicked a couple times, and on the screen appeared Bill. The camera seemed to be located right beneath the eagle sculpture near the office door. Maya could see two other people in the room, but understanding who they were was almost impossible since they wore long, black rain jackets with hoods. Was this a joke? Who wears hooded jackets indoors unless they are planning a robbery or some theatrical act?

"I did everything you asked, now get out of here!" Bill was furious, and Maya had seen him like that only twice before—once when she called him "Papa's little boy" because he hated when anyone reminded him that the newspaper had been bought by his father as a gift for his graduation ten years ago. The second time was when *Chicago Global* beat them in releasing an article about the state attorney who got caught with a drug dealing syndicate. They used the same pictures and story flow, so the whole issue had to be stopped in the press. Otherwise, it would have looked like plagiarism.

"Mr. Sawyer, we had a different agreement." The man who spoke held some kind of cane in his hands, and his voice sounded remotely familiar. It was hard to see or hear clearly from such a small notebook.

"I assume you heard our conversation. She's stubborn like a mule; I can't make her do something if she doesn't want to."

"That's your problem."

"I swear, if you don't leave, I'll call for security!"

The second man moved closer to Bill, and his shadow covered not only the chief editor but half of the office as well.

"If I were you, I would watch what I say."

"By the way, how is Clint?" asked someone who was not in view of the camera.

And again, that feeling of familiarity…Maya felt like she was starting to go crazy, but that was to be expected, considering that everything around her lately had been one unstoppable runaway train. Who were they? Why would Bill make any kind of deal with people like that, especially about her? What did they have on him? And Clint, Bill's bodyguard-slash-assistant, had been in a terrible accident last week and was still in the hospital. Did they take him out of the way to get easier access to Bill?

"I really don't know what more I can say or what I can do to help!" Poor Bill. His voice was trembling along with his hands. He was scared! Maya had never seen him like this, and that made her uncomfortable and worried.

"So, you want to say that you're not any help to us anymore? That's sad and disappointing," said the first man.

Maya really needed to take this video to her friends in the Media Lab. They should be able to get something from it before she published it or took it to the police.

"I am sorry, but you have to leave. I don't want anyone to see us together."

"Looks like he's trying to kick us out," said the second.

"The boy's ashamed of us."

"Just like his father."

Maya was losing her sense that any of it was real. Did those people always talk in order, like they had memorized a bad play, or was it just one person talking the whole time? The voices were different, but the intonation was always the same. What a freak show!

"What a rat!"

"When he was spending our money, he wasn't that ashamed."

"No, not at all!"

"I don't owe you anything!" Bill popped up from his chair. "It was my father who made the deal with you! Not me!"

"You share the same blood," said the one standing just out of view, and the shadows in the room became darker, almost snuffing out the light from the desk lamp. "His debts are your debts!"

"Get out!" In Bill's hand appeared the revolver he always kept locked in his desk. But this did not scare his visitors in the least. "I said get out! Or, I swear to God, tomorrow, the head of Nehushtan will be on the front page!"

"Miss Polanski," Vlad distracted her, "Please watch carefully now. Maybe you can explain what is happening."

Bill's hand moved from side to side, trying to keep all three men under the point of his gun. His face looked gray and completely transformed with fear. Why not just shoot the idiots? Not to kill them, but in the leg or hand, just to disable them!

"I warn you to watch your words. Swearing under God's name, that's something I take seriously..." said the first man.

"You don't leave me a choice," said the second.

"Doesn't he mean 'leave *us* a choice?'" wondered Maya out loud.

Bill stepped back, gasping for air as though someone had locked their hands around his throat. Slowly, his hand started to turn the gun toward his own face.

"No...Please..." wheezed Bill. "Please stop...I will...I will..."

He lost control over his body, and now his hand was stuffing the barrel of the gun into his mouth...

GUNSHOT!

Maya felt something sprinkle onto her face. Not understanding what was happening, she wiped her cheek and looked at her fingers. They were smeared with moist, red, viscous lumps that looked like strawberry jam.

Maya slowly raised her head, and what she saw almost turned her into stone. With empty eyes and a hole in his forehead, Vlad fell forward onto the table, his face landing in the plate of unfinished pancakes.

Startled and confused, Maya jumped away from the laptop as though the bullet had flown out from the screen.

Another shot! The laptop's screen exploded into a pile of sparks and smoke right in front of her. She twisted around, looking at where the bullet had come from.

In the doorway stood a man in a black rain jacket with a deep hood covering half of his face. This time, his gun, with its attached silencer, was pointed straight at Maya.

CHAPTER 6

Before, Maya thought the expression "life flashed before my eyes" was simply a figure of speech, but today was the second day in a row that she was watching her life in flashes, and that movie was getting old.

A buzzing droned on in her ears. The distance between her heartbeats became an eternity. All she could see at that moment was the hypnotizing aim of the gun and flashes, stupid flashes of the past. Everything she had done wrong, and all that she would like to have changed but did not for lack of opportunity—it all raced through her mind. Why right now?! She could not afford to be distracted with self-pity. There was no time for that! She had almost given up last night. Well, no more!

Jumping, she fell to the floor, stretching out like a cat, and immediately started to crawl.

Bullets, like hungry beasts, tore the upholstery to pieces in the booth where Maya had been sitting seconds ago.

Finally, everything returned to normal speed, and Maya felt the noise and panic. There was no more buzzing, just screams. What a silly part of human nature to yell when you should actually shut up and start moving!

But there was plenty of movement, and it seemed that the hooded maniac had come, not for a mindless safari hunt but for her and Vlad specifically. As she was sitting next to the kitchen, she realized that she had the fortunate opportunity to get away through there because she could hear cooks and waiters running away. Hugging the booth with her back, she tried to peek around and locate the assassin. He still stood in the doorway, like an unmovable Colossus, holding a deadly weapon in his unshakeable hand.

She could do it! She could escape, and he was not coming after her, at least not yet. But before running away, she had to take the USB drive that was still blinking in the destroyed laptop.

Taking a deep breath like a diver preparing to jump, she reached up and pulled the drive away. As payment for her boldness, two more shots flew through the air.

A sharp, burning sting hit her shoulder. She looked for a second just to assess the damage, and though it was just a scratch, it had begun to bleed profusely. It will be fine! She looked more, trying to find where the second bullet had hit, but saw no other marks on her body. At least she had the flash drive. Now, it was time to get away.

As soon as she pushed open the flapping door, her waitress, who had been hiding in the corner just behind it, started to scream like a piglet under the knife. She probably thought the killer had found her, and so she darted up and rushed forward instead of running away. But not for long…

Clap! Clap! Clap!

A heartrending scream broke down on a high note, and the lifeless body fell right in front of Maya, blocking her path.

"Shit!"

It was one thing just to move to the exit and something else entirely to crawl over a dead body.

Everything finally became quiet until Maya heard the sound of heavy steps on the wooden floor.

"Shit! Shit! Shit!" she whispered, moving one arm over the waitress, then the other. "Breathe…Just breathe…"

Boom…Boom…

The steps were heavy, as if a marble statue walked toward her.

She lifted one leg over, trying not to think about the body as the woman who had brought her food…

Maya threw up.

In some way, it helped her overcome her fear. She wiped her mouth and moved the other leg over. Clear of the waitress, she crawled as fast as she could. A bit further, and she was behind the grill.

Clap! Clap!

Dishes from a kitchen table exploded in porcelain rain. He was following her!

She needed to run. Crawling was too slow! It took all of her willpower to make the move, but she got up and ran toward the door with legs that were nearly numb.

CLAP! CLAP! CLAP!

The board with people's orders fell right behind her. Another bullet hit a boiling pot on the stove, raising up a cloud of steam in the room and covering her in a blanket of fog. Run! Do not stop!

With a roar, she charged toward the door, jumping and falling out into the alley behind. In other circumstances, if she could think clearly, she would have put something under the doorknob, blocking the door. Maybe it would not stop him, but at least it would win her some time. No, she was running like a crazy person, not caring where just as far away as possible. At first, her legs would not listen to her, but now they were moving so fast that she would never be able to stop them.

She had not yet left the alley when the colossus appeared in her way, blocking the exit. In the light of the street lamps, he looked even bigger. His rain jacket spread on the draft of wind, turning him into an angel of death whose wings covered half the sky. He looked like a child of shadows who kept growing, absorbing the light and air around him and, more frighteningly, Maya's courage.

Concentrating too much on the imposing figure, she failed to notice an old cardboard box in her way and tripped and fell onto the wet, muddy concrete. Impossible! The killer could not have gotten there so fast, especially with his slow, overdramatic way of walking. Maya yelled with all the air in her lungs and with all the pain and disappointment that burned from inside.

"What do you want?! Huh?!"

Maya slowly got up, keeping her eye on the assassin standing in front of her.

"Did you come to kill me? Then why the games?!" She backed up, hugging the wall until a trash container blocked her from going further.

Glancing back from where she had come, she thought of dashing back through the restaurant until another figure, an exact copy of the one in the alley, came out through the doorway. He had the same clothes, the same build, the same gun. Both of them started to raise their hands toward her, like giants, pointing at her with their ugly metallic fingers.

Not thinking anymore and acting on pure instinct, she jumped into the open trash container.

Claps sounded, and sparks flew as multiple hits ricocheted off the dumpster.

"HELP!"

No one would come to help her, and what was worse was that she had just put herself in the best position for her killers. Now they would not even need to lift her body out, as she was already buried in the trash. She was stuck! There was nowhere to run and no place to hide unless she could find a magic portal to La La Land under the piles of unfinished food and rotten peelings.

The sound of sirens approached from somewhere in the distance. But they were too far to save her unless her killers happened to be afraid of loud noises and flashing lights. Anyway, the cops would head into the restaurant first to check for any survivors there, and only after would they begin to search the surrounding area.

Only one thought gave Maya comfort—the hope that the cops would find her body before it was taken to the junkyard, where it would be disfigured by rats and homeless cats.

Footsteps. They were coming closer! She could hear them clearly like they were stepping on her tombstone.

A gunshot!

Something fell next to the trash container.

Clap. Clap. Clap.

Another shot was followed by another heavy thud, and this time, something hit the container on the way.

Trying to catch her breath, she looked up through the pile of trash, waiting for someone to look inside. Nobody.

There were no more footsteps or gunshots. Only the sound of police sirens drew closer and closer. Maya finally found the courage to get up and look.

Both of her would-be assassins lay dead in spreading pools of blood. Not so tough for statues, after all! They were nothing mystical, just really big men who had been killed by ordinary bullets. She looked around, trying to spot the cop who had saved her life, but the alley was empty. But Maya had the uncomfortable feeling that somebody's eyes were on her... from somewhere above.

Quickly, she looked up just in time to notice a man disappearing in the shadows on the roof of the building across the alley. It was dark enough and far enough, but Maya could have sworn it was the man she had seen on the bus from Lake City.

✶

She was done with running. What was the point? It seemed like nothing was up to her anymore. No matter where she went or what she did, death might come from just around the corner, and if she was destined to survive, help would be there as well, whether she was drowning or about to be shot. And who was the guy who saved her, anyway? Two shots—two dead bodies! Yes, he had the strategic benefit of shooting from the roof, but he must still know how to handle a gun. And why would he follow her all the way from Lake City? There were just too many questions for such a crazy day.

Dragging her feet, she walked past the police and their cars, who did not even pay attention to her, and she walked home. Eventually, they would access the security cameras, see what had happened, and then take a closer look at Maya. Since her dinner partner had been shot first, they might even notice how she stole the USB drive, that she still held it in her hand, and how the attacker came after her. This would doubtless bring the police to her door before too long. Until they came, though, she might finally have the chance to catch a little bit of sleep. Right now, she did not care whether they would be crooked cops or honest. She was done running for today.

Deep in the back of her consciousness, an inner voice was telling her to pack her most important things, grab her passport, and get as far away from Chicago as possible—maybe even out of the US. She still had an uncle on her father's side who lived in Warsaw. But what was the point? The police would report to all the airports in no time. She could not even call a cab without being tracked by the cops unless she found a taxi a couple blocks away, dressed as a bearded Asian monk, and paid with cash. No, she would stop running, at least until morning.

If Vlad was right, and influential people with lots of money were standing behind it all, then there would be no rest for her or her family. She could not go anywhere they might expect her to be. She needed to lie low for a couple of weeks, re-watch the video, analyze all that had happened, and then make her move.

Before walking into the hall of the apartment complex, she looked back at the police swarming around "ABOB" and the arriving journalists.

Fast. Impressive. Well, she was done for today, and she would check the news tomorrow.

"Miss Polanski! My Lord! What's happened to you?" The concierge was already peeking through his window onto the street when Maya approached, so he immediately opened the door for her.

"Long story..." she grumbled as she walked past him and straight to the elevator.

"Are you alright? Were you there?" He waved to the window.

"Yeah...They have unforgettable service," the doors of the elevator chimed and opened, "And if you ever go there, don't order the pancakes. They're deadly."

She walked inside and pressed the number for her floor.

Maya never could understand people with claustrophobia. What was so scary about a small, enclosed area? It was the best, she thought. There was nothing unexpected, and you could see and control the space around you. It gave her a false feeling of security.

She walked to her door and, only on the third attempt, managed to get the key into the lock.

The blissful silence and the usually calming darkness were disrupted by police sirens and flashes from the street. Even the sound-isolating windows could not guarantee a vacuum from it all. She walked inside and closed the door, pushing it with her back. "My home is my fortress," she thought.

Unless someone had already broken in...

Before she sensed the presence of the invader, strong arms pulled her around, locking one hand around her shoulders and covering her mouth with another. She tried to twist and slide down, but the attacker anticipated this move and clutched her even harder. She even moved to hit him with her elbow and stomp on his foot, but he maneuvered against those attempts as well. Screaming was useless as a wide palm was tightly sealed around her lips.

"Shhhhh. Quiet!" The domineering whisper squeezed her more strongly than the arms. "I'll let you go if you promise not to scream, okay?"

Not right away, but after a moment, Maya nodded, but the hands kept holding her with the same strength.

"You understand that if I wanted to kill you, you'd be dead already?"

Maya nodded again. It did sound logical, and she wanted to believe it…

"Okay, Maya…Just don't do anything stupid…"

As soon as his arms weakened their grip, she fell free and hit him as hard as she could below the waist, pushing him away. For a moment, he fell, whispering, swearing, and writhing in pain, but eventually, he managed to stand. It was just enough time for her to run to the kitchen and pull out the biggest meat knife she had. By the time he caught up, she was already standing with her back to a pantry. Holding the knife with both hands, she pointed the blade toward her offender.

"I thought we had an agreement?!" he hissed, still holding the wounded area with one hand.

"Did I do something stupid? I don't think so!" Maya smiled at the corner of her lips, not lowering the knife.

It was the same man who saved her in the alley, and she was right. He was the man from the bus. More than that, she now understood where she had seen him the first time. He was one of the journalists next to a Pattersons' house—one of the few who stayed behind and did not follow Brad. He tried to come closer…

"Hey! What do you think you're doing?" She waved the knife threateningly. "Or do you want me to cut off whatever's left in your pants?"

"Quiet!" whispered the man.

"Why are you hissing at me? It's my home, and I have…"

"Can you shut up?" He did not let her finish but just rolled his eyes and pulled out a gun. "Please?!"

"Oh. Okay. You should have just asked nicely from the beginning!" Now, there was no point in holding her knife. She was not Rambo, and even if she threw the knife, she would not get it anywhere near him. And she already knew that he was a good shot.

"Now, can you slowly walk back to the living room and stay away from the windows?"

"*Jawohl!*" She put the knife back on the counter and slowly started toward him.

He put the gun back into the holster hidden under his jacket and pulled out a small, black leather wallet, opening it to show Maya his ID.

"I told you I'm not here to kill you!"

Maya stopped and looked closer. Phillip Howell. Agent of the Federal Bureau of Investigation.

"FBI? Seriously? What does that change?"

Actually, it did change a lot. It was one thing to be in the same room with a stalker or killer and another thing entirely to be there with someone in authority, especially one who was there for her protection.

"Nothing if you don't listen to me. Stay away from the windows!" He pulled her farther inside the living room into a corner where her cat slept peacefully. "You need to change. You smell like dead fish."

"Oh, excuse me. If you would have hurried, I wouldn't have needed to jump into a second-hand sushi bar!"

"I can't protect you if you keep putting yourself in danger."

"Oh, so it's my fault that two maniacs killed the Russian geek right in front of me…"

"His name was Vlad."

"Whatever! And they almost killed me! By the way, since when does the FBI just fire their guns without any warning?"

"When we can't be exposed."

"So you're kind of undercover? Can you turn away? I need to change."

"So you can hit me with one of your vases?" Agent Howell gave her a look. "And not 'kind of,' I *am* undercover. And we hoped that you could help us."

"Sure, it's not like you were already using me as bait tonight!" Maya took off her sweater and sweatpants and threw them straight at Phillip's feet.

"Is that your blood? You got shot? Let me see!" Agent Howell took a step closer, but Maya stepped back.

"Are you a doctor now, too? It's just a scratch. If not, do you think I would have come home instead of going to the hospital?"

"Just let me check, please."

Maya released an annoyed sigh and turned her shoulder toward the agent.

Howell rubbed his hands together to make them warmer and carefully touched around the wound.

"Do you have vodka?" Phillip looked concerned but not worried.

"What are we celebrating?" Maya knew why he was asking, but there was something really pleasurable in torturing him mentally. "In the top cupboard. I'm not sure about vodka, but I am sure I have half a bottle of rum leftover from Independence Day unless Mr. Farts licked it dry."

"Who?" The agent smiled and went back toward the kitchen.

"My cat." Maya heard him turn on the water and open different cupboards. She was close enough to the door that she could try to run away, and maybe, if she was lucky, she would reach the elevator. No. He would catch up to her anyway. And as it was, she had begun to trust him. "So, did they come to kill me as well?"

"At first, we thought they needed you, that they had some kind of job for you. But after what just happened in restaurant, I'm not sure anymore what their plans are for you."

He returned with washed hands, a couple of clean towels, a first aid kit, and the opened bottle of rum.

"Take a sip. It should help."

"Doctor knows best!" Maya took the bottle and, trying to show off, took a large gulp straight from the bottle, like a pirate in an old movie.

It had been a while since she last had strong alcohol, and her whole façade fell apart when she started choking on the burning liquid.

"Easy, easy!" Phillip laughed. "A couple small sips will do just fine."

"Whatever," she snorted, handing the bottle back. "I think I already disinfected my sinus chambers and half of my brain."

"This will hurt, but try not to scream."

"Less talking more dooooooo…Shit! Holy Mother of…cats!"

He poured the alcohol onto the wound straight from the bottle.

"Shhhhh!"

"You 'shhhh!' I think I just peed my pants. Are you crazy?"

Phillip carefully cleaned up the wounded area with a towel.

"You'll need a couple of stitches, but it might work without them if you be really careful."

He took a gauze pad from the kit and applied some antiseptic cream to one side.

"Is the FBI investigating Bill's murder?" Maya tried not to look at her shoulder.

"It is a murder, you're correct. And yes, it is under our control, but the police don't know that yet."

"So Vlad was right. They have mole?"

"You could say that, but I tend to think most of them are under Nehushtan's control. You heard about him on the video."

"How...How did you know?" Maya pulled back a little.

"Hold still!" Phillip was almost done patching the wound. "We're the ones who removed that video from the servers, not the cops."

"So you have proof that it's murder, but still, the official version is suicide? Why?"

"Maya, the 'Head of Nehushtan' is an old sect. We've found records about them dating all the way from 1908. They have more than a hundred thousand members all over the world. We can't scare them off that easily."

"My God! You knew it, didn't you? About the meeting? And not from the recording, right?" Maya started walking closer to the door, forgetting that she was wearing only underwear and a tank top.

"No one thought they would kill him. It wasn't the first meeting Bill had with them, and Sawyer was helping us, informing us about the appointments. First, we kept a recovery team in the next office, and later, just an agent undercover as a cleaning guy. Most of the time, it was simple chit-chat. They would ask him to write particular articles, give him some valued inside information, or have him correct a storyline. We ended up leaving a recording device and an analyst in our office who would monitor the flow. When he reported code red, it was already too late."

"You're disgusting."

"I'm sorry?"

"Not just you, all you FBI guys! How dare you?" Maya lost it. "He was helping you! He was cooperating with you, and you couldn't protect him? And now you have the nerve to come to my house and..."

"Shhh!"

"No more! This is my home!" She flipped on the light switch. "So you think they'll come here now? Well, fine! Now you're here too, so you can take care of those idiots!"

"You don't know what you've done!"

"Sure, like your other agents won't come to the rescue."

"We need to leave! Now!" He pulled a pair of jeans and a jacket from the closet and threw them toward her.

"I'm not going anywhere until you tell me about Lake City. Why was I there? Why were you there, and what is so damn important about that town?"

"DRESS NOW!" Phillip pulled out his gun.

"Fine, shoot me!" Maya defiantly crossed her arms over her chest but grimaced because of the pain.

"You stupid cow! This is way bigger than you or me. No one's going to come to the rescue. No one will even report our deaths! The bureau can easily make this into a simple robbery with murder rather than admitting knowledge of the Head of Nehushtan!"

Maya doubted his words…But what if it was true? No, he must be bluffing!

"I said dress! Or you'll be running half-naked through Chicago!"

"Running from what?"

"From them!"

He grabbed her arm, causing her more pain, and pulled her a little closer to the window.

She barely caught her breath.

Outside, standing on top of several buildings nearby, Maya saw the silhouettes of a dozen men, all dressed in the same manner as the killers from the alley. They stood motionless as though someone had draped long, hooded jackets on top of statues. But they were alive, and Maya could swear that she felt the eyes of each one of them staring into her soul.

CHAPTER 7

L ife in the big city makes a person more flexible when it comes to transportation, and it especially gives you mixed feelings about municipal transport. And if you happen to live in Chicago, you know that the metropolitan "L" is so much more than just a bunch of old cars running over hundred miles of track both under and above ground. It is a legend and an attraction that could easily be placed up there next to Lake Michigan and the Willis Tower.

Her senior year, when Maya's roommate had those annoying wild nights of passionate love (which was almost every other night), Maya tried to stay at the library as long as possible. Afterward, she would pick a novel, a sketchbook, and a small cassette player and use her student pass for the "L," traveling for hours and hours. It was something sacred for her, almost ritualistic.

In those moments, she had the sense of being a part of millions, all while remaining unique. She was a huntress melting into a mass of people and an observer who watched, thought, and analyzed her surroundings. No matter which direction she traveled, she always found something of interest, something that would let her imagination go wild and creative. She wrote stories in her head about the people who traveled with her or about those walking outside. So many lives, so many stories, so many lines all crossed there on the "L."

Those days recharged her. They gave her the desire to be famous, to be the one who would come onto a metro car one day and find all eyes looking just at her with respect and jealousy. The "L" was her drug. It was the lover with whom she had the most complex and rewarding foreplay. She would let her heartbeat merge with the rhythmic rattle of the wheels, breathing in and out with the blinking of the lights. She could reach the highest level of nirvana in those moments when the train came up for air and then snuck back underground. And she would never forget those long and multilayered feelings of satisfaction and bliss that came at the end of the ride.

So much time had passed since then, almost ten years, to be exact. Maya could not remember when she last needed to use the "L" but seemed to think it was during some kind of parade downtown when her car got stuck in traffic just a couple miles from her office building. There she was, back again, looking for rescue and deliverance.

She found herself unable to relax all the way to the station and felt as though dozens of faceless watchers were following her and Phillip, prepared to strike one last time. Only when the doors closed and the cars started moving was she able to catch her breath and allow herself a little break.

"So, what now?" Maya, out of habit, put her hand into her purse to pull out the phone, but then remembered that the original had died after her swim, and the new one that she bought in the Minneapolis airport was now in a trash can next to the metro station.

"As soon as I'm sure we're not being followed, I'll take you to safe location."

"And how long will I need to stay there?"

"I'll get ahold of my contact, and someone from the FBI will pick you up. Unfortunately, I can't be seen anywhere around headquarters. And, Maya, please be smart and lie low."

"Are you sure this is necessary? Maybe we should go there now. We can get out on..."

"Okay, I'm only going to say this once, and you need to decide right now this moment. Not tomorrow, not in an hour. Now! Either you trust me and do EXACTLY as I say, or I get out at the next stop, and you're on your own."

"My gosh, FBI, chill! Let me be the hysterical woman in our duo."

"Do we have a deal?"

"Fine…" Maya hated when others told her what to do, but since her life depended on it now, she was willing to make an exception. "I'm just not sure I can hide for very long. I have some medical conditions…"

"Something serious?"

"Only if cancer is serious enough for you."

Phillip looked at Maya, trying to determine whether she was lying.

"I'm sorry, I didn't know."

"Don't sweat it, FBI. I'm sure that pretty soon someone from your side would find that out in my medical history."

"We'll come up with something, don't worry. And I'm sure we will have enough to start arresting them soon. The problem before was that they would only build their network, establish connections, and gather for secret meetings, but nothing criminal. Even Bill's murder was made to look like suicide, but now something has them on the move."

"Why are you looking at me like I'm that 'something?' I didn't do anything."

"You're wrong there. Something did happen. We just don't understand what it is yet."

Maya thought, searching her memory, but nothing came to mind. It must have been related to Bill and not her. He wanted to expose the clan to the public, and given their relationship with each other, perhaps they thought she might know more than she should.

"How powerful are they?"

"You've heard of the Ku Klux Klan?"

"Who hasn't? Wasn't the FBI created to weaken the KKK and change them from extremists to a book club of aging Boy Scouts?"

"Pretty much. When the government figured out how deep the roots of the KKK went on every level, they decided they needed the power not just to observe their moves but also to stop them once and for all, if necessary. Since then, we've had a special division that monitors all kinds of organizations. Everyone from the Masons to your run-of-the-mill Netsuke modeling clubs."

Maya smirked, but her mood quickly changed as she felt the cars slowing down to approach the next station. Phillip, too, became more serious, slowly putting his hand on a gun under his jacket and turning slightly to find the best vantage point. If someone were at the station, he would notice them first. And should they decide to walk on in, he would be ready.

Happily for them, no one was on the platform, and after a short stop, the doors closed, and the train started moving again.

"So, why did you bring them up? I asked how influential this Nehu-something Head is."

"Oh, yes. Well, what if I told you that many organizations, including the KKK, were sponsored by the Head of Nehushtan."

"You're kidding? They're that old? Do you know who's in charge?"

Phillip smiled, seeing how Maya went from being a scared little hedgehog to a shark who smelled a drop of blood in nearby waters.

"Believe me, you don't want to write about it."

"You think I could possibly be in more danger than I am already?"

"Bill tried, and you saw what happened. Maya, they are like a hydra. You cut off one head, and two new ones grow back in its place. From the beginning of time, those who had the most power, strength, influence, and money have been creating their own secret societies. Some prefer rituals, some secrecy itself, and some use their money for sinful satisfactions. But this isn't just some sect of religious, rich idiots. It's an order whose origins are mentioned back in the times of the Crusades."

Maya seemed intrigued.

"What is Nehushtan, anyway? Sounds slightly familiar, but I can't quite recall. Is it something Biblical?"

"Correct. In the Old Testament, there are stories of Moses taking his people into a promised land."

"Well, I only remember them walking through the Black Sea and food falling from the sky."

"Actually, it was the Red Sea, but that's a different story. While the Hebrew nation was in the desert, they were attacked by venomous snakes, and people were dying in agony. Millions of people! Moses couldn't help them all. It was just physically impossible. So God commanded him to create a bronze serpent and raise it up high enough that people in his camp could see it."

"Oh yeah, that's right. And everyone who looked at it was healed."

"Exactly. So the name of the serpent was Nehushtan."

"I see. But why just 'the head?'"

"Well, that's another story…"

"I'm thrilled!"

Phillip gave her a stern look, and she immediately raised both hands in surrender. Having forgotten that her shoulder was wounded, Maya felt a sudden, sharp pain strike her as punishment for her sarcastic gesture.

"We know how people like to assign mystical meaning to even the most common things but imagine here a huge serpent that helped perform one of God's miracles. Cultures of that time were used to having gods who looked like creatures of nature, and they had just walked out of Egypt, after all."

"If not a golden calf, then why not a bronze serpent?"

"Yep! Believe it or not, this snake was to become an idol for many centuries thereafter until the kingdom of Israel divided into South and North. The righteous king, Hezekiah, destroyed all of the statues and symbols of other gods. Nehushtan was cut into pieces and melted down, everything that is, except for the head. The priests of that cult, risking their lives, stole the head and hid it deep in the tunnels under Jerusalem.

"Many, many years later, the Church sent the Crusaders to find the Holy Grail. Templars who managed to reach the inner parts of the nearly-destroyed holy city were able to recover unbelievable treasures and artifacts, all of which were sent back to the Vatican. And as you might have guessed, the Head of Nehushtan was one of those artifacts, even though it never found its way into the Pope's residence.

"This treasure got lost, along with a group of twelve Crusader paladins. The French king swore to the Pope that they were his most faithful knights and wouldn't just steal a rare treasure such as that. But when they sent a search party, they found them all dead with no Head of Nehushtan and none of the other treasures they'd been hoarding. When they went to bury the bodies, they found snakes coiled up and slithering around in the armor."

The train stopped at another station.

Maya looked outside, but it was still empty, and even the last person sharing their car stepped off, leaving them alone. This was for the best.

"Interesting. No, seriously, I love how you talk about all of this. It's almost like it's not a legend but some historical fact of which you have proof."

"What if I do? Is that so hard to believe?"

"Ha! I didn't know there were many believers among the FBI."

"Many more than among journalists."

"Fair point." Maya smiled and leaned back into her seat when the car started moving again. "We see so many ugly truths around, maybe even more than you guys. And that makes me believe that if God does exist somewhere, then he forgot about us a long time ago. We're our own punishment. We're hell enough for each other."

Agent Howell smirked.

"Did I say something funny?"

"No. But your logic is interesting. The ugly truths that I've seen are actually what made me a believer. Our world is not just black and white. It has so many unknowns and mysteries that without faith, it would be impossible to process or move on."

A long silence grew between them.

Maya looked through a window to the sleeping city that stretched out like a blanket far into the horizon. She knew that the FBI agent was trying to help her, but the whole idea of being dependent on someone bothered her. And his whole story sounded like a sort of prank. When she was a kid, she loved to watch movies about archeology, lost temples, and magical artifacts, but in today's world, it was hard to believe that a large and complex cult network might grow to such power and influence over some stupid bronze head.

The agent sat across from her, but his attention was focused on the entrances between the cars as though he was expecting someone to walk in at any moment. More than awkward conversations, Maya hated awkward silences.

"No, I do believe in mysteries, too, like horoscopes! But not much more seriously than I believe in Santa Claus and his elves. And I need to clarify that I only believe in good horoscopes!"

"This is gonna be hard for you." Phillip gave her a sad smile. She could tell him anything she wanted and mock him for his faith, but he knew more than she could ever imagine.

"What is?"

"Surviving in this story," he said without a single tone of sarcasm, making the conversation take on a scarier feeling. She had offended him, and it seemed that he was going to hold this grudge for a while.

In that moment, Maya's smile disappeared, but not just because of Agent Howell's words. As they drew nearer to the next station, she felt she had seen something, even before the train exited the tunnel. It was like seeing an image, closing your eyes, and seeing it there again reflected in your mind. But this time, it was the reverse, and she saw the image in her mind's eye before seeing it in reality. Her eyes shut, she perceived the shadows of two men in hooded jackets waiting for her under a flickering fluorescent light on the approaching platform.

"Maya?"

Her face must have given away her fear. Yes, she was scared, but not because of the vision she had or because of the ordeal she had just gone through. Something deep within her started speaking. Somebody's voice, reassuringly, began telling her that everything would be okay, that she just needed to relax. It was not her subconscious mind. It was not Howell. It was the same voice she had heard on the video from Bill's office.

The train stopped, and there they were. Two men, deep hoods covering their faces, stood just where Maya had seen them in her vision. The voice inside became so melodic and desirable that her reflexes began to melt down like wax next to a flame. Colors disappeared, and her mind grew light and floated like the first time she started her painkillers.

The FBI agent slowly, as though surrounded by an invisible gel, tried to withdraw his gun. A couple passengers in the next car, not noticing any of the events unfolding around them, sat still like statues frozen in time. For a fraction of a second, everything seemed frozen, even Phillip. Maya stood up and took a slight step forward.

The voice inside told her it was okay and that she only needed to make a couple more steps. How silly she felt for having been afraid now that she knew that nothing bad would happen to her! She only needed to walk out onto the platform to the clan brothers, who stood calmly waiting to take care of her.

The sound of the words was sweet and inviting, like the waves of an upcoming dream in the midnight hour. She sensed that slight edge between sleep and reality when you know that you are about to fall asleep but are still conscious. She had come to the moment when the slumbery climax took control entirely, and she could no longer delay discharging into the world of blissful sleep.

Step. Step. One more.

Another...

She was about to leave the metro car when strong hands pulled her back, and the doors closed in front of her.

The sound of a slap brought her screaming back to reality.

Maya's cheek was burning. The fog in her mind was disappearing along with the voice in her head, and she began to recognize the concerned face of Phillip in front of her.

"Ouuuuch...Did you just slap me, FBI?"

"I had to." He did not seem to be sorry for it.

"Really? I think you've just been waiting for the chance. Did they teach you that in Quantico, how to beat harmless women?"

"You? Harmless?" He turned his face away, and she noticed a fresh, bleeding wound on his cheek. In that same moment, images and memories started rushing back into her head.

Images of Phillip pulling out his gun.

Images of her hands moving faster than his. With her right palm, she knocked the gun out of his hand, and with her left fist, she knocked him down.

"Ouch!" Now, she noticed the pain in the knuckles of her left hand. "But how...?"

"Still don't believe me?"

"Gosh...I feel awful. I'm not sure what happened. I started hearing that creepy voice inside, and...It's like some cheesy movie about hypnosis."

She was afraid to look at Phillip, thinking she must sound crazy. Maybe the cancer had progressed and moved into her brain?

"You're right. Hypnosis it is."

"So this is why Bill shot himself?"

"They are snake worshipers. Have you ever seen how a rabbit acts in front of a boa?"

"I took some psychology classes. A lot of doctors practice hypnosis, but there are so many factors involved. How was that possible if they didn't even have close contact? It looked more like some freaking voodoo!"

"I don't know what to say, to be honest. No one at the Bureau knows their full capability."

"Then how can you fight against them? Hold on! This doesn't make sense if they wanted to kill me and Vlad. Why not just do their mind tricks and make us open up our veins? Why send guys with guns?"

Phillip shrugged and stood up, taking his gun off safety.

"Do you want to ask them? I'm sure they'll be at the next station."

"Not really." Maya was not following what it was he planned to do.

"Then this is our stop."

Agent Howell pulled the emergency brake and brought the whole metro train screeching to a halt in the middle of a bridge. A couple shots fired through the window sent glass flying and formed their exit.

"Are you sure this is legal?"

It was the last thing she managed to ask before he grabbed her hand and pulled her outside.

*

She had been sitting in the corner of a half-empty apartment and, for the last five minutes, was brushing her wet hair. Normally, that would have been enough to calm her down, but today, she needed something stronger. Why had she not asked Howell to buy her some cheap booze?

Outside, the sky finally began to take on shades of the upcoming morning, and that alone seemed like a great gift from the universe. Surviving the last night had been a miracle. It would have been nice if she could turn off her brain and take a little nap, but that was nearly impossible. This was not the first time she had put her life into such a dangerous situation, but looking into the face of death with such unpleasant intensity was way beyond the norm, even for her.

Once before, she had crossed that road for an influential millionaire, and he turned her life into a living hell. But Sawyer had his own way of fixing the situation, and after a short meeting with the guy, the millionaire moved his business away from Chicago and left Maya alone for good. But now Bill was dead, and there was no amount of money in the world that could save her from the brainwashing snakeheads.

She had to agree that were it not for the FBI agent, she would not have made it very far on her own. Though the dank apartment smelled like urine and vomit and had been sealed off with yellow police tape, it nevertheless seemed safe. Who in their right mind would come looking for her in this ghetto where the walls were still decorated with bullet holes? Within the tiny walls, a few dirty windows, a floppy door, a table and chairs, an old mattress, and a half-living fridge furnished her new sanctuary. She was safe for now. But still, why could she not fall asleep?

It will be okay. She would be okay. Just have a little patience.

She took a deep breath and closed her eyes.

Cold and darkness.

Wet clothes pulled her down.

She wanted to scream, but there was not enough air. She was drowning. The darkness of the lake did not want to let her go. No, she would fight! She gave up once already! Was this a dream? She probably had fallen asleep after all. Well, now she needed to wake up.

The darkness was so real!

Phillip?! Would he come to save her? He might have been the one who saved her before and asked Valentina's son to take her inside…

And here he came! Light! A bright light and a strong hand catching her wrist. It might be Howell…No, it was not him.

A teenage boy pulled her out like she weighed no more than a cloud. His light hair looked like silver in the moonlight, and his eyes looked straight into her soul. She did not scream, and her urge to panic faded. His otherworldly blue eyes gave her a sense of peace. He was peace himself. But how could he be so strong? No. How could he pull her so high? He was not in the water. He was on it!

He ignored the laws of physics and simply stood on the water as though it had turned into rock under his feet…

Shaking, she felt herself leave the cold water of the lake and appear in a sunny room.

"Maya! Wake up!" The boy's face transformed into Howell's. "Are you okay?"

She jumped, but her leg felt numb from sleeping in a sitting position.

"Let me help you. Nightmare?" Phillip offered her a hand and slowly helped her stand.

"Sort of…" She did not want to appear weak, but her leg hurt like hell. "Did I say anything in my sleep?"

"Sort of…" Howell mimicked her tone. "I wouldn't be surprised if the neighbors already called the cops. You screamed like someone was trying to kill you."

"Interesting. Why on earth would I have dreams like that?" parried Maya sarcastically before hobbling over to the table, where she found some bags with clothing and snacks. "What have you got here?"

"Not something you would normally wear, I suspect, but it's for the best. Some jeans and a couple sweaters…and hair dye. Brown should look good on you."

"Forget it! No one takes down my red pride! Lemme see...chips, Coke, sandwiches...eww, tomatoes!"

"Oh, I'm sorry. Let me call the nearest French restaurant and order you some filet mignon for special delivery, Your Majesty."

"You're funny, FBI." She gave him a contemptuous smile, pulled the tomatoes from her sandwich, and began eating like she had never eaten before, which was surprising after her ordeal at ABOB.

"I see you found the shower?"

"Yeah. The water was kind of cold, but after my swim in that dumpster, my hair was full of fish fins."

"I hope I guessed your size correctly."

"I hope you saved the receipt. So what now?"

"Not much, you try to rest. I need to go check in with my people at the Bureau. Make a list of stuff you might need for a week, and I'll try to bring it in the evening."

Maya stopped chewing.

"You're kidding, right?"

Phillip picked up his sandwich, opened it, placed Maya's rejected tomatoes inside, and took a big bite out of it.

"Nope, not at all. If you stay here, at least I don't need to worry about protecting you for a while, so I can get back to doing my job."

"You think I can't protect myself?"

"No, you can't. Or have you forgotten what happened in the metro? You almost jumped out into their loving arms."

"Hey! It was a moment of weakness! Can't a lady afford one now and then?"

"A lady can, but you're no lady." Phillip took another big bite, and some mayo dropped onto the floor.

"You're a pig, FBI."

Maya knew he was right. She was defenseless against those people, but that was no reason to hide her from the world. She needed to act! She had to find a way to get herself out of this nonsense and not just sit around waiting for the FBI to catch them all.

"It's just for a week or so, I promise. Then I'll move you to a more comfortable place."

"Where? A great place like Lake City where I'll get covered by mold and dust? Heck, no! Oh, and did you forget about my health condition, or do you want me to die here from pain?"

"Doesn't look like you're in any pain."

That was strange. She had not felt any pain for quite a while, actually, but that did not mean she would not start suffering again at any moment. The doctor had promised a chance that the cancer would go into remission, but only after the chemo and surgery.

"Hey, you have no right to decide that for me. Let me help you. Do you know why they faked that resurrection and sent me to write an article about it?"

"By the way, resurrection wasn't faked. I read paramedics' report. I read coroners' papers. You know what that mean? Right? They cut her open. If she wasn't dead before, she wouldn't survive that."

Something inside was trying to talk to her. Asked her to let her inner feelings take over, but she was too proud and scared to admit that her logic was failing. Her dream. Her missing pain? Little girl and her parents who hide from the press…Everything was pointing in only one direction. But she can't agree. Otherwise, she will need to accept everything else as reality.

"Oh please, like they couldn't pay to paramedics or…you know they all might be part of that church! I'm sure there's something weird going on with it. I have a source…"

"Who, the girl from the hotel? The one who got dumped by the pastor's son and now hates the whole congregation? Sure."

"How did you...? Never mind. Still, I could be helpful to you!"

"Yes, by sitting quietly on your ass in here!" He finished the last of his sandwich in one bite. "How about I bring you some real food for dinner? I can call in an order and pick it up. Hmmm?"

"Fine!" Channeling all her anger, she stomped over to her corner and sat back on the old mattress. "Just bring me some clean sheets and hair conditioner. And as far as food, no tomatoes...and no pancakes."

CHAPTER 8

It was not clear whether Phillip had done it on purpose or if he had simply forgotten, but he hurried off without leaving any money for Maya. He just took the list and promised to bring things up closer to nine. That meant she had a whole seven hours to do what she planned and get back before Mr. FBI noticed her absence.

Luckily for her, Maya had memorized the company credit card, so she dialed a taxi service and prepaid, using the name of a secretary, Alison. Thirty minutes later, dressed like an ordinary stay-at-home mom in jeans and a sweater, she was on her way to the main office of the *Chicago Voice*. At one point, she was tempted to stop by her apartment and pick up some things she had not thought to get on their run last night and to ask the neighbor lady to watch her cat. It was way too risky, though, and who knew what prying eyes might be watching her place now? And regarding the cat, well, he had his ways of alerting all the neighbors of his needs. Perhaps she could ask Alison to go pick up some of her belongings and give the cat enough food.

But those were the wrong things to worry about for the time being. More urgently, she needed to call her parents and tell them that she was okay. It was likely that someone might ask them about her, but all they needed to do was simply tell the truth—that since Maya had left Alaska, they barely kept in touch.

Maya asked the cab driver to stop two blocks away from her office, allowing her to case the area first, making sure no suspicious people in black jackets or idle cops were waiting for her. Just as she suspected, there were two police vehicles parked right across from the main entrance. A couple of strange "citizens" scanned the area while pretending to read newspapers or listen to their music players.

No, better not risk it, even if they were not there for her. It was possible that there were general security reasons for their presence or that they were trying to prevent more accidents, but Maya was not taking any chances. She decided to go with her plan B, though it possibly meant a couple hours of waiting.

She circled another block and then turned down the alley behind a coffee shop, continuing all the way to a back door of the *Chicago Voice*, where there was a smoking area for the IT department. Since all of them had recently switched to vaping, and the company allowed them to do so at their desks, the employees barely left their chairs at all anymore. The only person who still utilized this area was Stan Cook, head of the photo department. He felt vaping was for posers and placed these newfangled replacements for cigarettes in the same category as cell phone cameras, non-alcoholic beer, and blow-up dolls.

Fortunately, there was no need to wait. He was right there, swearing like a sailor, making gestures with a half-finished cigarette in one hand and sipping coffee from a huge mug in the other. It sounded like the argument was not really job-related, or maybe he just was not particularly formal with his freelancers. Since Stan was using his headset, he could not hear Maya's footsteps approaching. When he finally noticed her, he jumped, startled, before slowly melting into a wide smile.

"I'll call you back…" He pressed the button, disconnected the call, took a sip from the mug, and gave Maya a long stare. "Girl, don't you know all the king's horses and all the king's men have been looking for you under every rock in the county?"

"Ha, what news! Guess why I'm not using the main gate!"

"I thought you turned tail and ran."

"Nah, I have some unfinished business. By the way, I need your help."

"I thought you'd never ask." Stan put on his sexy face and playfully moved his eyebrows up and down, leaning toward her.

"Ewww!" Maya theatrically waved a hand in front of his face, pulled the cigarette from his mouth, and doused it in his coffee. "Go get some gum first, or I'll make you brush your teeth. How many times have I asked you not to smoke in my presence?"

"Really? FYI, this is the designated smoking area…" He smirked back at her, not in the least irritated by her remarks. More than anything, he seemed happy to see her.

"Whatever."

"Hold this." He gave her his mug, pulled out the magnetic key card, punched in the code, and opened the door.

*

They walked together down the hall all the way to his office. On the way, he splashed the rest of his coffee and the drowned cigarette into the pot of an ornamental palm tree.

"Now I know who killed the bonsai tree next to my office."

Stan smiled mischievously, showing no sign of regret.

On the first floor, life had its own meaning. The technical departments were located there, so people were mostly staring at their screens, checking data, watching funny videos, or playing computer games, but no one was paying attention to her. Even on the busiest day, everything would have looked exactly the same.

Stan pushed open the door to his "chamber of thoughts" and maneuvered easily through old printouts and sketches on the floor, cleared a place for Maya, and refilled his mug from the coffee pot before jumping into his chair.

She hated this place. It reminded her more of a hamster's nest than the office of a department head. The walls were covered with cut-outs from old issues, some of his photos, a couple posters from computer games, and cheesy sci-fi movies. If you looked carefully, you could actually spot his diploma and a couple awards. Boxes were stacked into a formation that could easily have provided a lesson or two to the Leaning Tower of Pisa on how to beat the laws of gravity.

The whole floor was covered with everything that could lay around without rotting, including the empty boxes from old devices, receipts, folders with pictures, books, printouts of e-mails, and hundreds of albums filled with negatives. The carpet was visible only on the winding path to the coffeemaker located on top of a shelf and to Stan's desk, but the owner of this mess insisted that the chaos helped him clear his thoughts and cook up creative ideas. He was damn good, and that was why everyone seemed okay with such extravagance.

"So, is it true that the boss really bit the gun because of you?" Stan was neither a subtle nor tactful person, and demeanor was not one of his strong suits. "I always knew you were a femme fatale."

"What?" She looked at him, surprised.

"This place is like a hive today, and everyone's buzzing about it."

"Really? People think he killed himself because of me?"

"Everyone knew that you guys were…hmm…involved…"

"So people knew?" Maya thought they had been so careful about hiding their romance from others. Apparently, she was wrong, but who cared now? Bill was dead, and her colleagues thought she was the one who pushed him to do it.

"Oh, I don't care!" She needed to switch the subject. "I have something for you. Do you have access to our website?"

"Sure!" He was not surprised or worried and looked more entertained than anything.

Maya knew that Stan abused his access to the website because, sooner or later, someone always found little misspellings that he had entered into various articles. Originally, the rights to modification had been given to him, as with any other head of department, to update pages in case of breaking news or when the need arose to upload scandalous images. Today, she had something really fitting. Carefully, she removed a USB drive, speckled with dried drops of blood, from her pocket. At the moment, she was not even sure if it was Vlad's blood or hers or someone else's from the restaurant.

"Here's the truth about Bill's murder."

"Murder?" Stan slowly lost his smile. "You wanna say someone actually killed the boss?"

"But first, before you upload this on our site, make sure to copy it somewhere else. Upload it in a couple other places, like YouTube or Vimeo, and send a link to all social platforms. It needs to be done fast and simultaneously."

"You're scaring me, girl!" Maya sensed the excitement in his voice.

"Be ready. Someone will try to take this video down. Someone might even come to you with questions as well."

"Oh please…"

"No, Stan, this shit is real! I almost died yesterday because of it."

Stan took the USB drive, looking more serious.

"Is that blood?"

"No, it's strawberry jam, dammit! Yes, it's blood!"

"Yours?" Stan just then realized why Maya was so carefully and awkwardly moving her shoulder.

"Stan, you're starting to piss me off! Can you do it or not? I just want to be sure as many people as possible are able to see and copy it before it gets removed."

"I can ask Vlad. He can make it into torrent…"

"Vlad from the IT department?"

Stan nodded, waiting for her to confirm that she trusted the guy, but stopped, remembering that Maya never bothered to remember the names of "unimportant" employees.

"Do you know him?"

"I knew him..." She paused long enough for Stan to understand her meaning. "He's the one who brought that to me."

"My God...Maya...Why here? Why aren't you showing this to the police?"

"We can't. Not yet. I don't want this to get buried in secrecy or get 'lost' in an evidence room."

"Okay...yeah, you're right...Can I see it?"

"Go ahead. I hope there's not a passcode on this drive. Otherwise, it could get complicated."

With one movement, Stan pushed a bunch of papers and documents to the floor, freeing access to the USB port on his laptop. For the first time, Maya noticed that his hands were shaking. Stan's hands! This was the guy who took sharp, crisp photos even in terrible lighting. There was a time when she would have wished for her surgeon to have hands as stable as his.

"Well, let's see. There are about twenty files. Which one?"

"I have no idea. Let's start from the beginning."

Maya regretted saying so even before she finished her sentence.

It was the two of them. On the screen, Maya had her blouse open and her legs around Bill's waist. He was kissing her while she impatiently tried to unbuckle his stupid belt...

"Oh là là!"

"Turn it off!" Maya tried to reach for the laptop to do it herself, but the pain in her shoulder stopped her. "Please, stop it!"

"What? I thought that's the video you wanted to post to the main page!" Stan tried to add a tone of humor to his voice but noticed tears forming in the corners of Maya's eyes. "I'm sorry, I didn't know it was serious between you two."

"It wasn't. Try closer to the end."

"Hold on…" Stan changed the view parameters, and the video file icons turned into little preview images. Most of the files showed Maya and Bill. "My goodness, do you think I have a camera in my office too?"

"Everyone already knows what you do in your office after lunch, with or without a camera."

"Perverts!"

Maya smiled because Stan sounded proud, not ashamed.

He opened the last file. It was exactly the one Maya had seen at ABOB. Stan leaned so close to the panel that he could have left a nose print on the screen. After he finished watching the first time, he clicked on replay. Then two more times…

"Maya, what the hell?"

"I'm not sure. I mean, there's one possible explanation, but I'm not willing to say it out loud because it'll sound absolutely insane!"

"Well, it is!"

Stan pulled out his pack of cigarettes and lit one.

"What about the smoke detector?" Maya took it out of his hand, drew a long puff, and dunked it into his fresh cup of coffee.

Stan hit replay again.

"Okay…So, if this is not a trick…I mean, technically, he did kill himself, but this was against his will." Stan mumbled, looking at the screen, and tried to pull his thoughts together. "What should we do now? I mean… Yeah, you're right. We need to upload this and let everyone see."

"Stan, please tell me I'm not crazy. Is this all some kind of joke? Could Bill have just staged this as a performance?"

"Is your shoulder hurting for real?"

Maya nodded. But how easy it would be to think of it all as some kind of theatrical act involving a bunch of actors, including Vlad and some extras in the café! But she had not just heard voices in her head. She did, in fact, see people die right in front of her, and her shoulder had a real bullet wound. Bill would never hurt her like that.

"So, do you think you can handle the upload?"

"Pfff…Of course, but I'm worried about you. Maybe I should give you some time to leave. As soon as this video goes live, they'll know that you were here."

"I'm not sure they'd attack me in front of the whole office."

"Maya, if they can order a person to put a bullet in his head, then maybe they can erase memories. Or they might make the whole office hunt after you. Even me."

"Too much TV will fry your brain, Stan."

Stan did not even hear her, and his eyes sparkled as a thousand theories and ideas rushed through his head. Finally, his hope of advancing his career through catching a sensational story had become a reality. A flick on the tip of his nose brought him back to reality.

"So, the uploads?"

"Oh yeah! Already on it! What did that guy in the video say about Nehushtan's head? Isn't that Moses' copper snake?"

Maya stared at him with a slight smile and more than a little suspicion. This was a side of Stan she had never seen before.

"My adoptive parents were missionaries. Relax. But yeah, I'm a really smart guy, actually…Did they really kill Vlad? Damn it! I'm glad we at least have this!" He nodded toward the screen. "What's in that last file? You again?"

"I'm not sure. Click it."

This time, it was a recording from a hallway. Maya knew this place; a couple of times, she had needed to sneak into Bill's office through that hallway. She was aware of the camera but usually was more worried about people seeing her there. So often, we cease to notice technology, forgetting that there is always a person behind that digital eye. The picture was black and white and without any sound.

A flash came from behind the doors. That was Bill killing himself…

After a minute without any movement, the door opened, and two people, one in a hooded jacket and another in a long hooded robe, walked casually out into the hall. At any other time, Maya would have laughed at their outfits, but not today. Something was truly sinister in those cultish costumes and in the way one of the men walked. He was not afraid of being caught or of looking ridiculous. No, he walked as if he were the big boss of the *Chicago Voice*. His gait was normal and even strong, making the cane in his hand look unnecessary.

"Okay, now I'm lost…What a circus!"

"Stan, can you zoom in on his cane?"

"I can't do much here. Only if…Okay, let's pause here. I'll take a screenshot. Saving as a PNG. Opening in shop…Let's add some brightness and contrast. Clarity. Zoom…I would say that handle looks like…a snake?"

"Yep. And I could swear that I've seen that cane before."

*

She could have and should have just called for Alison and asked her to bring everything she needed from her office straight to the first floor, but Maya's head was so swamped with the flood of thoughts rushing over her that she went to the elevator and pressed the button for her floor. She knew that, no matter what, she needed to stay out of sight, but her sudden understanding of what was happening temporarily lowered her survival instincts.

She walked all the way from the elevator door to her office without drawing any attention to herself. Even though the chief had died, life at the newspaper kept going. Maya was not sure if people were even expecting to see her there, so if someone did catch her in the corner of their eye, they might mistake her for a visitor or freelancer who had come to share their stories or pitch ideas.

The sound of intense tapping on the keyboards and phones ringing filled the air from every direction and from the dozens of cubicles where her employees worked on new stories and articles. The commotion gave her a false feeling of security.

This was her territory, where she was the queen spider who sat in the middle of the web, pulling her strings and knitting together the best pages in the Saturday issue. She was a goddess, worshiped and feared. She was her own muse, inspiring and motivating her soldiers to conquer new heights. But what did it matter now? She had been gone, and it seemed as though no one even missed her. Tomorrow, next week, and in a month, the paper would still come off the press, and the thousands of people reading pages of the *Chicago Voice* would not even notice the difference. Vanity, vanity, all is vanity.

She walked in, closing the door behind her. Surprisingly, her altar was still empty, but how soon would it be before they placed someone else on her pedestal? To Maya's surprise, the office was still clean, and it seemed that the police did not think it necessary to turn everything upside-down. Either that, or they had not yet procured a search warrant. Well, that was their loss and her gain because whatever they found on her would almost certainly look suspicious.

Maya opened the bottom drawer of her desk, tossing through files and folders. With a click, the false bottom opened to reveal a hidden cache. There were documents under her alias, Loraine Flint or Lala Flint, including a passport, driver's license, and two major credit cards. Also, she retrieved a couple thousand dollars in hundred-dollar bills wrapped neatly in plastic. It was not much, but it would help her survive in the meantime.

In the archive room, she had another stash consisting of a suitcase packed with extra clothes, a wig, and another bag with cash. No, she was not a spy, but she had learned over the years that a good journalist occasionally crosses someone powerful and violent, and so it was always best to be prepared. She took a key from the archive that was taped to the bottom of a bonsai pot and was just about to leave when the office door opened.

"Miss Polanski?" Alison, Sawyer's secretary, looked more frightened than Maya.

"Sh-h-h-h. Come in. Sorry, Alison…"

Maya did not get the chance to finish her sentence when the girl burst into tears and rushed over, hugging her and burying her face in Maya's shoulder.

"Oh, Miss Polanski, I am so, so sorry!"

Maya was a bit shocked by the gesture but guessed the poor girl had finally found someone with whom she could share her fears and pain. But honestly, it was not a good time.

"There, there." Maya, trying to make the situation less awkward, patted Bill's secretary on the shoulder and tried to free herself from the unsolicited hug. It seemed the girl did not get the hint because she started crying even louder.

"I can't believe he's gone! What are we gonna do without him?"

Run the hell out of here, thought Maya, because if she did not manage to stop the hysterics now, the entire office would come to cry on her shoulder.

"I know, Alison, I know." Maya used a bit of force to escape, pretending that she was reaching for a box of tissues.

"This is some kind of nightmare!" Alison took a tissue and loudly blew her nose, and just then, Maya noticed how red her eyes were. The poor thing seemed really heartbroken. "He couldn't kill himself! I know it.

He was so alive! Such a great spirit! I saw him that night. Yeah, he was worried, but Miss Polanski, I swear he was so happy. Happy and beautiful people don't kill themselves like this!"

Well, Maya always knew that Alison had a crush on Bill, but hey, so did half of Chicago. And yes, she had written enough obituaries in her time to know that beautiful people do indeed kill themselves.

"Okay, listen up, dear." Maya really did not have time for this, but she might actually need more than one ally in this place, and who would be a better source of information than the front desk girl? "I know that it was not suicide, and soon everyone else will know it too."

"Are you serious?!" Alison's face finally stopped melting. Who wears mascara when you know that you are going to cry?

"Yes, I have proof, and I'll do anything to bring the bastards to justice."

"But how?"

"You just need to trust me and let me deal with it, though I might need your help."

"Of course, anything you need!"

"Actually…" Maya pulled the USB drive from her pocket. "I might make a copy of these files for you, and just in case something happens to me, it'll be nice to have backup."

"Are there more copies?"

Something was wrong with that question. Maybe it was how fast she asked it or some note of fear she noticed in Alison's voice.

"No, this is the original," lied Maya. "But bring me a couple empty drives, and I'll make a copy."

"Or I can copy it onto my desktop and bring it back." Alison stretched out her hand, but she already understood that it was not going to happen.

Maya felt a boiling wave of heat rushing from the depths of her anger as it filled her being, took control of her breath, and pulsed poisonous thoughts through her mind. She should have just given over the drive and walked away while she still had a chance, but too much had happened of late for her to remain under control any longer.

"All this time?"

"Maya, give me the USB." Alison stepped to the side, blocking the exit.

"Are you one of them? Or did they pay you to spy on Bill? What did they need from him? Money? The newspaper?"

Alison seemed surprised at first but then smiled and rolled her eyes.

"Oh, Maya, you have no idea what's going on." The secretary looked relieved and almost happy in saying so. "Just give me the stupid drive and go. You'd better move away from Chicago or even out of the States. Didn't you plan to go to Europe? Just stay there."

It was so strange. Maya had never noticed how deep was the color of Alison's eyes. Now, she could discern every subtle shade of blue that, layer by layer, was built into a spiral staircase leading far into her soul.

"Everything will be alright, Maya. We'll take care of it."

Spots of gold reflected in the blue ocean.

It was like sunrise on a beach, waking up after a whole night of dancing and love. When your body groans from heat and sweat, your breath becomes short, and your thoughts are clouded. Nude, embraced by the salted breeze. One jump away from pure satisfaction. The ocean…Endless waves of calm and peace.

Those eyes.

"…now just walk away."

Maya's hand felt empty without the USB drive, but she did not care. The ocean would take her away. Alison's voice resonated in the waves, blue like her eyes.

"Walk, Maya. You'll leave the building and walk straight up the street…"

A sudden beep on the intercom brought Maya rushing back to reality.

"Maya?! I know you're still there!" It was Stan. "The video's uploaded. We have a couple thousand views already!"

Anger distorted Alison's face. She jumped toward the table to see whose number was on the com, apparently not recognizing Stan's voice. That was more than enough for Maya to grab her Pulitzer award from the desk and bash Alison over the head.

The secretary fell to the floor, dropping the USB drive. Maya leaned to recover her lost treasure when the blue-eyed witch jumped on her from behind, and now they were both on the floor.

Polanski tried to push Alison away, but the girl was stronger than she thought.

Long-clawed fingers grappled at Maya's neck and pressed her down toward the expensive shag carpet. Dressed more comfortably than Alison, she was able to twist herself around and free her hands. She tried to shove the crazed girl off of her, but the secretary did not plan to give up that easily.

"I warned you! You could have walked away," hissed Alison, squishing the life out of Maya. "He asked me not to kill you, but this is your fault!"

Maya tried to grab Alison's hands and pull them away from her neck, but it proved impossible.

"I don't see anything special in you. Why? Why was it so easy for you, huh!?"

Everything started to go blurry. Black spots covered everything in Maya's vision, but she was not ready to surrender. Why had someone not come to the office by now? There was no way that someone had not heard them struggling.

"That's enough, Maya! Just listen to me! Look at me!"

Maya did not want to, but something inside her felt compelled to obey the command, and she looked back into the burning blue coals. She could not allow this freak to control her. She was not some rabbit who would cower in fear and let the snake bite her head off. Not anymore. Enough is enough!

With a roar and her last drops of courage, Maya raised her hands and stuck her thumbs into the blue flames!

An explosion of blood showered on everything around.

Alison jumped back, screaming in agony, pressing her palms to the bleeding holes in her face.

It took about ten seconds for Maya to catch her breath and stop coughing before she was able to get up, grab the thumb drive, money, and documents, and run away into the hall where everyone, frozen in place, just looked at her.

CHAPTER 9

In order to bring truth to society, a journalist often has to sacrifice personal comfort and peace. Could Maya call herself the most honest journalist in the world? Of course not. She had done so many things in exchange for little perks. Often, she would describe a hotel where she stayed in a better light if they agreed to waive her payment or place her in their best available rooms. For a free bottle of wine, her review of a restaurant could be as impressive as the bottle's original price. Maya had promised before to mention the name and make of her car in a write-up at least once a month in exchange for a new vehicle. She had received vases, silverware, furniture, discounts, and gift baskets from a host of different stores. Oh well…

Did she feel guilty? Not at all! Good businesses have good strategies, and she honestly wrote about how great they were. If others felt that, in reality, a business had conned its customers, well, they were free to write their own reviews, too. The only problem was that few would hear them, whereas Maya's voice was heard by thousands.

On the other hand, every journalist must reach for something nobler from time to time, whether in proclaiming a holy war against an unfair policy, trying to nail down a corrupt politician, or even unveiling a huge conspiracy. More often than not, a journalist would fail in such a task, but trying was all that mattered in the eyes of people. Each must choose his own Goliath to fight while praying to God that the giant will be too busy to thwart your attempts to catch him. And if not, you had better be prepared to fight to the bitter end, even if it turns out to be your end! And who knows, if worse comes to worst, maybe someone would write a ballad about your poor soul's brave struggle, or maybe just an article…or at least a flattering obituary.

Maya had been very lucky. She brought down one of the most influential mayors that Chicago ever had. The material provided by his assistant, Mr. Cloudy, destroyed his empire and brought Polansky to the Olympus of journalism. But now Maya was starting to understand that luck had nothing to do with it.

A couple years back, during the most heated period in her battle against Chicago's mayor, she had escaped to Florida for a couple months to wait out the chaos. Staying in her second home, she finished her third novel, met some of her fans, and had a short, mindless affair. She slept till noon, ate seafood with white wine for lunch, and had red meat with Burgundy for dinner. She drove for hours along the shore until she found the perfect empty beach and swam her cares away until her cravings for food or men would call her back to the city.

After everything settled down, she returned to Chicago, a hero with open doors to any branch of the journalistic industry. She even had an offer to host her own weekly show on a local channel or to become the main editor of a magazine based in LA. But she chose instead to stay exactly where she was because she had one hope and one dream.

One day, Bill would inherit everything from his father and would need to quit the publishing business to think about something bigger. Or he might simply cease to care about the *Chicago Voice*. But Maya, on the other hand, always had a soft spot for the paper. It would be a lifetime achievement, something to prove herself! Starting all the way at the bottom and rising to become the editor-in-chief would be the cherry on top of it all. After that, she could think about a TV show and everything else…But for now, actually, Maya needed to set the dreams aside.

The most rational option right now would be to leave the country. She could rent a car and drive to Canada under a fake name. She would stay there, somewhere in Montreal, for a week or two, call her agent in

Florida to arrange for the sale of her house, and move to Europe. Maybe back to Poland. She might even remember the language well enough to become an English teacher or a translator. Maybe she would never be famous again, but at least she would be alive. That is, unless the cancer made a sudden move, but even if so, Europe surely had some of the finest oncology clinics available.

But! There was always a big BUT in her life. The Head of Nehushtan had started this fight, had taken so much away from her, and made it all so personal. Could she really just flee with her tail between her legs? No. They had messed with the wrong woman. And with this thought overshadowing her survival instincts, she forgot about Canada and drove down the same road she had taken three days prior.

'Welcome to Lake City' looked like a joke, but Maya did not feel like laughing. Would Agent Howell think to look for her here? By now, he had likely found out that she was gone. Deep inside, she still wanted to see Phillip, but now it was up to him.

Maybe he felt relieved that he no longer needed to babysit Maya, but she had not asked for his help in the first place.

It was for the best. This way, he could work more efficiently and would probably catch the bad guys before she had the chance to kill them. Maya now knew who was the leader of the snakeheads. But in order to prove it, she needed to return to Lake City and find out why Bill had sent her there in the first place.

In five minutes, she was already in Valentina's neighborhood. The first time, she drove past the house slowly to make sure Phillip or a group of snakeheads were not waiting for her, and when she felt sure that it was safe, she stopped two houses away in an inconspicuous spot close to a little park. It was already growing dark, so she left her sunglasses and wig in the car and took out four shopping bags from the trunk instead. Maya hurried toward the door.

Even though she knocked quietly, the door opened almost immediately. Little Alice seemed like she had been waiting for her, or perhaps she had never left the door since Maya returned to Chicago.

"Miss Maya! Come in. Dinner almost ready!"

"Oh really? Well, that's good because I'm kind of hungry!" Maya could not help but smile seeing the little girl again. "Is your mom home?"

"Yeah, they setting up table and told to me watch the door!"

Maybe they had been waiting for someone else? Well, at least this time, she had not come empty-handed.

"Can you help me with these, sweetie?"

Maya gave one of the bags to Alice. It was filled with boxes of candy and an assortment of other sweets.

"This is all for us?"

"Yep!" Maya had not had much time to do any shopping, but on the way, she stopped by a market alley that boasted a small candy shop. She stepped inside, hurrying, and nearly bought them out.

"Can I have one?"

"Only after dinner!" Valentina stepped out of the kitchen and nodded toward Maya. She smiled but did not seem surprised to see her standing there. Looking at Alice again, she sighed, "I promise, I will let you choose first what box to open, but now give me bags, and show Miss Polanski where is restroom so she can wash her hands. And give her some slippers."

Maya was not planning to take off her shoes, actually, and did not plan to stay long.

"I hope I haven't interrupted."

"No, we was waiting for you." Valentina tried to smile, but Maya noticed a hint of sadness, or even sorrow, in her eyes.

"Really?"

"Michael said you will come for him."

Maya froze with a confused grimace on her face. Should she be amazed or scared? Was this part of a joke, or should she just relax?

"Sure, I'm just gonna go with the flow…"

"Excuse me?" Valentina did not understand whether Maya was talking to her or to herself.

"Never mind. So where is Michael? Is he home?"

"Not yet, but I am sure he will be shortly. Wash please your hands and join us to table."

"This way!" Alice took Maya's hand and led her down the hallway.

What a strange life she had. Using a fake name, running away from the FBI and a crazy group of fanatics, making decisions based on impulse and not on logic, taking the back roads, and still, she ended up in a house where everyone was expecting her.

Michael…

Who in the world is he? A new messiah? A wizard? An alien? He could not be a mere prankster. Gradually, she started to understand that the boy was truly something else, whether she liked it or not. He was something beyond her understanding. She felt like she was looking down on it all from above or from a different dimension. Her thoughts were rushing through so fast and venturing so far away that her conscious did not dare allow her to follow after them.

Out of the corner of her eye, she noticed the other kids sitting at the kitchen table and watching her with expressions of awe and fear. What had she gotten herself into? And who was she in this story? The savior or the villain? Or maybe both?

Alice flipped on the light switch in the guest restroom and turned on the water as if Maya would not be able to manage it herself.

"Here is my favorite soap! You can start, and I will bring you a fresh towel."

Alice ran off, and Maya just stared into the sink like she had forgotten how to use it. She could not help it! Her brain! It was completely taking over now! She could not fight it anymore! She had to let her brain calculate all possible outcomes and possibilities!

FINE!

If the Head of Nehushtan was really as powerful as Phillip says, then how did they recruit new members? Could anyone just apply and get accepted, or did you need to wait for your owl with a letter from the headmaster? Or perhaps not an owl…a little garden snake?

Could you teach a regular person those hypnosis techniques, or were they only after talented people? Was there a limit to the possibilities? Could a boy born with supernatural powers, coupled with the knowledge of the clan, end up as some kind of ultimate weapon? That sounded logical…ish…

Then why Maya? Why did they send her to him? Would it not be easier to send one of their own people to talk to the boy and explain to him how special he was and then try to recruit him after promising superior guidance and endless wealth? Doubtless, any kid from a poor foster family would love the chance to become something special…and rich. Or was Maya judging this too much from her own perspective?

But what if this boy was not just a miracle worker who could resurrect people and walk on water? What if he was some kind of prophet? What if he could see the real motives behind words and actions? What if Valentina had actually done something miraculous herself in the way she raised and nourished his pure soul?

But once again, why? Why was she here?!

Maya took a palm full of cold water and splashed it over her face.

Ravings of a lunatic! Craziness! Madness! She was losing her mind. It needed to stop.

"Miss Maya?" Alice was standing next to her with a towel in her small hands and had apparently been there for a while.

"So, where is your brother?"

"He is praying," answered the girl without hesitation. "He said you will take him away from us. Is that true?"

Actually, Maya had only planned to ask him a couple questions, but if he was a prophet, then that was probably true too.

"Do you wanna see your portraits?" Alice was the typical kid who could not entertain a sad thought for a long while.

"Did you see one in the newspaper?"

"No," Alice giggled, "the one that Michael drawed. Let's go, I'll show you."

Alice grabbed Maya's hand again and led her to the next room, where another boy was working on his homework. He quickly got up, greeted Maya, and left the room as though she was covered with a contagious virus. On the way out, he growled something to Alice in Russian, but Maya was not able to catch the meaning since her attention was captured by a drawing on the wall in the room.

Many…Many…*Many*…pencil drawings, in fact. They were so beautiful and clean that they looked almost like black-and-white photos. In three of the drawings, Maya noticed herself.

There she was in her living room, her legs crossed and sitting in her favorite chair, reading a book. Her cat napped peacefully next to her. Her hair was not done, and she wore the T-shirt that she only donned on days when she did not feel like leaving the apartment. She had such days so rarely, but she remembered this one in particular. It was the day before she felt her first symptoms of the cancer.

A glass of wine stood on the stand next to her, and a lamp—the same lamp she broke in a fit of rage after receiving the diagnosis. The drawing looked like Michael had been there and had witnessed it all, right across from her in her favorite chair, somewhere in the middle of the room. But this was no photo. There was no place to hide a camera there. He had seen this, even though he was not there!?

Another drawing of her looked more recent. She was in the middle of a vast darkness, swimming in black, zigzagging lines. Her hand stretched up to the stars, but there was no fear in her eyes. They were just dark, round circles reflecting emptiness.

A third picture. It was her for sure, but she did not remember this scene. She wore a torn dress, with her face bloodied. She sat on her knees under heavy lines of rain, cradling the body of a man…an old, old man whose face looked lifeless and gray on the white paper.

Maya held him with such passion as though he was her father or her child. The tears on her face were more pronounced than the rain, but how was that possible? She almost never cried, especially in front of people. Yes, there were so many people…So many faces stared at her through the wall of rain. Tens…hundreds…in black hooded coats. They surrounded her, and yet she seemed so lonely like the whole world had died with that old man in her arms.

Maya suddenly felt like someone sent a charge of a thousand volts through her body.

"He drew that last year," whispered Valentina, standing behind her.

*

Somewhere in the kitchen, the kids were trying to find the solution to their many great troubles: who would place the silverware on the table, who would fold and put out napkins, and who could be trusted with the glasses. Their voices seemed so distant like the house had grown to cover an enormous expanse. Maya felt like a tiny doll who had fallen from her plastic doll house into a big, new reality. The walls were spreading apart, making her smaller and smaller and moving everything into the background.

Sitting on the squeaky chair in the boys' room, in front of the desk, all she could see were the drawings. So many different scenes. Different people, nations, cities, and parts of the world. Most of those places she did not even recognize, but some of them gave her goosebumps.

Maya recognized a German train that had run off the tracks and a French plane that had crashed into the ocean a year or so ago. The whole world had gone crazy trying to locate the wreckage, and here Michael had the coordinates noted on the page. Many of these scenarios had already happened, and others seemed to indicate what would happen on different days in the future.

"Who is he?" Maya barely pronounced the words, afraid of breaking the deafening silence in the room.

"God's gift…" answered Valentina.

The foster mom sat on the corner of one of the boy's beds and carefully kept smoothing out the edges of the already perfectly straightened bed sheets.

"His parents? I mean, the biological parents? Who are they?"

"If only I knew…I was working in a small cafe next to the highway. Our locals get up really early, and they love to have breakfast there. Almost every day there is busy and crowded. I needed to get up around four AM to make sure by six we were open and had enough fresh muffins and biscuits. Other cooks would come closer to opening, so at times, I would be there alone.

"January was really snowy that year and really cold. The lake behind house was froze all the way through, and I used that as a shortcut on daily basis. As you know, our city is not big, so normally it is really quiet, especially in winter. But one morning, happened something that I didn't saw in thirty years of my life, and I hope I will never see again.

"On the bridge that crosses the lake, there stopped a car. It was so dark, no moon or stars, and new snowstorm was coming. They could not see me walking a hundred feet away, but I could see a man in long coat who walked around, opened trunk, took something from it and, without any hesitation, throw it from the bridge. After this, like nothing happened, he sat back in his car and left so fast, like demons was chasing his soul.

"Of course, I was curious. There is rarely anything happens here, so that was intriguing. I came closer to a deep pile of fresh snow that was holding something so precious and magical. I fell to my bottom right there. It was a baby. Small baby, maybe a week old."

"What an asshole!" Maya looked around sheepishly, making sure no kids had been within earshot. "Sorry, I couldn't help myself."

Valentina just smiled and continued her story.

"That's how Michael became part of our family. I helped in local clinic with my mom while she was alive, so I knew how to take care of a baby. I already had two adopted girls, so I decided to keep him. Of course I called to sheriff, and he stopped by, made a report, and sent notifications to everywhere he could, but no one was reported missing a little boy. So a half year later, I became his official mother."

"Oh, Valya, I'm just looking at you and feeling so proud. Not for myself. I feel ashamed of myself. I'm proud to know that because of people like you, there may be a chance for humanity after all."

Valentina smiled sheepishly and somewhat sadly.

"Oh, stop it. I am just a vessel in God's hands. For me, all of these kids are mine, almost like I gave birth to them, and they part of my flesh and blood. And for sure, they have a part of my heart. They give me happy days, but sometimes I do cry because of them, but I will not stop loving them. They are my little angels. God trusted me with their souls and lives, so how else would I act? And Michael…It might be so bad of me to say it, but I love him the most, even though I always understood that he is not from this world. He is so different, and I knew one day I would lose him."

Maya felt a deep desire to give Valya a hug, but her legs had turned into stone.

"I see you, and I understand now that all that he said is true, and you came here to take him away. I knew that would happen. I understand that I have no right to stop him, but my heart is breaking to pieces. The plan for his life is way higher than my selfishness…"

"And what plan is that?"

"I don't know…" Valentina quickly wiped away the tears forming in her eyes. "I just see those drawings, I see you…You almost drowned in this lake. How could that be possible? He drew you a year ago, and now you are here. He told us that you would come for him, and when you ran away that morning…I am not going to lie. I felt relief. But he said that you would be back today. And here you are…"

Valentina stopped, and silence again filled the room.

Maya really wanted to say something to help the woman calm down, but for the first time, she was simply out of words. At this point, she was just going with the flow.

She was no mother, and the closest thing she had to an adopted child was her cat, who was now abandoned in her Chicago apartment. Her bonsai trees would go yellow sometimes because she often forgot to water them. How was she supposed to comfort a mother who thought that she had come to take her child away?

The front door clicked.

"Мишка, Заходи! Мисс Полянски тебя уже заждалась!"

Maya did not need a translation. Alice had just announced to Michael that she was here, waiting for him. Both women sat motionless, trying not to ruin that last moment of peace before the storm came and started off a chain reaction.

From the voices in the kitchen, Maya could easily tell that everyone was happy to see Michael. But was he here for long? The kids loved him! He was their brother, and Maya was here to separate them…

WHAT THE HELL? Why was she supposed to do that? She could say no! She could just run out the door and never even talk or think about this again! But her legs were still like stone.

Her heart started beating so fast, as though she were about to meet the president or a member of some royal family. But why? He was just a teenage boy!

She heard the sound of a jacket being taken off and placed in a closet, followed by the sound of shoes being taken off. Quiet steps approached. A silhouette appeared in the hall. A gentle, calm voice said something to the kids in Russian. The water in the sink turned on.

Maya felt like the air in the room was vanishing. Anticipation was killing her.

And when she finally was able to overcome herself and stand up, Michael entered the room.

Blue eyes...

He walked into the room, and his presence came along with an avalanche of emotions. Maya felt like a huge, concrete block had hit her in the chest, knocking the breath out of her. She had forgotten how to breathe, and her heart seemingly stopped beating. She died under the gaze of those eyes. But this heavenly blue was different from the poisoned blue in Alison's eyes. These eyes did not try to suck her in and devour her. They just saw her. All the way through. She felt naked in front of this ten-year-old boy who gave her a fatherly smile. But she did not feel naked physically, but spiritually. All her thoughts, sins, motives, all of her, were under the microscope. She was transparent and scared. She wanted to cover herself, but there was nothing that could shield her from his sight.

A fire of shame in waves of a thousand explosions overcame her soul and mind. Maybe she should run away and hide, but she could not. Or rather, she did not want to.

Why? Was this her mind playing another trick? Was he one of them? The strongest one? The one who would control her and make her his puppet?

No...Before she heard her own voice yelling for her to wake up and before her conscious mind was suppressed. But now, she still felt that she had a choice, and she wanted to stay. She wanted this fire to burn all the way through until she was so clean that she had no more need to hide, no more feelings of shame.

Security cameras, lie detectors, hackers. Those were all a joke compared to the gift this boy had. He knew all her secrets, but he did not judge. He just smiled. He was happy to see her finally.

"Hi!" He finished wiping his hands on the towel and laid it over his shoulder. Stretching out his hand, he warmly introduced himself. "I'm Michael. Sorry you needed to wait on me."

A whole eternity passed before Maya was able to overcome herself and shake his hand.

"That's fine," her voice cracked. She tried to smile, but it looked more funny than friendly. "I'm Maya."

What was going on? She felt like a teenage girl who had finally met her rock star. Blushing and giggling like she was no older than Alice, she finally managed to look away from Michael. She felt like a child, like someone who had burned and been reborn from ashes.

Is that how you lose your mind? Is that why she never felt pain anymore, because the cancer had finally taken control of her brain? She held Michael's hand and could not let go. If this was not brainwashing, then it was all something that she would never understand. The strange feelings were more than just friendship and more than love. She felt deeply that no matter what, she had to do everything in her power to help, support, and protect this person. Before, she would have considered such emotions a sign of weakness, but now she understood that only a strong person could accept it. This was a calling!

It was just like the apostles, Peter and Andrew, who heard the call, left their parents, nets, and fishing boat, and followed Christ. It was like the calling that changed Matthew, making him leave his high-paying government job for the life of a traveling disciple. It was like the calling that Elisha heard that burned his plow and caused him to go after the prophet Elijah.

And this time, the calling found Maya here in a small town far away from her normal life. This calling was coming from a young boy with the bluest eyes, and no matter what happened, she was willing to answer this call!

She raised her eyes to meet his, and the deep blue gaze welcomed her.

*

Dinner was no different. Catching somebody's eye is as easy as feeling a light touch. Sometimes, even when we are surrounded by people, we can feel that someone is looking directly at us. And normally, we can discern whether the look is one of curiosity, hate, or flirtation. But when you are popular, and everyone is looking at you, it is easier to spot the one person who is not watching.

In the beginning, every public figure is flattered with all the attention, but it can become annoying very quickly. A look is like a touch. One touch can deliver comfort, passion and mark a gesture of friendship. But when everyone pokes and grabs you from every corner, all you want is to be invisible, at least for a while.

Many times before, Maya had experienced long and obnoxious stares, as if people were trying to drill a hole in her head or memorize the exact placement of each freckle on her face. And whenever you confront that stare, the other person moves their eyes away, pretending that they were never even looking at you but rather studying their sleeve or the dust on their shoes.

Today, Maya was on the other end of the staring game, and she could not help it. She knew it was rude, but she could not take her eyes off Michael. Everything about him was so fascinating! He was like any normal kid who laughed and joked at the table with his brothers and sisters, passing food, complimenting the mother's cooking, sharing stories, and making funny remarks. But behind it all, somehow, he was so different. His hands, smile, even the sound of his voice were filled with energy and peace. Maya even forgot that she was hungry and only looked at her plate when Michael glanced at her.

If someone were to ask her later what they talked about over dinner, she would not remember. She smiled a couple times at Alice's stories and nodded in agreement during a couple conversations. But all the time, Maya was in a different reality. She had found herself in one of those moments where you want to plead with time, saying, "Stay, thou art so beautiful!" It was a big family, but everyone was so close. There was so much noise and yet so much peace. What a bizarre feeling! She envied Valentina. The socialite was envious of the foster mom.

Dinner finished, and before Maya realized it, the table was wiped and cleaned, and only a vase, some sweets, and two cups of tea remained on it. Valentina took the kids, and they left for an evening church service, leaving Maya alone with Michael. As soon as the door closed behind Valentina, Maya's heart started beating so fast that she nearly fainted. Her fingers grew roots around the cup of hot liquid, and her eyes bounced around, unable to anchor themselves on any one thing and rest. The last time she was that worried was for her job interview at the *Chicago Voice*.

"Are you afraid of me?" Michael asked casually and without any condescension. He was genuinely curious.

Maya tried to laugh, but the noise that came out sounded more like a loud, hysterical hiccup. She wanted to fall to the ground in shame, and her face turned as red as a fire engine.

"Afraid? Why...How...you think so?" Oh God, could she feel any more embarrassed?

"Miss Polanski, I will not harm you." The words were so earnest and thoughtful, and Maya simply believed them.

"Are you capable of harm?"

Why was she asking that? She could tell by his look that he would not harm a fly. Or was he just an innocent-looking flytrap?

"Depends on what you consider to be harm. For some people, hearing the truth can be as deadly as a bullet in the chest."

Maya blinked. She blinked fast. Was this real? A boy talking about truth that can kill?

"Whose words are those, Nietzsche's?"

"I don't know. Did he also feel that way?"

No, Nietzsche never said those words, but she wanted to see Michael's reaction. Was he really that smart or really that skilled at hiding his feelings? And why was she not ready just to accept his supernatural ability?

"By the way, I wanted to say thank you," she said, changing the subject...or perhaps testing him. "It was really brave of you to jump into ice-cold water for a stranger."

"You would do the same if you saw your friend in need, wouldn't you?"

Maya choked on her prepared question. She was trying to coax him into talking about his ability to walk on water or about how he managed his trick with Vikky.

"Probably...for a friend. Yes. But not for a stranger. They're not my friends."

"How do you know if a stranger is a friend or enemy if you don't know them? If you don't do anything good for them?"

Maya smirked.

"Well, as long as I have money and am willing to give to others, every bum will be my friend, and they'll be happy to call me one. But are they really friends?"

"Every day, you pass by many people who are richer than you are, and they might be happy to have you as a friend. Money doesn't buy happiness."

"Oh, believe me, it does!"

"So you think you can buy true joy?"

"And you think not?" Maya smiled. All her nervousness faded. She loved debates. And on the subject of money, well, she knew a little bit more than a boy who lived in a foster home.

"I think money can bring some pleasure but not joy."

"Aren't they the same?" Maya smirked again.

"How would I know? I'm just a boy who lives in a foster home." Now Michael smiled, and Maya's smirk disappeared.

"Good one. Are you reading my mind, too? Well then, you'll already know what I want to ask you. How? How did you get me out of the water?"

"Miss Polanski…"

"Just call me Maya. I'm not your boss and not your teacher."

"I don't want to be disrespectful."

"Oh, to hell with respectful! Apparently, I'm your friend, so there's no need for all this 'miss' nonsense! Just Maya!" She was losing her patience. And deep inside, she wanted to have at least one little victory in her verbal battle with the boy.

"Fine. Maya…I'm not going to answer your question. Simply because you are not willing to hear the truth. At least not yet. But I can't just say what you want to hear."

"Wait…what?"

Maya felt like this boy had just slapped her or put her on the spot.

"You are not that easy, Michael, are you?"

"More tea?" He smiled and stood to pick up the whistling teapot.

"Are you kidding?" Maya felt like her blood was boiling, and her head was about to start whistling, too. "Some freaks made my boss send me here to investigate the resurrection of a girl, and they still killed him. I almost drowned in that stupid lake outside your house. I'm on a hit list, and I'm running around like a fat turkey in open season. Do you know how many times I almost died this week?"

"You still look alive to me."

"NO! Don't even joke with me now! I saw you! I saw how you came to me! On the water! Not swimming, not rowing a happy little pink boat, or riding in a yellow submarine. You walked! I saw it! And you pulled me out of the water. How?! I guess that's routine for you, but guess what! It was not the only freaky thing that's happened to me lately! My secretary almost killed me in my own office. I can't go home. And you're saying I can't accept the truth? None of it? How about those drawings in your room? No comments there either?"

"Not yet." Michael was still so calm and carefully refilled his cup.

"You know what? Fine!" She jumped from her seat. "I have plenty of other things to worry about. I'm leaving, and screw all of this. Your miracles, clans, snakes, FBI, zombie girls—to hell with all of it! Like I need this crap! I'm leaving, and we'll just see how your pictures become reality if I never set foot in this house again!"

"You're right about that," admitted Michael.

"Oh, really?! You think so?"

"I know that you'll never set foot in this house again. And neither will I...Just don't be scared."

"Of what?!"

"Maya, trust me, everything is under control. Just don't panic!"

With a loud explosion, the front door blew inside the hallway. The house trembled like it was about to fall apart. Maya's head jerked around at the sound of shattering glass as a smoke bomb flew inside through a broken window and clattered on the ground beside them. Before she had time to react, it began releasing a thick cloud of smoke. Gasping and choking, she felt the fumes pulling her toward unconsciousness. The last thing Maya could remember before fainting was the image of dark, hooded silhouettes walking toward them through the smoke.

CHAPTER 10

They did not beat her, pour ice-cold water on her, or even handcuff her.

She just woke up sitting in a wooden chair. On the opposite end of the table in front of her sat someone else, but she could not see that person's face as a blinding lamp was shining into her eyes. The light was giving her a headache, and she felt like a porcupine was crawling up through her throat. This was probably a side effect of the gas they used to bring her down in Valentina's house.

Maya tried to figure out what to do next. Should she pretend to be weak, drowsy, and unable to understand what was going on, or should she attack her abductor with words like, "Do you have any idea what you've done? All of Chicago is going to be looking for me!"

"Would you like some water?" someone asked in a soft and disgustingly compassionate voice. It sounded like an older man.

"Where is Michael?"

Silence.

Maya closed her eyes for a moment since the lamp was so bright and put all her energy toward listening. The old man across the table sighed deeply. It seemed that they were alone in the room.

"Drink. Here, this is herbal tea with honey." A strong hand with old, loose skin came out from the shadow and into the light, moving a cup toward her. "Miss Polanski, we're not here to harm you or cause you any further trouble."

The hand disappeared again into the darkness, but Maya noticed a slight sparkle in the shadow.

"I'll ask you again: where is Michael? What have you done to him?"

"He's alright." With the same fake compassion, the man added, "We will not harm him either."

"Sure. A gas bomb and a raid on a foster home is the most peaceful way to invite someone for a tea party."

Another sigh.

"I agree, it was a bit much, but we needed to use caution. Over the last couple of days, you, my dear, have caused us a lot of trouble."

Maya started to laugh.

"Did I? I caused you trouble? Really? Was I the one trying to kill your guys? They needed to use caution, sure. Aiming a bullet for my head is the perfect way to protect yourself!"

"Maya…Let's not make a big deal out of this. If you knew why you were here, you would understand that we've been the good guys from the beginning. It only seems like we were hunting you. No, my dear, all we wanted was to reach out to you, to protect you."

"Oh, seriously? Damn, what a dummy I was! How silly of me to run away from your mother freakin' killers who tried to cap me in the alley behind the café! Thank you, thank you so much! Even though I'm sitting here in God-knows-where, I feel way better now, knowing that you're the good guys!"

The old man started to chuckle.

"Oh, Maya, I was always so fond of you. But, really, we need to leave this all behind and move on; we have so much to do together."

She wanted to let loose with another venomous line, but her throat was on fire. She glanced at the cup of tea. Well, if they planned on killing her, they would not bother with poison. Trying to mask any hesitation, she picked up the drink and took a sip. It did feel better.

"You see? No harm. And if you cooperate, you can even get back to your life today. You can go home, and all this will be behind you. And tomorrow, you can be the new chief editor of one of the biggest newspapers in the States."

"And what do I have to do? Sign a contract in my own blood, or just sell my soul?"

The old man let out another little laugh.

"Not much besides cooperating with us. Since Mr. Sawyer's gone, we need someone we can trust."

"Not much?"

"Yes, well, we need a little favor from you today, only to prove that you're willing to work with us."

"So…?" Maya was losing patience. She wanted to hear it out, to know why all of this started and what exactly she could give them that no one else could. Perhaps this would finally answer the riddle she had been trying to put together.

"You need to convince the boy to stay with us and explain to him that for a boy with such extraordinary ability, it'd be better to stick with people who can teach him and protect him from this cruel world."

"Uhmmm. Are you mistaking me for his mother or sister? I only just met him today!" As soon as the words left her mouth, Maya felt a hot wave go down her spine. She should not have mentioned a mother or sister. These idiots might just decide to go after Valentina or, even worse, after Alice.

"Maya, who do you think we are? Do you think we're some kind of animals who would torture a mother in front of her kids?"

Now, it was a cold wave. He could read her mind, too.

"Let me go! Right now!"

"Easy, Maya. There's no reason to worry."

"Take this stupid lamp away!" Maya finally started to feel what she should have felt all along—rage! That always helped her overcome her fear.

"Relax. Have more tea…You have no reason to worry…"

"You're repeating yourself!"

The old man made a sound sort of like barking.

"The lamp is for your own good. If you don't see my eyes or hands, you won't have to worry that I'm manipulating you with hypnosis."

She did not see the faces or hands of those men at the subway station when they tried to make her jump out of the car at the next stop, either.

"I will not help you until I know that Michael is safe and you've finished explaining everything to me."

Silence. The man was thinking.

"I would try to explain, but I'm afraid you wouldn't believe me right now. You need to understand that there's so much more to this world, more than you're ready to believe or accept at this point. There are laws of another realm that exist beyond your understanding that would make life so much easier for Michael, much more so than his mother ever could. And with his help…We can't make him do anything. He must want to help. Otherwise, it will not give us the desired result."

"Are you insane?"

"In some ways, yes. But wouldn't a person with eyes sound insane to the blind as he tries to describe everything he can see?"

"If you want his help, you're doing a great job attacking him and destroying his home. If someone did that to me, I willingly help them!"

The old man chuckled again. Maya lost it.

"That's enough! Put this stupid lamp away, Cloudy. I know it's you!"

The chuckling stopped. The light from the lamp went off, and the regular lights in the room came on.

The interrogation room was not as big as it seemed before. And Maya found that she had been wrong; besides herself and Cloudy were two more men in the room, standing next to the wall behind him. In their black hoodies, they looked like mannequins or statues with clothes.

"You recognized my voice?" asked the old man whom Maya knew really well after the mayor's case. He did not look upset or surprised and seemed more happy than anything. He looked at her so carefully and patiently that she almost felt his eyes trying to see into her thoughts.

"No, it was the stupid knob on the end of your cane. I noticed it on the video of the night you murdered Bill, and believe me, tomorrow, your face will be in all the morning newspapers."

"Oh no! What should I do now?!" Cloudy put on a scared voice, looked toward his guards in shock, and started to laugh. "She's good, right? So brave! I love it!"

"Keep laughing. You think I'm bluffing?"

"I know it, dear. Just drop it, okay? And I repeat: I am not here to harm you. All right? I am your friend. Even more than that—I am your biggest fan. Or have you forgotten all my help?"

"Can you explain why? You're a man with so much power—why not try to become mayor on your own? I'm sure with your gifts, you could be President. Why? Or for your job, do you need access to higher authorities while remaining less visible?"

"I was right about you. But what should I do with you now since you know so much?"

"Are you threatening me? Going to give me a gun and make me blow my brains out?"

"Pfffff…Maya, please, how many times do I need to tell you that I don't want to cause you any harm? We need you alive and well. We need your cooperation, and we will get it from you somehow. Either you'll choose to help…or we'll find a way to motivate you."

"So you are threatening me!?"

"Motivation can be pleasant. I can make your life a dream come true. For you and for your family in Alaska. For your nephews who'll be leaving for school in eight hours and twenty-five minutes. Or we could protect your parents' house from any unfortunate gas leaks, and they might even win a vacation for a safe cruise to Europe."

Maya jumped from the chair too fast, and her head spun, still sick from the attack. Before she managed to jump on Cloudy, his bodyguards had already grabbed her and pushed her back down in her chair.

"If you dare touch any of them…I swear…"

"Sh-h-h-h-h, wait a second, don't swear yet. You see, I value such words more than you might." Mr. Cloudy got up from his chair and gestured to his guards to step away from Maya. "Believe me, I'm not a bad person, and I don't like to do bad things to others. I love to help…"

"Freaking Mother Theresa…" growled Maya.

"Almost." Cloudy smiled. "I hope you remember how I helped to boost your career."

"Drop it! I get it; you have connections, and I owe you. I see where this is going. So, theoretically speaking, what would I need to do in exchange for my freedom and Michael's…and for your promise to leave my family out of this?"

Cloudy seemed pleased.

"Just a very simple thing. I need your solemn oath."

"What?" Maya gave him a look that had the whole spectrum of expressions from amusement to hate.

"As I said, I value an oath more than anything. You will just swear to me that when the time comes, you will say and do exactly what I tell you, no questions asked no hesitations, and no delays. One simple task."

Maya still thought he was joking. He kidnapped them just to make her swear a simple oath? Sure, why not. As soon as they let her out, she would disappear into thin air, and good luck finding her and making her fulfill her vows! And after all, she could cross her fingers or toes or say "just kidding!" and then to hell with him and all his demands.

"So what do you say? Do we have an agreement?"

"Fine. I swear."

"No, no, that's not enough. I want you to understand it. I want you to mean it. Say it this way: "I swear on my mother's heart, on my father's mind, and on the life of the one I love that I will fulfill my oath no matter what I am asked to do.""

"How kindergarten of you…"

Cloudy did not find this funny. He was serious and anxious.

"Say it!"

"Okay! I swear on my mother's heart, on my father's mind…" Something strange was happening inside her. Fear opened its eyes and looked right at her. "…on the life of the one I love…" What if this was not a joke? What if those words were somehow real in some other dimension, and by saying them, she was signing up for a terrible bargain? "…that I will fulfill my oath, no matter what I am asked to do."

Emptiness. Cloudy stretched out his fingers and carefully crossed her heart, slicing her in half and removing something precious and invisible from within her.

"Very well. Now they will take you to Michael. You can rest and have something to eat."

*

137

The boy was sitting on the floor next to a large bookshelf, peacefully reading an old book with fancy binding and pages, yellowed with time, that barely held together. The room was poorly lit by a single torchiere lamp in the opposite corner, which would have made it seemingly impossible to read anything, but he still managed. Two antique couches stood next to a sturdy oak desk and a tapestry, half eaten by moths, and long, dusty grommet curtains framed the boarded-up windows. Maya was surprised that the place had electricity and that it did not smell moldy. So much wealth and history, hidden and alone, kept its own pace of aging. In all of this, Michael seemed so foreign and small, like a lion imprisoned in a cage made from cardboard. It was not the walls but his own humility that was holding him there.

As soon as Maya was pushed into the room, he put the book aside and headed her way.

"Are you alright?" he asked with such concern, like he was the adult there and not Maya.

"I wanted to ask you the same, actually." She carefully looked him over, and her eyes stopped at a spot of blood on his sleeve. "Are you hurt?"

"No, this isn't my blood…One of them cut himself when he climbed through the window."

"I hope he bleeds to death!" She started to shake off her clothes as though she were covered in dirt and dust, but there was none. The snakeheads must have transported them there very carefully, but she still felt so filthy. "Are you sure they didn't hurt you?" She studied him more closely and carefully took his hand to turn him around so she could look at his back.

"I'm fine. Thank you, though. I told Valentina that you were a good woman." Michael smiled, and Maya felt awkward, releasing his hand and stepping back a little. "So what did they want from you?"

"They want me to convince you to help them with something."

"I see…" Michael did not sound surprised, but he turned and walked back to his book. Was he upset? Did he know what would happen? If he knew, then why did he ask her?

Maya felt confused and guilty, even though she had not asked him to do anything yet.

The best thing for now would be to go to the bookshelf and choose a book for herself, lie down closer to the lamp, and rest for a while. Or maybe she should try to peek through the holes in the boards over the windows and try to determine where they were. She needed answers.

She drew closer and sat next to him on the floor.

"Michael, do you know what they want from you?"

"Yeah," answered the boy without raising his eyes from the pages.

"And…?" It seemed like he was not planning to share this information. But she was here because of him, so a little bit of trust would have been nice. "Okay, I see. Well, let me ask differently. Can you help them with whatever they need?"

"I can."

"And…? You don't want to do that? Right? Is it something bad?" She needed to keep herself calm. If she started yelling at Michael, he might completely shut down.

"What I desire or not isn't relevant." He looked at her again.

Why did she feel electricity go through her whole body every time this child made eye contact with her? Those young eyes held so much elderly wisdom in them. Her anger dissolved like ice in a cup of hot tea, and her words melted away in the useless attempt to reason with him.

The door opened again. Two men walked inside the room, and Maya stiffened up, prepared for anything. One of them stayed in the doorway, and another was carrying a tray with hot food.

"Here's dinner," he said, looking at Michael. "If you need anything, I'll be right behind the door."

Maya could swear she heard something unusual in this guard's voice. Fear? Servility? Compliance? He looked at the boy like Michael was his boss and not Cloudy.

"How is your hand, Marty?" Michael took the tray from his hands.

The guard melted in a smile, and a hint of red touched his face. He pulled up his sleeve and showed his hand to Michael.

"Like new!" The man snickered like a little girl.

Hand? Is this the one who cut himself climbing through the window? But what were they talking about? Maya did not see anything, just a pink line of virgin skin from the wrist to the elbow. It was a scar, but perfectly stitched! No, actually, it seemed glued together…

"Good! I'm really glad." Michael placed the tray on a table and picked up one plate to give to Maya. She was so shocked that she took it without any hesitation.

It was a simple TV dinner, warmed up in a microwave. It seemed that their hosts did not plan to starve them to death. But if they wanted to secure Michael's allegiance, they could have offered something better. Or had the guards decided to give away their own food? Or maybe Cloudy simply was not a gourmet.

"Well, I'd better go," Marty said, almost asking for permission.

"Sure. And be safe. Better go home tonight. It might be dangerous to stay here."

The guard nodded and left the room in a hurry. Only after the lock made a double-click was Maya able to breathe again.

"Who the hell are you?"

Michael shrugged his shoulders like he did not understand the question, or maybe he did not want to understand. He seemed preoccupied with some other, more important task. Maya saw how he closed his eyes and his lips moved as he asked a blessing for the food.

She waited until he had finished and then asked him again with a little bit of force in her voice, demanding an answer.

"What did you mean 'it might be dangerous here?' Hmm?"

Michael picked up a spoon full of beans, ignoring Maya's rage.

He ate a scoop. Another…

Maya reached out and struck his arm, and the third portion, together with the spoon, flew into the bookshelf, spreading the beans into a funny pattern.

"I am talking to you, damn it! Why? Why are you ignoring me?! Is this a joke for you?"

"Maya, have some food. Those beans are really good. Who knows when we'll next have a hot meal?"

"Apparently, you know! That's enough!" She rushed on him like a storm. He seemed too old to get a spanking, but he was too young for her to slap him. "I am not your toy! You will respect me, or I will teach respect since your mother clearly didn't. If not, then in the morning, I will agree to their terms and let them do with you…whatever…their…sick…minds…want!"

"It's so funny how humans like to say in anger things that they actually don't mean."

Maya choked on the rest of her words.

"Humans…?"

Michael got up, picked up his spoon, wiped it on the corner of his shirt, and went back to his plate.

"Eat, Maya, eat. And we should try to get a little nap. We'll be leaving with the sunrise."

*

The rest of the evening was spent in silence. Maya did not give up on her attempts to learn the truth, but she decided to apply a new strategy. Passive-aggressive worked well on most people she knew, but who knew if Michael would even notice that anything was different? Would he care? It seemed like he was only telling her what he wanted to tell, nothing more and nothing less. Patience was not her strongest suit, but what else was left to try?

She decided to get some rest. Before turning off the lamp, Michael prayed quietly for a good five to ten minutes, but no matter how hard Maya tried, she could not hear what he was saying. To avoid looking bad, she repeated one of the prayers she used to say before bed when she was a kid, but since it was a really short prayer, she repeated it three times to make it seem more respectable.

After Michael settled in on his couch, Maya turned the knob on the torchiere, and the lamp light dimmed into darkness. Her sofa was not as terrible as it looked, or maybe she was just so tired that she barely cared anymore. It was a great feeling to stretch her legs. Even the thin blankets that are normally served on long flights would now seem soft and comfortable. Maybe she should take off her shoes, but she felt way too tired to move.

Who would have thought that she could fall asleep while being imprisoned on an old sofa and under a synthetic throw? Maybe Michael's prayer helped her.

Ha! What a silly thought!

She felt the world disappear, and she slowly melted into a dream...

BOOM! The room jolted.

Maya jumped to her feet but fell right back down when the room shook again.

There was no one around her. Michael was not asleep but was standing next to a window, whispering a prayer, and a weak light was coming through the wooden panels.

What was happening? Had she really slept for a couple hours and just had not realized it? What was causing the shaking? Was it just her falling in and out of deep phases of a dream?

No! The walls trembled again, and dust flew from the books and into the air.

Another hit, and this time, the lamp behind her fell to the floor. This was not a dream! Was it?

"Michael?" She got up and started walking toward him, but he kept praying.

Golden rays of morning sun streaked through the gaps, turning their prison into a laser show where sparkles of dust made the room seem voluminous and unrealistically beautiful. Light pierced the darkness, and the walls could not hold them anymore.

A loud clap like July thunder rolled into the ancient room and the wall where Michael stood crumbled apart, letting the fresh air and the new morning inside.

There was no more barrier to their freedom.

CHAPTER 11

Maya was only able to turn around and look when they had walked a good two hundred feet away. In the same moment that her gaze fell on the house, the rest of the mansion collapsed and turned into a pile of brick and wood covered in dust.

The house was not alone on the street, and Maya could count at least ten other homes built in a similar architectural style and equally as luxurious. But only Cloudy's house was now lying in ruins. Had there been an earthquake?

Michael kept walking along the sidewalk, ignoring the destruction behind him. He seemed calm and casual as always, perhaps even a little bit happy, like a child on an afternoon walk to the park. Maya, on the other hand, felt terrible. Yes, they had been imprisoned there, but at least it was warm and cozy in its own way. Now they were outside, and the early autumn in Chicago was a bit too chilly for a walk in a T-shirt. Luckily, she had slept in her shoes because the rest of her belongings were now buried under the remains of Cloudy's mansion.

"Did you do that?" Maya tried to catch up to Michael.

"Do what?"

Of course he would play dumb again, but after what Maya had just seen, she knew she had better stay on his good side.

"We should call 911. There might be survivors."

Michael stopped and looked at Maya with an expression of surprise. Then he smiled and continued his walk.

"Ha! For a moment, I thought you really cared about your kidnappers."

"*Our* kidnappers, actually…Why is that funny?"

"Maya, you don't care about them. And we were alone there. They all left shortly after you fell asleep. But if you want to make a call, go ahead. I won't stop you."

"Fine, yes, I do need to make a phone call. I think I know where we are."

It seemed that they had not bothered to search her. The fake license and some cash were still there.

"As soon as we see a café, we're going in. I need coffee…and…do you know your home number?"

"Yes, but we're not going to call them. It will just upset Mom."

"More than finding an empty house with a broken door and smashed windows?"

"Believe me, it's better this way." For the first time, Maya noticed sadness in his expression. "And we'll find a nice breakfast place in a few minutes. They should have a phone. Do you have enough money?"

"For breakfast, yes, unless you know how to turn stones into eggs and bacon."

"You might not like it…it always turns out really salty."

Michael smiled and walked ahead, leaving Maya to decide whether he was joking or not.

*

As Michael had predicted, they walked out from the alley facing a small café. In the same moment, a whole squadron of police and fire vehicles raced toward the subdivision they had just left. Evidently, a randomly destroyed house cannot go unnoticed for long.

There were not many people inside, but the only available waitress was busy with another customer, so Maya and Michael opted for the cleanest-looking booth next to a window. Digging through her pockets, Maya found roughly three hundred in cash, which would be enough to eat and maybe find a nice room for a couple of nights. But then what? The rest of her savings were now in the trunk of a car parked next to Valentina's house.

"Back to square one," sighed Maya, understanding that she now had to make an unpleasant phone call.

"Something smells good. Like cinnamon."

"You're funny! You can foresee an earthquake, but not what's cooking in the kitchen. Here's twenty. Order us something, but just make sure they give me milk for the coffee and not half-and-half."

"Okay, but she won't come for another five minutes."

"Well, then, I hope you won't run away in that short time."

Michael started laughing like she had said something silly.

"Laugh as much as you want, but if I don't get my coffee, I'll like you even less than I do now." Maya left some money for the boy and went to the cash register, where they had a radio phone resting on its charging base. Without waiting for permission, she picked up the phone and went to the restroom. After making sure she was alone, she dialed 911.

"911, what is your emergency?"

"Good morning, my name is Maya…" She stopped. Phillip had said that Nehushtan's people were everywhere. What if they had ways of monitoring the emergency lines?

"Ma'am? Are you alright?"

"I would like to speak to FBI Agent Phillip Howell."

"I'm sorry, ma'am, you need to dial Chicago's FBI division…"

"But…I have no idea what their number is, and I really need to get ahold of Agent Howell and just him."

"Are you 3521?"

"Yes, I am!" Why had Maya not thought of that on her own? It was the witness protection code, and every journalist knew that.

"Then you should follow procedure and call the specified closed line."

"I can't!"

"Are you in danger? Do you want me to send a patrol?"

"No, please, no cop cars...Please just pass this message to Agent Howell. It's about Copper Snake. Give him my coordinates and tell him that I'll wait for him for the next hour or so. If he doesn't show, I'll try to call him tomorrow."

Maya hung up and took a deep breath. Well, now she needed to wait. Hopefully, they would be able to pass her message straight to Howell, but would he be able to get to her within an hour? If he was really mad at her, he would be there in under thirty minutes.

Maya refreshed herself, washed her face, and fixed her hair, thinking again about the wig that she had left in the car. But after all, she needed to look less noticeable, and right now, she looked like a typical mom who had brought her son to breakfast before school. She left the phone in the restroom and walked back to Michael, who had just finished ordering.

"Coffee with milk on its way." The boy smiled.

"Thank you," said Maya with a note of sarcasm. "I see you're in a good mood."

"Yes. Richard is here."

Maya followed Michael's gaze and noticed a man standing across the street looking toward them. It was no hooded freak, not a bum, not a millionaire in a fancy suit, nor a cop. Just a regular, ordinary man, around fifty years old, with such a common look that if he had not been staring fixedly at the café, Maya would not even have noticed him.

"Do you know him?"

Michael shrugged in such a way that it could have meant either yes or no.

"Okay, let me ask it this way—should I be worried?"

"No, he's a friend." Michael waved to the man, but he might not have seen them since the window was covered with one-way reflective film.

"A friend like Martin, the guy you healed, or a friend like another one of your own kind? Someone bringing you a message from the mothership?"

Michael looked at her with a judgmental smile, but she did not expect him to answer. He never did.

"Should I go get him?"

"No, he must find the courage to come to us first."

The waitress brought a glass of orange juice for Michael and a cup of coffee for Maya and told them that breakfast was on its way. For a moment, Maya decided to let everything go and eat whatever the boy had ordered for them, hoping for the best. Richard would be a nice guy who would give them money and a new fake ID, or perhaps Phillip would arrive and take them to safety without yelling and lecturing her too much. She added sugar to her hot, steaming cup and then poured a little bit of milk from a separate cup. As soon as she took her first sip, her face changed, and she understood that the day was already spoiled!

"Holy udder! How hard is it to give a person a milk and not half-and-half?"

"I swear I told her!" Michael choked on his juice and started laughing.

Maya did not think it was funny, but the boy seemed to lose his brakes. He laughed so loudly that it became contagious, and even she could not keep herself from grinning.

"Fine, laugh. I'll take your juice, and you can have this butter coffee."

He kept laughing and pushed his glass toward her, but she just waved it away, not having been serious.

"Oh, he's coming!" Michael's attention switched back to the man outside, and by that time, he was already at the door of the cafe.

"What's your third eye see? Will I get a chance to have my toast and eggs at least?"

"Ummm…I ordered some pancakes."

This time, it was Maya who laughed hysterically.

Richard walked in and looked around until he noticed Michael. Maya could not tell if he was scared or happily surprised. Either way, he froze in place, afraid to make a move. Maya noticed that he held a backpack that seemed too big for school books but too small for camping needs.

Michael waved to the man again, and Richard smiled and waved back hesitantly. After a couple of deep breaths, he found enough strength to take the first step in their direction. Then another. One more. And there he was, standing right next to them.

"I am so sorry!" His voice trembled. "I'm sure this might sound crazy, but I was asked to bring this to you."

He lowered the backpack and placed it next to their table.

"Thank you," said Michael.

"Wait a second. Who told you? What is this?" Maya looked at the fully-stuffed bag, full of curiosity.

"My son…It's a couple of warm jackets. I wasn't sure what it was for, so I also put in a blanket and some canned food."

Michael opened his backpack without any hesitation and pulled out a nice letterman's jacket. It was not new, but it smelled fresh and clean. Maya saw a woman's coat as well. That was really thoughtful, especially since it kept getting colder outside, and Maya's cash was limited.

"Thank you, Richard," said Michael. The man froze again, stunned by the fact that the boy knew his name.

"Your son?" Maya would not let that go. "Did he see us walking here this morning?"

"I'm not sure how he could. Well, he told me last night in my dream."

"What? In your what?"

"In my dream," repeated Richard, though he kept staring at Michael. "Three years ago, we got into a car accident. My wife and I got away with some broken bones, but our son…he was paralyzed…"

The man looked at Michael again, this time with an indescribable sadness in his eyes.

"My boy…he can't move. At all. He can't speak. He's alive and conscious, but…but…please…"

"So your paralyzed son told you to bring us jackets in a dream?" Maya hoped that if she repeated it, it might make more sense. Nope. It did not.

"Yes! And he also said that you might help him. Is that true?" Maya was not sure whether there was more hope or despair in his voice.

"Of course we'll help!" said Michael. "Take us to him."

∗

The coat was warm and comfy but definitely not new. Maya could smell a strong, sweet aroma of peony and French lavender on it. Who in their right mind would wear a perfume like this? The madame of a crosswalk brothel or a retired opera diva? Along with this mix, she could imagine a feathered boa, a box of white face powder, and a fat, fake beauty mark.

It was most likely Richard's wife's coat. Maya wondered what she must have said when her husband decided to take her clothes to some stranger. Maybe she was still asleep when Richard left, or maybe they were both crazy, and she was used to his "visions." Or…maybe they really were desperate. Oh well. No matter what, it would be hard to surprise Maya with anything now.

Before they left, she demanded that they stay to finish breakfast and wait exactly one hour. Phillip did not show up, and no one ever called back. Maya went back to the restroom a couple times to check the phone since the waitress had not even noticed it was missing.

She was not sure if they could have gotten hold of Phillip that fast, especially since he was working undercover. But at the same time, they did not send any cops…Or perhaps they did, and maybe one of them was there somewhere in the café eating doughnuts and watching her? Oh, how she hoped that Agent Howell would appear! Then, she would not feel as lonely, and at least he would understand and believe her story. She should tell him about Cloudy as soon as she had the chance, she thought. Now, when things were getting even more complicated, it seemed that an ally like Phillip could help her preserve her sanity. No one else would believe her.

After an hour passed, they went to Richard's car, and he drove them to his house, which was about twenty minutes away. The whole time, he and Michael were talking about something, but Maya was too preoccupied with her own thoughts and let it all pass by.

The inside of the car was warm and relatively clean, even though it was not new, and Maya started to feel sleepy again. She turned the radio up a little bit louder and began to switch channels until she found one with the latest news. She was hoping to hear anything about the shooting in ABOB, or the attack on *Chicago Voice*, or the earthquake, or perhaps some other event that she had not yet heard about. What could be worse than a journalist who was behind on the news? Nothing struck her interest, and it all seemed to be the same boring stories as always.

When they pulled into the driveway, Richard's wife was already waiting for them. The house was brick, one of many like it in the area, and it suited her really well. She was a dry, bleached woman with gray hair, and she stood leaning against the door, looking absently off into some corner of space far beyond this universe. She seemed younger than Richard, but she had less life than he did. A tired veil covered this former beauty of days gone by, and her current appearance was like a reflection in an old, clouded mirror stored away in some dark, dusty attic.

"That day, Valery drove the car," whispered Richard. He stopped the engine, but it seemed like he was in no rush to get out. "Before, I liked to have a drink or two after lunch. Not always, but sometimes, after classes. I teach chemistry at the college. We had some problems…no more than any long-married couple, but that day, we fought, and she found me in the bar next to campus."

Richard looked at his wife, who seemed not to notice their presence, and then back to Michael.

"She was a strong woman, way stronger than I am. She always supported me, and Dan pushed us forward."

Richard kept talking and looked to see Michael's reaction as if waiting for the boy to change his mind or frown at him in judgment. But he neither interrupted him nor offered any feedback. He just listened.

"It was a rainy day, and it was really late. The car just slid off the road. I'm not sure if I would have handled the situation any better if I'd been driving, but this just broke her. When we found out that our boy was paralyzed, she practically turned into stone. I know I deserve this. I should be in Dan's place, and with God as my witness, I'm ready to give anything to change places with him! Anything. Do you believe me?"

The next thing Michael did shocked Maya, but not Richard.

The boy stretched out his hand and began gently stroking Richard's balding head like he was his father. Richard started to cry like a child.

"There, there," whispered Michael without any irony. "Everything will be alright. God heard your prayers. He knows you've repented."

"I am so…so sorry."

"He's not mad at you! He knows your heart!"

Maya, if only she could, wanted to melt through the car door and get as far away as possible from that scene. Richard could not stop crying. It was all something that he had held in for a long while, and now that it had finally broken through, it would flow till the last drop escaped.

Michael just whispered words of comfort and reassurance, and Maya could barely process it all. Eventually, the boy hugged the man, who then started to sob on his shoulder, burying his face in the letterman jacket that probably belonged to his son, Dan.

Maya looked at Valery, who finally seemed to notice them, but she was not curious enough to come any closer. What exactly had made her this way? She was alive but empty. Pain, guilt, exhaustion? None of those, or perhaps all of them together? Like anyone else, Maya knew what depression was and had faced that destructive old "friend" once or twice in her life. She even remembered its most recent visit. When she was first diagnosed with cancer, she did not believe it. There was anger mixed with fear, but after a couple weeks, that blue guest came to her doorstep.

He came during the night while a hangover knit her guts into macramé, and he lay right behind her, being the "big spoon." He told her it was okay to be sad and that it was fine to be alone since he was there for her. He gave her permission to let go of fear and sadness and told her that emotions did not matter. She just cuddled with him, without lights, and the heavy curtains pulled over the windows. She had no food or water, no sense of time, no thoughts. She just took long, deep breaths and stared at the more-than-usually interesting picture on the empty wall, staring until her eyes got tired.

But she did have Bill, who came to her apartment challenging her. He thought she had the flu and brought her chicken soup and told her she could stay home for a while. Everyone at the office wished her a fast recovery. That was the moment when she told Bill to go to hell with his soup, and the depression was kicked out through the same doorway with him. Maya showered, dressed, went back to work, and decided to fight to the end. But Valery seemed to have become one with her blue ghost.

"I'm sorry," said Richard, looking at Maya and wiping his tears.

"That's okay." To be honest, she had stopped noticing him and his sobbing.

"Let's go inside. Valery baked some pie yesterday, and I can make fresh coffee. Real coffee, not that stuff they serve at the cafe."

"And I'm sure you have milk?" Michael smiled and looked at Maya.

"What else am I here for?" Maya tried to force something like a smile and, after a long, deep sigh, stepped out of the car.

It was still chilly, even though the sun had risen high above the rooftops, and the day promised to be bright and warm. Not a single cloud...Cloudy... Maya growled inside. She was still mad at the old fart who had tricked her, used her, and made her promise something that might come around to bite her later. She was not sure how she could send a message to Alaska, to her family, to warn them about the danger they were in.

"Careful, please. I really should fix this but haven't found time." Richard walked first along the brick path leading to the house. A long time ago, it might have looked really pretty, but now time and rain had moved some bricks to the side, popped one up in a spot, and sunk in another. It was a good thing that Maya was not wearing heels.

"Valery, look! He's here! He's really here!" started Richard ingratiatingly, trying so hard to wake up her emotions.

And it did work briefly. She turned her gaze in their direction and stared at them, really looking at them. First, she glanced at Michael, then at Maya, but the whole effort did not last long, and her interest soon disappeared as easily as the November wind took the last leaf from a tree.

"Good morning!" This was not Maya's first time visiting a stranger's house, and normally, she was able to win their affection and trust in no time, whether for an article or for a personal favor. But today was different, and she was only there as an attachment to Michael, so perhaps she would limit herself and just let the boy do his work. But what if Valery suspected they were just a couple of swindlers?

"Honey, you're freezing!" Richard carefully hugged his wife. "Have you been here all this time?"

She nodded.

"Come on, don't be shy, come on in!" Richard opened the door, gently directed his wife to go first, and then stepped aside to let Michael and Maya walk in.

Inside the house, it was warm and smelled like someone had spilled a tank full of medicines in the middle of a bakery. Maya detected vanilla with alcohol, brown sugar with penicillin, and cinnamon and iodine. The light was dim, and the air was stuffy. But at the same time, it did not look scary or dangerous, just sad and abandoned. It was like the owners had left a long time ago, but their ghosts were still here, giving the place the vague sense of being occupied.

"Valery works from home now. She bakes for a couple places, and I deliver the orders before work. Baking helps her relax."

Maya did not want to be mean, but did the people who bought her goods know they had been baked by a zombie? Who knows what went on inside Valery's head? What if she decided one day to add some unusual ingredients to her cupcakes or pies?

"I'll go start the water boiling. Sit, please. Val, honey, bring our guests some pie."

Valery, without a word, turned around and headed toward the garage where she must have set up her bakery since Richard had left the car outside.

"I'm so grateful that you came. Last week, Valery...I started to think I was losing her. Two days ago, she went to take a bath..." Richard turned and looked to make sure his wife had not come back, "...and when I came to check on her, she was just sitting and watching the water run over the top. And the water was too hot, but I'm not sure if she even felt anything."

"Don't worry, everything will be alright," Michael assured him.

Maya looked at him with a mix of judgment and disapproval. How could someone make such promises to people who might be so greatly disappointed? Even she would not have said so, and God knows how much she lied to people to get what she needed. Or was the boy convinced that he could fix whatever was going on there?

Michael looked back at Maya, smiling and confident.

"Where is he? Where's Dan?" Michael asked Richard, though he kept his gaze on Maya.

"What are you doing?" whispered Maya.

Richard's hand started to tremble again. Was he afraid of the same thing that Maya was thinking? What if everything was just a joke. What if nothing happened and the boy he had brought inside was just insane or just a prankster? What if it was not the will of Heaven, or there were no miracles, no supernatural resolutions, and he ended up spending the rest of his days living in guilt, looking on at his paralyzed son and his wife, who was losing her connection to reality? Deep inside, he hoped to stretch this moment out a little longer, that moment when he still had hopes for a better outcome instead of facing a cruel reality.

"He's there, in his bedroom." Richard cautiously took a step away from the kitchen, forgetting about the boiling water.

Maya thought about running away, grabbing the keys Richard had left on the table, getting into his car, and driving until the gas tank was empty...but Michael was still looking at her with childlike excitement.

"Fine!" hissed Maya to the boy, and she got up to follow Richard, with Michael walking right behind her.

Were it not for a machine beeping quietly and the monitors that showed Dan's heartbeat, blood pressure, and other numbers indicating the presence of life, Maya would have thought that the person in the bed in front of her was a medical dummy. His pale skin, the blue rings under his eyes, and the sharp lines of his cheekbones made him look like a mummy.

Two bottles of some medicine were connected to his veins through long tubes. Is that how they were supporting his life? Is that really life? Richard said he was conscious but that he could not speak or move. Before, Maya thought that nothing could be scarier than prison, but now she knew differently! In prison, at least, you can walk, stand, or sit in your cell. You can scream at night or sing in the morning. Here, you were a prisoner in your own body. Maya would have given up after a month or so, or she would have lost her mind.

"How can you afford this?" Maya asked without thinking how cruel it might sound.

"We can't, well, not anymore. He was on my insurance, but the bills were ridiculous. We had a couple sponsors who were helping us out, but last week, they closed their account."

Richard started crying again, and in that moment, Dan opened his eyes.

She expected to see signs of pain and a call for help, but she was wrong. Dan was definitely stronger than Maya. He looked on with hope, and Richard was right. The boy was conscious. When he saw Michael, Maya could swear that his lips moved, just barely, giving a reflection of the beautiful smile he once had. Did he really understand who had come to see him? Had Dan really spoken to his dad in a dream about Michael? Once she read in *Chicago Twilight* that people could communicate through…Stop! She could not start believing in this mumbo jumbo! Fine, she was here! Fine, she was open to anything that might happen, but she would not believe it until it really happened.

"Do you believe that he'll walk again?" asked Michael of Richard, but then he looked at Maya as if he wanted the answer from her.

Oh no! She was not going to be responsible for that. If he wanted to do his "voodoo" dance around Dan and whisper magic words or sacrifice a goat and two doves, he could do anything he wanted, but she was not going to get involved! Because if nothing happened, she did not want to be the one guilty of the failure.

"I believe!" said Richard, though there was more despair than faith. "I believe with all my heart!"

It is so easy to promise to give away your shirt or your last piece of bread for a loved one when there is no real threat to their life. In a moment like that, you might even compromise with your conscience and say that you believe when you really do not.

No…Maya knew that Richard did not believe. He wanted to, she knew that! He would give away his own life to believe it, but he was just a human filled with doubt and guilt. She made a step toward the door, unable to see the faces of poor Richard and his son when nothing happened. She would wait outside. And even if the boy did get up from bed, Maya would invent an escape for her logic. She would just believe it was all a show, that Dan was never paralyzed, and that they had just played on her emotions.

"Take his hand!" Michael said it so powerfully that Maya's heart skipped a beat. Her father used to talk to her like that when he had asked her to do something many times already in a kinder voice, but she refused to mind. She panicked and froze in place.

"Maybe I'd better go check on Valery?"

"Take his hand, Maya." He did not raise his voice, but she could not say no.

Timidly, and fighting with her very nature, Maya crossed the room and carefully took Dan's cold hand. She had touched a dead body before, at her uncle's funeral. She was curious how a human felt after life had left its vessel. This felt almost the same, maybe a little warmer, but there were no muscle reflexes, no movement. Even a good actor could not fake that.

Maya covered Dan's hand with hers. He had such cold fingers. For a moment, she felt a desire to squeeze them, move them closer to her body, breathe on them, and try to warm them up. What nonsense!

"Really good, Maya." Michael came to her, smiled, and closed his eyes...

...and placed his hand on Maya's shoulder.

Why? Was he not supposed to lay his hands on the sick guy or proclaim something in a powerful voice, like "Get up and walk again!"

No. All he said was, "Father, show your mercy."

Fire! A wave of liquid fire covered Maya, crushing her shoulders and filling her body! The flame did not hurt her, but she hurt from the inside out like a hot compress soaked with medicine and pepper. Bliss and light, in overwhelming flashes, rushed through her nervous system, making her feel alive. She felt like the whole world just opened new horizons to her. She felt every cell in her body, every single hair, and the pores on her skin. She saw all the colors in the gray room, like acrylic paint, soaking through the cracks and gaps of the small bedroom, making the area around expand as wide as the universe.

Maya could not stand, but she could not move either.

Holy fire was going through her, cleaning and repairing all her thoughts, blood cells, and DNA. Oh, how long she had waited for this transformation, how long she had dreamed and hoped for it, even though she had never experienced it before. It felt like meeting your soul mate for the first time or that eerie calm you feel when you walk into a strange place and yet feel at home. It was the love you feel when your child is just born or when your parents hug you for the first time after your birth.

Maya forgot how to breathe, move, speak, or think!

Fire. Everything was covered with blessed fire.

If that was hypnosis, then let it go on forever and never end!

So much fire and light! She wanted even more! But could she hold it? Oh no! A little bit more, and the fire would burst her into molecules, spreading her in everlasting transformation. She had to let the fire go through her. Otherwise, her body would disappear.

She had to give it away, and then she would get more! How did she know that? Had the fire given her knowledge? There was no time to ask, even though she had the whole of eternity floating through her. Give! She must give it away! The more she gave, the more she would receive!

She could not hold it anymore anyway!

The flame went out through her palms into Dan's cold fingers. Light, like a waterfall, was crashing into Dan's motionless body, and Maya felt like a new portion of energy had filled her.

She felt like a pump and started laughing and crying at the same time! She knew that Richard might think she was crazy and that Michael was next to her, proud as any teacher, but all she could see right now was Dan and his tears.

Dan's body rose from the bed, but not in levitation. His muscles pulled his body into an arc, and he took a deep breath like someone who had just been pulled to the surface from beneath a deep river. Had Maya done the same when Michael pulled her from the lake?

Now, the fire burned in both of them.

An avalanche of holy fire covered every muscle, every bone, and every nerve. Maya could see the invisible. She saw how cells gained life, how blood began to circulate, how broken bones moved back into place, and how the bruises from spending a long time in bed dissolved.

They both gasped! It was like both of them had just been born a second time. His breath became faster, and the monitors connected to him started freaking out. He was like a fish trying to breathe outside of water. He would need to learn so many different things again. He cried! He cried out loud. Maya could hear Dan's voice, and she stepped back, disconnecting from Dan.

The fire slowly melted in the air, leaving a warm sensation throughout her whole body. She looked at Dan, then at Richard, who was on his knees crying as well. Michael stood next to him. But how? When?

When did he take his hand from her shoulder? She noticed in that moment that Michael looked very serious, as though he had matured in a flash. He looked at her, not as a kid, but as a mature and thoughtful teenager who had done some noble and honorable deed.

Fingers, still cold, touched Maya's hand. It was Dan who looked at her, crying.

"Tha…thank you…" said Dan, and he started to cry even more upon hearing his own voice again.

CHAPTER 12

Phillip showed up right on time.

Maya was barely balanced on the edge of reality.

At any moment, she might pass that critical line where you end up in a straight jacket and in a room with padded walls and warm pudding for your main dish. After the miraculous healing, Richard helped his son get up from the bed, and not only was the young man able to stand up, but he started walking as well! Valery, of course, fainted, and poor Richard was torn between an unsteady Dan and a wife who was now flattened on the floor.

Maya sat silently on the side of the bed, watching the spectacle as Dan and Richard rushed to assist Valery. Yes, his steps looked awkward, and he was as stable as a newborn foal, but he walked! There were days when Maya slept longer than usual, and her whole body would feel numb and as useful as a doll's, and here a boy, fresh out of paralysis, was moving across the room right away after spending a couple years as a vegetable. A walking miracle. Literally!

At first, this thought made her smile, and then she started to giggle, but when Agent Howell invited himself into the house and appeared in the doorway, she started to laugh hysterically.

Oh, his face!

That priceless look. Before, she might have been the one staring around in confusion, but now she was a part of the absurdity, and FBI seemed lost in the middle of a freak show.

At first, Maya did not even notice the gun in his hand, and more likely, when he heard Valery's scream, he assumed the worst, and his reflexes took over. After analyzing the situation, he lowered his weapon, but from the look on his face, Polanski could tell he was willing to kill her right there and without waiting for the Head of Nehushtan to do the job.

Did that scare her? Not at all. Any other time, maybe, but she knew he would be angry as hell, and she was honestly just happy to see him.

Maya finally overcame herself and tried to sound as innocent as possible when she began to speak.

"So, are you going to say anything, or will you just keep staring at me until the end of time?"

"You know…" He looked like he was prepared with a long speech that he had recited in his head over and over on the way there.

"I'm sorry." Maya smiled at him as sincerely as she could. "And I am not often sorry about anything."

He waved her away dismissively and put the gun into his holster.

Over the next twenty minutes, she tried to explain everything to him, starting from the moment when she escaped from the safe house. Phillip tried not to interrupt her, and only from time to time when his eyebrows would scrunch together or the corner of his lips would raise up in a cute smirk, would Maya try to find better words to explain herself.

It seemed that the attack at *Chicago Voice* did not surprise him, but the assault on Michael's house was confusing. He kind of understood the reasoning behind Maya's trip to Lake City but was totally skeptical of the earthquake story.

He listened to her carefully, almost like he was trying to read between her lines. Maybe deep inside, he was afraid that she was playing him, lying in some way. Now and then, he would look over at Richard, Dan, and Valery, who did not even seem to be paying any attention to him or Maya. The unconscious woman had finally come to her senses, stopped crying, and was now gazing at her son. All three of them sat on the floor holding hands and sharing smiles and tears.

The agent kept looking at Michael, who was now peacefully drinking tea in the corner of the living room, and with each new revelation about his miraculous abilities, Phillip looked more and more concerned.

"...and then you showed up."

Phillip closed his eyes, trying to digest all the information.

"I know this all sounds crazy, but hey, who else is going to believe me if not you? And after all, I believed your story."

"Don't you think this is all really strange?" asked Howell quietly.

"Which part?" Maya smiled.

"All of it...I mean, it all looks like some beautifully staged play. How do you know this Michael is not part of Nehushtan?"

"Why would he be? They need him, and they want to use me as a recruiter, which makes no sense to me." Maya stopped smiling. "Hear me out. I know this is crazy. I mean, ape shit crazy! As I was telling you everything just now, sometimes I would surprise myself at how insane it sounds. But at this point, I've decided to turn off my brain and let my guts lead me."

"And your guts are saying this boy is a saint?"

"The Snakeheads sure aren't. I can feel it. I talked to Cloudy, and when I was with him in the same room, I could feel how evil he was. I might not be the smartest woman in the world, but I do know how to read people. And Michael is his total opposite."

"I don't know, Maya. But if you're saying Cloudy is in charge of the clan, then we are not safe here. If I was able to trace you down, which was actually really easy, then they'll be able to as well. I told you they have access to the police, and they own some people in the FBI. It took me less than ten minutes to get the security footage to see which car you got into and to find the address by its license plate."

"Okay, let's move then…But Michael is coming with us."

"Uhmm. No, he's not."

"Yes, he is! Or I'm not going either."

Phillip looked at Maya with a strange caution. Then he looked at the boy who was now talking to the parents and their pale son around the kitchen table.

"Did he brainwash you?"

"If he did, I would not say so anyway. You need to believe me. He's a good kid. I'm not sure how much of a kid he is, though."

"What is that supposed to mean?" FBI's look went from caution to alarm.

Maya lowered her voice and moved closer to the agent.

"I think he's…an angel."

"Maya…Have you at all considered that everything that's happened to you over the last week was staged? At all?"

"Here we go again." Maya sighed.

"How about your cancer? Do you feel any different?"

"That's not your business!"

Maya wanted to get mad, but her conscience started speaking to her. Agent Howell was right. She had no pain, no symptoms. But since when? When did she stop noticing the pain? She looked over at Dan, who had been paralyzed before and was now walking again. A wave of joy rushed through her veins.

"Do you think he healed me?"

"Or...You were never sick? They might have given you something to cause the pain."

"On a daily basis? FBI, I think you're starting to lose it."

"There are plenty of ways to simulate pain. Even your painkillers could create an addiction effect. After they wear out, you would start to feel symptoms until you took another pill."

"I'm sorry, Agent Howell?" Valery called from the kitchen.

"Yes?" Phillip replied a little too roughly, and the poor woman almost dropped the plate from her hands.

"There's a man outside our house. Is that your partner? You can invite him in for..."

Phillip did not get a chance to reply, and her words were cut short by a crashing sound like someone had thrown a small stone through the kitchen window. Valery's shoulders jolted like something unpleasant had touched her. She turned toward Dan, looking at him for the last time to make sure he was okay, smiled, and fell to the floor.

Maya could not understand what happened. Only after seeing a puddle of blood quickly spreading from under Valery did she raise her eyes toward the window with its small, round bullet hole and see a man in a black hoodie with a gun in his hand.

"Get down!" Phillip jumped on her, and they fell together onto the floor. "Everyone, stay down!"

A couple more shots broke the window completely.

Howell, holding his gun, crawled to the window and fired a couple shots in the air, hoping to scare off the attackers. It was one thing to kill the unarmed, but completely another to try to survive in the crossfire. Maybe they fell back.

No. A couple more shots from different directions buzzed by outside.

"He's not alone." Howell did not seem surprised.

"Valery?" Richard, finally realizing what had happened, stepped closer to his wife and touched her hand, then her shoulder, and then the big, red stain on her chin… "Valery! Help, help her!"

Maya crawled closer to the woman and touched her neck, feeling for a pulse.

"Hold on, love…" He tried to press on the wound, hoping to stop the bleeding.

Phillip slowly tried to peek outside, but as soon as he raised himself high enough to look, about ten more gunshots rolled in from outside, and a shelf on the opposite wall exploded into small pieces.

"FBI, I need your phone!" Maya slowly removed her hand from Valery's neck. "We need to call for help. She's dying!"

"You need to leave!" Phillip fired a couple more shots. "Take them and go!"

"So you don't think this is staged anymore?" She was boiling with anger.

"Go! NOW!" If Agent Howell could shoot laser beams from his eyes, he would have burned her alive with the look he gave her.

"Please don't leave me…" Richard started to cry.

Maya wasn't sure whether he was talking to her or to his dying wife.

"I can help," said Michael, coming over from his chair like nothing had happened before that moment. "I might need a moment…"

"No…" whispered Valery, fighting through the pain. "You can't…"

"Honey, but…please, let him!" Richard did not know who he should ask for help. He kept stroking her hair, kissing her forehead and seemed to shed more tears than she shed blood.

"He can't waste himself. You know that…" Valery's eyes were closed, so it was hard to understand whom she was talking to. "You must protect him. You must…"

Michael sat on the floor next to her and took her hand.

"You already did so much for me." Valery opened her eyes, and they were full of tears. "I believe again. I believe in His love."

"I will see you soon." Michael smiled at her and then kissed her hand.

Valery took a deep breath, and the pain left her.

Her eyes looked up somewhere beyond even the ceiling. A smile touched her lips, and her face became radiant with a heavenly glow.

"I see Him!" she said in a trembling voice. "Oh, He is so amazing…Oh, Michael, He is so proud of you. He values what you do. Don't let anyone make you believe otherwise…"

Valery closed her eyes and stopped breathing.

For a moment, everything stopped in time. Even the wind seemed to calm…

But not for long.

New shots from outside landed much closer. Howell got up and fired a good answer in their direction, which led to someone's short, painful scream.

More gunfire answered back to Phillip, but he was fast enough or lucky enough to dodge it.

"Maya, that's enough. You need to leave. Do you still have a key to the apartment?"

She nodded.

Who knows? Maybe it was an adrenaline rush, or maybe she was just growing accustomed to combat. It did not take much for her to jump to her feet and pull Michael up as well.

"Richard, let's go. Get Dan!"

Richard stood up, but instead of helping his shocked son, he went to one of the bedrooms.

"RICHARD!?" Maya was not sure what was happening, but there was no time for figuring it out. She pulled Michael toward Dan, but both of them looked lost. "Michael, help me. We need to get him out of here. Do you hear me?"

Michael did not answer, but he quickly stooped down to help Dan up, throwing the latter's arms around his neck. Either the boy was stronger than he looked, or Dan was even lighter than he looked. Maya thought for a moment that Michael looked a bit taller and more mature.

Richard returned as fast as he had disappeared, holding a rifle in his hands and an ammunition belt over one shoulder. He was no soldier or warrior, just a chemistry teacher, but he knew how to use his hunting rifle. Maya's dad had often taken her and her four brothers hunting, and she could tell that this guy knew what he was doing.

He walked straight to the window, fired two shots, and ducked out of view before shots fired back toward him.

"Richard, go with them. I can handle this!" Phillip changed a clip.

"No, you can't. I think there are at least five more out there." Richard was calm, and that made him look almost scary. He looked like Death, or at least its slave, with his bloodless, pale face and empty eyes. Agent Howell seemed to recognize that look, and he knew that this man was ready to die at the window to avenge his wife.

"You need to go...For your son. Take the keys from my car. I parked in the alley. Take them out of here!"

Richard darted back up to the window, fired another two shots, and ducked down again before the new line of shots answered him.

"Richard...Please?" Maya was afraid to come after him, but if they wanted to get out of there alive, they needed to do it now.

"No. They'll never make it to your car. I have a better idea. Dan, your Jeep is in the winter garden! Show them the way!" Richard's lips trembled, but not his hands, as he pulled a set of keys from his pocket and threw them to Phillip. The agent caught them in one hand as if by reflex. "You can protect them better than me. I will try to hold them off as long as I can."

"I'm not leaving you…"

"You are! You brought them here! Because of you, my wife is dead. Now at least save my son!"

Maya thought Phillip might try to shift the blame onto her, maybe suggesting that Maya's irrational decision to call 911 led them to her…But Howell did not say a word and just nodded. He began to move toward Maya, and on the way, he stopped to feel for Valery's pulse. She was dead indeed.

"I am sorry…" said the FBI agent.

"Protect him. That's what's important. I know you understand that." Richard's voice was cold as steel, and it was his last wish, asking for Phillip to guard his son's life. Or was he not talking about Dan?

"I know." Phillip squeezed the keys in his hand so tightly that his knuckles turned white. Then, turning again to Maya and the boys, he rushed them to the back door.

There was no backyard. The house was built on the edge of a small park, and only a line of bushes and a big, glass greenhouse marked the edge of Richard's property. A small alley stretched for half a mile in both directions.

The Jeep Wrangler was parked in the middle of the gray, glass building where nothing had grown for the last couple of years. There were just piles of books, garden tools, empty glass jars, and spider webs. One of the walls opened up as wide as a garage door, which was how the vehicle had been parked inside in the first place after the accident with Dan. Surprisingly, the jeep was clean, and none of the piles of junk blocked its semi-new tires. If this was Dan's car, then Richard must have tried to keep it clean and maintained with the hope that one day his son would be able to drive again…Or maybe it was out of guilt.

Maya helped Michael pull Dan into the back seat.

"Buckle up, boys!" she yelled as if a car wreck were the most dangerous thing that might happen to them that day. But in a vehicle without doors, the last thing they needed was to lose someone on a sharp turn or a bumpy alley road.

Phillip looked at the big pile of keys, trying to guess which one started the engine.

"That one," squeaked Dan, pointing to a long key with a blue ribbon tied on the end. Words were still causing him pain, but speed was crucial now.

One easy turn and the engine started with a strong roar and the passion of a horse that had been kept in the stable for too long.

Gunshots fired anew toward the greenhouse, but this time, only one shot from Richard's rifle could be heard firing back.

For a brief moment, Phillip froze and then looked back at Dan.

"I'm sorry, kid..."

Dan looked down, seemingly in acceptance, and closed his eyes.

The FBI agent switched gears, pressed the pedal, and the Jeep lurched back into the alley. Phillip switched gears again, and the vehicle sped down the uneven, dusty road just as three hooded men rushed into the backyard.

CHAPTER 13

The freeway. Hundreds of cars were moving in both directions, creating the best sort of protection and defense. It seemed that if they kept driving along with the flow, they would be fine and safe. They were one car amongst thousands, and they could go as far as the road would take them or jump out at any exit. No one would know where they were. Four absolute strangers became one unit. Maya felt an odd connection to all of them, even to Dan…How strange her life had become now! She needed all of them and needed them to be alive and well.

Secrets and death can unite people better than a family bloodline.

Yes, they needed to keep driving as far as the old Jeep could handle such a chase. Richard had maintained the car well, but if it had been in a garage most of the time, how long would the engine be able to keep up? The road. Movement. Farther and farther. New streets and buildings, cars and people. No one knew them. They could easily pass for a family on a trip. Maya and FBI could be the parents, Michael their son, and Dan—her younger brother.

Maya glanced into the rear-view mirror, making sure the boys were alright, and kept playing with thoughts of how old she would have been if she had given birth to Michael…It was so strange, and the boy looked older than she thought he was. He looked almost the same age as Dan. Maybe if Dan were not sick, he would be bigger and stronger, but right now, Michael, who was what? Twelve? Thirteen? Looked like a high school student.

Well, she was too young to be the mother of a boy that old, but maybe a stepmom? FBI seemed older. He could be a parent.

"What?" Phillip noticed her curious look.

"Nothing…Was just wondering, how did they find you?"

"Me?" FBI was on edge, and if a stare had physical force, she would have been pushed out of the car. "You understand that if you listened to me and stayed in the apartment, none of this would have happened?"

"I know…" replied Maya quietly.

"Really?"

"Yes…God…You think I'm having fun with all of this? You wouldn't believe how much I wish this were all over and that I could get back to my routine work at *Chicago Voice.*"

Phillip just smirked.

"What?"

"I don't think that'll happen anytime soon. If Cloudy is the one behind all of this, then I'm not sure any of us will ever have a routine life again. He warned us, so be prepared. I'm not sure who this boy is, but if he needs him, he won't stop."

Maya, normally strong and determined, now felt crushed. If she were there alone, she might even allow herself an occasional moment of weakness. She'd close the curtains, turn on some loud music, and cry into a pillow. But not now. Maybe she would have that chance later.

"So, should we go back to the apartments?"

"It's not safe anymore. If they tracked you through 911, then it'll be the same for me. They know we're working together. It will only be a matter of hours before they pull my GPS tracking history, find out where I was, and connect the dots."

Mayas squeezed her hands so no one could see that they were trembling.

"Then what now? Can we go to the police? Straight to the FBI? A news station?"

"Not until I know for sure who we can trust. We need to find a safe spot. I'll also try to secure us some bulletproof vests."

"The last time I talked to Cloudy, it felt like he needed us alive. I'm not sure what changed."

"They only need Michael alive," answered Dan, which made both Maya and Phillip turn to look back.

Michael seemed so peaceful as if he was not actually covered in blood or just escaping crossfire with them. Blissful ignorance. But how did Dan know anything about it?

"What do you mean? Do you know something?"

Dan stared back at the FBI agent with so much anger and hate that Maya thought the weak boy would try to hit Howell.

He probably blamed Phillip for the death of his parents, but that would be unfair. Were it not for FBI, they would all be dead. Maya needed to switch the topic to something else and would ask Dan what he meant later on.

"How much gas do we have?"

"Less than a quarter," replied Phillip, who kept gazing at Dan through the mirror.

"Then we should stop, get gas and some food, and maybe new clothes." She pointed to the blood spots on her top. "And Dan can't just walk around in his pajamas."

"We can't use cards...I might have some cash, though," agreed Phillip.

"I have a little bit as well."

For the next five minutes, they drove in silence. Phillip kept switching lanes and looking back, though Maya was sure that was not necessary. If they had someone tailing them, he would have gotten lost a long time ago in such busy traffic. But she let FBI do his job, and he was already irritated with her.

When the gas indicator finally lit up, Phillip changed lanes again, swerving in front of another car, and turned onto a freeway exit at a sharp angle. His sudden actions made at least half a dozen drivers unhappy, according to the sudden choir of klaxons.

The gas station was almost empty, which suited them perfectly, and there were only a couple cars parked next to a McGregor's Hamburgers attached to the small convenience store.

"Okay, boys. You stay in the car. Dan will only draw attention. What is your shoe size?"

"Ten…it was ten…I think."

"Sounds good."

"Maya, you can't go."

"Give me your jacket, and no one will see the blood spots. I'll be fast, and you can get gas."

Phillip smiled. It seemed that this side of Maya entertained him, even though he still wanted to kill her.

"Maya, your face is in every news segment. Do you really think a jacket will make you less noticeable?"

She did not like it, but Phillip was right.

"Well, then you go inside, get me a new T-shirt or sweater, and maybe some hair color?"

"Okay. Here's my jacket in case anyone comes close. How much money do we have?"

"Mine and yours. Barely two hundred. How much gas should we get?"

"Take a full tank," said Dan. "I think I know a safe place where we can spend some time."

Phillip was unsure but tried not to say anything.

"My dad has a lab on the college campus. It has electricity, heating, water, and even a couch."

"Will they let us in?" Maya liked the idea of a place with a couch and warmth.

"You see this long key on the chain? The lab is in the basement of the science building, and today is a weekend, so we should be fine."

"Okay. Let's do it…" Phillip looked at Dan again, like the two of them were having a mental wrestling match. "In the meantime, stay here. I'll go buy some food and clothes. You get gas. Just, Maya, please behave."

"Jawohl, mein Herr!"

Phillip rolled his eyes, left forty dollars with Maya, and left.

"Get me some nuts!"

"You're nuts enough without them…"

Maya raised her middle finger toward him, but Phillip did not notice.

"Something smells nice," said Michael, finally, looking toward the McGregor's. "Is that a restaurant?"

"You've never had fast food?" Maya tried to remember if she had seen any big, golden arches on any signs in Lake City. Nope…

"To be honest, after three years, maybe I shouldn't, but I would kill for a hamburger." Dan looked guilty saying it, but Maya could see how he almost drooled at the thought.

Maya waited until Phillip entered the store, then zipped the jacket and leaned toward the boys.

"So, should I get a large order of fries with your hamburgers?"

*

Maya knew she would be better off saving the cash for more important things, especially as no one knew how long they would be in exile. But on the other hand, she was a person who believed in living for the moment. If you have the chance, get everything possible out of life because there might not be a tomorrow. If God was merciful enough to let them see the sun of a new day, then he would find a way to feed them and provide for their needs.

Before, Maya's god was herself. She believed that she was capable enough to find a way to "keep on rowing." Now, though, after Michael's appearance in her life, she had started to think that maybe her good fortune had been God all along, guiding her to success and helping her survive.

"Let tomorrow worry about itself," she said to herself. Maya paid for twenty dollars worth of gas, and with another twenty, she ordered a few cheap meal combos from McG's, including frozen coffee for herself and milkshakes for the boys. She even bought an ice cream for FBI since he needed to chill out a little.

No more fearing tomorrow. They would get through it! She got through cancer, for Pete's sake. Or...

Maybe she had been slowly poisoned by the pills, and when she took the painkillers, she was causing her body to imitate the symptoms. Or had Michael cured her when he pulled her from the lake? But that was the exact same day that she lost her "painkillers."

She sat down at an empty table, watching as her order was assembled, and tried to remember how it all began. She analyzed every moment, every symptom. Could Bill have put something in her drink to trigger the first pains? Everything could have been a masterful play in which she unknowingly played the lead. She could explain everything logically if she tried hard enough...almost...or she could just accept the fact that there are miracles in this world and that Michael was the miracle worker. But in that case, she would need to accept everything based on feelings and faith.

Faith...She had never had any. Well, she had faith in science. She had faith in herself. She had some faith in a couple friends and her parents but not in anything supernatural.

But Michael…He was different, and she could feel it. And if she could not yet accept that he was an alien or an angel, then she had to agree that he was at least a very unusual boy. He had a set of skills that others just did not have. She could accept that! She remembered five-year-old prodigies who could play the piano or violin; she had written a column about it. She remembered a boy on TV who could name the capital of every country. Indigo kids existed, and some bad people had wanted to kidnap one of them.

Perfect! That was logical, reasonable, and believable. And no matter what, she owed it to this boy and his mother to keep him safe until he could go back home. That is something decent people should do, and it was about time Maya did something nice for someone else.

Her stream of thoughts was broken by a quiet whispering. Maya was sure someone had said her name. She looked around, but no one was there.

Was it the snake worshipers? No, she had not heard it inside her head. She heard it with her ears.

Maya looked at the girls in uniform who were still packing her order. Yes, she had ordered a lot, but it should not have been taking so long.

"We're waiting on fresh fries. It'll be a couple more minutes. Sorry for the wait," said the manager, almost as if he had read her thoughts.

"No problem." Maya smiled, understanding that she had really screwed up.

What exactly had made her understand it? Maybe it was the fact that half of the staff had moved to the back of the kitchen, or perhaps it was the full containers of fresh fries already sitting on the tray. It might have been the scared look on the smiling face of the manager or the fact that the TV was currently showing Maya's photo with a note reading "armed and dangerous."

"You know what, I'll just take this, and you can keep the fries." Maya picked up the half-filled sacks of food and rushed to the door, but it was already too late. Police lights appeared from every direction, and soon, the nearly empty parking lot was swarming with cops. Maya could see at least six police vehicles from her vantage point.

Suddenly, the whole crew fell on the floor, and the few visitors moved under their tables.

"MAYA POLANSKI! WALK OUT WITH YOUR HANDS RAISED WHERE WE CAN SEE THEM!"

Maya looked around, hoping to find a way to escape, but it seemed that this time she was out of luck.

She smiled. It was all so theatrical like she was in the middle of a cheap soap opera or a cheesy police sitcom. She had seen it hundreds of times. Faceless cops. Identical cars. Noise and lights. And she was the only one different, the only one with an actual role. The rest were extras, and she was the leading star.

Slowly, she removed one of the hamburgers from its wrapper and took a large bite. At least she would not go down hungry.

"Thanks for the great service. Here's your tip!" Maya threw the change that she held in her hand onto the counter, and, taking another bite, left the hamburger and went outside carrying the sacks of food for the boys.

She walked freely and with confidence, not as though she was about to be arrested, but the way one would when receiving the greatest award in television history.

More police vehicles arrived, and she thought that soon, all of Chicago would be there just for her!

"HANDS! I NEED TO SEE THEM!"

She did not believe that they would actually shoot her, but she still lowered the sacks slowly to the ground.

"What's wrong? I just stopped for a milkshake. Is that a crime?"

"DO NOT MOVE!"

She was not moving. She knew something would happen, and soon. She could feel it. The knowledge of the future was as real as that of the past. It was as if she had already seen the ending of this movie and knew that it had a happy ending.

"What is going on?" Phillip came up from the store holding a pistol in one hand and an open badge in the other.

The police saw it and relaxed for a moment.

"I'm Special Agent Phillip Howell, this woman…"

But something happened. As soon as he spoke his name, all guns switched their focus from Maya to Phillip.

"SLOWLY DROP YOUR WEAPON AND STEP BACK!"

"I'm an FBI agent!" repeated Howell, not understanding what was happening.

"DROP YOUR WEAPON!"

The police officers were not kidding. Maya was not sure, but it seemed like the clan of snakes had finally grown tired of Phillip's interfering and decided to get rid of him. Interesting. What back story did they create about him? A crazy agent who had gone rogue? A terrorist who pretended to be with the Feds? Things were just getting exciting.

"Check my badge! Call the office! Ask for Agent…"

"DROP YOUR WEAPON, OR I WILL SHOOT!"

Two more police vehicles appeared in the parking lot.

Maya looked toward the Jeep, where Dan was barely able to keep Michael inside. Something would give…It was like the moment before a storm. You can feel the coming thunder. You can smell the ozone as lighting begins flashing along the horizon. Maya always had good intuition, but what was happening right now was beyond human senses!

The world lost its colors and sounds. Everything felt like a performance that she observed from inside her body. The cops made Phillip drop his gun and get on his knees before they pushed him onto the dirty asphalt, nearly breaking his arms behind his back as they prepared to cuff him.

Now. NOW. Something was going to happen...NOW!

Oh yes! She knew it like a spider rushing toward its prey. As soon as the web trembled, the predator was on its way.

A truck raced toward the scene, ramming through the wall of police vehicles. It had no recognizable markings or license plates. Taking no damage and losing no speed, the black military-standard truck plowed a corridor all the way to her. When there were only a couple feet left between them, its brakes squealed, and it spun ninety degrees, blocking her from the police.

As funny as it might sound, she knew that the man who sat behind those tinted windows was looking right at her. He was calm and determined. He was not afraid of anything.

All attention turned to the driver. All weapons pointed toward the vehicle. But even an army would not have intimidated the one behind the wheel.

An unusual silence fell over them all. Maya could hear only the wind rushing through the power lines and the rustling of a trash bag behind the gas station. She heard someone's prayer from inside the restaurant and her own heartbeat. Everything became a world of shadows and sculptures. Had her perception of time changed, or was something supernatural happening again?

The black door opened, and a shadow stepped out. It was not a man like any that Maya had seen before. He was tall and slender but shaped like an athlete, and he walked toward the police in a movement that seemed theatrically smooth. For a moment, she thought he was not walking but sliding across the parking lot, barely moving his legs. There was something so snake-like in his manners and look that Maya had no doubts about who this man was. Like a serpent, he was dressed and yet naked at the same time. The fabric used to make his hooded robe was thinner than silk and darker than void. She could see every curve, every muscle in his body. He was like one of those mannequins used for studying biology. Under the clouded sky, his robe absorbed the light and reflected nothing.

The police stared blankly at him, like a bunch of mammals frozen in front of a boa. His cloak began to spread on the wind, becoming longer and lighter. The breeze revealed the truth about the visitor, and just as Maya had thought, he was naked under the silk. The fabric rose higher behind him, like two black wings that covered the sky, sucking out the last remaining sound. One of his wings spread over the gas station, and another covered the sky above the police.

Maya had seen a naked man before, and nudity had never shocked or confused her. If anything, it would wake up a desire in her, something natural and tempting that she usually kept hidden but would release as a long-strangled storm when the situation allowed. But right now, the nude body called to her soul, not to her flesh. She felt a desire to fall on her knees and worship this dark angel.

Another gust of wind pulled the hood from the man's head...

A reptile with the body of a human? No! He had a human face, but instead of skin, his slick head was covered with scales. They shone in the gloom, like diamonds dipped in oil.

"You are not who you think you are..." said the angel, and the sound of his voice grew with power and momentum. It crashed like a wave on the walls, cars, fueling platforms, and surrounding people, returning with an echo and repeating itself hundreds of times in Maya's head.

"The world is not like it was before."

The beautiful fabric swam on streams of air and delivered the words and transformed them into symbols that spoke deeper than ears could hear. Maya felt motion and sound, love and hate, and eternity in a heartbeat. The being inhaled and exhaled with every movement, his endless silk wings covering all the world around.

"Fear does not control your hearts. Blood cannot pay for you."

Maya saw the cop's eyes, their pupils slowly spreading, creating dozens of black holes reflecting the angel's silky wings. Maybe her eyes were reacting the same way, or perhaps only those who had direct eye contact were becoming hypnotized. She could not tell.

Maya understood that this creature was trying to control her mind, and he was successful. She could not move her sight away from his flying robes, but she knew that she needed to fight.

"Life is an undeserved gift," the mind controller said, slowly raising his hand and twisting open his palm as he twisted reality.

"No..." whispered Maya, understanding what was about to happen.

The police finally moved from their frozen position and lowered their guns. Slowly, as the puppeteer pulled their strings, the weapons raised again, pointing toward themselves...

"No...No...No..." whispered Maya, trying to regain her voice.

All twenty policeman held their own guns under their chins.

They had no fear, no regrets, no will, no consciousness.

"NO!" yelled Maya, finally finding her voice!

The snakehead kept his torso and hand still but slowly turned his head to look at her. Was it surprise she read into his yellow eyes? No, he was not a reptile. He was not an angel. He did not have scales, but just tattoos that covered his head, imitating snake skin. No, his cloak had not covered the whole sky. It was just long, silk fabric moving on the wind, nothing else. He was just a naked guy...perhaps somewhat smaller than an average man, with a weak outline of muscles. He stood, his arms raised in a dramatic fashion, and looked straight at her while the illusion faded away.

He knew that she could see him like he really was. He smirked and, in a spiteful gesture, dropped his palm.

Twenty simultaneous gunshots shook the air!

They fell like puppets whose strings had been cut by a resentful master. Such a cynical and pointless death! What was the purpose of it? Just a demonstration of power? He could have made them forget his presence or sent them all away, thinking they were kids or monkeys. He had the mental ability to make them do anything he wanted, but he made them kill themselves.

And he did it simply because he could.

All the sirens stopped.

"You sick son of a snake!" Maya felt anger and adrenaline rushing through her veins, making her heart race like that of a wild mare.

The snakehead moved toward her with interest and a sense of challenge. He was inspecting her, reading the movement of every muscle in her face. He inhaled her emotions and absorbed her rage. His ugly face was covered with scale-like tattoos all the way down his neck and shoulders. She had seen too many freaks in her lifetime to be afraid or disgusted. But what made her sick was the realization that he had come here for her and had killed all those men to get under her skin.

He glared into her eyes, and it all started again.

Those eyes! Those damn yellow eyes started to change into blue! It was the same cold, hypnotizing blue that wanted to drown her before.

"Don't look into his eyes!" Phillip finally raised his voice, probably because the visitor had switched his attention to Maya, and FBI started getting control back over his mind.

It seemed to be too late. The eyes were stronger, deeper, more desirable…

Howell reached for his gun that the cops had pushed aside from him.

"Where is he?" a familiar voice whispered inside her head.

Maya felt like her eyes were swirling, spinning the world around her. Why? Why was Phillip so slow? She could not fight those blue talismans much longer.

"Where is Michael?" The man stretched his hand toward Maya, and his appearance started to melt and mold into a new form. The cloak became alive again and transformed into tentacles, or snake tales, and moved toward her paralyzed body. He had her!

Before her eyes, the naked freak show morphed into a god with a snake-like head. He grew taller, stronger, more masculine. His jaw moved forward, splitting under the nose. The tattoos faded, letting his shining scales move to the surface.

Dozens of snake-like limbs touched her, attempting to find the weakest spot in her thin mental armor. She felt intense pain as sharp, invisible claws grew through the limbs, impaling her skin.

It could not be true! But how could she feel the pain?

"Tell me where he is, or you will know how painful illusions can be!" He was reading her thoughts. There was no mistake…

"Leave her alone, or I'll shoot!" Howell was still weak and kneeling on the ground, but both his hands gripped the gun tightly. From this distance, even a bad shot could make the kill.

The snakehead turned his head around in the blink of an eye like only a serpent could do.

Maya still felt the pressure from the illusionary limbs around her torso, but the mental attack weakened. That meant only one thing. The visitor switched his focus onto Phillip, who suddenly yelled as though he had been impaled through body, soul, and spirit. FBI fell onto his back and began to aim the gun at his own head, his eyes still fixed on those of his opponent.

When the snakehead had his fill of causing pain, he made Phillip open his mouth wide enough to slip the gun inside.

"Why? Why are you doing this?" Maya was still paralyzed but able to speak.

"Give me the BOY!" whispered a choir of voices in her head, but she could swear that the choir was led by Cloudy. "Where IS HE?!"

"I'm here! Let them go!"

Michael finally managed to escape the car where Dan had tried to keep him safe as long as he could. The miracle boy approached the stranger in just his T-shirt and jeans. He looked so young and defenseless compared to the killer illusionist.

"NO. Michael! Run! Run away! Dan! Take him! Take him out of here!"

Dan tried to run after Michael, but with one quick lash of his wrist, the snakehead mentally crushed Dan, dropping him to his knees with an anguishing pain in his head.

"Enough!" said Michael, quietly but with authority. In that same moment, Dan's pain disappeared, and Maya was released from her illusion.

"Is it really you?" smiled the snakehead, trying to analyze the boy. "I don't see why they're all so defensive of such an ordinary-looking child."

"Let Phillip go and leave."

"You're so scared. So confused..." The snakehead moved toward Michael, looking him straight in the eyes.

"Michael! Do not look at him! RUN!" Maya tried to move, but it seemed that the stranger's power had drained her of all strength, and she fell down like a bag of meat and bones, barely able to twist to one side in time to protect her face from the unavoidable impact.

"You just made a mistake." The visitor kept walking toward Michael, pushing on him mentally and closing the distance.

"Go away. You already did so much harm." Michael made a step toward the snakehead, looking into his eyes, but not the same way anyone else would have. Hypnosis did not work on the boy.

"Oh...You're not so simple after all." The naked man, in his black, draping cloak, smiled again, but the smile soon began to fade.

Each took one more step, and now they stood right in front of each other, an arm's distance, and both held eye contact. From anyone else's perspective, it looked weird and wrong. A freak and a teenage boy fighting a mental battle, surrounded by dead cops, a paralyzed woman, a barely conscious young man, and an FBI agent biting his gun.

Something in the air changed. Thousands of voices began chanting inside Maya's head. The choir of serpentine voices grew louder, trying to say something, cheer the stranger on, or frighten the others…

Maya could feel goosebumps begin to cover her body. Was it her feeling coming back? No, it was more than just a feeling. The air became charged, like with static. She could see little sparks on the edges of metal objects. Their mental duel was changing the physical world.

Suddenly, the snakehead shrieked and fell to one knee, like something heavy had fallen on his shoulders.

"IDIOT!" heard Maya inside her head. It was the voice of Cloudy and only his this time.

Silence. The chorus retreated, leaving the battleground as the snakehead dropped the other knee and then fell onto his side, hugging the dirty asphalt but keeping his sight on Michael.

"Why are you here?" asked the boy, so calm and casually. Maya knew the answer would follow immediately.

"You know why you came…" wheezed the defeated visitor.

"Why?" Michael was actually curious. Maybe he did not know himself.

"If you do not join us…we will…we will have to kill you…" The man tried to wrap his body into the black silk strips of his cloak, but he never took his eyes off Michael. "You can't stop the ascent of Nehushtan…"

"Where and when will he be reborn?" Michael leaned toward the snakehead, making sure he could not break eye contact.

The visitor began to shake. Huge drops of sweat came through his tattooed skin, and he started gasping for breath, like a fish that had gone from the lake to the frying pan.

"Ug-g-g-h-h-r-r-a-a-a-a-a!" screamed the snakehead, clinging to the ground.

In any other situation, Maya might have thought that the man was having an epileptic attack, but she knew that was not the case. The visitor, who did not appear so magnificent now as when he arrived, looked like a vagabond covered in filth and scraps of cloth.

"Sto-o-o-o-o-op!" he yelled, hoping for mercy.

"When and where?" asked Michael again.

"A-u-u-u-u-ug-g-h-h-h-r-r-r-r!"

The snakehead squeezed his hands so tightly that blood started dripping from his palms. He continued writhing until he had managed to turn his head around and lock eyes with Phillip.

"PHILLIP NO!" Maya understood what was happening, but FBI could not resist.

In a flash, Howell pulled the gun out of his mouth, stretched out his hand, and fired the whole clip.

All six bullets hit the snakehead, and he finally relaxed, motionless, a pool of blood spreading on the ground.

"Blood is not a payment for death..." he whispered, still looking at Michael. "Nehushtan is laughing at you."

The mystic died without letting his secrets go.

Maya was not sure how to feel about that. For one agonizing moment, she thought the cultist would make Phillip shoot Michael, but instead, he sacrificed himself. Why? Or did they really need this boy alive, even if they did not have the power to control him? But as confused as Maya was, Michael seemed even more so.

Maya tried to stand. Her body belonged to her again, though she had a headache worse than she had ever had with any hangover. She felt like she might throw up at any moment.

"Are you okay?" Dan came over to Michael, carefully touching the boy's shoulder.

"Why did he do that?" Michael asked Dan as though he might understand it all more than any of them.

Dan had no answer. The only one who could have given an explanation was currently losing his blood, which flowed in a stream, joining those crimson pools flowing from the policemen.

Maya, fighting nausea, staggered over to Phillip, who was still staring at his smoking gun like it was a prosthesis, a part of his body that went out of control against his will.

Just then, Maya noticed many pairs of curious eyes peeking through the windows of the gas station and restaurant. How much had they seen? What exactly did they see, and what did they understand? Had they been close enough to experience the illusions cast by the dead visitor? Well, that was not her problem. Right now, she needed to take care of those who were close to her and get the hell out of there.

"Can you stand?" Maya put her hand under Phillip's chin and moved his face away from the dead visitor and toward herself.

"I...I didn't want to."

"I know." Maya carefully ran her hand along the side of his cheek, but he did not even notice.

"I was so scared...I thought he would command me to..." His cheekbones tightened.

"Kill yourself?" finished Maya for him. Maybe it was the same thing Bill experienced when Cloudy visited his office.

"No...I was afraid he would command me to kill Michael...or you."

Not understanding why, Maya pulled Phillip toward her and hugged him passionately, the way one would a person you loved. She wanted to protect him from his thoughts and fears, to let him know that everything would be fine, that she was there, that she understood and was ready to help.

She was no less scared than he, and she had never been a hugger, but right now, she wanted to be stronger and enjoy the closeness of the moment, perhaps melting into it forever.

But there was no time to be weak. Especially right now. And it was too early for rest as well.

This thought gave her the strength she needed to pull Phillip up to his feet. They needed answers. They needed to know what was going on. Michael was stronger than the snakeheads, and if they could harness his skills, then maybe they could fight back instead of running away.

"Michael!" Maya turned toward the boys. "You resurrected that small girl. Right? Can you resurrect this snake, dude? Then we could…"

"He can't!" Dan interrupted so roughly that Maya choked on her ideal plan. "Michael, you know that, right?!"

Michael slowly raised his eyes and looked at Maya, and she saw tears.

"It's not about what I can or can't do. It was his choice. He chose to die. But them…" Michael looked at the dead police officer, "they shouldn't be dead. They should live…"

"No…No. NO! Michael, please don't!" Dan was begging Michael as if he were about to waste all their savings on nothing. "It's too many of them! You have to save yourself!"

"Get behind me, Satan!" said Michael so strongly that even Maya stepped back.

Dan stopped talking, and for the first time, his pale face went red. If Maya had been standing further away, she might not have noticed it, but she could swear that tears appeared in Dan's eyes just then.

"They should live. It's not their time yet," said Michael more softly. "Maya, go to the car and wait for me there. Give me a few moments."

For the first time, she had no desire to argue. She helped FBI get up and, holding him, waved Dan toward the car. She leaned to pick up a bag of clothes that Phillip had purchased from the small store and retrieved his badge from the ground. After she helped Phillip get in and buckled him up, she looked at Dan, who had turned into a ghost again.

"He can't, he really can't…" he whispered to Maya.

189

"Believe me, this kid is tough. I'm not sure we really understand what he can and can't do. Sit here, I'll go pick up our food!"

Maya turned to walk back and froze in place.

Another illusion!

Or was it real this time?

Michael approached the police vehicles and raised his hands in the air…What was so strange about that? Nothing…until sparks of light appeared in the air, creating a perfect arc that rose and covered the whole area where the dead policemen lay.

The arc grew in volume and spread.

A humming thunder was born under this glowing sphere, and it shook the cars and bodies.

Another clap of thunder, stronger, mightier, shook the ground, making the dead move. At the same time, the police sirens flashed on again! Maya felt the ground vibrating under her feet. Another earthquake? The second in one day? Or was this just another localized demonstration of power?

Dust, dirt, and small bits of trash were picked up into the air and started to swirl around inside the golden sphere created by Michael. Maya felt a physical pressure on her ears, like that on a plane during takeoff. She flew so often that she recognized the feeling immediately. The atmospheric pressure was changing rapidly, creating the feeling that soon, the whole street would fly off to Heaven.

The strangers looking through windows froze in place, but not from amazement. They froze, like in those movies when the superhero moves faster than everyone else. But Maya was not a superhero, or had Michael made her into one?

The small cyclone, strong enough to pick up boxes and other litter, made a tunnel from the sphere all the way to the sky…

The sound of a thousand trumpets and the crashing of waterfalls filled the air, and Maya had to plug her ears from all the noise. It was a most magnificent and terrifying experience. It felt like something great was coming, something much bigger than all of her existence and understanding. The presence of Someone was so real that she now felt stupid for ever questioning His reality.

Not understanding why, she fell on her knees and started to cry like a little girl who had just seen a long-lost parent.

A bright beam of light covered everything!

The people in the windows moved but in a strange way. They moved like characters in a film that was put on rewind...

The blood became alive! It moved! The streams of blood began moving back toward their containers. The earth shook again, and all of the policemen flew from the ground as if it had bounced them upward. The bullets flew back through their heads and back into the guns. Time was going backward! They all turned, aiming toward the military-class vehicle...

The cyclone disappeared. The humming was swallowed by the sound of police sirens. Only the golden sphere remained, shining from inside.

Michael lowered his hands and turned toward Maya.

"He can't..." The words suddenly repeated in Maya's head, and she understood why.

Michael...Yes, it was him, there was no doubt.

But he was not a teenage boy anymore. He had the same clothes, the same hair, the same eyes...But now he looked older, similar in age to Dan. He was not a teenager anymore.

Time? Had that fading golden sphere made time spin one way for the cops and a different way for Michael? But for them, it was only a change of ten...twenty minutes? How did Michael look five or six years older now?

"Let's go, Maya...They will wake up in a few minutes."

Michael smiled and walked toward the Jeep.

Maya followed.

Right now, she had even more questions than before, but she was not sure she should bother him with her ignorance again.

She just followed him…and she was glad to follow.

CHAPTER 14

Richard's lab looked like an oversized storage unit that was filled with the strangest sort of things and left without purpose or order. It was likely that those who had left the maps, books, slide boxes, old posters, and models of chemical elements would never come back for them. But at the same time, this room had its own character, and it reminded Maya of her school days when she would have to make those kinds of rooms somewhat clean again for her detention.

They carefully brought Phillip inside and placed him on a small couch next to the wall where Richard probably stayed late grading papers or, if he was one of the sorts of professors that Maya knew, where he would "grade" his students.

Despite all the dust and cluttered items, the lab was functional. It had a desk with a computer and a couple boxes marked with different class names. Two of the six tables had glass bulbs filled with some liquid and a collection of tubes, which were mostly empty. You could tell it was a chemistry lab by its distinctive smell, but who knew if it was used by the students or if Richard worked on his own projects here?

"He seems worse..." Dan touched Howell's forehead. "He's burning up."

Since the mental attack from the snakehead, Phillip was barely conscious. He would wake up for a couple of moments and then faint again. Maya wondered why she had recovered so fast. Maybe all of her previous mental encounters with them had begun to build some sort of immunity, making her more resilient against hypnosis.

"Are you sure we're safe here?" Maya knew that just about any place would be better than attempting to drive further or finding a hotel when their faces were all over the news.

"Should be." Dan looked outside through the small windows located just below where the wall met the ceiling. "Campus is almost dead now, so I'll go move the Jeep a little farther, somewhere by the dorms, and that way, we won't draw so much attention in the middle of the empty parking lot."

"Okay. But change first."

"I'll be fine. It's the weekend. There's always someone walking around in pajamas."

"Still, we don't need the extra attention." Maya went to the bag and pulled out a pair of sweatpants and a gray sweater, tossing them to Dan. She then grabbed more, exactly the same colors, for herself. "Awesome, now we'll all look like clones."

"I might need some too," said Michael, shyly, because he had not just aged, but he had also grown a good eight inches taller, and even though the jacket that Richard had brought them was now perfect on him, the T-shirt underneath was way too short.

"You got it!" Maya threw him another sweatshirt. "Also, I'm glad you're talking again…Though, your new manly voice is kinda freaking me out."

Michael blushed like a teenage girl.

"Will you be okay here? I'll try to stop by the supply room and see if I can get us some blankets and canned food."

"Sounds good…And before you leave, can you log into your dad's computer? I need to send a couple e-mails."

"I can try…Dad never could remember his password." Dan walked over and lifted a box of pencils under which was a sticky note with the password "Dan1el&032" scribbled on it.

"Oh, that was easy. Thank you."

"Just be careful. College networks aren't so safe."

"Don't worry, I know how to send e-mails through a proxy server. You can go now. Michael, can you tidy up a little? It'd be especially nice if you'd move those boxes up there so we can block the windows. I don't want someone to come wondering why the light is on."

Without saying a word, Michael started cleaning. Dan left, and Phillip was still unconscious, so Maya sat in front of Richard's desk, entered the password, and opened the web browser page. First, she opened a page that created a rabbit hole of proxy addresses, making it nearly impossible for anyone to find her real location. She sent a short email to Stan on his personal account, asking him what was new in the office and requesting some contact information since her phone was long gone. Not being sure how often he checked his mail, she sent him a spam-like message on his phone through an online texting service reading, "Douse your cigarette in coffee!"

Then she opened a page of local news just to find out what they were all saying about her. There was no need to look very far. Her picture and one of Howell were right on the home page. Apparently, they had been placed as a warning not only for Chicago and the whole state, but they were also on America's Most Wanted list now. There was a picture of Michael as well, with an amber alert, and this way, they had become not just criminals involved in multiple homicides but kidnappers as well. Maya knew that if you were some kind of bank robber or a husband who had killed his wife and her lover, you could flee through small towns, and no one would care much. But if you were a child predator, then even the police could not save you from the angry hands of society.

"Smart move, Cloudy…Smart move," said Maya to the screen.

"Any news about Dan's parents?" Michael had already blocked the two long windows, and now, if they needed to turn on lights in the evening, their presence would be less noticeable.

"Nothing yet. But I wouldn't trust anything it says anyway…Hmmm, but this is interesting."

"What is?" Michael began moving stuff away from a corner next to the sofa in order to make a "bed" for the others. There was an old-fashioned radiator that might provide them a bit of warmth and peace while they slept.

Maya did not answer. She had just found out why the cops had switched their attention from Maya to Howell when he showed his badge. Cloudy had come up with the story that FBI Agent Phillip Howell was killed on a mission two years ago and that his body had been found a couple of days later with no clothes, badge, or gun, and so whoever was helping Maya Polanski was impersonating a Federal Agent, and might in fact be the suspected killer of the real Howell.

She refreshed the page, and "Breaking News" appeared. There was a picture from the gas station with the dead cops and Maya and Phillip holding guns. "Chicago Couple kills 17 policemen and 24 civilians, leaving no witnesses."

"Oh, we are so screwed!"

"How bad?" asked Dan, walking into the room holding a pile of emergency blankets.

Michael also moved toward Maya.

"Not sure you wanna see this, Michael…Maybe it's a lie, and the police and witnesses are all alive." Deep inside, Maya hoped this was just another media twist, Photoshopped with a loud title to put more people after them. But she knew that if the real cops were alive, they would have told the truth, and the witnesses would have come forward. Could Cloudy risk that much?

Phillip began to moan in pain. Maya grabbed a plastic cup, filled it with some water, and sat down next to the agent. It took a lot of effort to make him drink.

"He's burning up…Did he get shot, maybe?" Maya started looking for bullet wounds they might have missed, but there was no sign of blood.

"They killed them all after we left?" Michael finished reading the article. "But why?"

He really could not understand. How do you explain to the most innocent person the great capacity for evil in this world?

"They just didn't want anyone left who could tell the truth," tried Dan.

"So...Is this because of me?"

"No!" yelled Maya, jumping in. "Michael, this is not your fault. Those people are just bad, really bad!"

Michael was looking at the screen with its fake picture.

"But they're lying. I brought them back to life!"

"I know. Dan knows...Maybe after FBI is better, we can contact some of his friends, and they'll help us figure this mess out."

Phillip moaned again as if in agreement. Maya took an old T-shirt and soaked it with a bit of cold water. Gently, she pressed it against Howell's forehead. She tried to calm him down, and then a crazy idea came to her. She closed her eyes, trying to remember how it happened when she had helped Dan and tried to send some light into the suffering agent.

Nothing happened...But Dan and Michael seemed to notice her attempt.

"Am I going to get older too?"

"No, you won't," said Michael, who came beside Phillip and touched his hand. "I hope you'll see the difference."

After that, Howell's face changed, and he exhaled deeply as if someone had removed a heavy weight from his chest. His moaning stopped. He fell asleep, quiet and peaceful. Maya did not even see sparks of light or the movement of magic in the air. And Michael looked exactly the same. Maybe now would be a good time to ask him for an explanation of how it all worked, but then he got up and left the room before she could say anything.

"He'll be okay. He just needs some time," said Dan, grabbing a couple of blankets that he had brought. He covered Howell with one, gave Maya another, and wrapped himself in the third as he sat down next to the warm radiator.

Maya stood, went over to the huge lab sink, and washed her face and hands. After a pause, she just put her whole head under a stream of water and splashed around like a heron in a sparrow's birdbath, washing her hair. The soap was terrible, with the generic smell of all cheap antibacterial soaps, but it gave her a feeling of cleanliness and unusual warmth. She wiped her hair with paper towels, picked up her blanket, and joined Dan in the corner.

The sound of rain falling started outside, pelting the windows. Maya could hear heavier drops hitting the street, beginning a long conversation with the empty alleys of the old university. From the sound of it, this was going to be a long conversation. They would argue all night long, with the thunder and cold wind, flashes of anger, and crying on the glass panes, leaving lines on the dusty windows.

"He'll get all wet," said Maya, trying to hear if she could detect any lonely footsteps outside the windows.

"Rain...Wind...Earth...Fire. What can they do for him?" Dan was absorbed with thoughts of his own, barely paying attention to Maya.

"So..."

"So what?"

"How does it happen that a guy who was a breathing mummy for the last couple of years knows so much about all of this?"

"About Michael?" Dan smiled sadly. "Not sure you want to hear my answer..."

"Go ahead, amaze me."

"You're not going to believe it anyway."

Maya looked at Dan with an expression that could freeze hell over.

"If I had a quarter for every time I heard that...Cut the crap! What do you know!?"

Dan turned so he could see Maya better and took a deep breath, trying to decide on the easiest way to start his complicated story without getting killed by such an impatient lady.

"Have you heard of Job? A man who was righteous and holy before God?"

"Believe it or not, I did go to Sunday school, so yeah, I know about Job."

"Once, three strangers saw a vision, the exact same vision, and they began to see it every day over the course of nine months. And when all three of them met, they were terrified and confused but felt blessed to be prophets of a great gift that was coming into the world."

Maya looked straight into Dan's eyes. He had no reason to lie and seemed absolutely serious. She had sometimes seen a dream over and over, but it would often have different outcomes and different twists, and it never happened more than three or four times, certainly not over nine months.

"Continue."

"Sadly, no one believed the three. All three were Christians. Two of them were women of faith, and both told their pastors about their dreams, only to be met with disbelief."

"And the third...?"

"He was a pastor himself. But no matter who he talked to, most people would say it was just some kind of parable, a story bending in his soul. But then he met two pastors who told him that they had heard that same story already, and that's how they all met."

"And will I hear that story today, or do I need to subscribe to your services first?"

"One day, in front of the White Throne came many angels. They told God about all the great things they saw in the world, about the lives of his children. They told about the faith they saw, about the good deeds and miracles, no matter how big or small, and the Almighty was pleased to hear it.

But among those angels came Satan as well. He stayed quietly on the side, smirking about his own business. Then God asked him:

"What is wrong? Or did you not see all of these great things that people do in the name of My Son?"

"Of course I saw," answered Satan. "Not all of them have enough faith to make miracles, but those who do often become famous, popular, and rich. They are well respected, and their fire burns hot and bright. Your angels are always around them, so even I cannot come close enough to challenge their faith!" The evil one gave God his widest smile. "But it is easy to do miracles in the name of Your Son when they can pay for them with blood that they did not have to shed themselves."

"And they do not need to. The blood of My Son is payment for every soul, covering all sins and allowing for any miracle."

"Of course, You are right...All I am saying is that this is why people make miracles. If they had to pay for the healing of others with their own blood, I am not sure they would be willing. Maybe for their family...Maybe for their close friends...But not for their neighbor, not for a stranger."

The Almighty looked at Satan and knew he was lying.

"But you are God! You believe whatever You want, and if Your people start breaking Your own rules, You find a way around it. You said the punishment for sin is death, but instead of killing them, you allow your Son Jesus to be killed. But was it even worth it?"

"It was, it is, and it will be! And I will prove you wrong."

"So be it. Behold, there is a woman who has just become pregnant. The father of the child does not care about her and will not remember her name in the morning. She is weak and will die when she gives birth. Give power to this unborn child, power like none of your people have had. Give him the gift of your faith that he might perform any miracle possible. But...let him pay for those miracles himself."

"And what kind of payment do you want from him?"

"An eye for an eye…that has gotten tiresome." Satan smiled. "But let him use his own time, his years, the source of his youth for any supernatural act that he will do for others. Little miracles will age him by a day, and big ones—by a year."

"I see what you are trying to do."

"Because You are God, You see all! But let the angels witness how quickly this human will stop using his gift for others, turning into a selfish creature who will not pay the price to help others."

Maya listened intently. She always liked a good parable, and the story of Job always fascinated her. The whole concept of bad things happening to good people might be explained by some eternal games being played in Heaven. While some might see Job as the story of a strong soul who was able to stay fast in his faith till the end, Maya saw a story about how cruel God could be, allowing Satan to play with the lives of His faithful servants. In that story, she found a great reason not to be a follower.

Yes, she did believe in God, but in her own way. She might believe there was a king somewhere in Africa. He existed—good! But she did not really care about it.

"Let's pretend that's true. Then how does it all relate to the Nehushtan clan?"

"It was just a vision. I don't have all the answers, but the one I did have, I gave you. But if I try to think about it logically, I know that snakes are not the most holy symbol. Maybe they are trying to sabotage Michael's mission, to make God lose."

"Then why do they need me? Just to convince him to be selfish? Well, I can do that for sure."

"You still don't believe me…I can't blame you."

Maya shrugged her shoulders. On one hand, it all would explain Michael's power and the whole hassle around his persona. And she had already pushed the boundaries of what she could accept way beyond what a normal person would. She saw the golden sphere and how the police under it came back to life. If that was not a miracle that could change one's perception of the universe, then what would?

But the whole concept of God making a bet with Satan…It was a good moral story that could be published in a religious book and placed in the "faith literature" section of the library. No more, no less.

"When Mom told me the story about her dream, I didn't believe her either."

Another wrecking ball smashed the boundaries of her disbelief.

"Valery was one of those three?"

"Yes. The other two were the pastor in Lake City's 'New Life Church' and Valentina, Michael's adopted mother."

Hundreds of new questions began to circle through Maya's head, and she was not sure which to ask first.

"Hold on…You know Valentina? Wait? So your mom knew there was a boy who could save you all this time and didn't go for help?"

Dan looked at Maya, and she knew deep inside that he probably asked himself this question every day while he was paralyzed.

"What do you think would happen to Michael if all the people who knew about my accident found out about my miraculous recovery? Do you think people would leave him alone?"

"No…of course not." Maya tried to place herself in Valery's shoes, trying to process how she would feel. Could she be mature and humble enough not to drag a little boy into her house and make him heal her son? Even if that boy would not just age, but die…? And then another thought struck Maya that raised goosebumps all over her body. "How old were you when your mom told you about this since you're able to remember it so clearly?"

"Her visions stopped the day Michael was born, not long before my car accident…about four years ago."

*

The storm roared through the halls of the old church building, shaking the foundation and the broken stained-glass windows. Police tape overlapped construction warning signs, and some doors were sealed with restriction notices. There had been rumors that the mayor planned to turn the historical building into a shelter for teenagers, but the remodeling kept being postponed due to high criminal activity in the area.

A lonely, shadowy figure appeared from the long alley and crossed straight through the abandoned church's garden to the side entrance where the seals on the door were already broken. At this late hour, most of Chicago's more cautious citizens would have avoided such an area, but this man was more than just human, and little in this world could scare him. The shadow from his cape, spreading on the wind, created cover and absorbed the light all around. Even the statues of the saints lost their human-like glow and turned back into carved rocks. If darkness were a living creature, this man could be her son.

He pushed open the door and walked into a hallway confidently like he was the archbishop and not a servant of hell. The creature in human form walked down the long hallway and turned toward the stairs leading below.

His steps were quiet and light, and only the most careful listener could have detected the slow rustling of snake scales against the marbled floor. Despite the inky darkness, he did not miss a single step, and when he reached the bottom, he almost instinctively found the doorknob and pulled the gate open.

With a creaking noise, the old metal grill let him into the crypt.

"You're almost on time," said an elderly female voice, as squeaky as the gate's hinges.

"I am here, and that's all that matters," answered the man with a slight tone of irritation.

"Of course…Shall we begin?"

Without waiting for an answer, the old woman clapped her hands, and a thousand candles in the room lit up, filling the crypt with a blinding bright light. The man hissed, and for a brief moment, his eyes sparked with a yellow glow, the pupils shrinking into thin vertical lines. It took him a minute to calm down before his eyes returned to their human shape and blue color.

A new table and two chairs had been set up in the middle of the old crypt. Under the glow of the candles, the ageless woman, covered with layers of scarves and golden jewelry, was placing cards on top of strangely drawn maps.

"Really, witch? Next time, save your cheap tricks for the circus."

"So spiteful, snakelet, taking away this last joy from an old lady. You know we are not allowed to perform in front of people."

"I'm here for information, not a show."

The old witch was dressed in fairly modern but somewhat eccentric attire. After pulling her long, silver hair back and tying it into a knot, she tugged up the sleeves of her wax-covered sweater.

"Fine…Sit down, then. Who are you looking for now?"

"Are you a seer or not?"

The witch smirked at the hooded man, imagining what terrible things she could do to him were it not for the rules she had to obey. Slowly, she began to shuffle the old deck of cards in her hands, keeping her eyes fixed on her guest.

"I'm in a bit of a hurry," said the man, ignoring her invitation to sit.

"I know, but the cards are not newspapers. You can't read everything in the first headline. I'm sure Maya knows all about that."

This time, the visitor smirked at the old witch's words. He lowered his hood and sat down across from her. She kept on shuffling and looking across at her visitor. He was not a mere pawn and was almost definitely higher up in the chain of command, as indicated by the layers of tattoos covering his shaved head and jawline.

"Was it painful, your first scale?"

On reflex, the man touched one of the tattoos behind his ear, remembering. He had been about six years old when they found him and offered him a place in the charter school with full scholarship and financial support. He was only a child, and the alcoholic who was his biological father had access to the funds, much of which he drank away. The boy was not scared but happy to have his own room instead of a corner mattress in the small trailer, as well as a clean bed he did not have to share with fleas or bugs.

That same day, he got a tattoo. The Tattoo, actually! The witches always used potions and elixirs for their rituals, and some of them, centuries ago, had invented a special formula for the ink with powdered bits of the real Nehushtan's head. It was just one scale behind each ear, but it hurt as though someone had pierced through the skull and scarred his brain. Six out of ten died after the ritual. He survived. He suffered a couple weeks of fevers and agony, but then rebirth was not an easy process. That day, he also received a new name—Asmodeus XVII, but the others just called him Asmo.

He saw that some of the clan members had more than one tattoo, and it scared him, but the elder boys assured him that after you "hatch," the new scales just grow through the skin. It did hurt a little, but the pain was more pleasure than suffering.

Many years later, someone opened his father's eyes to the truth about the school, and he came to the conclusion that they were not paying enough for his silence. He foolishly decided to blackmail the Nehushtan clan, telling them that if they did not pay him triple, he would go to the newspapers and tell them all that his son had been taken away, along with many other boys, to be used at the school to pleasure wealthy elites.

Asmo was not sure what made him angrier, that his father thought he had sold him as a sex slave or that he wanted more money for it.

Well, it was a mistake that his father paid for with his own life. The clan made the teenage Asmo kill his own father. Was it hard? Not at all! He did not even have to move a finger. All he did was make his father thirsty, so thirsty that he could not stop drinking. He would empty bottle after bottle, drowning himself. He cried. He even wet himself but kept drinking the cheap booze until he passed out unconscious.

The next week, when police came on reports of a strange odor, they found his swollen body and wrote down "alcohol poisoning" as the cause of death.

On the day his father died, Asmo hatched. Five new scales appeared on each side of his head and neck, and since then, his skills had become much more powerful. None of his teachers ever doubted his potential. He showed all the signs, and while his mind-controlling abilities were maybe not the strongest, his techniques were so very creative that he never left a trail of his own thoughts injected into his victims.

Hatching was significant for each member of the clan, as it was the source of power and the basis for ranking members. New scales would grow only after the most challenging tasks, and the more scales you had, the stronger you became. Duels and mental combat among members were encouraged by the elders because practice outside of the school was prohibited and could be punished by death. The Head of Nehushtan was a secret organization, potentially able to overthrow any government, and such was their ultimate goal. But until then, they needed to keep a low profile, and only the elders were allowed to use their skills in the open.

Until the last week, that is…

"I don't remember," lied Asmo. He wondered if he would have enough power to compel the witch to read the cards any faster.

"Hey, hey, hey!" The old seer looked down at him. "Don't you dare."

A strong sorceress could feel mental waves. While the nature of their magic power did not come not from ink, they still served the same master. Members of the clan often tried to force each other into submission, sometimes for fun, sometimes as proof of dominance, but with the witches, such actions could end very badly. If you tried mind control on the old hag, her entire coven would come after you.

"So...Did he hatch?" The witch raised her eyes again from the cards and looked at her visitor. "The Great Snake, has he hatched?"

"You're the seer here."

The witch did not like him; he could feel it, but that was normal. They were allies but not friends. She looked straight into his eyes as though she was the one able to control his mind. She glared, but her hands always remained on the cards, shuffling and laying them out across the map.

"So, can you find him?"

"I can see all of them, but I'm not sure you could handle them all on your own."

Asmodeus XVII was indeed one of the youngest among the elders, and he had hatched fairly recently, but his scales grew at an exponential rate. Who was she to know what he could handle?

"What a waste of time..." He tried to stand up, but the witch's hair moved as though every curl were a snake, and the flames of the candles rose up to the ceiling, filling the crypt with the orange glow of hell. An unseen force pulled him back into his chair.

"Sit quietly!" hissed the seer with a strangely deep voice. Her fingers grew longer, bending at unnatural angles while she continued to shuffle the old, rune-covered cards. The images began to change so quickly, like in a child's flip book where the still pictures would turn into an animation. But what he saw was more than stick figures. The images were unbelievably realistic and detailed. The map spread across the table began to magnify, focusing in on an area where four dots were glowing. He knew where it was and could probably get there in an hour, maybe less.

Asmo humorously wondered if the witches were the ones who invented the GPS system as it is now. Then, the cards showed him three of the four sleeping inside a basement room. The images, though mere drawings, revealed even the smallest details, like the wrinkles around Maya's eyes, the blue rings under Dan's, and the tears in Phillip's...

"Show me the boy!"

The witch smiled but did not lose eye contact with her impatient guest. Her fingers flipped through the deck of cards, and her deformed fingers rearranged their order until the elder of Nehushtan could see a young man walking under the rain among tall, old trees.

"Are you sure that's him?"

The witch did not answer, but what happened next with the images stunned them both. The young man on whom they were spying through the moving cards seemed to hear the question and turned his face to look straight back at Asmo.

All of the scales on his skin activated as they did, only in moments of dueling or mental attacks. The boy was challenging him through the distance, through the cards. Among the clan members, only a magistrate like Cloudy could have done something equal, and the majority of members, even the elders, required direct eye contact with their victim to perform mental combat.

The witch grew pale and started wheezing as though something crushed her insides, but her fingers continued to flip the cards, some of which began to fly off the deck.

Asmo tried to move, but the charm the witch had placed on the room was still in effect. His skin began to burn, and it was most definitely not a pleasurable pain. He felt every single tattoo, felt how they began melting under the sight of the young man.

The hag began to scream, her eyes turning red as though she were staring straight into the sun. Her strength and control failing, the cards split more and more from the deck, covering the table, the floor, and the old shelves. Hundreds upon hundreds of cards filled the air, though her deck never changed in thickness.

The candles burned fast and hot like each one was connected to its own gas line. The seer could barely breathe, and her dry old body jerked around in convulsions, her voice shifting from a deep wheezing into a high-pitched note. She reacted like a fish thrown into a hot pan... Asmodeus felt the same. His tattoos burned like a wire net that had made contact with high-voltage electricity.

"Sto-o-o-op this! STOP!"

The witch could not hear anything except her own shrieking.

Asmo made another attempt to overcome her charm, and this time, the gravitational force weakened and allowed him to raise his hand. Fighting through the burning pain, he pushed the table over, knocking down the seer.

She fell together with the chair, and a pile of her cards buried her.

With a strong rush of wind, all the candles dipped into darkness, leaving the glowing scales on Asmo's skin as the only source of light. A sudden silence covered the room, and only the distant raging of the storm outside reminded them of the reality of their circumstances.

The snakehead, for the first time in many years, felt powerless and scared, and apparently the witch felt likewise. Like a beaten dog, she whined helplessly on the floor, covering her blinded eyes.

"You old frog, how could you let him see us?" If he were not so weak, he would have smacked her across the face.

"He is beyond my power...beyond yours..." she cried, curling into a fetal position.

"I will send someone for you. I need to go."

The old seer did not try to stop him but lay whining and whispering spells and wicked prayers. It was possible that she might die, but that was not his business. If so, he would explain everything later to those concerned, but for now, he needed to contact a magistrate before it was too late. The whole clan was in active search, with all eleven elders looking for the boy and Maya.

But was he strong enough, and how many elders could he contact by morning? One of them had already died in a stupid battle next to a gas station. He knew him personally, Lucio XXI. Though crazy in his own way, he was much stronger, and yet he still had fallen.

"The conclave…Tell them. They might not know. The Great Snake is hatching…We all need to be prepared. Everyone needs to know!"

Asmo stopped in the doorway.

He had not seen any point in killing the old witch until now.

He turned back and approached the broken, blind woman whose gray hair resembled the bleached strands of a spider's web covering the floor around her.

"The conclave…"

Asmo bent his knee, carefully taking the witch's hand. Her pulse was weak, and her breath was heavy. She would be dead in minutes, or maybe hours…Or maybe not. She was a witch, after all, and they were known to recover from things far deadlier than a staring contest with holy fire. But he could not risk it.

"Not yet," said Asmo. In his hand appeared a two-bladed dagger, like a long meat fork, slightly curved in the shape of fangs.

As he struck straight into her heart, the seer tried to scream something for the last time, but when he pulled out his weapon, the woman exhaled without a sound.

"No one can know yet…"

He stood up, wiped the bloodied blades on the side of his sleeve, raised his hood over his tattooed head, and left quickly and without a sound like only a snake could.

CHAPTER 15

Phillip jumped upright on the couch, trying to retrieve his gun.

"Bad dream?" Michael looked as though he had been waiting for him to awaken. The boy sat on a high stool next to a relatively clean table, finishing up his breakfast. Swiveling, he positioned himself right in front of the couch where the FBI agent had been sleeping.

Maya and Dan slept on the floor next to him, wrapped in cheap blankets like hamsters in a messy nest, squeezing closer to the old radiator, which was now barely warm. He looked back at Michael and, choosing his words carefully, whispered, "Is this because of me?" Howell could see the change in the boy's appearance. "Was I that bad?"

At first, he thought the boy would not respond, being so occupied by his breakfast cereal. But then he looked up at Phillip, and the agent felt ashamed for even having asked.

"You would have recovered even without my help, but it might have taken a little longer."

"Thank you." Phillip lowered his eyes.

"You're welcome."

"It was terrible. I don't know how to explain it, but it felt like the agony would never end…"

"Then I hope you make the right choice," responded Michael, shoveling in another spoonful of cereal. "Hungry? I got some milk and a couple boxes of cereal from Samantha. She works in the cafeteria and was nice enough to give them to me."

Phillip nodded like he understood who this Samantha was or why she would bring them food from the university kitchen. The agent got up as quietly as possible. Wrapped in a blanket, he moved over to Michael, taking a seat right next to him. The cold floor burned his bare feet, but he did not care much about it at the moment.

"Did you tell her?" he asked, lowering his voice as much as possible.

"No. That's your job." Michael smiled sadly.

"I wish I could fix everything..." Phillip glanced at Maya, who was sleeping so peacefully. She looked harmless, but in reality, she was possibly the most dangerous person he had ever met. Her passion, her recklessness. She was a sleeping volcano, and he was not sure if he wanted to be the one to wake her. Literally or figuratively.

Some people can sense another person staring at them, or maybe his thoughts were too loud because Maya woke up and looked straight at Phillip. It was fairly unexpected, but he did not blink or look away. Her reaction was beautiful as well. She smiled at him, and he blushed. Yes, he, who had not had an uncontrolled emotion for such a long time.

"That's cute, FBI. Looks like your cheeks aren't the only things happy to see me."

Howell, remembering that he was dressed only in underwear and a blanket, turned away from her quickly, feeling his face burn with embarrassment.

"Oh, relax. I count it as a compliment. Your clothes are there. I needed to undress you." She hopped up, picked up his pants, and threw them at him. "You were burning up last night, and I had to wipe you down with a cool, wet cloth."

"Thank you," said Phillip, still not looking at her while putting on his pants.

"No, no, thank you," said Maya, smiling and winking. "So, what's for breakfast?"

"Apparently, someone gave Michael a couple boxes of cereal."

Maya looked at Michael, remembering the conversation they had had with Dan the night before, and, seeing his face, felt like the gears in her head were grinding and straining to understand the change in his appearance. She just recently met the teenager, who looked like a young man now, and in reality, he was just a four-year-old boy. So how should she communicate with him? His body transformed quickly—yes, but did his maturity level keep up? Maybe everything about him that she found strange and odd was just normal, childlike behavior. But he did not cry for his mom, play with toy cars, run around picking fights with Dan, or jump on the couch. It was all so complicated.

"What time did you get back?" asked Maya, sounding to herself exactly like her mother.

"Maybe an hour ago. We might need to leave this place. They know we're on campus."

"You saw them?" Maya, who did not bother to make her own bowl of cereal, picked up the one that Phillip had just poured.

"Not with my eyes..." It seemed like he did not plan to finish that sentence.

Maya took a spoonful and gave herself time to finish chewing while assembling a line of thoughts.

"Okay, Michael. I get it. No more doubts about it. You are not like us, which is not a bad thing, but you really are different, and that's great! Yes, I still don't understand a lot of things, and the events of the last week have proven for sure that my worldview is not as broad as I thought. But, honey, we're in the same boat now. If you need to withhold something about your life or mission, that is okay. But if we're talking about the safety of the whole group, try to keep us in the loop."

With that, she took another heaping spoonful.

Maya could see that her words reached the target. He was thinking and was trying to decide on something that no normal four-year-old ever would.

"We can go to my grandparents'. They have a farmhouse in Idaho. It might be safer," offered Dan, who had woken up a moment before.

"Not really. After everything that happened at your parents' house, all of your relatives, and especially the really close ones, will be under surveillance."

"Well, I might have a nice place for us…" Maya smirked. "I have a house that no one knows about."

"Are you talking about your beach house in Florida?" Phillip smirked back at Maya. "The FBI has known about it for a while now. I'm sure the snakeheads know about it as well."

Maya opened her mouth, wanting to say something, but nothing came to mind. She seriously believed that she had outsmarted everyone and that she had a great a backup plan, but apparently, it was just another delusion.

"We can't hide forever," stated Michael. Normally, he was calm and almost emotionless, but today, troubling thoughts were written all over his face.

"If only we knew what they need from you…and me. Then we'd know what to do next." Maya was obviously fishing, figuring that if Michael was ready to involve them more, he might just need a little nudge.

"You're right. They need me and you. But they don't need Phillip anymore, and Dan, he's in danger now."

Maya was shocked to hear a straight answer. It was not quite what she was after, but it was more than she hoped for.

"Okay. You want to split up? You think they'll be safer without us?"

Both Dan and Phillip stopped moving. One would think their opinion would have some value when they were talking about their very lives, but they both knew that right now, it was better to trust Michael.

"They will not survive without us. We can't leave them behind."

"Are you sure about that?" Maya knew he was sure. Otherwise, he would not have said it, but she needed to hear the confirmation for her own assurance.

"I know why they need me, and it's more than likely that they will use you to leverage me...But they have all they need from Phillip and Dan... They are just unwanted witnesses now."

"Right..."

Maya took another spoon of cereal, though her stomach was now as heavy as a boulder.

"Michael, as you know, this is all really new to me. I didn't ask for it, wasn't looking for it, and if God is real, then with Him as my witness, all of this is overcomplicating my life to an unbearable level. If there's even a slight chance for a happy ending—I'd like to know now. I need some kind of hope. And if the only way to achieve the best solution is to blindly follow you, I'll shut up and do exactly what you say. I won't question you, bother you, or bore you with my nonsense. BUT! If we can work as a team, if we can get out of this shit alive and together, please tell us! Let us help! We don't know what you know for sure, but we might have other suggestions that could prove useful. Does that make sense?"

Michael was not upset, and he even smiled back at Maya.

"You have a plan already." It was not a question. He knew it.

"Hell yes! I always have a plan! If you say we can't hide, then we need to fight!"

"Interesting. And how do you plan to do that?" Phillip, who was still recovering from the last fight, was more than a bit skeptical.

"We're going to Cambridge!"

"Cambridge? What's wrong with this university?" asked Dan, smiling.

"Exactly! This place reminded me of it. I have an old friend who works there, and he's a genius! A bookworm with a phenomenal memory! His senior project was about cults in America. I'm more than sure he'll know something that could help us.

"There's not much public knowledge about the Head of Nehushtan, so I wouldn't be so sure."

"That's okay. If there was ever a leak or any cross-reference, he would remember it. He works better than any search engine. And remember everything. Everyone calls him "Gigabyte." You've heard about photographic memory? That's Charles. He's a freak! But the coolest freak in the world. And if he's ever read anything about a clan with the power of hypnosis, he'll be able to point us in the right direction."

"If you say so."

"Everyone has a flaw. We just need to find their weak spot, and then we might at least have a chance."

"Fine. If we leave now, we might get there before midnight."

"Hmm. I'm not sure my Jeep can handle it," said Dan, feeling guilty. "I'm sure Dad took good care of it, but it had problems with long-distance travel even before."

"Then we'll borrow some new wheels." Maya picked up Phillip's gun, playfully adjusting it in her hand. "So, are we ready for a road trip?"

Phillip stood and carefully took the gun out of Maya's hand.

"Cambridge it is…Even though I think it's just a waste of time, that's better than hiding here."

*

Rain had poured the whole night long, giving summer its last rites and paving the way for autumn. It washed away all of the warm colors from the sky and knocked down the last leaves from the trees, making the campus grounds look pathetic and naked. Even the sun was a washed-out, de-saturated blob spilling behind the curtain of clouds.

If humans could hibernate, Maya would have taken the opportunity, and even the small, dusty lab would not have posed any problem. She would wrap herself in plenty of blankets and hide next to the warm radiator until the storm, winter, and cult hunting were passed. Who knows? Maybe by spring, no one would even remember that she exists? Though it was dusty, and not enough light passed through the blocked windows, the old brick walls at least gave her the illusion of protection and a temporary peace. Outside, it was windy, wet, and already very dangerous.

Four members of the Nehushtan cult stood casually next to the Jeep. Its tires were punctured, and a strong smell of gasoline fumes hung in the air. They did not even pretend to hide, and they were not worried about what people might think of them. They just stood under the rain, quietly waiting for the runaways to venture closer.

"Apparently, we need a new car sooner than I thought," noted Dan.

"There was no need for them to ruin all the tires and the gas line!" Maya hated these kinds of senseless vandalism, and although they would be better off running, this provocation just enraged her.

"Should we go back inside…?"

"They want to talk," answered Michael, moving forward.

The four men, in their soaking-wet hoodies, talking amongst themselves, froze suddenly and spread their shoulders in one synchronized motion as Michael approached.

"You'd better step aside." Michael kept walking toward them, but they held their ground like deaf and blind mannequins, frozen under the pouring rain. "You will return to your master…"

"You must come with us. There is no other way," spoke all four in unison.

217

Their voices were different. One of them was deep, scratchy, old, while another had the higher pitch of youth, but they all spoke with the same familiar intonation.

"You have no hold over me! You can't control me."

"We know…But you will come if you value their lives." All four raised their hands and pointed toward Dan and Phillip.

"They're under my protection," insisted Michael, cutting them down. For the first time, Maya heard a note of anger in his voice. Maybe it was because he had grown up and his voice had deepened.

"If you walk away, they will all go too…forever." It was not even a threat but more like a simple fact that Cloudy was stating through his messengers. Fear found the weakest spot in Maya's armor, and she felt his slippery, cold fingers underneath her soul. Not thinking, she moved closer to Phillip and squeezed his arm like a little girl.

"We are all leaving, and none of you will try to stop us!" This was a command, not a suggestion.

"Surrender, and they will live." One of the men snapped his fingers, and a flame, like a burning flower, appeared in his palm.

Just then, Maya realized why it smelled so strongly like gas. The water in which they stood was not just rain. If he were to drop this "flower," all of them would be consumed by fire.

"You're not going to do that."

"Come with me, Michael, and I promise that Phillip and Dan can go free."

Maya was not surprised. She knew Cloudy would not let her off so easily, but maybe they should surrender after all. They had escaped before, and they could do it again. It might be easier to do if it were just her and Michael.

"Cloudy's controlling them…Can you counter his charm?"

"I could if it had been done against their will. But all four chose to submit to him."

"He must be somewhere close." Phillip looked around cautiously, scanning the roofs and empty windows. "Even for him to control four people at the same time, he would need visual contact with them."

"Come with me. I'll ask you one last time."

"Maybe we should run in different directions? That might make him lose focus?" Dan was ready to run long before then.

"No…You must stay with me. Otherwise, I might not be able to save you. There might be more than these four around."

"I'll count to three, Miracle Worker," said all four in sync. "One…"

"Please stop. Don't do this!" Michael was not scared and did not sound like he was begging for mercy.

"Two…"

"You don't understand what you're doing!" There was so much compassion in his words.

"Three!" The man with the flame lowered his palm and touched the ground. The three others threw black dust into the air, which made the flame go blue and grow in intensity.

Maya's first instinct was to close her eyes, but she knew that if she did, she would miss another miracle.

The roaring flames moved toward them. First, they would burn Michael, then she and Phillip, and even if Dan decided to run, the blue flame would catch up to him.

With his gaze fixed on the attackers, the miracle worker raised his hand, and a soft light surrounded him. A swooping force from heaven hit the ground where Michael stood. Maya, Phillip, and Dan were knocked away from him, and the wave pushed the flame back toward the cult members…

Their waving cloaks instantly caught on fire. Blue hell surrounded them, but they did not even move. Maya saw agony in their eyes, but their bodies were not under their own control.

BOOM!

Dan's Jeep exploded, throwing the snakeheads around like puppets.

Screams! Having lost visual contact with their master, freedom returned to the men just in time for them to feel the searing blue heat devour their flesh. Their screams did not last long. Whatever they had added to the fire made it burn stronger, killing them quicker and evaporating their bodies. A couple moments later, there remained nothing but four piles of ash left on the wet, rainy ground.

Michael turned back and seemed to mumble something to himself. He did not look older, proving Dan's notion that only miracles for the good of others would make him age. Self-defense did not count against him… But something else shocked Maya. Michael was crying. It was not rain. It was tears. He cried for those who had tried to kill him. Did he feel guilty? Could he have stopped the flame without turning it against the attackers? Or maybe it was not he who had stepped up for their protection.

Would she ever understand the depth of his character? Could she ever develop a nature of compassion and a willingness to sacrifice herself for the sake of others?

"Are you okay?" Michael approached Maya and extended his hand toward hers.

"Are YOU?"

He shook his head, but it did not seem like he planned to share what he felt with her right now.

"Well, at least we have a car now." Phillip nodded toward a black sedan that was parked off to one side, similar to those they saw next to Richard's house.

*

Cloudy's trembling fingers slowly moved along the knob of his cane as though he was trying to read some kind of Braille written on it. He and one of his "brothers" were looking through the window of an empty classroom at Maya and her friends as they got into the vehicle and escaped, again, leaving behind the burning Jeep and the remains of their fellow Nehushtan warriors.

"Magister...We must report. The Conclave needs to know what happened. This boy is stronger than we thought. And we need to call for a trial against Asmodeus. He killed a witch, and they will not forget it... The Conclave can..."

Quicker than a striking snake, Cloudy separated the cane's knob from its wooden shaft, releasing two sharp metal blades...They pierced into the other man's neck, and the light of life faded from the eyes of his faithful follower, along with his dangerous suggestions.

"Very soon, I will be The Conclave. The Hatching is near."

CHAPTER 16

Over her rapidly rising journalistic career, Maya had already crossed the USA from the Atlantic to the Pacific at least five or six times on wheels. Rapid pressure changes always hurt her ears, and all of the taking off and landing made traveling by plane simply too uncomfortable. Of course if she needed to get somewhere fast, she could always suffer through it, but if there was no hurry, she would rather drive the long hours than defy gravity.

Partly, it was her personality, and she preferred to be in control. That way, she decided what time to leave and how fast to drive. She stopped in cities on the way if she felt like it or took breaks at scenic viewpoints. She would zoom into a rest area for a bathroom break or simply take her lunchtime flirting with other travelers.

The romantic in her drew inspiration from the waving stripes of the highways. Un-driven roads, forgotten small towns, unpainted lakes, the lives of ordinary people, and forests with creatures rarely seen by humans—all of it spoke to her artistic self. It taught Maya to absorb her surroundings, to process them through the prism of her mind, and then splash them all onto paper.

There was no doubt that her life would never be the same, but if she had to choose between hiding in some peaceful cave for the rest of her life or living on the run, she would always choose the latter. She was made for freedom, a child of wind and fire, untamable, and she would rather die fighting than give up and settle in under a rock.

Trying to be as careful as possible, she changed lanes and exited from the freeway. Everyone was asleep, even though it was barely getting dark. For the first stretch of the road, Phillip had been driving, but for the last five hours or so, she was in charge. Maya would agree with the snakeheads on one thing—they knew how to choose a vehicle. This set of wheels was the finest she had ever driven, but no matter how comfortable the seat was, her legs were begging for a stretch, and her shoulders were getting stiff.

A rest area was hidden among the old, tall forest, but compared to the damp, foggy woods of Oregon, this area was dry and bleached. The trees were not as tall, and they did not grow as closely to each other. Still, one could feel the surrounding protection of nature. The parking lot was almost empty apart from a couple trucks in the distance that might be settling for the night and an Asian family who were taking pictures next to the rest area map. An old male couple shared a sandwich under a brightly lit pergola.

Maya stepped outside, and the fresh scent of autumn in the forest brought chills and goosebumps to her skin. In a couple more weeks, it might even start to snow. Once, she had almost gotten stuck on one of the freeways. Because of a snowstorm, they had closed the road for the night, and she was prepared to trade her car for a sled and reindeer. But being stuck turned out not so bad after all since she was traveling with Bill. They went back to the closest town and rented the last available room in a cheap motel, where they channeled the built-up stress and frustration into a more productive and passionate solution. That is how their romance started if it really was a romance…She did miss him, though.

He was the reason she was involved in all this nonsense. If he had gone to the police right away or simply warned her before sending her out…A little heads-up would have helped her a lot. Maybe they could have run away before it all escalated into this unmanageable mess. But how could she blame him for keeping secrets when she had not told him anything about the cancer? She was not mad at him. Disappointed, yes, but not mad.

She went to the restroom, which was surprisingly cleaner than one would expect from a state property in the middle of nowhere. Another surprise was hot water in the sink and simple but pleasant foaming soap. Gosh, she had seen worse restrooms in hotels. She spent a good five minutes with her hands under a stream of warm water, washed her face, and noticed how little she actually needed in order to recharge.

When she walked outside, Michael was leaving the men's room.

"Oh, what were you doing in there? Or do saints also need to poo—" she choked on this last question, seeing his shocked face. "I'm sorry...I'm sorry that was stupid."

First, it was a smile. Then he smirked. He looked straight at her, his face slowly blushing, and lost it. He started laughing. It was so loud and contagious like only small kids can laugh! Dimples appeared suddenly on his cheeks, and tears in the corners of his eyes.

Maya could not resist and joined him in the laughing madness. The old couple was gone, and the Asian family was about to load into their van, so there was no one to judge, no one to care. Maya laughed to the point that she had pain in her ribs. She could not stop. Oftentimes, she would release through crying, but it seemed that her emotions decided to overflow on her this way instead. A couple times, she would start to calm down, but when she looked at Michael again, they would both start from the beginning.

"Freaks," sighed Phillip on the way to the restroom. His tone was more one of humor than of negativity, and that made Maya break into a new round of laughter.

It took a while before either of them was able to look at the other without recharging their hysteria. Phillip was checking the car, and Dan scraped together all the change he was able to find and spent it all in a vending machine to get a couple bags of chips and pistachios.

*

The evening was getting colder, but Maya did not feel like climbing back into the car. She and Michael settled under an oddly shaped sculpture, sharing one of the bags of chips, and they were the best chips she ever had. Despite everything, she was enjoying this moment. Yes, there were so many unknowns on the way, but right now, she felt peaceful and calm. It was almost like the days when she would go camping with her dad and brothers, the days when life was simple. Even back then, a bag of chips was the best food in the world. A strange impulse made her scoot a bit closer to Michael, and she laid her head on his shoulder. He was not bothered at all and even scooted closer to her...

It was such a small gesture, but there was so much in it, like when your child gives you a hug for the first time or your mean sibling suddenly apologizes for hurting you...Maya felt like crying.

"It's so quiet here, almost unreal."

"Almost like home."

The wind blew the treetops gently, and some nocturnal bird flew up into the air.

"You probably miss them? Your mom...and your brothers and sisters." Maya had to keep reminding herself that Michael was just a four-year-old boy. If she had needed to leave home at the age of four, she would have been devastated.

"I know they are safe. For the next three days, they will stay at church. Pastor will watch over them."

"And how about after? Do you think we'll see them after?"

Michael smiled at her, like a wise old man, realizing that she was innocently trying to pry some hidden knowledge from him.

"You will know everything in your own time."

Maya just shrugged and leaned back on Michael's shoulder.

"Fine. Then tell me what you think about our road trip. Do you like to travel?"

"We never went anywhere. Our van couldn't go far, especially with all of us."

"But where would you like to go?"

Maya pulled a couple more chips from the bag and gave the rest to Michael.

"I don't know. There are so many countries and so many people. All of them have their own thoughts and desires, which created their cultures and traditions. It's probably impossible to go everywhere."

"I knew a guy, a photographer. He traveled all over the world. I think there's no country on the map that he hasn't visited."

"Of course you can visit all the countries. The earth is not that big. But to live, to experience, to understand the people—why they do what they do, why they worship their gods or destroy the temples of their neighbors, how their language evolved, what sounds make them feel brave, and what music puts them asleep…Why a certain combination of spices makes a dish their favorite, and what recipes they keep as secrets or pass along only to family…What meaning the moon cycles have for their heritage, and why some animals are sacred…How do you understand all that after just a brief visit? There's not enough time in one human life to fully understand your own family, let alone the whole world."

Maya forgot how to breathe.

"That is deep shit for a four-year-old."

"Thank you?" Michael smiled at her again. "Age is just a number…"

"Please stop. One more nugget of philosophy, and my brain will self-destruct. Just tell me what you would like to see. Just one simple thing. A country, city, place. Anything human, like maybe something…"

"The ocean." Michael did not have to think long about his response.

"Really?"

"Yeah. Mom has some pictures in her album from when she was a child, and her parents took her to the ocean. It was so beautiful. And she seemed so happy. So yeah, I would like to see the ocean. I'd like to walk on the sand and hear the sound of the waves..."

The cold wind around Maya started to smell like seaweed, and the taste of salt filled the air. Somewhere, far away, she could hear seagulls calling and the faint echo of the roaring surf.

"Would you go there with me?"

Maya just nodded, afraid to say anything, as though the sound of her words might destroy this magical illusion.

"Because what is the point of going to the ocean if you can't share it with people you love?"

And that was it. Maya pushed her face into Michael's shoulder and started sobbing. A kid who just three days ago was nobody was now one of the most valuable people in her life. She wanted to squeeze him and not let go, to hold him till the end of days! If the snakeheads dared to come, they would have to kill her first before they could take him away.

As soon as they were done fighting the cult, they would go south! They would go far away from everyone, so no one would even dare to seek Michael or his gift. Maybe they should leave even now! They could easily cross the border and go live in a small Mexican town, and she could raise him as her own son! She would forbid him to do any miracles! Not even for her! She would find the best girl for him to marry, and he would see his kids grow up! He would age normally with them and would die long after Maya, like any normal person.

"Is she okay? Is she crying?" Phillip's voice sobered her up, and she momentarily distanced herself from Michael.

"No, I'm not...It's just my contact lenses."

"You don't wear contacts."

"Not anymore, but my eyes miss them!" She wiped her face really quickly. "Go-go-go! Can't you see we're talking?!"

"We'd better get back on the road unless you think we should sleep here. It might be safer than any hotels."

For a moment, the thought of a bed, even in a cheap motel, sounded so good and tempting, but if they were on a search list of the most wanted in America, they would need to face Nehushtan's clan faster than she could put her head to the pillow.

"We can keep going. I'm still okay."

"I had a good snooze, and I can drive as well. The question is how rested we want to be when we arrive at our destination."

"That's true. But the car is too small for all of us to comfortably spend a night."

"GUYS! Guys! GUYS!" Dan ran out of the restroom, holding a phone in his hands.

"What, did you just discover social media? I know you were in a coma, but…"

"NO! It's not even my phone!"

"Ewww?" Maya still did not seem to get it.

Phillip did, and he came and took the phone from Dan, checking the screen.

"I found it in the stall!"

"Ewww again!"

"Looks like it belongs to one of those Asian guys who just left, and luckily for us, they did not bother with a password." Phillip was already looking through the settings.

"Is there any internet connection?"

"Just one bar with 3G, but that'll do it."

Maya pulled the phone from Phillip's hands and thoroughly wiped it with the end of her T-shirt.

"I really need five minutes, and I hope the owner will not be back before then."

"Hopefully, you know what you're doing." Phillip looked concerned and reasonably worried.

"Relax, FBI. I'm waiting for a reply from my friend. I wrote to him from Richard's lab. He was supposed to get a hold of Gigabyte."

"Okay…But we'd better leave. Like now."

Maya followed the direction Dan was looking and was barely able to refrain from swearing. The highway patrol was just exiting toward the rest area.

"Be smart." Phillip's voice was colder than the wind. "Everyone get inside, but play it cool. He's just on rounds. Otherwise, there would be way more."

No one needed to explain it twice, but when someone tells you to play it cool or act less suspicious, apparently, your body becomes stiff and your actions stupid. All movement becomes jerky and unreasonable. Destiny decided they had enough on their plate already, and the officer in the car barely glanced at them as he moved toward a group of parked trucks. Maybe the clan's black vehicle was not reported stolen, or the patrol officer had not bothered to memorize every face that showed up in the system, but Phillip was able to leave the parking lot freely and drove them back onto the interstate.

"Great! And people like that are supposed to protect us from criminals?" Maya was relieved and definitely scared, but it was not in her character to admit weakness.

"He's a good man. He just didn't see us. I thought it would be better for everyone that way."

Dan, who was sitting in the front with Phillip, turned back and looked at both Maya and Michael. It was not certain if there was more judgment or worry in his look, but Maya felt exactly the same way. Maya nodded to

Dan, letting him know that she understood, and he turned back. The last thing they needed was to make Michael close up again.

"Sweetie…You can't do that." She sounded exactly like her mother, which made her cringe a little. "You can't waste your energy on little things like this."

"Maybe you're right, but I didn't want anyone else to get harmed."

"But you harmed yourself."

"Not really. If I do something for myself, then it's fine…"

Maya looked at Dan, remembering their late-night conversation.

"How do you know?"

"I can feel it…" Michael turned his face toward the window, looking out at the darkened forest.

"Feel it? Does it hurt?"

Michael kept looking out at nothing in particular, but Maya could see his reflection in the window. She wondered if he was lying to her…if he could even tell lies. Was he capable?

"I do feel something, but it's not related to pain."

"How about regret? I know when a billionaire walks outside on a street full of beggars, he could easily give a hundred-dollar bill to each of them, and at the end of his walk, he would barely notice a change to his bank account. But if a man who works three jobs gives a part of his income to an alcoholic on a street corner instead of his family, I get mad!"

Michael smiled. In his eyes, Maya probably seemed like a child trying to find answers to questions far beyond her understanding. Maybe there were no answers to questions like "Where is the end of the universe?" or "What is the purpose of life?"

"How many billionaires do you know who walk around the streets giving away hundred-dollar bills?"

What could she say? He was right. She had been invited plenty of times to different charity events, masquerade balls, and auctions where the wealthy of this world would throw money to the wind. How much of their finances actually went to a poor family like Michael's or to veterans or animal refuges? All of that was just to show off and to buy more power or simply to launder money before tax season. Rich people liked to stay rich, and the main key to getting more was not giving it away.

"Sacrifice only has meaning if it costs you something personally, and when you give it away, it brings you joy and relief knowing that others might have more need for it than you do."

"Sounds like masochism to me," answered Maya, rolling her eyes. "You really want to tell me that you feel relief when you get older? Fine, I can understand that when you're four years old or even a teenager covered with acne. Everyone wants to grow out of the ugly duckling stage, but right now, you look like you're twenty-twenty-five. If you keep going, then really soon you'll die from old age! What joy and relief is there in that?"

"But what about Dan? He could walk around and enjoy life again. I think that is worth a couple of years, and even when I'm gone, he will still remember me. He is not mad at God anymore for what happened to him. And I only exchanged a couple of my years for decades of his. In all that time, he'll be able to do so much more than I could do in just a couple."

"Listening to you, one might think you'd decided to run for the 'New Messiah' title. Aren't you scared?"

"I'm not trying to be Christ. That's impossible!" He faced her again. "You want to know if I am scared? Of course I am! I'm terrified! I'm afraid of making a mistake. What if I don't have the bravery Jesus had? His sacrifice was unique, and He paid the whole debt for all humanity, for everyone who's ever lived, is alive now, or will live in the future."

"But He was the Son of God…He was a Miracle Worker."

"But He was a human, too. He also had fears and doubts, but He was able to conquer them. You say He was a Miracle Worker, but He gave other people the ability to make miracles, too. Maybe not as big as His, but still. And you know what makes me angry? That others can do what Christ did—love others, be compassionate, be a shoulder to cry on and a helping hand for the fallen—but they don't do any of that when they could, and they wouldn't even age when they did so."

"And funnily enough, we actually enjoy killing time."

"You know what I think caused the most pain to Jesus? Even more than those nails on the cross? He paid with His own life to make all of us better, but we're wasting that gift. And no, I don't think it's funny. I think wasting time is a great tragedy and a sin against Heaven."

Maya did not feel like smiling. Jesus, for her, was always a friend of religious freaks, the perfect baby from Christmas cards, a symbol of somebody's faith. And now...

The car suddenly became so small. Everything around her shrank and felt airless. Maya opened the window a crack to let in a little bit of fresh air, which caught the attention of Phil and Dan. Their looks made the space around her even smaller. More than that, she felt like Jesus Himself was looking at her from Heaven.

No! Jesus was there, right there, sitting right alongside Michael. The way he talked about Him made Him so real and so present that she could barely handle being there. She needed space. She wanted to run and hide. Jesus Christ, the Name she uttered so many times in swearing, was there, had been there, all the time. He saw her. He knew her. He knew everything about her. And now He was so real and present that an open window was not enough.

"Stop the car!"

"What?" Phillip glanced at her in the mirror, but the expression on her face made him pull over to the side.

Before the car had completely stopped, Maya had already opened the door and started running away toward the forest.

Run! Run further away!

Where?! Who knows?! But away! Away from the car! Away from the moon and sun. Away from Michael! Away from his Christ!

Air…Who had sucked all the air away? The huge, endless forest pushed toward her, building walls and grabbing at her clothes, stretching out its dry hands to scratch her face and pull at her hair.

She ran…It was so dark, and there was nothing to breathe. If she could not run, then she would walk…crawl…just move away! Away, away, away!

The crunchy sticks and old leaves tried to swallow her ankles. The cold, rocky earth was supposed to be good for running, but instead, it held her feet like a swamp, making each new step an impossible challenge.

No! She had not asked for all of this! She had her own life. A beautiful, bright, independent life where everything was under her control, and she did not need supernatural help! The natural was perfectly fine. She took so much of it. She was above average. She could plan, build, and move how and where she wanted, and now…He was looking at her. He was real.

No! No. It was easier and simpler without Him. She did not need Him. She made herself the way she wanted. Why should that change? She always had a plan! Even when she became ill, she still had a plan. A vacation. Doctors. Surgery. A low chance of success, but still a chance. Yes, she would be sick for a while or even the rest of her life—maybe she would not be able to work or even write, but there was a plan, and there was no place for Him!

A step! Another step! Go, Maya, go! Run away!

Why did she feel like He was still next to her? Why did she feel like He came here only because of her?

No, she was going mad. Too much had happened over the last week. Anyone could lose their sanity under those circumstances, and she was sick on top of it all! Maybe there were no more symptoms, but she was ill. Something was not right. None of it was right; all of it was so abnormal. She was not normal. Not anymore. He was here!

An old, fallen tree was in the way, and it was too dark to see it in time. Maya fell forward at full speed, tumbling into a pile of old leaves and freshly grown mushrooms. Somewhere in the night, an owl screeched, and a small bird flew away from a bush nearby.

The sudden silence crashed around Maya...And only the sound of His sigh was audible. It was so vivid. She could not handle it anymore.

"A-a-a-a-a-a!" she screamed from the depths of her lungs.

The roar echoed...The pain of loneliness and emptiness squeezed her dry.

The void that had always been inside, around which she had built a nice paper wall, finally broke through, revealing itself. She never admitted that she needed someone, and she especially did not need Him! She had a perfect life!

If she kept repeating this, maybe He would go away. No, He was here because He knew she wanted to talk to Him. Fine! She would talk to Him if that was what He wanted.

She rose up from the ground, still on her knees but not lying in the dirt anymore. If He was there, she would look at Him! Oh, she had a lot to say.

"WHY? Why are You doing this?" she yelled, angrier than she thought. "Why do You need me? This world has plenty of people who would love to kiss up to You! So many who would be pleased to do anything for You! Why me?! I am not the right person for this, simply because I will never be able to understand You. How? How could You look and do nothing when we were killing Your Son? If You didn't care about Him, how can I believe You might care about me?"

"And how about Michael? Why are You doing this? Is this really just a game for You? You are that bored? You are selfish...ageless..."

"How can people believe in Your love? You are mean...spiteful...

Why do I care? I know You don't!

I don't need...I was fine so many years without You! Why would I need you now?!

No! I don't! I don't need...I don't...I..."

She wanted to say it, but she could not. Something inside held her back. Something was changing. Her tightly squeezed fingers slowly spread, letting dirt and leaves fall to the ground. She pushed back, lying on the ground but facing the sky. She couldn't because if she said it, it would be a lie.

"I...I am...I'm sorry..." whispered Maya. "I'm trying to find a reason to hate You. That way, it would be easier to live. Yeah, I can't understand You, especially how You didn't wipe us out when we killed Your Son. We deserved a flood, fire from the sky, or a vacuum instead of oxygen, but You kept putting up with us? Why?

...I never asked You for anything. Even when I knew that I was sick, I did not bother You, but today, I don't care if You hate me or think I'm a hypocrite, but I'll ask You. And I swear, if You answer, I will never bother You again. I'll try to pay You back. Not sure how, but I honestly am going to try. Please...Do not kill Michael. Take his curse away from him. He's not supposed to pay for others with his own life. I don't think that pleases You. Wasn't the life of Your Son enough?

But even if You need this to happen, change it! If someone needs to pay, I can...If this is so important, put this curse on me, but please... please...let Michael live his normal life. I am already dying. Let him live. He's a good boy, and our world really needs a person like him. There are so many like me already...I know that for a fact. Show Your mercy. He cannot die for others. He can't..."

No one answered.

CHAPTER 17

She had lost track of time. It was more likely, actually, that she had simply fallen asleep right on the cold ground, and time, place, feelings, and all things simply ceased to exist. There was a time, back in college, when she had tried some illicit drugs just for the experience.

While the feeling of euphoria lasted, it was all fun and exciting, but the following drop and inability to control the situation scared her enough to conclude that it was not for her. Being a control freak was already a strong enough drug. She did enjoy a good glass of wine, or even two or three from time to time, but when she was prescribed painkillers, she specifically asked for one that did not result in drowsiness.

Right now, she felt a high like never before. She was calm, clearminded, and sensed the greatest peace she had ever experienced. Part of her believed that it was because she had found Him, but the more rational part grumbled somewhere in the back of her mind about her cancer taking over her senses and sanity.

"Maya!" Phillip's voice seemed to call from another universe. "Maya!"

She was there, lying in the old grass and dry leaves, pondering when it might have rained last in those woods. Such thoughts seemed far more important than coming back to reality.

"MAYA!"

She looked in the direction of his voice and saw a little spark of light coming from between the dark shadows of ancient trees. If she lay there really quietly, perhaps the FBI would walk right past her. Maybe in an hour or so, he would give up and go back, or maybe sooner, depending on how much battery life was left in his phone. What else would he be using to make that shining little spark?

The dying moon crept up from behind the clouds, turning the surroundings into an abstract painting with a dominant blue and chaotic black, like in those overpriced paintings where the artist spills ink onto the canvas and lets gravity do most of the job for him.

"Maya!?"

He was closer. To his credit, he was a good agent with decent tracking skills, though when someone like her rushed through the woods like a cow, breaking every branch in her way, one would hardly need a wide skillset to track her down.

"I'm here!" she replied, not even considering standing up.

Before, his steps sounded cautious, but now he rushed toward her voice, and the bright light in his hands hit her right in the eyes.

"Turn it off!" It was indeed the flashlight on his cell phone.

"Are you okay?" Phillip moved the light away from her face and shone it on her body. "Did you hurt anything?"

"I don't think so...just my ego." She stretched out her arm for him to help her to her feet.

"Good, it was too big anyway." He grabbed her arm and tried to pull her upward.

"Oh really? You think so?" She shifted her weight and, instead of getting up, pulled him down.

Not anticipating her trick, Phillip fell headlong toward Maya but managed to land on one knee and an elbow to avoid a collision.

The cell phone flew to the side, skittering over some leaves until it stopped, shining into his face. His suddenly very cute face. No, even before she had noticed how attractive he was, especially with the scruff growing on his cheeks and adorable jawline. Maybe it was regulation in the Bureau to be clean-shaven, and what a pity that was because, after a few days on the run, his short beard added such a sexy alpha male look to him.

"I think you might be crazy." Phillip smiled, noticing her gazing longingly into his eyes.

"I think I hit my head a bit too hard..."

She pulled him closer and found his lips with her own.

Time melted again. Hours, days, months, and ages flew past them. The world died and was reborn again. Nations rose and cultures blended, but for Maya, nothing existed anymore apart from his lips, which tasted like the awakening of a new era. Waves of desire and shame crashed against each other within her, like two oceans that met in the middle of a human-shaped vase.

At first, his lips felt so cold and distant, afraid and even trembling, but then they began to respond to her every move. They bent, attacked, curved, and slid...Those lips were a symbiotic addition to her own, and they adjusted to hers as though he was reading Maya's mind.

She felt his breath, the scruff on his cheek, his hands and elbows, his knees, his torso...He was so close to her, and she felt wanted. She raised her hands, not sure what she would do: either push him away and stop this madness or pull him even closer. She knew he was waiting for a sign from her. He was such a gentleman, and that made her desire even stronger.

Maya should have known better. Sex always complicates matters. If she let it happen here in the forest, then no matter what it meant, things would not be the same afterward. Right now, there were enough complications in their story, but his hair, his body, his lips...

She let her fingers comb through his hair, and it was softer than she thought. The tips of her nails dug slightly into his scalp, and his lips moved more aggressively in response. It was exactly how she liked it!

He kissed her cheek, her neck…

Goodbye, rational thinking! Oh, there was no more thinking at all.

His kiss on her neck made her skin come alive. Her breath grew shallow. This would be the first time she had made love in the woods, and there was not even a tent or blanket between them and nature. She opened her eyes. The damn flashlight was still shining right on them.

Whatever. She did not care! The boys had better stay in the car, though! She stroked Phillip's hair, letting him know that he was doing everything just right. She kissed him on the cheek and pulled him closer and closer. She pulled on his ear…

Scales…

The little source of light still shining on them revealed a couple scale tattoos behind Phillip's ear…

Ice fell on her and rolled from her toes to the tips of her hair. She lost her breath now for an entirely different reason, and thousands of panicked thoughts washed over her mind, screaming louder and faster than the beating of her heart.

Phillip stopped, sensing that something was wrong. "Is everything okay?"

It was not easy to keep any semblance of calm.

"I'm…We need to stop." She carefully climbed out from under him.

"Did I do something wrong?" He looked at her with such confusion and perhaps even a bit of shame or guilt.

"No. No…" she lied, trying to act as natural as possible. "We shouldn't. The boys might come…"

Tattoos like a snake's skin! They were exactly the same shape and size as those of the clan members. They all had those tattoos, all of them! Some had fewer, some had more, but they were all the same...Why did Phillip have them? Maybe it was an illusion? Just some dirt that had stuck when he fell to the ground?

"Yeah. You're right. I'm sorry." Phillip stood, avoiding eye contact.

All this time? Was he one of them all this time? That was how they found them so easily everywhere they went! Of course! How blind was she?

Not anymore.

"Don't forget the phone." Maya leaned down to adjust her shoe and pointed toward the shining gadget. As he turned to retrieve it, her fingers slowly moved toward a heavy-looking branch on the ground.

"Right..."

The agent took a couple steps, bent his knee, stretched out his arm...

Maya had never played baseball, but she had swung a bat before. She put so much strength into her hit that the sudden crack startled her.

Phillip, not expecting anything, tumbled down into the old leaves without any movement or sound. The cracking had come from the branch and not from his skull. Maya leaned closer, picked up the phone, and shone it toward Phillip's head. Only a couple tattoos were behind the ear, but a long chain of them curled and spread far back into his hairline.

Maya jumped back.

He was one of them. Under his hair, he might have hundreds of tattoos.

"You son of a witch!" She kicked him, trying to overcome the emotions that were tearing her apart. Why was he doing all of this? Why had he saved her so many times? Was it all a grand, theatrical act?

She raced back through her memory, trying to remember every step, every detail. Nothing he had said could be counted as truth. Did he even work for the FBI? But he had the badge, the gun...

The gun! Right. Maya bent down again, pulled the gun off of him, and rifled through his pockets.

A snakehead! She kissed a snakehead!

Why was she so stupid? Did Cloudy start this game? How did he get the information to them? Would they find him soon? Had he already had a chance to report back to them about Gigabyte and their destination?

Phillip stirred. Squinting, Maya could just make out the vein on his neck and saw that it was still pulsating.

She stood slowly and thumbed through the cell phone's recent call history. There was a call to a Chicago number about thirty minutes earlier.

So dumb! So naïve! So clueless! Well, not anymore. Her teeth ground together at the thought of having been played so easily.

She needed to get to safety.

He made her trust him, even fall for him. Was it that easy? Was she that simple-minded? That predictable? Tears streamed down her face, but she briskly wiped them away and forced herself to snap out of it. It was her own fault, after all. She had always known when to admit her mistakes, no not to others, of course, but she always had to be honest with herself. He was a huge mistake. He was her flaw. But she would soon fix that!

"You motherfu…"

*

Dan woke suddenly at the sound of a gunshot emanating from the forest.

Another one sent his heart into a gallop. He looked around, noticing that he had been left alone. Fighting the desire to hide or climb behind the wheel and drive away, he simply sat in place, frozen in fear.

The car shook a little, and he realized that someone was sitting on top of the trunk. Shaking, he leaned closer to see who it was and heaved a sigh of relief. Dan opened the door and stepped outside.

"Michael, did you hear that?"

"The shots? Yeah, I did." Michael was looking intently up at the sky, but he did not sound worried or even concerned. As usual.

Dan walked around and climbed up onto the trunk as well.

"Should we be worried?"

"Not about Maya..." Michael looked at Dan and smiled. "But if I was you, I wouldn't ask her anything...especially for the next couple hours."

Michael jumped down and headed back into the car.

"Come on, Dan, she's coming, and we will need to leave immediately. You'd better get behind the wheel. She'll be in no mood to drive right now."

Dan knew it was best not to argue, and so he went straight to the front and adjusted the driver's seat and mirror. Before he started the engine, he froze for a moment.

"Just her? Not Phillip?"

Michael did not answer, but just then, the passenger door opened, and Maya jumped inside with a look that explained more than actual words.

"Drive! Now, now, NOW!"

Dan nodded and pressed the accelerator, flying onto the empty road.

Maya breathed so heavily from anger that she thought she might start to spit fire. Dan tried to look at her from the corner of his eyes and understood why Michael had told him not to ask her about anything. She was a total mess. Her jaw muscles turned into steel pistons, like those that move the wheels of a steam engine. Her face went back and forth from being pale to flushed.

"You need to calm down, or you'll have a stroke," said Dan as carefully as possible. Maya glared at him with such a look of ire that he thought she might just tear his head off with her bare hands.

"I told you…" whispered Michael timidly. Maya swung her whole body back to face him.

"Did you know? OF COURSE you knew!"

Maya fought so hard not to let the hysteria take her over completely.

"How could you do that? You helped him even though you knew he was a snakehead!"

"What?!" Now Dan looked shocked.

"Shut up and drive!" snipped Maya.

"Why did you help him!?"

"I could see that you cared about him. I saw you wanted to help…"

"I trusted you! I trusted him! You're supposed to tell me!"

"Are you mad at me or at yourself for caring for him?"

Maya squeezed her hands into fists until her knuckles turned white.

"NO! Do not even! Shut up! I don't want to hear a word from you anymore! I am DONE listening to you! I am SO done with you!" Maya heard Dan inhale as if he was about to say something, but she cut him off before he could even let out a peep. "And you too! We get to Washington, and we're done!"

"You don't mean that!" Michael tried to touch Maya's shoulder, but she was faster.

"Don't even try to use your voodoo on me, miracle freak! If Phil…" she tried to say his name, but her mouth almost filled with bile. "FBI was one of them! I doubt he even worked for the FBI. Liars! All of you! Liars! Do you have scales too?!"

Maya reached out violently to look behind Dan's ears, and he was barely able to keep the car in the same lane.

"Okay. Clear! You can stay!" Then she pivoted again and grabbed Michael by the shoulder. "How about you?"

243

He smiled and leaned forward so she could see more easily.

"I'm not one of them, but if it will help, you can check."

For a moment, she hesitated, but then she pulled on his ears and peeked around behind them. He was clean as well…

Either the knowledge brought her relief, or he had tricked her. In touching his ears, something happened to her. It was as though someone had shot her with a huge dose of sedatives.

"Fine…you can stay too…But I'm still mad at you. Both of you!"

"What did I do?" Dan attempted a smile, feeling the change in Maya's voice.

"Nope! Zip it and drive. And you, Michael…I'm very disappointed! I want you to promise me that you won't keep anything from me ever again. Please! Because I'm afraid I'm going to lose my mind before this is all over!"

Maya did not expect Michael to answer her, but he nodded.

"Okay. I promise."

"Really? Okay…Then tell me something you know that I don't."

He nodded again and smiled sadly.

"I'm going to die, Maya…I must. But I think you already knew that. But what you might not know is that it will happen sooner than you expected."

CHAPTER 18

Washington DC is one of the most-visited cities in the world. Every year, millions of people come to see the capital of the greatest country on Earth, the defender of freedom, the very symbol of democracy, and so on and so forth...Maya hated all this hubris built up just to support an illusion, a fictional image. She knew too many political figures who were after nothing more than money and lofty titles. While average citizens kept buying into the epic performance of that overpaid, entitled drama club with their pre-written speeches about the American dream and freedom for all, the rest of the world was scared of and annoyed by the United States.

One thing was true, however—DC was the perfect city to get lost in. With all the technology available for navigating traffic and analyzing crowds, it was still difficult to locate someone in the massive flow of gawking tourists, especially if someone were looking for you in the Boston area and not here.

About an hour after they left the forest, Maya finally received the long-awaited e-mail and told Dan to move toward DC at the next fork. They arrived right at sunrise. After a quick search, she opened the map and set up the coordinates. The GPS navigator brought them to a landfill with piles of old, rusted cars. In its own way, it looked beautiful, like a forgotten city made from crushed metal and broken glass.

"Are you sure about this?" Dan had tried to keep quiet the rest of the drive since Maya's breakdown, but now he felt that it might be his last chance to talk at all.

"Yes. We need cash." Maya leaned toward Dan and honked the horn a couple times.

"I don't like this. This place looks sketchy…It looks like the place where people go to die."

"I'm sure you're right, and, more than likely, no one would ever find your dried-up corpse here."

"Thank you…I feel better now."

From behind one of the towers of junk, a man walked out dressed in jeans and a long sweater, all covered in dark stains that might have been blood…or just oil.

"Stay here…I'll be back."

Maya checked her pistol, tucked it behind her belt, and slowly walked out toward the newcomer.

"She's nuts!" Dan looked back through the rearview mirror at Michael, who did not seem worried about her. "Or maybe I am…"

"Don't worry, she'll be fine."

"Okay…okay."

Maya talked for a few minutes to the emotionless scab, who looked at her like he could not decide whether to rape her before or after murdering her. At one point, this "dude" raised his sweater to scratch his belly, but Dan was convinced that he was actually showing Maya a gun tucked into his jeans.

A couple times, he glanced toward the car without any big enthusiasm, but Maya just kept talking and talking. She was good at that…or even great because after a moment or two, the guy smiled, displaying a row of golden teeth, and nodded in agreement.

Maya nodded back to him, and they each left in a different direction.

"What was that?" Dan was not sure why Maya looked so happy. "Don't tell me this is your genius with the photographic memory."

"Pffff. Of course not. Okay, boys, get out of the car!"

"Why?" Dan wanted to argue the matter, but Michael had already opened the door and stepped outside.

"*Schneller!*" Maya took the key out of Dan's hand. "Just trust me, and in the name of all the saints, including Mickey, just keep your mouth closed. Let's go!"

Dan wanted to say something more, but with the release of just one sigh, Michael signaled that he had better not.

In another few minutes, a scratched but respectable-looking blue sedan pulled up next to them. Normally, you would expect to see an old grandma driving this kind of vehicle on a Sunday morning, but this car was being driven by the same man with whom Maya had been negotiating. He stepped out, leaving the engine running.

"Okay, lady, here's your wheels. The plate is clean, but I would avoid the cops anyway."

"Is it still hot?" Maya gave their key to him.

"Not really, six or seven months. But you never know."

"True." Maya nodded like she flipped stolen cars every weekend as a hobby. "And the money?"

He smiled like he had hoped she would forget but then pulled out a folded collection of twenties.

"Six hundred. You can count 'em."

"You look like a trustworthy person." Maya looked at him with her most flirtatious smile and pulled Dan and Michael toward the running car before anything happened. "Pleasure doing business with you!"

The man smiled back at her, spinning the key on his finger and thinking how successful he had been. In her own way, Maya felt ashamed because she knew that sooner or later, the snakeheads would come to claim what belonged to them.

*

Of course it was not the best vehicle in the world, but it drove fairly quietly and without drawing any unwanted attention. It died just once at the stop light but started up again fairly fast. No cops or cult members were after them. After making a couple loops through the downtown, Maya finally found a reasonably priced parking garage and pulled into a space on the ground floor.

"Okay, guys, here's two hundred for you. Try to kill some time until four." Maya counted out some of the twenties and gave them to Dan. "Buy some hats right away."

"But it's not sunny..."

"Dan, you're pissing me off. Go blend in with the crowds. Always be around people. Eat something. I'll see you at four sharp, left of the main entrance to the Library of Congress. Do you understand?"

"Yes. Four o'clock next to the library...Where are you going?"

"I need to run some errands and clean up a bit, and they might be looking for the three of us together anyway...Watch after Michael."

Maya pulled out the phone they had found at the rest stop, placed Michael up against a white wall, and took a picture of him. Then she waved to Dan to do the same.

"What's this for?"

"Shush and smile for Auntie Maya."

Dan bent his pursed lips into some form of a smile, and Maya took a picture of him as well.

"Maya! Why did you take pictures of us?"

"I'm going to make a huge poster of you to place above my bed...For new IDs, of course, you dum-dums! Okay. See you soon, and don't let him do anything stupid!"

"I know..." Dan was not thrilled by the idea of separating, but Maya was already too cranky, so he reluctantly agreed.

"And I will watch after him," smiled Michael.

"I know you will. Guys, please stay away out of trouble. Get yourself a cheap watch…"

"Four o'clock. Got it."

Maya nodded and briskly walked away from the parking garage.

Dan waited until she disappeared, looked at the money and the car, pondering the idea of taking Michael with him and leaving Maya in DC, alone. Finally, he rejected the idea, put the cash in his pocket, and smiled at the miracle boy.

"So, are you ready for a field trip?"

"And for breakfast!"

*

Time passed by quickly. They followed Maya's recommendation and stopped by a small kiosk where they bought two hats and two sweaters with a silly "I LOVE DC" printed on them, along with a silhouette of the White House. They had breakfast in a famous cafe chain, both enjoying overpriced and overly-sweetened coffee with hot sandwiches and chocolate croissants.

For a person who came from a small town, Michael was acting fairly normal around the unstoppable stream of tourists and business people who passed them by. Dan, who had grown up in Chicago but spent the last couple of years in a state where he could only hear the voices of his parents, seemed overwhelmed and nervous by contrast. Maybe in a week or two, when they would be out of this mess, he would try to call his grandparents and tell them that he was alive and well. Maybe one day he would even be able to visit his parents' grave…or maybe, at least, he could be buried next to them.

The duo spent most of their time walking around Capitol Hill. Even Dan had never been there before. For lunch, they grabbed a couple hot dogs and ate them on a bench next to the Reflecting Pool. All the time, they were talking about meaningless things and abstract topics. A few times, Dan felt like asking something deep and getting an answer that only Michael could give him, but he soon felt ashamed and sent the thoughts on their way.

How many people got the chance to speak to a saint? How many would give away half of their belongings just to get an answer or miracle? Here, Dan could ask anything, but then how would he be any different from everyone else? Maybe later, someone would judge him for not taking advantage of the opportunity, but right now, he just wanted to be a friend, a person whom Michael could trust, and not just another abuser of his abilities.

At ten minutes before four, they had made their way to the Library of Congress. Dan had decided that it would be better for them to arrive early than listen to Maya's magnificent swearing later. She did make them wait. A few minutes later, she appeared, and oh, did she look different! She was dressed like a businesswoman or a politician, with an elegant pantsuit, matching shoes, and a beautiful haircut. She must have used all of her money on the look. When she noticed them in their hats and matching sweaters, her face squeezed up like she had suddenly bitten a lemon.

"Such a lovely couple...of idiots." She rolled her eyes and gestured for them to follow her.

They did not go through the main entrance, and instead, they walked around the side where someone was already waiting for them. The man, standing awkwardly in a mismatched suit and glasses, looked more like a comic book character who ran a government lab or worked for an evil genius. He was short with a visibly balding head, an un-tucked shirt, and an unbuttoned jacket. Every few seconds, he looked at his watch like his life depended on it.

"Giga, we're here," Maya said in a loud whisper so only he could hear.

"Maya..." He looked at her with joy and adoration. "Oh my, Maya, time has no effect on you, does it? Gosh, it's been what, three years, two months, and six days since I saw you last? You haven't changed a bit."

"And I see time's had no mercy on you at all."

They both laughed, and Gigabyte opened his arms for a hug. Maya not only hugged him back but also planted a kiss on his cheek and then his forehead, leaving marks from her lipstick.

"I feel alive again! The most beautiful woman in the world is standing here with me after all this time!"

"Oh, stop it, you flirtatious old fox!" She blushed, which was new to see, and carefully wiped the red lipstick off of her old friend. "So…Did you make it?"

"I knew it. You're here for business. No love for your old Charles."

"I'm sorry, honey, but this time I'm really deep in it…Up to my ears."

"I believe you. I follow the news. Here are your badges."

Gigabyte pulled three visitor badges from his pocket, each showing a high clearance level similar to the one he had on his own jacket.

"I thought you were making us passports." Dan took his badge, looking back at his own unhappy face.

"No," sighed Maya. "This is our last chance. If he can't help us, no one can."

Dan was not sure who this "he" was that Maya talked about since it did not sound like she was referring to her friend Gigabyte, who stared at the boys with a sarcastic grin similar to Maya's.

"Guys, you might want to take those sweaters off. People who work here don't normally wear them."

"Couple of idiots," snorted Maya playfully.

"Okay. Let's go inside. There will be two security stops. Just scan your badge, and you should be fine. He'll be here in an hour or so, but we should be able to get to his section during the shift changes."

"Thank you, Charles…"

"If I lose my job because of you…"

"Then at least you'll get a free room and three meals a day in a high-security prison. Maybe even a hyperactive roommate."

Charles laughed, fixing his glasses, and it did not seem that he was too worried. In fact, he appeared amused, like it was some sort of game.

"I hope he still remembers me."

"How could anyone forget you?" Giga smiled and opened the door to let everyone in.

Before walking in, Dan could not control his growing suspicion anymore, and he grabbed Maya's arm, looking straight at her.

"Who is *he*? Who are we meeting here?"

Maya looked back at Dan and, with maximum satisfaction, answered in a most nonchalant tone, like it was no big deal.

"The president, of course."

CHAPTER 19

They walked through so many corridors that Maya would probably never be able to retrace her steps if she needed to. The timing was perfect, however, and the library had more than enough people to get lost in the crowd and blend in. At this time of day, though, most people were too tired to pay attention to another visitor with a blue access strip. Ordinarily, if someone had made it inside with this access level, then they clearly had a right to be there.

But in another hour, that might change...

Maya had briefly met Mark Turner, President of the United States and previously a senator from Illinois, at an event organized by his campaign right before he won the election. Back then, everything was so simple, and he was just a powerful man who offered her a drink and a couple of compliments. She had played on his ego, flattering him for a chance to write an article.

Nothing happened. Absolutely nothing. It was just a great conversation with laughs and mild flirtation, and then he went on to become President, and she became the head of her own column. She never went after married men anyway unless she was desperate or unaware.

When Gigabyte replied to her e-mail saying that he had recently moved to DC, working for the government and spending most of his hours at the Library of Congress, the gears in her head started to spin and devise a new path that might not have been foreseen by their pursuers.

One year ago, during the Fourth of July celebration, a huge tragedy shocked the nation and spoiled festivities for everyone, but especially for the president and his family. His son, a boy of ten years, was tired of being followed everywhere by security, being limited in his actions or, where he could go or whom he could see. He decided to pull a spiteful prank and sabotage the fireworks display behind the White House…Well, long story short, the boy ended up in the hospital with multiple burns and a broken spine, leaving him paralyzed from the waist down. His recovery was long and painful.

Not only was the son's spine broken, but it seemed that Mark's spirit was as well. He had changed so much visibly. There was a noticeable weight loss, and his hair had gone almost entirely silver in the last year. The fire in his voice had turned into smoke. Even though everyone pitied the man, the whole country wished he would step down from the presidency and let the vice president take the reins, especially since she was already running things in the Oval Office while Mark spent most of his time with his broken family.

"Are you sure they're coming today?" Maya knew that if Giga was not sure, he would not have given her false hope, but there was so much at stake.

"Yes," whispered Charles. "We got the security note. He brings his son in for new books…Okay, we're here."

Gigabyte opened the door to a room full of shelves, old books, and a reading table. Compared to the rest of the building, this room was significantly colder, and the air felt dryer, probably for the safety of the books. Maya felt safer here as well.

"What's in here?"

"This is the broken room," smiled Gigabyte. He closed the door behind them and pointed toward the reading desk with four chairs. A pile of books rested on top. "The camera in this room is dead. I'm not sure if it's on purpose, or it's just careless stupidity, but we can stay here until we go see Turner...But he'll still have his personal security. You understand that?"

The boys took the chairs closer to the wall, but Maya was still recovering from the nerve-racking walk in the government facility. She looked around, searching for any surveillance that Giga might not have noticed before.

"I do...I do...You know, we are screwed no matter what, but you don't need to stay here with us."

"Well, if what you're saying is just one of your pranks to get an interview with Turner, then, yeah, I'll leave now."

"I wish it were."

"Normally, your pranks are funny...but I'm scared for you."

"Believe it or not, I'm scared too. And not many things in this world scare me." Maya smiled sadly at her friend.

"If this is all true, you shouldn't be scared. You should be terrified."

Dan looked curious. He knew that Maya had been sending e-mails back and forth with Giga, but he was not sure how much she had told him.

"Melodramatic much? Or did you find something?"

"Well, I do remember a lot of legends that have popped up here and there." Gigabyte suddenly looked very serious, almost like he was going into a trance. "I brought a couple books that I was able to find on such short notice, but there are more...many more..."

Maya picked up one of the first books, a French edition about the Crusades. She carefully flipped through the pages until she noticed a small bookmark and opened the book to that page. She only knew a couple words in French, but the illustrations spoke for themselves. There was a large drawing of a snake's head, as well as what she guessed was the French word for Nehushtan, spelled almost the same as in English.

"Stories about a shadow clan building up networks of power throughout the world have been spotted in different sources, but not as many as I expected. I'm sure some books have been destroyed altogether, and I've noticed that others have missing pages. Who knows how many were never allowed to be printed?"

"Were you able to find what I asked?"

Gigabyte looked at Michael like he was silently answering a question in his own mind. How much of Maya's story was true, and could this young man be the subject of the epic hunt?

"Yes…They're waiting for the Hatching."

Maya looked confused and concerned.

"You see, Maya, some people are born with a natural talent for music or painting. They see and hear the world differently. Yes, of course, you can learn how to play the piano or how to hold a brush and blend colors, but for some, it's all so natural. They just do it the way that feels right to them, without having to learn."

"Charlie, cut to the chase."

"So. There are kids born with the 'Gift.' It's an ability to bend the physical world and reality with their will."

"It's called 'Faith,'" added Dan.

"Well, if you're religious, then yes, that's the closest explanation."

When Maya sent her messages to Gigabyte, she had been expecting something rational, something proven, or theories based on historically documented facts. This was not what she had in mind, and more than that, the last thing she needed was for Dan and Giga to start arguing semantics and theology.

"Continue."

"So, our whole world is structured on certain unchangeable laws. Water in a pot will be still until you blow on it, drop something in it, or make it boil."

"Yeah. But we can't make water boil just by blowing on it."

"You just don't know how." Giga smiled. "You can use kinetic energy to increase the temperature of different items, like sticks. If you rub them against each other quickly, they produce heat. So imagine if some people had the ability to move the sticks of the universe to create the unimaginable."

"Then what about the laws of physics?"

"What about them? These people just know a better formula."

"So resurrection? How do you explain that?"

Giga shrugged. "If I knew, I would open my own resurrection business. Better ask your little friend."

Michael did not seem interested in the conversation, even though most of it was about him. He had left his chair and begun wandering around the shelves, pulling book after book from the long rows, flipping through the pages, and placing them back.

"That's not physics! It's a miracle of God made possible through Michael's faith!"

"Hey, I'm not saying you're wrong," smiled Charles. "But what if faith is also one of unknown laws? Maybe science just hasn't found a way to convert it into a formula."

"This is sacrilegious! Not everything can be measured!"

"Even your teacher tried to measure faith...by a mustard seed."

"That was an example, trying to compare it to something so small..."

"ENOUGH!" whispered Maya angrily. He slapped the book closed. "Both of you, stop it! Physics, faith! I don't care! It's beyond me or any logical thinking. Okay? All I want right now is to know whether we have some proof so I can tell Mark something besides old Bible stories."

"Well, the most interesting might be this..." Gigabyte seemed to know Maya long enough not to be offended by her outrage, but Dan was now sulking like an offended puffer fish. Selecting one of the books and handing it to Maya, Giga continued, "They have their own hierarchy. There's a magistrate who watches over and guides the most talented and promising, but if they become too power-hungry, he simply kills them."

On the page displayed to Maya, there was an old gravure showing a man in priest-like robes sticking a long, two-bladed dagger or fork into a boy's scaled head.

"They kill their own members?"

"Yes. Imagine a pawn that knew at some point it might become a bishop or queen, but before it gets to the finish line, it already starts acting the way a queen would, not just putting itself in danger, but compromising the whole plan."

"The Hatching? The Hatching is a plan? Or King? I'm confused."

"No...I don't think their plan is just to save a 'king.' It's something bigger. Maybe to gain total control on every level. Maybe to stop being chess pieces and step outside the game. Turn people into their own personal chess pieces. They want to change existence as we know it."

"The Apocalypse. The reign of the Antichrist," added Dan.

Maya rolled her eyes. "I feel like the Apocalypse has already started in my head. Any more, and you'll see me spitting hellfire. I asked for something that I could take to the president! What is a Hatching, then?"

"If we come back to the chess game, one of these pawns might become a king...An ultimate king...Or Antichrist, if that's easier to believe. Then it's game over."

"And you're saying they do not know which of the pawns will become this king?"

"Correct...They might suspect. They might be making a bet. They can even create perfect conditions for it to happen, but they have to be really careful. If they guess wrong, they could end up with some pawn becoming a crazy rook or knight."

"Has it happened before?"

"Many times. One of the most interesting to me was a certain British earl named Alexander. He was sent to Russia as a child and raised with Czar Peter the First. He later rebelled and turned against the czar, joining the side of Peter's sister, Sophia. Apparently, he thought of marrying her later and becoming Czar himself. What a mess! It caused a revolution!"

"Revolution...Yeah, the president will like that."

"So, you really believe that Michael is one of these Hatchings or Hatchlings?" Now Dan's eyes rolled, and he became the skeptic. "Look at him! Does he look like..."

Dan froze. Maya followed the direction of his stare, and her face changed dramatically.

Michael was gone.

"The king has made his move..." whispered Giga, with mixed feelings of excitement and fear.

"He is not the Anti..." Maya choked on the phrase, understanding how unreasonable it sounded. Picking up a few books and shoving them into Dan's arms, she rushed to the door. "He's not THAT king. I know it! But we need to find him before anyone else does!"

"If you leave now, security might notice you and escort you from this wing." Giga tried to stop her, but she had already run into the hall.

"Without Michael, our meeting will be pointless! Which direction is the security room? We need to ask them to look for him!"

"I thought you didn't want any extra attention?!"

"Security room! NOW!"

Giga sighed but hurried after her.

"Dan, you take those books and go to the main reading room if everything—"

An alarm filled the air, cutting Maya off.

All three of them froze in place, looking around, confused by the sudden disturbance.

"What now? Fire?"

"No, it sounds like we're on lockdown…" Once again, Giga looked more excited than scared. "I bet your king got to the president already. Checkmate! The Apocalypse is here, folks!"

"STOP IT!" yelled Maya, shouting over the alarm…and it did stop.

"That was fast." Dan almost melted into the wall, and even his face turned the same color as the paint behind him. Were it not for the books he was hugging as protection, he could easily have blended in with the background.

"Giga, where is Mark supposed to be?"

"Through this hall, on the left…Just follow me!"

CHAPTER 20

It was not as far as she thought, and Gigabyte had indeed found a perfect hiding spot for them. After a couple of turns and a quick sprint down an empty hallway, Maya walked into a vast, bright room, three levels high, which probably served as a VIP section for high-level guests.

It was one of those libraries built more to impress visitors with its sheer grandeur rather than for any practical use. The spiral stairs leading to the upper floors served more of an aesthetic purpose than anything. She could easily picture some rich, eccentric protagonist in a film sipping coffee in front of the crackling fireplace on a foggy winter morning. Maybe his nemesis would murder him here on a gloomy, tempestuous night, with only the thousands of books as silent witnesses, watching his blood spread across the expensive Persian carpet, powerless to help.

But right now, Maya was in a different kind of story. This was an action flick!

Her sudden appearance made everyone freeze for a brief second, like statues at Madame Tussaud's.

Four men in dark suits stood, guns drawn, aiming at Michael, who was trying to move closer to a boy in a wheelchair. Maya had seen pictures of the president's son before. It had been all over the news and tabloids when the tragedy occurred. Now, she barely recognized him with his dried, pale figure and multiple burns and scars covering his face. He sat motionless in the chair, barely paying attention to the goings on.

261

His father, Mark, the great, confident, and smiling knight-in-shining armor, was also little more than an empty shell of his former self. Maya could at least detect the fear in his eyes while his son remained emotionless and distant, not unlike herself when she had first given a try to her strong painkillers.

Maya never asked herself what the results of that trauma might be. He was paralyzed from the waist down, with scars spread over the surface of his whole body…was he still in pain? Eventually, one can accept the trauma and even the loss, but not if there is a constant reminder in the form of unrelenting pain. That is why Mark could not leave his family for long periods of time and ended up slacking on his responsibilities.

There are so many things a person can notice and assess in just a split second…but you cannot stop time any longer.

"Freeze!" Now two of the Secret Service agents pointed their weapons at Maya and Gigabyte.

One of them spoke something into a small microphone on his lapel, placing one hand to his ear. One needed not to be a genius to know that the room would soon be teeming with agents and police and God-knows-who else they could squeeze in there.

"On the ground, or I will shoot!" yelled one of the agents who was shielding the president with his own body, his gun aimed straight at Michael.

"Mark!" yelled Maya, suddenly finding strength from somewhere deep inside. "Let him…Let him help!"

The president did glance at her briefly when she first appeared, but his eyes had since locked on his son and the strange young man who was approaching him. Now, when he heard his name, he turned his eyes and tried to match her face to the hundreds of thousands of images in his memory.

"Do I know you?!" The fear slowly gave way to new feelings of confusion and distress.

"Yes. It's me, Maya Polanski…we met…"

"*Chicago Voice*, right?" His voice softened, which could only be a good sign, but all four agents seemed to tense up even more.

"Sir, we need to take you away."

"It's alright, guys…" Mark even cracked a weak smile. "Miss Polanski, what's this all about?"

"Sir, she is red!"

Maya noticed another agent quietly reporting something about them.

"Mark! He can help him…" Suddenly, her voice sounded so calm and unnatural for their current situation. "Mark, please. Let him help."

Reality split itself into multiple segments. There was an outside world and an inside one. Somewhere out there, government forces rushed toward the library and would appear any moment. There was also no doubt that Cloudy and his people had received word of her presence there and were on the move as well. But these were all problems for the outside world.

Here inside, they also started dividing. Gigabyte and Dan had been pulled back into the hallway by someone, and that was okay. Maya could not worry about everyone right now. Right now, it was her and the president. A crippled boy and a miracle healer who took another small step toward him. A pair of guns and their targets. So many things to keep track of…but the most important thing now was to let Michael make another sacrifice.

"Maya…?" Mark looked at her with a desire to understand. He wanted his fear back, but something would not let that happen.

"Trust me…Everything will be alright."

All of the agents turned slowly toward her. She was the main suspect now. They needed to protect the president from her. Yes, his family, too, but the president was their first priority.

"I don't understand? Why?" Mark searched his mind for some kind of logical explanation, but it eluded him.

"Mark. We're here to help…And to ask you for help as well."

The president nodded as though she had just offered the most logical explanation he had ever heard. Even the agents seemed in agreement. They still kept their eyes on her but were no longer aiming so much as staring with guns in hand. The looks of fear and alertness gave way to what one might consider looks of awe.

"Pe-e-e-erf-f-f-fect," whispered a wind, echoing along the ceiling of the library.

Maya felt goosebumps at the familiar voice. Was it Cloudy, or just her imagination playing with her? Of course it was her paranoia. She had just been thinking about him. But he could not know exactly where they were, could he? She had indeed heard his voice in her head before, or at least she thought she had. He had tried to control her mind at other times, but before, there had always been…

"Maya? Do you want me to do this?" Michael now stood right beside the poor child. "Isn't that why you brought me here?"

"Seriously? Now you're going to protest and throw a tantrum?" Maya knew that Michael saw right through her, but she was too ashamed to admit that she had set this all up for one purpose. Yes, she planned to use him…or rather his talent, but just to gain their trust. They were in trouble. BIG trouble, like she had never imagined possible. Here, they had the chance to ask the president for help… "Michael, we need this. I'm sorry!"

"Please, don't hurt Denis," pleaded Mark in a cracked whisper.

Maya sighed. Maybe it was all a mistake, especially right now when the great and mighty leader of the Free World was just a father—crushed, scared, and absolutely desperate.

"You could have just asked me…" Michael did not even blink. Still looking at Maya, he stretched out his hand and gently touched the poor boy's forehead.

Miracles. Could one possibly grow used to them? Even if they became an everyday occurrence? Nothing seemed unusual anymore in this new world of hers, and such miracles should be the new norm, or so one might think. She had seen him heal and walk on water. But why, all of a sudden, were her insides collapsing into a void? It felt like the tiny, invisible strings holding her together all snapped at once with the cry of a dying violin as an unmerciful hand jerked them away.

Was this all a mistake?

It was. Not just maybe.

She opened her mouth to tell him to stop, but a wave of warm air already rolled out across the room. Pulses of bright light shone, their source deep inside Michael's heart, or deeper...or perhaps they came from Higher? No, he was using his own power. The day they healed Dan, she felt how the power rushed through her like she was a perfect conductor. But Michael, on the other hand, and to continue the allegory, was a powerful battery using his own charge, even if that power had been placed in him by something divine.

He looked emptily at Maya, waking up senses of guilt she had almost forgotten. And while shame demanded that she lower her eyes, she could not allow herself such weakness. If she made Michael sacrifice a part of his life, the least she could do was to be brave enough to share this moment with him.

It did not take long. The power that Michael used barely changed him, and maybe some of those present in the room would not even notice a difference. But Maya did. Who said that only your own sacrifices result in pain? Making others pay for your mistakes should scar your soul...but only if you still have one.

The scars on Denis' face faded away along with any signs of burned or transplanted tissue. His eyes slowly adjusted to the light, and the fogginess from his medications faded away. His shoulders stretched, and Maya noticed him moving his knees.

The boy gasped for air, like he suddenly surfaced from underwater, like babies do coming into the world. He focused first on the young man who slowly removed his hand from his forehead and then on the surroundings, trying to remember how he got there in the first place. Then he looked at Maya in an attempt to find a familiar face, but only after he turned his head far enough to see the president did he find one.

"Dad?!" Tears ran down his face, suddenly, like in the dramatic movies that Maya hated so much.

Mark and his guards stood just as before, motionless and silent.

Denis moved in the wheelchair and noticed that his legs responded, which almost scared him, as he had given up on the idea of that ever again happening. He looked back at Michael, and this time, his fear changed to amazement.

What a clever boy! He might have a bright future if he had understood what had taken place so quickly. And now he had a future again!

"Can I?" For some reason, he felt that he needed to ask Michael's permission, and Michael simply smiled back at him.

Denis jumped from the chair and ran toward his dad, giving him one of those biggest and strongest hugs that only kids can give. Still not understanding what had taken place, Mark finally found the ability to move and fell to his knees, hugging his son and burying his face in his shoulder.

The guards finally relaxed and lowered their weapons, feeling awkward and out of place, unsure as to what they should do next.

"I'm sorry..." said Maya, mouthing the words silently and looking at Michael.

He did age a small amount, and there was now a wrinkle appearing on either side of his blue eyes. Against her will, a treacherous little tear ran down her face and pierced straight into her heart. Something else had changed in Michael's appearance. It grew colder and more distant. Before, when he looked at her, she felt like the sun itself was shining just for her, but now, a wall stood between them...a big, thick, invisible wall of ice.

"I thought you were different," whispered Michael.

Maya wanted to say something to him, but the president finally released his hug and started looking over Denis intently, examining every freckle and each eyelid. Everything was back to normal, and all the scars were gone. He hugged his son again. Next, he turned to look at Maya, and his face was changing as well. He had emptied all of his tears onto Denis' shoulder, though his eyes were still red and puffy.

"Maya...How? How is this possible? It's...a miracle."

"I know." Maya offered a weak smile to the father and son. "But this miracle needs your help."

The president looked at Michael, who was still standing in the same spot next to the wheelchair...the empty wheelchair, and he nodded.

"Of course. Anything I can do..." Mark noticed the stern look of one of his bodyguards and hastily corrected himself. "Anything within reason."

"We need protection. Like, high-level shit! New names, new lives, and the fewer people who know about it, the better."

The president looked confused but then seemingly remembered an important detail.

"Maya, I think I saw you today in the news..."

"Mark! You just saw what this boy can do, right? Now think! What would people do for access to that kind of power?"

Mark's lips thinned into a straight line, and his eyes moved back and forth between his son, Michael, Maya, and his security. He was thinking, trying to come up with a plan.

"You need to tell me more."

"I would love to, but please take us somewhere safe first, away from here."

"Yes, of course. Is it just you and him?"

Maya turned back to where she had last seen Dan and Gigabyte but could not see them. Had they run away or perhaps been taken by the library security? Maybe that was for the best, as it might be safer.

"There are two with me here in the library, but we can look for them afterward."

"Then let's go to my car." Mark stood up and beamed, looking at his son. "When Mom sees you, she's going lose her mind!"

Denis matched his father's smile and tightly squeezed his arm like a small kid. The president melted from this gesture, and Maya felt another tear running down her cheek. All of this emotional stuff was definitely making her softer, and she had not yet decided whether that was a good thing.

"Okay, guys, right this way." Mark gestured for Michael and Maya to follow and started walking with his son toward one of the doors leading out. Before reaching it, something first banged on the outside loudly, and a round of gunshots answered back.

All four agents returned to their normal selves and acted faster than Maya could understand what was happening.

"Dad?" Denis squeezed his father's hand even harder.

"Don't worry, everything will be alright." The president freed his hand, pushing his son away from the big windows, already viewing what was happening just outside. "Maya, are those the people who're after you?"

Maya ran to the window and looked out. About a dozen men in black stood outside, forming a line next to the president's motorcade, and about half a dozen men in uniform lay dead on the ground.

She blurted out a vulgar line of curse words, describing a most exotic and biologically impossible act involving snakeheads and a herd of elephants, which made not only Denis and Michael turn red but the president and all of his guards as well.

"Yes…that's them."

"Sir, we should use route B," suggested one of the agents, gently pulling the president toward the door Maya had come from.

But someone walked in through the very same door, blocking their way.

"Too late." Phillip Hall, dressed the same as his clan members, stepped into the light.

Maya took a step toward him as well, trying to comprehend the hurricane of emotions crushing all of her hopes and dreams into nothing. He had shaved his head, displaying a large number of scale tattoos coming from behind his ears and reaching all the way to the crown. Maya noticed a large bruise on the left side of his head, obviously the result of her attack in the forest.

Phillip noticed her stare and involuntarily touched the wounded side.

"I hope it still hurts," Maya hissed, walking close to him, perhaps closer than she should.

"It does," answered Phillip, nodding with a sad smile. "It was a nice swi—"

Maya channeled all her frustration into a fist and punched him on the right side to balance out the bruising.

Either Phillip did not expect such a strong swing, or Maya had placed enough force into the hit that FBI tumbled to the floor, caught off guard.

"Mamma mia, such drama!" rang the voice of Cloudy, theatrically loud to announce his presence.

He casually leaned over the rails, looking down at them from the third floor. He had probably been there for a while, observing everything that took place, whispering into Maya's ears. He was not alone, and some younger man stood behind, far enough not to be able to see his face but close enough to notice his shaved head.

Even though Maya's fist still hurt from the sucker punch, she jumped toward the next guard and tried to wrestle the gun from his hand. If he had been a typical policeman from some small town, she might have succeeded, but he was clearly well-trained, and she failed to secure the weapon for herself. The agent pushed Maya away and turned the gun on her.

"Shoot him! Shoot this son of a snake!"

The agent looked even more confused, glancing around between Maya, the president, and the elderly gentlemen, trying to decide what to do.

"What are you looking at? Shoot him?!"

"Do I know you?" The president seemed puzzled by the new visitors.

"Yes, we met a couple of times when you were in Chicago. Actually, we met at the same party where you met Miss Polanski, but I can't blame you for remembering her but not me. After all, that was the plan."

"Sir, this is Albert Cloudy..." started one of the agents.

"Mark! This is him!" Maya sputtered from anger. "He's the one who's hunting us!"

Cloudy rolled his eyes and waved toward them sarcastically.

"My dear, for hunting, you need to track the prey, and in your case, I always knew exactly where you were. With all the chaos you cause, it's more simple observation than hunting."

If it had not been for the metal detectors they passed at the checkpoint, Maya would have brought the gun she had taken away from Phillip. He had accidentally shot a couple times from it when she bashed him over the head, but there were still five bullets left...She would only need one! Cloudy was in plain view. She could not miss!

"Oh my world, Maya, seriously? Control yourself, you're so predictable." Cloudy shook his head like a disappointed parent to an unruly toddler. Then, switching tone, he looked straight at the guard closest to Maya and, in a voice filled with ice and cruelty, commanded, "Give it to her!"

The security agent turned white, and his eyes voided themselves of any sign of consciousness. Without hesitation, he turned to Maya and stretched out his hand, holding the weapon by the barrel for her to collect.

At first, she stared, confused. Was she really that predictable, or had he read her mind? Did he really think she was not capable of murder? Well, they would soon find out!

She grabbed the gun. The safety was already off, and all she needed to do was aim and shoot.

And she did.

Once! Twice! Again and again, until there was no more ammo. Even then, she kept on squeezing the trigger, hoping that more bullets might appear if only she tried hard enough.

"Satisfied?" Cloudy had not moved, not even flinched. He neither bled nor did he even seem alarmed.

Every single shot would have been lethal, but the problem was that the bullets never reached his body. They were, in fact, still on their way, levitating in the air. They trembled at the pressure of confronting forces, one that had released them and another that stopped them in place.

"Now it's my turn!"

Something like haze moved through the air. All of the flying bullets turned and raced back, killing each of the security agents. Maya had seen a lot lately, but this was beyond her understanding. Her ears continued to ring from the sound of the shots, but instead of fading, the noise echoed and hummed, growing louder and aggravating a pain in her head.

"What are you?" The president moved in front of Denis, shielding him.

"The one who made you President and the one who can change that. So, I would recommend that you step aside and keep quiet for a while."

Maya still held the gun in her hands, looking around at the fallen security guards. She understood that no one in the world would believe her story, that she tried to kill the bad guy but killed four innocents instead. She had a smoking gun in her hand, and any jury would find her guilty.

Yet something else was bothering her, and she could not understand what it was.

"Okay. Now, Maya…" Cloudy finally turned and started down the spiraling stairs, followed by one of his apprentices, "…time to honor the oath you gave."

"What are you talking about?" Maya felt an overwhelming stream of anxiety clouding her judgment and reflexes.

"The Oath. You swore to me that you would say and do exactly what I tell you."

"You're a psycho…"

"We're all a little bit psycho, my dear." Cloudy stepped down onto the same floor and made his way closer to Maya. "And you are no exception."

"Let them go…please, and I will do what you want…" Maya could not stop looking over the dead bodies. Mark looked scared and helpless, but nevertheless, he had now positioned himself in front of Michael as well as Denis, protecting them both. In the corner of her eye, she saw Phillip, already on his feet, walking toward the president. She thought she heard him whisper a low and quick "Count!" to her, or maybe she imagined it.

Count? Count what?

The paces between her and Cloudy?

The books? Windows? Heartbeats? What?

"We will all leave here soon," droned Cloudy, "You just need to let Michael go with me."

"Not gonna happen."

Cloudy shrugged his shoulders but did not look too surprised. He gestured toward his helper, who pulled a phone out of his pocket, offering it to Maya.

"You remember the words you swore on your mother's heart...?"

Maya felt a sudden heat hit her in the face. She broke out in a sweat, and every single hair on her body rose like a startled cat.

"Don't you dare touch my parents!"

"Me?!" Cloudy gasped, followed by an overdramatic sigh. "Never! I would not do such a thing! But you, on the other hand...Did you think you would simply repeat some silly words to an old fool and nothing would ever happen?"

Cloudy took another step toward Maya, and his face changed. Before, he had always seemed aristocratic and well-mannered, displaying occasional smirks and rolling his eyes. He would have made a perfect fit as a show host for retired drag queens. But now his face looked like it was carved out of coal, icy but with glowing sparks of hellfire in his eyes.

"Take the phone," insisted Cloudy with a tone that would not accept rejection. "The number's already entered. Just hit call. Your mother has had a heart attack. Good thing your dad is around."

Maya pulled the phone out of the apprentice's hand and touched "dial."

The next few minutes felt like they happened under a trance. Her dad was indeed on the other side of the line. As soon as he realized it was Maya, he bombarded her with questions and complaints, telling her how much they had been worried.

It took a lot, even screaming over the phone, to make him listen. She ordered him to look for her mom. He did not sound happy, of course, but he went. Even though she wished he would hurry, he took his time, preaching all the way about all the troubles she had made for the whole family, about the police and the FBI already contacting them, and a patrol car outside of their house around the clock. He did not forget to mention the news they had seen on TV and how much it was upsetting her mother...

Then he screamed. He yelled his wife's name. Maya could hear the phone drop to the floor and her father calling for help. If there were cops outside the house, they would come running, but Maya wished her dad would call 911 on his own. Then she had the idea to call them herself, but before she could, Cloudy snatched the phone from her hands with serpentine speed.

"Don't worry, everything will be fine." Cloudy reverted into the sweet old man. "Just do what you were asked, and all will be well."

"And if not?" Maya felt two different energies fighting over her emotions. One wanted to rebel, seize the gun and start smashing the old fart's face until there was nothing left resembling a person. The other was talking sense, trying to calm her down and urging her to consider her surroundings.

"If not...oh well. Your mother will die sometime tomorrow, and since you swore on your father's mind, the poor man will lose it. Dementia, most likely, and it will take him away quite aggressively. But he will not die. He'll live a long, long time, so you can watch him over the next few decades and remember what you've done."

Maya closed her eyes, feeling the ground under her feet begin to sink.

"I can't tell him to go with you; it's not within my power."

"You're wrong. I saw what you did over there with the president's son. Great job! Now, I want you to convince him to live life how he wants. You know that way, he will not grow any older, so it suits everyone."

Maya looked toward Michael...But he was not there! Mark and Phillip were still present, but Michael and Denis were nowhere to be found. She felt relieved but scared at the same time.

Cloudy smirked, looking at Maya, and then beckoned for Phillip to come closer.

"The boys are gone, I know. Your idiot lover decided to help them leave during all the ruckus, thinking I wouldn't notice."

"He is NOT my lover!"

"But he is the one you love," smiled Cloudy, pulling a little blue vial from his jacket pocket.

"Love him? I've known him less than a week…"

"Yes? But you did not kill him in the forest. And even now, looking at him, you do not feel any hatred."

Maya glared back at Cloudy, trying to prove how wrong he was, but his grinning eyes saw right through her.

"Who knows? Maybe I misread some of the signs." Cloudy shrugged, trying to look defeated. "Then you won't care if I kill him."

"I DON'T care! But why kill your own man?"

"He was mine. Oh, believe me, he was one of the best. Loyal, smart, talented—look at all those scales he has on his scalp, and each one means a lot…But you ruined him. Now, I have no need for his service. Can you believe it? He thought he could trick me. He came after you left him, telling me you planned to escape to Florida! Oh, what a naïve, loving fool!"

Cloudy looked at Phillip and stretched out the hand holding the blue vial. Phillip froze in place and then took a step back, trying to resist the command. Cloudy's face flinched like he had bitten something very sour, and Phillip's will and resistance melted like ice in an oven. He came, took the vial, and opened the cap. With fear in his eyes, he drank it all to the last drop.

"Okay, I think I'm done here." Cloudy looked at everyone present, assessing whether he had forgotten anything. "So, Maya, find the boy. He's still in the building. I can feel that. Talk to him. He could have such a wonderful future; do not take that away from him. Then come back to me. I'll be waiting."

Phillip buckled over suddenly and moaned in pain.

"Help him!" Maya dashed over and caught Phillip before he could fall.

"Aha! I knew it!" Cloudy smiled, looking toward the president like he had made a bet with him, but Mark avoided eye contact, too scared to react. "No worries, it's a slow-acting poison. He'll have about six hours but should take the antidote before then."

"Where can I find you?"

"Now we're talking!" Cloudy grinned his widest. "I think I'll visit the White House. What would you say to that, Mr. President?"

"It would be my honor..." sighed Mark, his voice empty and cold.

"Perfect! I'll see you there, my dear. Let's go! I've always wanted to take a ride with the president's cortege!"

CHAPTER 21

As soon as the door closed behind Cloudy, Maya grabbed Phillip in an angry huff and dragged him toward one of the doors that could only be a restroom. She wanted to swear but understood that doing so would not help. After all, she had only just discovered how powerful mere words can be. Maybe she could call down a torrent of curses on the annoying old fossil, but with her luck, he would only grow stronger.

"What are you doing?" Phillip felt weak, but he could still walk. Maya, who seemingly thought otherwise, shoved him closer to the toilet.

"Express initiation to the two-fingers club!"

He looked at her like she had completely lost her mind.

"Two fingers down your throat! Now!"

"Maya this poison…"

"I said, NOW!"

Phillip tried to argue but soon conceded defeat and began trying to empty his stomach. Maya found a fancy-looking glass on the sink counter near the towels, filled it with water, and brought it to him.

"Drink and repeat! Maybe it won't save you, but it might slow down or lessen the effect. We need more time!"

Knowing better than to argue again, he followed orders and repeated all that Maya had commanded him to do.

"Stay here! I'll go get Michael, and maybe he'll have mercy on your treacherous ass!"

"They're in the broken room," managed Phillip, between heaves and with a tone of shame in his voice. "That short guy said you would know where it is."

"I do…Stay here, and do not stop!"

Maya ran back through the empty VIP room and into the hall. The room could not have been too far away, but the doors were all so alike. She could easily miss the right one were it not for the sound of Dan and Giga's arguing voices.

"You idiots! I could hear you all the way down the hall!"

"Who cares!" Charles laughed, catching Maya off guard. The disturbing tone in his voice signaled that her friend was about to lose his marbles.

"The building is empty! Everyone is gone!" Dan, on the other hand, was still white and shaking even more than before.

"Evacuated?" Maya looked around and was both surprised and happy to see Denis seated in the corner, but she could not see Michael. A knot instantly developed in her gut.

"Where is he this time?" Her question was not addressed to anyone specific. Neither Dan nor Charles seemed to have any idea where or when he had gone.

"I have no clue! I thought he was with you…Maya, he was there with you, the president, and this kid. Phillip pulled us away."

It seemed like Dan was expecting a better reaction, or even any reaction at all, but Maya was not interested.

"Charles, we need to find him!" Her voice cracked. As much as she tried to keep a look of bravado on her face, Giga could read real panic in her eyes. Furthermore, whenever she called him by his actual name, he knew she meant business.

"We can always follow our old plan and go look in the security room. Maybe he just wandered off somewhere?"

"He left." The quiet voice from the corner grasped their attention immediately, but it seemed that Denis was not planning to reveal anything else.

"And do you know where?" Maya covered the distance between them in less than a second, unsure what to do next—beg on her knees or shake the boy so he would talk faster.

"I think so...He asked where the nearest hospital was. I told him about the one where they treated me."

"Was he wounded?" Maya tried to remember if any of the bullets had hit Michael. She shot six times...But there were only four bodies, and all of them were shot in the head. Cloudy did not miss. Then where did the other two bullets go?

"Maya..." Dan whispered, barely able to keep his composure.

How could she be so stupid? Of course he was not wounded. He was a Miracle! He is the one who heals wounds!

"He said...It would be easier. Then you wouldn't have to make an impossible choice."

She felt a sudden shortness of breath and the sensation of all her innards shredding into chunks. Guilt and desperation rose up in a whirling tide, nearly drowning her.

*

A storm swallowed the city. Like an unleashed beast, it ran above the heavy clouds, rumbling its invisible chain behind it and striking blinding flashes of light every time the chain struck against a pillar of heaven. There was no way anyone would arrive at their destination on time today. Washington DC had lost its power and dignity.

In these endless lines of vehicles that formed growling rows of mechanical veins, everyone was equal. The rain and wind, in their flirtatious dance, paralyzed not only the freeway but all major roads connected to it, leaving the entitled politicians from Capitol Hill stuck in the same lane with the hardworking single mother with three jobs. Yes, their cars were in very different price ranges, but what was the point if you could not move an inch?

Miles and miles of honking, glowing, steaming machines contained the most diverse and unpredictable animals. The populace resembled an experimental collection, brought in for a test to see how much its subjects could endure in their pretty cages, hating the cars in front for not moving, despising the ones behind for creeping closer, and being thoroughly annoyed with those on either side who happened to move faster than they.

"Are we moving yet?" Maya had probably asked that question for the third time in the last five minutes. "What is going on?"

The taxi driver did not even bother to answer this time. He had likely decided she was crazy and not worthy of another explanation. For the hundredth time, he asked himself why he bothered to pick them up. Maybe he had been enchanted when he first saw her, a beautiful, rain-soaked, but respectably dressed woman. It was only after he stopped that he noticed her skinhead, junky boyfriend.

"We need to get to the hospital!"

"No shit," answered the driver in a perturbed whisper.

"What did you say?" Maya caught him sighing. Through the rearview mirror, she looked like a person on the edge…Maybe she was high as well? Again, he didn't bother with a response.

"What was wrong with the last two hospitals I drove you to?"

In any other situation, she might have come up with a good story, something interesting, intriguing but wholly believable. Something about a rare blood type, or a lost brother, or even a secret operation. Then the driver would not only find the fastest route, breaking all traffic laws, but he would also refuse to take her money. Not now, not today.

Phillip shivered and, from time to time, would release a quiet moan, becoming tense as rock and clenching both arms around his stomach. At first, he tried to sit up, but now Maya made him lie down, placing his head on her knees.

"Hold on, FBI…we're almost there," lied Maya. For all she could see, there was neither any movement nor any sign of a hospital.

"You should have left me…" whispered Phillip.

"Oh, please!" Maya cringed at such a cliché. "Try something better."

"You're losing time, Maya. You really should go alone."

"I change my mind. Just shut up before I vomit…Gosh, no more cheesy movies for you, FBI."

"I'm not FBI…"

"No shit," answered Maya, mimicking the driver's intonation. "I'm not sure you're even a Phillip."

"I'm not," said not-Phillip, smiling. "I know he was a real agent, and I just fit the profile."

"You mean there were no snakeheads in the Bureau already?"

"No, there are…They have people everywhere."

Maya smirked, hearing his use of "they" instead of "we," but decided to play along. Deep inside, she knew that not-Phillip was telling the truth. Yes, he was a member of their clan, and more than likely, he had come into her life under the orders of his leader and not because fate had drawn their hearts together. Still, she knew that he was not evil. She just knew it. Maybe that is why she could not kill him in the forest. Or maybe she was just a fool who had fallen for him in a matter of days, thinking he was a knight in shining armor, even though he was only a cheap traveling actor wrapped in tinfoil.

"Count…? What was that about? Back in the library. Count what?"

"Maya, Cloudy is not as powerful as you think."

"Stopping bullets and redirecting them is some powerful voodoo, I would say."

"Exactly! How many times did you shoot at him?"

"Six…?" Maya tried to follow, but it still did not click in.

Phillip's face changed from an expression of encouragement to a grimace of pain, and his face and forehead broke out in beads of sweat.

"How far are we?!" Maya hugged not-Phillip, bringing him closer to her own body in an attempt to absorb a part of his pain and misery.

"Listen, ma'am!" The driver seemed to have had enough and turned back to face her. "You better shut the hell up, or you can take your skinny ass out of my car and…"

Phillip's shivering turned into a convulsion, interrupting the taxi driver, and something inside of Maya snapped.

"Drive," she uttered calmly but with an unusual strength. An unseen power surged from every cell in her body, passed through her veins, raised the hair on her neck, and released a faintly visible wave all around her.

Something happened, something that she could not explain, but the driver froze in place like a motionless puppet. His eyes lost all signs of life and merely reflected her will. It felt oddly similar to what happened with the security agents when she commanded them to stop, but this time, it was exponentially more powerful.

Smash!

Their cab moved, hitting the car in front.

The stunned driver never removed his gaze from Maya, but his subjugated body had pushed the accelerator to the floor. Still not turning his head, his hand switched the gear to reverse and pressed the pedal again.

Another smash!

The air filled with the sound of honking and screaming, but paying no attention to the distraction, the driver continued shifting back and forth, hitting the car in front and behind until there was enough room to exit the traffic and drive on the sidewalk. All the while, his eyes and face remained frozen in a disturbing fashion.

Never breaking eye contact with Maya, he threw the car forward, picking up speed, knocking down trash cans, newspaper kiosks, wet cement signs, and anything else coming his way.

Strangely, she did not feel any guilt or concern, perhaps because there were no pedestrians out in such crazy weather. Only people looking for death would be outside in a storm like this. Their first headlight broke in an attempt to shove the other cars out of the way, and they lost the second, colliding with the bench at a bus stop. As it was built so close to the curb, they had no other choice but to drive right into it.

A power flew through her and right into the motionless face in the seat in front. Somewhere behind the wax mask of her puppet, she sensed a deep fear. At first, he had emanated anger, but now, there was only uncontrollable panic and terror. Somewhere deep inside, this man who had become her tool was screaming, begging her to stop, but she could not. At first, she had used her own energy, mixed with the pain radiating from the man in her arms, but now the power was drawing a charge from the hysteria of her prisoner.

So much power!

It felt like it would not end, and the more the driver lost his mind, the more control she received. The stronger the emotions he released inside, the stronger she became! Is that what it felt like to be the spider when the prey fell tangled and helpless in her web? She did not need to do a thing and just waited patiently, watching him jiggle in the sticky mesh, growing more confused, tangled, and weak. Doomed.

Faster! Faster! No laws, no barriers. Who cared that the road was blocked? Roads were for the weak, for the common man. She was different. The masses around could only be jealous of her freedom. They would have been frightened to be in her place, to lose their comforting laws of nature. But not Maya! Not anymore!

They passed so much anger in the other vehicles as they sped by, and she found that she could easily stretch out that web, harnessing their anger into more power. Her own will bleached theirs, and she fed off their emotions as they all came under her command.

Somewhere in the city, Albert Cloudy smiled...

Maya jerked out of her power trip like she had been shocked by electricity. She released not-Phillip from her arms and lost mental contact with the driver, making him fall limp and deflated. He slid over to the passenger's seat, releasing the wheel and removing his foot from the pedal. Just before the speeding taxi drove into a hedge, Maya noticed tears streaming down the driver's face and that his hair had gone entirely silver.

The painful realization of what she had done hit her stronger than the brick wall hidden behind the hedge. It was the north wall of a hospital. The hospital!

CHAPTER 22

She seemed to black out for a while. It could not have been longer than a minute or two, or the paramedics would already have come unless no one saw what happened. What about the cops? It would have been impossible not to notice a car driving forty miles per hour on the sidewalk. But even if the police were to show up, they would arrest the driver, not her. Only if he was still alive, that is. Not-Phillip was still breathing on her knees, but it seemed that he had passed out as well, either from the hit or the pain.

Maya reached out to check on the driver, but her leg answered with a stabbing pain, restraining her movement. She cursed under her breath and looked down to see what had happened. Her knee was stuck between the driver's seat and the door, which was now buckled and deformed from the impact.

Holding her breath, she tried to push the seat forward, giving herself a bit of room, but her leg started burning even more strongly. She needed help. Most of all, she needed time and a little bit of luck. Deep inside, she knew that Michael was there, maybe within a radius of a hundred feet. She really hoped she was not too late.

"Hey, FBI!" She carefully stroked her companion's face. "We're here."

He moaned in response but did not wake up.

"Phillip, come on!" She gently slapped him on the cheek a few times. "Whatever your name is, you can still be Phillip to me. Come on, I need your help."

Moaning and squinting, he stirred and looked around.

"We got it. This is the place…I can feel it." Maya wiped the sweat from his forehead and noticed something strange. She had smudged the tattoo scales on his temple.

She raised her fingers, inspecting them more closely. The sweat dried almost immediately, and small flakes of skin and ink flew up into the air like dust. Was his body rejecting the tattoos? Was he shedding his skin like a snake?

"Go. I'll wait here." Phillip closed his eyes, but Maya shook him, not letting him sink back into unconsciousness.

"I'm stuck. You need to help me get out!"

For a moment, she thought he had slipped away, but suddenly, he rolled onto his side and stood, drawing on the small reserve of strength he still had inside. Floating from side to side, he analyzed the situation. Visibly fighting nausea and pain, he pushed the front seat with both hands. Maya yipped from the stinging pain but freed her leg. Nothing was broken or even bleeding, but her leg was pulsating in agony from her ankle to her knee.

The door on her side was smashed and arched in such a way that opening it would be impossible. If Phillip were to pass out again, she was not sure if she would be able to rouse him.

"Get out! You're in my way. Phillip, move your ass!" He heard her, but she was losing him. He stopped moaning, his face twitched a bit in discomfort, but his sweat stopped running across his face, and he went pale. "Don't you dare! No!"

Maya pushed against his shoulder, trying to prop him upright, but the pain in her leg stopped her once again.

Phillip's head slowly tilted in the other direction and began to fall sideways.

"No! NO! NO! You can't! You can't leave me now! Not after all this! You hear me?!"

She slapped him across the face. Then once again.

His eyelids moved in an attempt to open. The corner of his lips flinched like he wanted to say something to her or at least smile.

"Please…" Her voice cracked, and tears filled her eyes. "Not now…Not now…I can't do this without you…"

First, she released a pulsating sigh, and then a small squeak escaped her mouth as she tried desperately not to cry. The overwhelming wave of sorrow searched everywhere for release.

"You can't leave me right now…"

Maya knew she had no right to give up, though her spirit screamed and threatened to accept defeat. It would be entirely too easy to allow herself to have this moment of weakness, to get comfortable, or as comfortable as possible, in the back seat of a crashed car, place her head on Phillip's shoulder, and wait. She could just wait for help while the rain grew stronger and stronger and the wind bent the hedge like long blades of grass. She could wait and listen to the slowing of Phillip's breath and weep when his heartbeat came to a stop.

Cloudy told her that she had six hours, but barely two had passed. Maybe Phillip would still last for a while longer, although unresponsive. She could wait till it was all over. Michael would be gone. Cloudy would kill her parents. If she was lucky, he would kill her as well because she was too cowardly to take her own life but not brave enough to live the rest of her life with all that had happened. Yes, that would be the easiest way…

"Phillip!" screamed Maya, punching him in the chest with both fists! "Up! Now!"

No. Cloudy would not win! She was not about to let the old son-of-a-monkey have the victory over her. Yes, she might die, but at least she would die standing as Maya Polanski and not as a sobbing cow doomed to the slaughter, lying in a car, helpless and waiting.

"Get up!" She hit him again, but this time, before her knuckles impacted his chest, she somehow knew he would open his eyes. It was like she saw it before it happened. She saw it, not with her physical eyes, but with her... imagination? Faith?

He indeed opened his eyes and gasped, like someone who had casually fallen asleep and suddenly awoke, startled.

"Why? Why didn't you just leave me alone?" wheezed Phillip through the fog of pain and weakness.

Maya sat stunned.

Slowly, she gazed over her hands and then at Phillip. Something was happening. Somehow, she was changing. She wished she knew how she had managed all of these strange happenings: controlling the agents, controlling the taxi driver, making Phillip wake up. She was onto something, but there was no time to analyze every step or experiment a little more to understand how it happened. Would she be able to do it again when she really needed to, and not just when these spontaneous sparks of power released on their own?

Phillip, with great effort, raised his head and examined the door, trying to find a handle. On the third try, he finally managed to pull the handle and pushed the door open, letting wind and rain rush inside.

She helped him get up and almost shoved him outside. For a moment, she thought he would tumble onto the wet grass and broken branches of the hedge, but Phillip held onto the door and kept himself upright. Maya, on the other hand, fell as soon as she tried to place her weight on the injured leg.

The cold whipped her face with stinging drops of rain, and her relatively dry clothes became soaking wet and muddy in seconds. She did not have the energy to swear anymore. In the insanity of the moment, she even giggled at how all the shitty events in her life would not give her a break.

"Come on!" said Phillip, weakly and barely maintaining his balance. He still managed to bend down and grab Maya's arm, helping her stand.

"Thanks!" she yelled, with a distinct note of sarcasm, over-shouting the storm and accepting his help.

Her next move surprised even her. She opened the front passenger door and leaned across to the taxi driver, checking his pulse. He was alive. The guy was a jerk, but he did not deserve to die or even go to jail. Maybe she would be able to convince the police that he was trying to save their lives or that she had forced him to drive like a maniac at gunpoint. Later, she would deal with that—much later.

"Let's go!" screamed Maya. "We'll see if we can make it to Michael before we fall apart!"

*

Maya thought climbing out of the hedge to the sidewalk would be the hardest of their next tasks, but she was wrong. As soon as they turned the corner to see the front side of the building, they beheld utter chaos.

The square in front of the main entrance was jammed with people. Under the rumbles of thunder and gusts of omnidirectional rain, the screaming and shoving crowd looked like something written in Dante's pen. At least a couple hundred people tried to force their way closer to the doors while another hundred silently looked on at the madness unfolding.

Maya looked toward the ambulance entrance, and while the door over there seemed less burdened with people, it was being guarded by two police vehicles and multiple cops.

"Shit..."

"We'll have to go through the main doors." Phillip saw the police as well, and he knew that by now, their faces would likely be memorized by every single one of them. Even if there were security or police at the main door, they had a higher chance of blending in with the crowd.

"Just hold on!" Maya gritted her teeth and started toward the boiling crowd, ignoring her own pain and propping Phillip up with her arm and shoulder.

She lost all sense of time and divided the distance into steps—little bursts of movement through the wall of the city-swallowing storm. It might take minutes or hours, she would never know, and the pain in her leg increased tenfold, but she kept walking. Numerous times, Phillip started to choke when he breathed, and six times, he almost slipped off her shoulder. Twice, they nearly fell when a gust of wind hit them from behind. But NOT ONCE did they stop to take a break, and NOT ONCE did they allow themselves a moment of doubt.

"HELP!" yelled Maya when they drew closer to the throng, but like an evil joke, the wind changed direction and swept her words far away, smashing her face with cold, heavy drops. She did not plan to stop or slow down until someone heard them. "HELP!"

This time, a couple did hear them and even turned to look, but the expression on their faces was a mix of annoyance and fear. Maya sensed that they were not about to help the newcomers, and she was right. They turned their faces back toward the main entrance like nothing had happened.

"Let us in!" screamed someone from the crowd.

"I have cancer! Please! Let me in!" cried a woman from the end of the human mass, hoping someone would allow her closer to the door. "I have three kids. Please, let me through!"

The people ignored her, pushing forward on their own.

"Is he still there? My son…He needs to help my son!" shouted a weeping man with a pale, sickly child in his arms.

Maya and Phillip finally made it to the cluster, and Maya tried to squeeze on through, but the people stood so close to each other that moving forward was impossible.

"Another's coming!" yelled someone, and from the main door, a young couple ran out. There was nothing unusual about the girl, but the young man was bald and wearing a hospital robe under a light jacket.

"Is he still in there?"

"Is he coming outside?"

People screamed from every direction toward the young couple, scaring them a bit, but it seemed that both of them were crying with joy. Now, they could get married and live happily ever after.

Somehow, Maya knew that they were school sweethearts and that they had survived a long-distance relationship while each attended a different college. She knew they planned to get married in the spring and had already bought a house when he was diagnosed with blood cancer a couple months earlier, and the doctors were not sure if they would be able to help him. The young woman still wanted to get married, but he did not want to leave her with massive hospital bills when he died. But now...

How did she know that?

"Please! Let me in. I need a new lung!" screamed a man not far from her, but he was lying. He needed a new liver because he had been an alcoholic for eleven years, and it was only when his health started going downward that he...

How did she know all this?!

"I need to see him! My son died! I need him!" shouted another from the crowd, and Maya could feel the pain of loss. Somehow, other people's memories and thoughts were filling her, and she could see in her mind the image of a little boy lying in a puddle of blood at the bottom of some concrete steps.

More and more voices came from nowhere. People's voices and pain and memories filled the air and penetrated her mind. It became difficult to breathe and to process it all. She closed her eyes in an attempt to shove the unwanted images out of her brain, but like hundreds of simultaneously running TV sets playing different channels, they grew louder and louder, trying to shout over each other.

"SHUT UP!" yelled Maya. This time, resentment and anger filled her cry. Either by her will or just coincidently, the wind took her scream and delivered it to the ears of everyone standing in her way.

A dead silence fell over the crowd. Even the sound of rain was absorbed into a vacuum. They all stared. Everyone. Every single person, old, young, man and woman. Even those watching the ruckus from the sides now looked toward Maya.

As a new gust of wind blew, an old and nearly-forgotten memory filled her mind. This time, it was her own. When she was a child, she had strange dreams. They had been so creepy and unrealistic that it was not surprising that her brain tried to erase them. The dreams haunted her for a long time and almost always consisted of the same event. How funny. You can live life never thinking about something from your past when suddenly an invisible force triggers the memory, and you find yourself reliving the moment so vividly.

In her dreams, she was always a small girl, no older than three. She argued with her grandma, asking for something in a store. It might have been a doll or a silly stuffed animal. Grandma, embarrassed by her behavior, took her outside to the street. Then Maya yelled! So loudly, so angrily...demanding to have her way. The world froze. Everyone in the street looked at her, and only at her. On both sides of the busy road, somewhere in a city in Eastern Europe, the people forgot what they were doing or where they were going. They stopped their conversations and even their thoughts. They looked at Maya like nothing else in the world deserved their attention.

Then they started walking again. They kept looking at the little girl while they moved in the same direction, slowly at first and then faster and faster. Soon, they were all running toward her. She would wake up screaming. A psychologist whom she had seen back in Alaska when she was still in elementary school explained that it was just her brain's way of asking for attention. That was his explanation of the dream, and he was partly right.

But right now, the dream was coming true. It was not in Europe, and she was not a child, but everyone looked right at her...and then they moved. Hundreds of emotionless people, who only a moment ago were ready to break down the hospital door, stepped aside and formed a path so Maya could walk through.

An intense pain pierced her head, but she started forward regardless.

"How?" Phillip, who might have seen many strange occurrences in his life, stood confused.

Maya's face grew cold and angry, and she turned back to grab Phillip and pull him along with her. He stared at her, like everyone else, only he was not under her spell. He glanced around at the frozen faces, the host of people who were as good as mannequins, and then looked back at Maya.

"No…" Phillip shuddered, frightened. He had never seen this Maya before. Who was she? What was she?

"Don't stop, we're almost there!" Maya took her focus off of the entrance and switched her attention to Phillip. The crowd shifted slightly in response.

"Maya, don't do this. You need to stop now."

"I don't know what you're talking about." But she did know. It was just like in the car with the taxi driver. She could feel every single person standing in the square.

Phillip pushed away from Maya a bit and grabbed her by the ear, looking behind it. His expression revealed so much, but Maya did not need to ask what he saw. She knew. She did not know how, but she could feel it. Small scales had appeared there, multiplying and covering her scalp.

"You can't be…Don't use it!"

Maya shook off Phillip's hand, and he nearly fell but stepped aside. The people around then mimicked Maya's every movement.

"Don't act like you didn't know!" Maya glared at Phillip with a deep sense of irritation. "If I'm one of you, why didn't you tell me so?"

"…tell me so?" repeated the crowd.

"You're one of us?" Phillip took a step back.

"I don't know!" yelled Maya, her voice joined by the hundreds of voices around her. "Stop it!" she yelled again, and the crowd remained silent.

"You saw those damn marks, right? Or is the burning sensation on my scalp just my imagination?"

Thunder rolled like a gigantic barrel that had been loosed somewhere from the top floor of the hospital.

"You didn't know?" Phillip, confused and afraid, felt a rush of adrenaline, giving him the strength to stand on his own, even under the sweeping rain.

"Of course I didn't know! Are you stupid, or has the poison finally made its way to your brain? Why would I run from you and try to get away if I had known?!" She hurled more abuse at him and was not really sure what made her angrier—the fact that he could not keep up or the fact that she did not even know who she was.

"I don't know! But you're using power from Nehushtan!"

"Oh really? You think I didn't figure that out on my own?!" She boiled with anger, but the argument was taking her focus away from controlling the masses around her. The swarm began to return to their senses.

"How?!"

"I don't know! Maybe I caught it from you?"

"It's not a flu! You have to be tattooed with the first scale by the clan!"

"I don't care. I'm going to get Michael with or without your help, and I'll stop him even if I need to make a pact with the devil, so help me—"

"DO NOT SAY THAT!" Phillip cut her off.

His words shook her stronger than the thunder, and she lost the final bit of control she had over her puppets. Hundreds of eyes continued to look at her, but differently now. They remembered everything that had just happened, even though they had not been able to do anything about it. First, they stepped back with fear and then looked around, sipping up bravery from each other.

"She's trying to stop the angel!" screamed one woman suddenly.

"She's a demon!" shouted another voice, and many soon repeated the accusation.

"Kill her! Kill the devil!" screamed yet another. The whole mass rushed toward Maya and Phillip.

CHAPTER 23

Crowds—even the sound of them was unnatural and scary, like the calling of a crow or the movement of wind through a dead orchard. Though comprised of people, something about a crowd is inhuman and wild. Maya always thought that when people got together, they lost a bit of their personality. They acted, moved, thought, and even breathed as one huge creature that could easily be triggered into a frenzy.

In a crowd, a person could allow his nature to move him completely, doing those things he might never otherwise do on his own. Right now, the wave of people surrounding Maya wanted to kill her, and, to be honest, she understood why. Not only had she killed Alyson, she had gouged out her eyes as well. She shot at Cloudy six times. She would want to kill herself, too, were she in their place, especially for what she was becoming.

"RUN!" yelled Phillip, and using all his remaining strength, he jumped into the people rushing toward them.

Even though the force of his jump was weak, it was enough to make a few lose their footing, and they began falling like dominos, tripping over each other, trying to get up again, and then knocking others down in the process. This moment of distraction did not last long.

Maya hesitated and then ran back to the main door only to find something else in her way. Behind the glass doors stood a cluster of security personnel holding a barricade, which they moved only to let people out. They were armed and just as frightened as those outside.

Maya decided to beg them to let her in, and if they denied her entry, she would use her newfound power over their minds. That same power filled her more and more with each passing moment. She had no doubt that as soon as she commanded them to open up, they would obey.

But they did so on their own.

"Hurry inside! Are you okay?" asked one of them, barricading the door again just after she squeezed through.

"Yes, thanks." Maya could not understand what was happening.

"You're Maya, right?" asked the same man, and the rest of them looked at her like she was the one who now gave the orders.

"Yes," she cautiously answered.

"Michael…He told us you'd come. He said…" The guard looked at the others, almost waiting for their approval. "He said you're the one who will collect his body."

Maya felt like the earth had dropped from under her feet.

"Ma'am, what's going on? Who is he?" asked another guard. At the sound of his question, a vision flashed through Maya's mind, and she began to see their collective memories of Michael's appearance at the hospital.

A young man walked through the main door, made his way to registration, and asked where he could find children's oncology. Upon receiving an answer, the youth started toward the elevators, ignoring their calls to come back and fill out the papers for a visitor's badge. A light flashed. Now, the guard was in oncology, and something unbelievable was going on. Kids, one by one, were running away from their rooms. He knew those faces. He had seen these kids before. He knew their colorful pajamas and bald heads. He even knew some by name.

But these were not the same children. They were smiling. These were not the forced smiles they put on to calm their weeping parents, nor the respectful smiles they displayed when the doctors came to tell them about a new round of chemo. These were not the smiles they wore for journalists when the Wish Foundation came to help them fulfill a lifelong dream before the end. They were smiling. Really smiling!

"You didn't stop him?" Maya asked the question, but she knew the answer.

"How could we?"

"Where is he right now?" Maya was crying again, but her hair and face were already so wet that no one could possibly notice anyway.

"That last couple was from the sixth floor," answered a female guard.

"Thank you," blurted Maya, and she hustled toward the elevator as fast as her leg would allow.

Before she reached the elevator, the doors opened, and an older couple stepped out. They were both in their sixties and when they noticed her coming, they moved out into the hall to let her in. For a moment, Maya's eyes met with those of the gentlemen, and images of his memories flashed through her mind.

He sat next to a bed, waiting for Death to come and take his love away from him. He sat and prayed that the inevitable would wait just a minute longer. He gently caressed her hand and looked lovingly at her curly, gray hair that had once been golden. He prayed for just one more smile on her wrinkled face, which to him was as beautiful as the day they had met. He was not ready to say goodbye. They had been together forty years, but it was not enough. He wanted at least one more day. And tomorrow, he would pray for yet another.

The door opened, but it was not Death come to take her. It was Life in the form of another old man who came and placed his hand over theirs...

A light shone through the old man wearing the funny "I love Washington DC" sweater, and then he left as quickly as he had come.

"I hope he'll help you too," whispered the gentlemen to Maya before the doors closed.

She was late.

Hospital elevators are known for their speed, and usually, when covering five or six floors in a matter of seconds, Maya's stomach turned. Today, though, Maya felt like each second took forever, and as soon as the door opened, she jumped into the hallway, completely ignoring the pain in her leg.

So many people! All of them pushed each other, trying to get somewhere, or rather to someone, and Maya knew who it was. She dashed into the swarm of people without hesitating to use her elbows to rough her way forward. Most of those in her way were still pale, sick, and fairly weak, though they fought savagely for their chance to reach Michael. She heard swearing, crying, and begging from all around. One woman she needed to shuffle aside started to scream like Maya had broken her arm or rib. A man tried to grab for Maya's hand, hoping her momentum would help pull him forward as well, but she shook him off harshly and dived deeper into the frenzy.

The storm outside raged more strongly than earlier, and even over the screaming inside, she could hear the rain hit the windows in the empty rooms to the side of the corridor. Thunder rumbled back and forth across the roof like an angry teenager throwing flickering matches across the sky. It was just a question of time before one of them might strike the building. Something outside exploded in a bright flash of light, and the hospital fell into darkness.

If people in a crowd became more like animals, then darkness multiplies the effect exponentially. Shouting and begging turned into weeping and cries of agony. Panic gripped everyone tightly, condensing and hurling the stampede toward their target. At the end of the hall stood a man touching anyone who approached him, and each time another came into contact, bright light released through his hands, mirroring the lightning outside.

Red emergency lights came on, indicating that the backup generators had kicked in. While they would provide enough electricity for the most essential areas like the ER or life support machines, they were not enough to provide adequate lighting in the hallways. The new, dim light, rather than calming the masses or stirring their sense of shame and humanity, merely sent people into a rage. Maya lost her footing and found herself crushed between the man in front and those who were pushing from behind. The pain in her leg reminded her of her own existence, and she would have screamed, but no one would have heard her voice in the blending cacophony of noise.

"Back off!" yelled someone. "Please back off!"

Maya punched the man behind her with her elbow, trying to make some room, and then pulled herself upward in order to get a better view forward. She was almost there. Only five or six people stood between her and the doctor who had just shouted. He was trying desperately to keep people away from someone standing just behind him. Maya could just see that someone, his gray hair, his scared eyes clouded with cataracts, his dry skin as thin as crumpled papyrus, and his sweater reading "I love Washington DC."

"Michael..." whispered Maya, almost afraid to admit who it was she saw before her.

People kept rushing forward, pushing the doctor and Michael closer and closer to a wall.

"Touch me! Heal me! I'm here! Please, cure me!" demanded the crowd.

Each time he touched, healed, and cured, he grew weaker and older. Those who received his magic light stopped fighting and yelling, and with a smile on their faces, they were absorbed by the others who rushed over them to receive their own miracle.

"Michael!" tried Maya again, but her voice betrayed her. It cracked on the first note, and she could barely hear herself.

She shoved harder and drew a little bit closer.

"MICHAEL!" she yelled as loudly as she could, and the old man stopped to look her way.

He was so old, perhaps the oldest person she had ever seen. Strands of long, thin, gray hair draped lifelessly around his weary, frightened face. On his own, he probably would have fallen by now, but the doctor protecting him had placed Michael's shaking arm over his shoulder, propping him up.

"Maya…" There was no surprise in his voice, only acknowledgment. "You came…"

The woman in front of Maya froze for a second, likely caught off guard by his ability to speak. It was easier to continue draining the life from an objectified old man than from a conscious human being whom you killed bit by bit with your own need. Maya used the opportunity to shove the lady aside and finally reached Michael.

"What are you doing?!"

"It's okay. Your parents will be okay."

"Michael, you're killing yourself, and that is NOT OKAY!" She grabbed him by the elbow, shocked to feel the thinness of his arm through the sweater. His hands were barely there, just thin bones with precious little tissue or muscle.

"You need to take him away from here," whispered the doctor with a look of awe and fear in his eyes. "I don't know…I don't understand. In twenty years of…"

Maya knew what he wanted to say, but she did not care and had no time for it.

"Just help me! We need to get him out…"

"It's my turn, bitch!" A man with a burned face hit her so hard from behind that she tripped and fell into one of the open rooms. "Do it!"

The belligerent patient grabbed Michael's hand and pulled it toward his face, and even from a distance, Maya could hear how the bone in Michael's wrist cracked. He groaned from the pain but still released his light, healing the ungrateful man.

She had never had children of her own, and maybe never would, but in that moment, she understood why some mothers would kill to protect their children. Maya stood quickly and looked around for any kind of help. She noticed an emergency kit in the room. Digging through a couple of plastic trays, she soon found what she was looking for. With one tear, she ripped the packaging off of a scalpel. Faster than a cobra, she jumped back into the hallway, positioning herself between Michael and the others.

"BACK OFF! ALL OF YOU!" Maya held the scalpel and waved her hand about so everyone could see it. "I swear to God, if anyone takes another step, I will cut them to pieces!"

A young man jumped to grab her hand, but Maya was faster. Adrenaline, or her newly discovered powers, helped her evade his attack, and she struck out at him, cutting the attacker's shoulder. It was not a deep wound but significant enough to let everyone know that she meant business.

"I said back off!" hissed Maya. Looking over her shoulder, she instructed the doctor to take Michael into one of the empty rooms.

Desperate people in need of help can place the entirety of their hope in another's promise. When that offer of help is ripped away before being realized, the reaction is often very ugly. Almost fifty people, who had nothing else to lose, now stood before Maya, their hope torn away from them.

As soon as Maya turned to see that Michael had been taken to safety, they moved on her, not caring about the weapon in her hand. She was ready. She could feel each of them, see their thoughts, and so she calculated their movements before they happened. With one jump, she snuck into the same room and shut the door, pulling the lock into place.

Muffled screams of fury and devastation echoed outside. In the relative quiet of their new surroundings, Maya drew several deep breaths to regain her composure and strength. She needed all the bravery she could muster to turn and look into Michael's face. He sat on the empty hospital bed, which had probably been occupied just an hour ago.

Based on the pictures taped to the wall, someone's grandmother had been there. She was deeply loved and greatly missed by those at home.

She was gone now, and not in the world over the rainbow, but home and probably already in the arms of her surprised kids and grandkids. Maya hated her for it. This unknown lady who had rushed out, leaving her Sudoku book and reading glasses behind, was one of the reasons why Michael now looked like THIS! She hated every single smiling face in those photos.

Why did they get to feel happiness while Maya felt only profound grief over losing a beautiful, innocent, and precious boy? Her boy. The only real and pure thing in her life.

"How could you do this?" asked Maya, trying to control her anger. "Did you want to punish me? Was that your plan? Well, mission accomplished!"

"Maya, this was meant to be," answered the old man, cradling his broken hand.

"Can you explain to me what's going on?" The doctor seemed a genuinely nice man, and he really was concerned about Michael. He did not understand, but he did care. At the same time, though, he was not stupid. He saw how the boy who was healing his patients grew older and older with each touch. He saw it and did nothing to stop it.

"Call for security and make them clear the hall. I'm taking him away from this hell hole!"

The doctor nodded in reply, understanding that he had better keep his questions to himself. Moving to the intercom panel next to the door, he pushed a button. At the same time, something banged loudly on the door. And then again!

"Freaking animals!" hissed Maya through her teeth. "Call security! NOW! Before they break the door down!"

"Maya..." Michael's voice sounded gravelly and dry, reflecting the suffering and weight of someone else's many years. "Let me be. I can still help a couple of them."

"NO! You are not touching anyone! I'm taking you with me."

"I can't go anywhere…I'm tired. So tired. Please, just let me stay here."

Maya swallowed the lump rising in her throat and would have broken into tears were it not for a new series of blows crashing against the door. No matter how fast the security moved, those creatures in human form would be there sooner.

She stood and walked over to a glass door which opened onto a small balcony. Whose stupid decision was it to build a balcony high over the concrete ground below in a wing that housed cancer patients? She could not believe that no one had ever tried to jump and end it all. She pulled the lever, but the door did not open.

"It's locked, but it can be opened." The doctor scanned his badge on the lock panel, and something clicked. "It's in case of a fire. There's a fire escape."

"And you're just telling me this now?"

"But he can't walk on his own, and his hand is broken!" For the first time, the doctor raised his voice, and while it got her attention, she did not listen to him. Instead, she pulled the lever again and slid the door open. The force of the wind rushing inside pushed her backward as if the storm on the other side had been waiting for just this opportunity.

Everything flew into the air! A blanket on a visitor's chair rushed up to the ceiling, accompanied by a couple plastic bags. Papers from the chart mixed along with the photos and circled all over the room in a vortex. Maya's hair and clothes were soaked again in no time.

She looked outside at the sturdy metal fire escape.

"WE NEED TO GO!" she yelled back. "THEY WILL KILL HIM! CAN YOU HOLD THEM OFF A BIT LONGER?"

The doctor, tussled by the raging elements, looked at Maya, at the tired old man, and then to the door where the banging had begun to increase in intensity. He nodded in agreement.

At first, Maya thought she might need help carrying Michael, but when she went to the bed to help him up, she noticed straight away how light he had become.

"I'll take you out of here! We'll go to Cloudy. He will fix this. I'll make him fix it!"

"He'll do no such thing," answered Michael.

"Oh, he will. He needs you! He has no choice!"

"Maya…It was never about me. You know that, right?" Michael looked her in the eyes, and that eerie wisdom she always saw in him before finally matched his appearance. "You should understand that by now."

"Why? How can you be sure?"

He just smiled and caressed her wet hair. Time froze for a moment, and there was nothing else, no one else. Just Maya and Michael, who was still a child in the old man's body. She could almost hear Giga's words in her head about the perfect conditions for creating the Hatching, about those chosen to change the game or perhaps become an Antichrist.

Memories long-trapped in the back of her mind rushed forward. The childhood dream about when she had asked for the toy did not end with the mindless multitude running toward her. They kept on running, crashing through the display windows, breaking the doors, and knocking others over on their way to retrieve the toy for her. She commanded, and everyone who heard rushed to execute the order, not caring about their own safety or any obstacles.

That same evening, Albert Cloudy had come to their house and offered them a shocking amount of money and the opportunity to move permanently to the United States. All he asked in exchange was permission to tattoo small scales behind Maya's ears. He even promised that she would not remember the pain.

"Am I…the Heir?"

Michael nodded again, feeling guilty and ashamed as if he was the one who had chosen that destiny for her. As if he was the one who had tattooed her or made her life into a living hell over the last week.

"I'm just the tool they used to help you fulfill your purpose."

"We'll see who the tool is! Let's go!" Maya grabbed Michael. Fighting the wind and rain, they stepped toward the small balcony and turned to thank the doctor who was trying to barricade the door with chairs and the rolling hospital bed.

"If they wanted a snake, I'll give them one!"

She had just helped Michael outside when a clap of thunder echoed her name through the sky.

"MAYA!" repeated everyone and everything with the same familiar intonation.

Maya looked up as a reflex but then followed Michael's stare downward to find what was waiting for them below. A perfectly formed double line of black-hooded followers of Nehushtan closed off the square in front of the hospital, dividing them from hundreds of people who, ignoring the storm, stood in place looking upward at Maya.

Right below the balcony, she saw Cloudy with Phillip lying near his feet.

"COME DOWN, MAYA!" rumbled the thunder, along with the voices of the clan members and surrounding people now trapped under Cloudy's spell. "THE TIME IS COME!"

"Forget it!" she yelled back.

"LET ME HELP YOU! I WILL GIVE YOU A NEW LIFE!"

"Shut up!"

"I can give Phillip back to you," said Cloudy's voice inside her head. The skin on her scalp and neck began to itch. "You have nowhere to run. It's all over."

"IT'LL BE OVER WHEN I SAY SO!" screamed Maya, and the thunder laughed in response to her naiveté.

"Can you do anything? Can you stop this?" she asked Michael. Her skin started to burn.

"I can't," answered Michael sadly. "But you can."

"Me?"

"And only you."

At that moment, the door to the room gave way. The mob in the hallway rushed inside, climbing over the bed and ignoring the poor doctor who barely managed to jump out of their way. They tripped over each other but kept running forward, crazed and determined. Before Maya could do anything, they jumped on Michael, pulling and pushing him at the same time. She tried to shield him, but someone slipped on the wet floor and sent a wave through the heap of people, knocking her out onto the metal staircase. And Michael...

He gasped, flapped his arms, and flew...like a bird or an angel. Only he did not fly upward, but down, straight onto the concrete below.

CHAPTER 24

"**D**id he touch me? Could you see? Was there a light?" asked a lady wearing old sweatpants, a bleached T-shirt, and a messy ponytail. She seemed to want confirmation from everyone there, and that was more important to her than the fact that she had pushed Michael over the rail.

"What have you done? You stupid cow!" yelled a man standing nearby. "You killed him! BEFORE HE HEALED ME!"

"No! No! He can't die. He's an angel. He can't die! Can he? He can't, right?" exclaimed another young man, going into hysteria.

Only Maya looked silently downward where, next to Cloudy, lay not just one but two men who were dear to her heart. Maybe she was imagining it, but Michael's hand appeared to move, touch Phillip's, and release one final flash of light into the world. Even from here, Maya could hear Michael's heart stop beating.

"Go! Move out of the way. I'll go down! Maybe he's still alive!"

"Maybe he can still heal even if he's dead…"

"Yeah, I've heard that! Like saints. You know, and relics. They keep them in churches, and people say they can heal!"

"No…" whispered Maya, but everyone heard her. "You're not going to touch him."

She felt a hot wave move through her spine, and a strange sensation overcame her body, releasing adrenaline and pumping blood so fast that she could hear each beat, like drums, raising their war call in her ears. Maya had heard and even used the expression about one's skin crawling, but only in that moment did she really understand the feeling.

In her case, it was not figurative. She felt chills run through her veins, turning her blood toxic. The tempo continued to rise, and at the very moment when Maya thought her heart would burst through her chest… it all stopped. She became calm and renewed, cold and rational. She was in control of…everything!

"Move over!" shouted the man who was upset about Michael dying before he had his chance to be healed. He pushed those in his way and grabbed a metal bar, trying to climb from the balcony down to the same platform where Maya stood.

She raised her eyes, and he stopped. Then he took a step back.

Everyone stared at her, and she could feel it. That was exactly what she wanted. She moved up from the fire escape, never breaking eye contact with the man, tasting fear and anger fighting inside his mind.

"Come on. Take one more step!" hissed Maya, surprised at the sound of her own voice. They had killed Michael. They killed him and did not care. If she did not stop them, they would tear his poor body to pieces and make them into their idiotic relics. "One more step, and I…will… kill you!"

"You can't…" mumbled the man, inching backward until his back pushed against the balcony. "You can't stay in our way."

"Can't I?" Maya felt a painful urge to stretch all of her muscles, bend all of her joints, and pull her wet hair back and out of her face, but she only clenched her fists instead.

The sound of tearing flesh echoed with the thunder.

"What are you?" Now, the man was completely terrified. There was no more sense of anger but only pure animal fear. He would not look her in the eyes, and all of his attention was on Maya's hands.

She followed his gaze and looked down at her fingers. Her skin, like the façade of an old building, began to crack, and a strange fiery glow shone from the resulting faults. Maya raised her hands closer to her face and then pulled away a piece of torn flesh, allowing the skin beneath to feel the fresh air.

It was silky smooth, dark as obsidian, and glowed with red-hot lines like the scales on a snake. It was not frightening but beautiful, almost like the artwork of some ancient alien civilization. Burning lines flowed through precious dark stone. What a shame to hide such beauty under human flesh!

Maya took a deep breath, like a dragon about to spit fire, sucking away almost all of the oxygen from the surrounding area. The group on the balcony watched her with increasing fear and panic. One can take all the air out of a tightly sealed room, but not from an open space! Did this creature, now controlling them, have the power to do the unthinkable? An invisible orb surrounded Maya, and all those caught within it fell under her complete control. The heavy rain hit the edges of the sphere and turned into steam, disappearing instantly.

When Maya exhaled, all her clothing and skin burned off in seconds, turning her into a dark, glowing statue. She seemed to levitate as gravity lost its power around her. One man, the closest to the edge of the balcony, managed to look away from Maya's glowing, hypnotizing eyes and looked down to evaluate whether he could survive the fall or end up as dead as Michael.

"Go ahead!" Maya grinned. "Try it."

He looked back at Maya and then, without hesitation, bent and dropped. Miraculously, he managed to land on a tall hedge and not on the concrete.

"Why?" Maya heard in her head. The disappointed voice of Cloudy continued, "You could have made him jump, and then he would have died."

"I saved that for you," answered Maya, with the voices of all those left on the balcony.

"Good!" echoed the crowd below, with Cloudy's intonation. "Now, come with me. I have so much to tell to you. So much to teach you."

"You have nothing for me!"

"Really?" This time, the question came from the people on the balcony.

Maya felt the invisible connection she had with them disappear. She could still feel fear inside of them, but her access to it was blocked. Upon Cloudy's silent command, all of the remaining souls on the balcony turned away from her and, using all their strength, climbed to the edge and started hurling themselves off. They flew like ragdolls further than the hedge and landed in a perfect circular formation at the feet of the old clansman.

Only seconds later, the rest of the people who watched Maya from the hospital room ran out like wild animals and leaped to their deaths. Every one of them! And lastly, even the doctor who had tried to help Michael flung himself downward.

Maya turned her head slowly, like a cobra before striking. She glared down at Cloudy, who had stepped away from Phillip and Michael to admire the newly formed pile of bodies. From there, on the sixth floor, she could see that they had formed a pattern similar to the one she had seen in the books—a serpent coiled inside of a hexagon.

"Still think I have nothing to teach you?" Cloudy's voice laughed in her head. "Come, I'll even let you say goodbye to them."

Maya stared, speechless, at the old man who had the power not only to kill so many people with his thoughts but also to make them form a specific symbol upon landing, like some kind of perverted art installation. Maya knew that in order to control someone's mind, he needed to have personal eye contact or at least contact with one of his followers. He had used her. She let him use her as a channel. She had been angry, yes, but she did not want to kill those people even if they were guilty. Michael would not have wanted their death. More so, some of those people had been healed by Michael, and now his gift was wasted.

Her glowing appearance started to fade away slowly, transforming back into a tired and soaked woman standing alone and sad on the fire escape. Why bother with illusions if there was no one left to see the image she had created. She looked at her hands, and they were her own again, except now they bore the scale tattoos on them. Something had, in fact, happened. Her fury and thirst for power had spread this disease through her body.

"Come down…" Cloudy's words echoed in her head. "I've waited for this my whole life."

She seemed so lost. When there was nothing left to fight for, why bother?

No…After a moment of deep consideration, Maya decided that she was not giving up so easily.

She had never understood kamikaze pilots or suicide bombers. But a pilot whose plane had been shot and was soaring downward to the end knew at least to steer his plane toward the nearest target. A soldier surrounded by the enemy, with only one grenade left, knew what to do. So did she. If she was destined to die that day, then she would take Cloudy with her.

"Don't be stupid," croaked Cloudy angrily.

She had him.

One little drop of fear was all she needed.

A roar of desperation and insanity boomed out from within her, exploding like a new nova star. A wave, like a sonic boom, fanned out from around Maya, hitting the buildings and trees. Every window in the hospital shattered, creating a deadly spray of splintered glass and rain. Her voice broke the sky, and her cry was followed by a chain reaction of multiple crashes of thunder. Her body burst again into flame and heat, revealing the same godly statue. This time, however, she shone fire-red with black scales coiling around her form.

The fire escape turned red in seconds, remembering the days when it was born from molten ore and shaped on the anvil. Waves of heat swirled around her radiant figure. She was no longer human. Bright and incandescent, she covered her surroundings with a blinding light. The metal frames could not hold their shape and started to bend and melt, stretching like the strands of a spider's web, carefully lowering Maya down to ground level.

"I know this is an illusion," hissed Albert Cloudy.

Maya took the first step onto the wet grass, which steamed and turned into ash around her feet. The nearest trees caught fire. When she stepped onto the concrete, it cracked, leaving charred craters instead of footprints.

"This is an illusion…Illusion!" repeated Cloudy.

She could not see him. He hid behind the mixed crowd of black-hooded followers and ordinary people caught under his spell. They all watched her in horror, and through all of their eyes, Cloudy watched her as well.

"Come. Come to me," said Maya. Her voice formed waves of heat spreading from her mouth.

The mass of people stared as the otherworldly creature walked into the circle of bodies. When she reached the center, she stopped to look at the two familiar, lifeless faces at her feet. Stretching out her hand, she touched them, and the bodies of Michael and Phillip were instantly consumed in flame. The rest of the circle caught fire as well.

"It's not real! It's all an illusion, all of it!" Cloudy was no longer trying to convince his followers but himself. "She is toying with you. It's not real!"

Maya raised her glowing hands, and the flames grew bigger, throwing ash into the air. Smoke covered everyone, falling down over the black hoods, absorbing the fear and panic radiating from them.

"I am the Heir!" said Maya, straight into their minds. "I can do all! Give me your loyalty!"

"Don't listen!" yelled Cloudy into the minds of the crowd. He was trying desperately to regain mental control over them, but his voice was distant, like sound trying to break through radio static.

"He betrayed you. His fear and weakness make you vulnerable. You don't need a leader like this."

"WEAPONS!" screamed Cloudy, this time with his real voice.

The people jerked in unison like they had been shocked by an electrical impulse. Released from his control, they awakened to real life. Cloudy understood that he was losing contact with his puppets and decided to release them.

All illusions faded instantly. Maya was not a glowing sculpture; the fire escape was still intact, and even the glass windows were unbroken. There was no fire, only bodies forming a circle and Phillip walking away. He carried the body of an old man in his arms.

"You see? Idiots! She fooled you!"

The horde who earlier had blocked him from view stepped aside, staring at him questioningly. This exposed him to Maya as well. Those who were not clan members began to retreat, slowly at first, and then ran.

"No, I didn't. My show was for you and you alone. Or did you think you're the only one who can use others as transmitters?"

"As your magister, I order you to draw your weapons!" Cloudy boiled with anger, looking around at his brothers, who clearly were not rushing to his aid. "In the name of Nehushtan, KILL THE HEIR!"

No one moved.

"Your illusions are weak. I know what you did in the library. Now I know. You made me think you stopped the bullets and redirected them. In reality, I aimed where you made me think you were standing, and your lackey killed the agents in the next moment."

"That's true…" confirmed one of the men, lowering his hood and revealing his tattooed face.

"So what? I'm your magis…" Cloudy started.

"She won the duel. She remembers your moves." Everyone nodded in agreement.

Something happened to Albert's face as if he had smelled something disgusting. He jerked his shoulders forward and, in one fast movement, pulled out a double-bladed dagger and stabbed it into the eye of the arguing clansman.

"Anyone else want to challenge me?"

The brotherhood looked down at their fallen member.

About six of the snakeheads drew their weapons and took steps toward Cloudy.

"Do you think she's the first heir to lose its mind? Do you think I was made a magister for nothing? Do you really think she...or any one of you could win a duel against me?! THINK AGAIN!"

Cloudy burst into a cloud of smoke, and in his place appeared a monstrous wyrm. The creature moved fast and gracefully, and in a few strikes, it killed all six of those who had drawn their weapons against him.

Maya looked at their fallen bodies and saw wounds that could only be left by a dagger, while the others saw something much more gruesome.

"GET HER!" roared the monster.

Maya tried to break Cloudy's illusion, but the moment he had killed one of his own, caught everyone off guard and released enough fear for him to regain control. Now, taking the image of a giant snake-lizard, he had enough terror to maintain that control against her attacks.

"Bri-i-i-ng her to ME-E-E-E!" rumbled the beast, but still no one moved.

He glared around, spitting flames into the air and harvesting more energy...But all Maya saw was an old man with a dagger in hand, looking around for support.

"Fine, I'll do it myself!"

The others saw the dragon leap forward at Maya, opening its jaws to expose sharp teeth that could sever her head clean off. But Maya saw

Albert running in her direction, his arm stretched out and waving the shining dagger. Mustering all his strength, he aimed straight at her head.

The blades fell clean through Maya's head, dispensing her own illusion, but with enough inertia to swing the curved blades down until they stopped just in front of Cloudy's chest. He had stopped just in time to avoid stabbing himself, but when Maya's decoy images had completely faded, he saw that she was not alone.

Phillip, who stood right next to her, caught Cloudy's wrist. Grinning, he helped him finish the move, shoving the blades right where the heart would be.

The image of the dragon floated away. The old man stumbled back, looking startled and confused. He was certain that she had been right in front of him. He was positive that Phillip had died. But she had outmaneuvered him, and he had not anticipated it. Albert looked into Maya's eyes with both fear and hope…

Maya raised her arms, looking up into the sky, and whispered something. The inky black sky gave way to sunlight again. A bright aura fell behind her onto the bodies lying in the circle, and a glowing dome formed around them, filling them with life. Everyone in the circle began to stir, and stood slowly.

Cloudy tasted blood on his lips and felt a fog overcoming his mind. The glowing dome disappeared, taking with it every single tattoo from Maya's face.

Cloudy raised an arm, trying to touch Maya.

"This isn't real. Is it?"

But he never heard an answer and fell dead, as anyone stabbed through the heart would do.

EPILOGUE

Maya watched how the rays of sunlight, broken by thick palm leaves, turned the living ceiling over her head into a myriad of glowing diamonds. They sparkled here, overflowed there, creating a rhythmic, dazzling glimmer that soothed her, carrying her heart and spirit to a place of refuge.

She lay in the hammock that stretched between two old, strong palm trees and let the ocean breeze caress her skin. Inhaling and closing her eyes, she allowed herself a moment simply to absorb the surroundings. Somewhere nearby, a small group of children laughed and told jokes in Spanish. Even though she had learned it back in high school, today, her skills amounted to a few simply worded phrases about food or directions. Phillip spoke it much better and received constant compliments from the locals, who were so impressed with the gringo who knew their language. It greatly annoyed her…Still, she felt proud because that gringo was her gringo, and all those beautiful Latina women and a couple of the men would need to kill her first before they had a chance with him.

Maya could hear a couple of parrots high in the crown of the tree, cracking palm seeds and chattering, probably about her, and wondering whether it was safe to come closer or better to stay away.

When her eyes were closed, her hearing became sharper and more reliable. Maya could hear every crash of the waves running over the white sand, rolling little shells back and forth, and taking her worries deep into a world of corral and uncharted depths…

*

...Even from there, Maya heard his heart stop beating.

Her first urge was to kill them all. Every single idiot who had pushed and pulled poor Michael deserved to die. And then they argued over whether or not he really could die. The blind fools, could they not see? He was dead...They should have been in his place.

Actually, she felt confident that she could merely command them, and they would all jump from there, falling to their deaths. She could even tell them to jump and bend in the air such that they would land, forming some dark, twisted pattern on the ground. They deserved to die. They deserved it!

But did they really? Who else deserved death? Maybe she deserved to die. She was the one who brought Michael to the Library of Congress just to use him, just to get help from the president. Maybe she was the one who needed to jump from there to pay for her own mistakes.

No. Michael would not want that. Neither would God...

"Yeah, I've heard that! Like saints. You know, and relics. They keep them in churches, and people say they can heal!"

"No..." whispered Maya.

She needed to do something. She needed to stop those awful people before they did something even more unforgivable. On her command, they would all die! She could harness more than enough power. Maya felt the burning sensation stretch from her head and down her entire body. "You're not going to touch him."

The tattoos covered her neck, her back, and began stretching across her shoulders, making her much angrier and tipping her brain into berserker mode.

But Michael...He came to those people, people who did not deserve his help or compassion. He came to help and to give himself away to heal them. He healed her! And after her breakdown in the forest that night, she had understood that God did the same to His Son, not out of hate or cruelty, but to rescue undeserving people like herself. Those who accept

His calling ought also to serve those who do not deserve it—out of love! It was all about undeserved love. God had given her that love freely. Michael had demonstrated the same love through his sacrifice. How could she accept such love yet refuse to give it to others?

Peace. Suddenly, she felt calm and renewed, cold and rational. God was in control of…everything!

Only one little thing was bothering her—Cloudy. His manipulative grin, that child of evil, that man who respected no laws of people or of Heaven. He was trying to penetrate her mental barrier. She could feel his long, cold, slimy fingers, like tentacles, crawling around her head, probing every inch of her skin, trying to find a weakness to breach in order to manipulate her. She needed to play it cool. She needed to make him believe that he had her.

"Oh God…help me!"

In the realm of the invisible, she grabbed those tentacles and squeezed them until they became part of her. An illusion. She would show Cloudy an illusion!

She would have to be careful. He needed to believe that Nehushtan had overtaken her. She knew how, but it was risky!

"Dear God, help me not to screw up!"

First, she created the glowing arm and the peeling flesh to reveal an unnatural form. It scared the surrounding people, but that was vital to her plan. Maya knew that Cloudy would feel their fear, and he needed to believe that everything was going according to his plan.

It was a little spectacle for one viewer.

"God…oh God!" whispered Maya, continuing her performance.

Now the hardest part—she had to move the people to safety!

A sphere covered her and everyone on the balcony. Cloudy would see her clothes and skin burn away, turning her into a floating monster. He would see the people overtaken with fright, pushing each other to get away from her!

"I'll tell you this once!" said Maya. "If you want to live, run and hide! If any of you leave the building before I tell you it's safe, you will die!"

They looked around at each other, waiting to see if anyone had the courage to say something.

"Leave now, or I will make you leave!" With those words, Maya allowed them to see her as Cloudy saw her in that moment—a dark figure defying gravity with glowing red scales and eyes that burned like fire!

The crowd fled the balcony and adjoining room so quickly that even Maya was surprised with the result.

Next step! She could not let Cloudy suspect anything.

"Go ahead!" Maya grinned. "Try it!"

She created the image of a man bending over the balcony and falling onto the tall hedge below. It was a test. She wanted to see just how deeply she could control Cloudy's visions. Killing the man might seem too out of character for her, and he might call her bluff.

"Why?" Maya heard in her head. The disappointed voice of Cloudy continued, "You could have made him jump, and then he would have died."

She had him.

"Thank you. Thank you!" she said, deep inside her heart.

She needed to push a bit further. She had to make Cloudy accept Maya's thoughts, believing them to be his own. The cruel desire she had earlier to kill those people—that would fit Albert perfectly. She sent the thoughts into his mind.

It worked!

Maya felt him stretching his tentacles, trying to grasp and manipulate the minds of the phantom people she had created. The real crowd was long gone, and all he saw was a mirage. He commanded them to jump, landing in a circular pattern.

He was convinced that the illusion was real, but when he began to walk around and inspect the pile of bodies, Maya became terrified that he would discover her deception. Was she strong enough to keep him fooled? He looked up again, seemingly satisfied. Success! Furthermore, Maya knew that Cloudy was controlling the minds of the poor people standing below. They would see everything just as he saw it!

Now, she needed him to feel a sense of desperation in her. Easy! Anything to get closer to the degenerate old wretch…

*

"Maya!" someone called.

She opened her eyes, trying to remember where she was.

"Señora Maya?" the same voice came from the other side of her house.

"I'm here, Juana!" Maya stretched in the hammock, allowing the sunshine to sweep away the rest of her dream.

A young girl, no older than fourteen, walked around the side of the house with a basket in her arms, looking confused.

"Over here, sweetie," called Maya, waiving.

"I saw your boys, Señora Maya," said the girl upon spotting her. She was the neighbor's daughter and often came over to lend a hand around the church building in return for some help learning English. Maya had to admit that Juana spoke English far better than Maya spoke Spanish. "Señor asked me to bring this and to tell you that they go to the beach."

Maya looked in the basket, where there lay a stack of tortillas, some fruit, and a dozen eggs.

"Can you take it inside, please?"

"Sure, Señora."

Maya had asked her over a hundred times just to call her by her name, but the girl would only blush and shake her head in disagreement. Well, maybe in another couple of years, she would succeed in making an American out of her.

"Oh, and here is a letter for you!" Juana handed Maya an envelope and, with mischief in her eyes, added, "I didn't tell Señor Phillip about it, in case it is from one of your old boyfriends."

"Go already!" Maya laughed, and the girl walked back to the house giggling.

Maya looked curiously at the stamp and postmark. It was from Washington, with an address that Maya did not recognize, but she could tell from the handwriting that it was from Charles. It was written to the "Church of the Risen Christ" with a little note reading "for Lala."

"Giga!" Maya smiled even wider and hugged the letter closely.

Now she knew why she had had the dream. For the first month after the events in DC, she had that same dream almost every night. Now, it would come as a sort of premonition whenever something related to that day was on the horizon.

*

...Cloudy hid among his own when he saw Maya descending the fire escape. Of course, in his mind, it appeared that the molten frames were stretching downward, lowering her to the ground. It was a masterpiece of illusion, and she was proud of that little detail.

She remembered how hard it was for her to approach Michael and Phillip. She did not know for sure what she would discover, and she could not risk allowing her emotions to control her. She had to finish what she had begun.

"Maya?" Phillip barely held his eyes open, and they quickly filled with tears. "Michael...He's dead."

Maya nodded.

"I'm so sorry," whispered Phillip.

Maya nodded again.

"Phillip, you need to get up and take his body away."

Phillip looked over at Michael, and his tears began to flow freely.

"I don't know if I can. Maya, I don't know."

"Get up!" Maya stretched out her hand and grabbed Phillip's wrist.

She did it on a level of intuition, as a reflex, but also from divine inspiration. Maya did not know what she was doing exactly, but she just knew that she was supposed to do it. She felt warmth and perceived a glow, similar to how she felt in the small room where Dan was healed. She let the light and warmth travel through her hand and into Phillip. Not wanting Cloudy to see, she created the illusion of their bodies igniting at her touch and fire consuming them.

Phillip stood, not understanding how he had found the strength. He had no idea what was going on, but crying, he knelt and gingerly lifted the broken body of the old man who once had saved his life. This same man had tried to heal him again just after his deadly fall but died before he was able.

Maya reached to close Michael's eyes and lovingly kissed him on the forehead.

"Can you do it? Can you do the same for him?" asked Phillip, hesitating.

Maya wanted so badly to say yes, but she knew that this had been Michael's choice. He came here for a reason and did what he thought was right.

"Go. Take him inside. Try to find Doctor Hall; I think that's his name. He'll help you take care of the body."

"Come with me!"

Maya smiled sadly in response.

"I need to finish this."

"We need to finish this!"

*

Maya fought her way out of the hammock and walked back to the house.

"Stubborn idiot," she whispered in the air, remembering how Phillip had taken Michael's body into the hospital only to come right back outside.

Even today, Maya was unsure if she could have done what Phillip did. Yes, she really despised Cloudy, and he was truly evil, but would she have been able to kill him? She knew that had it not been for "FBI," they may not have had their happy ending. People still died that day, and so many suffered as a result of Cloudy's actions. To be honest she had made the last of her illusions, the dome of light resurrecting people, purely out of spite. She wanted Cloudy to see the people he thought he had killed being resurrected—by her. Now, no matter which circle of hell he inhabited, the bulk of his suffering would be in trying to understand which events had been an illusion and which were real.

Juana left, having sorted out the groceries. Maya took a knife and carefully opened the letter. There was not much inside, just one handwritten page and a few clippings from different newspapers.

"Dear Lala…"

Charles' familiar scribbles made her tear up. Those were fun times when they called each other "Giga and Lala." If she could be sure that they would be safe, she would head to the airport in a heartbeat and fly to see him, just to hear him call her Lala again in person. Sadly, there was still so much at stake. They had seen each other again at the White House the day after the storm, and the following morning, after the strange events at the hospital, they all agreed not to communicate unless something absolutely vital came up.

The first year went exactly according to plan. The president had helped Maya disappear for good, but she had been dying from curiosity.

Unable to resist, she had written a little note to Charles. Since then, they exchanged letters once a month, praying that no one would be found and harmed as a result.

"I hope my note finds you in good health and a good mood. I'm not sure if I should tell you this, but better safe than sorry. As you remember, your book club was dismissed, even though you had become their honorary president. However, I've since come across more information and some rumors suggesting that your book club here in the States was just one of many around the world. I have reason to believe that the heads of these other clubs are looking for you. I'm not sure what their reasoning is. Perhaps they want you to take the place of their former head, or perhaps they want to 'repay' you for all you did..."

The morning after, when the president's escort picked up Maya and Phillip and took them to one of the safe rooms in the White House, she knew that nothing in the world would ever be the same. So many people disappeared. The FBI was indeed investigating the secret organization, and only a select group knew about it. After the nightmare in the Library of Congress, Mark had wanted to fire everyone for not keeping him in the loop, but so many influential people turned out to be in the clan, and investigators could not risk exposure. When Cloudy died, everyone who had been on the FBI's radar simply faded away. Where they went and how they disappeared, no one could tell. That is why they made the decision to relocate Maya to foreign climes.

"...On a positive note, I decided to send you some clippings from *Chicago Voice*, and I really hope that my suspicion is just paranoia.

With love,

Giga.

PS: I saw your parents last month. They both seem healthy, and they still believe in their hearts that you're innocent."

Her parents. Those poor old folks. She had agreed that it would be better to spin the story that Maya and Phillip were two runaway criminals who had kidnapped a boy. That would be easier than trying to explain everything about a secret clan with the ability to control minds.

The people in the hospital were told that because of the storm, there had been a gas leak, and everything that had happened was just a mass hallucination. A couple months earlier, however, Giga had sent Maya a clipping from the tabloid *Twilight Chicago* in which a taxi driver told a story about the day of the storm and how a witch controlled his mind to make him drive on the sidewalk. He did not reveal his name or go to the police out of fear that no one would believe him.

Maya wondered what Giga had sent her this time. She took out the first clipping and a big smile spread across her face. It was Dan with his dad, Richard. Dan was ecstatic when he found out that his father had survived. The article mentioned a victim of crossfire in Chicago and how, after a long recovery, he was able to stand in support of his son on his graduation day, which had been delayed as the boy had been in a coma.

The second cutout announced a new suicide clinic in the name of Bill Sawyer that had opened in Chicago, with a twenty-four-hour hotline and active programs offering support to the families of those who had lost their loved ones.

A third snippet featured a column from the Saturday issue, which was still published under the name of Maya Polanski. It was a fairly entertaining article about the latest analysis of societal changes.

The fourth had a photo of Mark Turner with his family and team, announcing his bid for a second term. He deserved it. What happened that fall had changed him for the best. He became the leader everyone needed, and while Maya did not know all of the details, the changes he had implemented were bringing the United States' global image back to a more respectable level.

His wife and son looked so alive and happy. Well, maybe one day she could sneak through the guards again and finally get her interview.

"Damn!" Maya inhaled sharply.

Dropping the rest of the pages, she moved closer to a window, holding the photo up closer under the better lighting. One of the men, who might have been part of the new campaign team, stood next to the president, resting his hand over the head of a long cane—a cane whose handle was shaped like the head of a snake.

Maya dropped the clipping and began to breathe rapidly. Searching her memory, she tried to recall each detail of that tempestuous night. She watched Cloudy die; she saw his dagger pierce clean through him! And the cane that concealed his dagger...what had happened to it? Nausea squeezed her throat.

She ran across the room, tearing straight into a bedroom where, under one of the loose floorboards, she had hidden a bag of cash, three passports, and a mobile phone. Scooping it up in her hands, she darted over to the closet, where she retrieved two duffle bags she had already packed for just this sort of situation.

If a snakehead had made his way that close to the president, then none of them was safe anymore.

Carrying both bags, she grabbed the keys to a Jeep hidden about two miles away in a wooded area. Maya left the house, letting the screen door slam behind her, and headed to the beach. She paused only a second to turn on the mobile phone and then jogged the rest of the way.

The only call on the phone had come from Doctor Hall, and she remembered it more than any other detail. They were just finishing a conversation with the president when it rang.

"Hello?" answered Maya.

"Hi. This is Doctor Hall..."

"I know. You're the only one who has this number."

"Oh...Okay. I'm calling you with regard to our friend."

Maya stood and walked over to a corner of the room.

"I thought we agreed that you'd take care of his funeral after everything he did for…"

"I know, I'm sorry…But…"

"What?" Maya was losing patience.

"His body…It's gone."

"What?!"

"…"

"What do you mean it's gone?"

"I don't know what to say. I came to the morgue ten minutes ago. Security called me about some strange explosions of light. I came, and his body was gone."

"Did someone steal it?"

"I'm afraid so…"

"Damn snakeheads!" hissed Maya. "Okay, thanks for calling. I'll take care of it."

"Sorry, there's something else…"

"What?!" Maya no longer tried to mask her frustration.

"There's a boy here. He's looking for you."

"What?" repeated Maya for the fourth time. "What boy?"

"I don't know. Blue eyes, about four years old. He knows your name. Should I call the police?"

"Ask him what his name is."

She heard the doctor ask, and she heard the answer. Maya almost fainted right there in the White House.

*

Maya cleared a row of palms and stumbled out onto the beach, where she could see Phillip, who was playing in the water with a small boy. He would pick him up in his hands, raise him above the waves, and then toss him as high as he could, allowing the boy to fall back into the water, giggling and making as many big splashes as he could.

She stopped in her tracks and watched them play. She knew that as soon as she called them, this moment of joy would have to end. Five more minutes. Who knew when he would be able to see the ocean again? He had dreamed about it for such a long time. A little bit longer. Just a bit more…

But now they really needed to go.

"Phillip! Michael!"

September 2015 – October 2019

Made in the USA
Las Vegas, NV
23 October 2023

79078996R00190